The Fates of the Princes of Dyfed

By Cenydd Morus

Illustrations by
R. Machell

AC y mae bodau sydd gymaint yn
fwy na dyn ag y mae dyn yn
fwy na'r bacillyn lleiaf welir drwy
y chwyddwydr cryfaf. Mae y gal-
luogrwydd i ymddadblygu hefyd
yn anfeidrol. Mae y meddwl dynol
ar y ffordd mawr i ymddadblygu yn
dduw. Dyma ffordd Duw o greu
duwiau, sef drwy ymddadblygiad.
Mae Duw erioed yn eu creu.—*Index*

ARYAN THEOSOPHICAL PRESS, Point Loma, California, U. S. A.
THEOSOPHICAL BOOK COMPANY, 18, Bartlett's Buildings, Holborn Circus, London

COPYRIGHT, 1914, BY KATHERINE TINGLEY

THE ARYAN THEOSOPHICAL PRESS
Point Loma, California

To Katherine Tingley

Leader and Official Head of the
Universal Brotherhood and
Theosophical Society,
whose whole life has been
devoted to the cause of Peace and
Universal Brotherhood, this
book is respectfully
dedicated

PREFACE

How far the story is taken from the Four Branches of the Mabinogi, and to what degree it has elected to go its own way, need not be enlarged on here; now that that great old Welsh book has become a popular classic, with cheap editions both in Welsh and in English. Suffice it to say that from that source come the main framework of the plot, and, I hope, the whole spirit and atmosphere; and that there is a mint of phrases recurring through the chapters, which have been boldly lifted from Lady Guest's translation, and set in here without quotation marks, footnotes, or other acknowledgement. Why not? Such phrases were probably a part of the stock in trade of all the old story-tellers: "Names of Adornment," such as we find listed in the Triads; and belonged rather to Wales and bardism than to any one author. Other phrases, again, have been taken from Llywarch Hen and Taliesin, and from the druidical writings of the School of Glamorgan. Further, if Morgan Llwyd o Wynedd had not called his book *Llyfr y Tri Aderyn*, "The Book of the Three Birds," it is doubtful whether the various parts of this story would have found subtitles with so native a flavor as the ones that have been given to them. As to how much of it may be borrowed from Irish sources: it would be difficult for the writer to say; since it is rather a long time since he had access to books of Irish mythology, and the latter presents itself to his memory rather as a rainbow-hued and beautiful illumination, than in any detail. To read the Mabinogi aright, one must read it in the light of that ancient, proud and beautiful civilization which the Irish stories reveal so much more fully, and with so much less admixture of foreign and medieval elements; just as, to reconstruct the Celtic pantheon at all, one must work by the light of all Aryan mythology. In the days of Pwyll Pen Annwn there was little distinction between Cymro and Gwyddel, or between the Clan of Hu Gadarn in the Island of the Mighty, and the Family of Dana in Ireland.

The Mabinogi, as it comes down to us, and as it appears in Lady Guest's wonderful translation, remains such a classic, such a masterpiece of style, such a storehouse of ancient treasure, that it may be asked: What right has any one to imply that such and such an incident goes unrecorded in it, or is recorded incorrectly? But one must re-

member that the Mabinogi was very old before it was written down;
that bards had told and retold these stories a thousand times between
the days of their prechristian origin and the twelfth or thirteenth
century when they were written in the form in which we have them.
Would they have suffered no change during those ages? It is certain
that they would; from being the record and exposition of a mythology,
they would have become mainly a source of entertainment; their
pristine purpose would have become obscured; their day star would
have dwindled to a rushlight. Supposing we knew nothing of the
Greek mythology, but what might have remained as a tradition with
the troubadours?

The deepest truths of religion and philosophy had their first recording for the instruction of the peoples, not in the form of treatise, essay,
or disquisition, but as epics, sagas, and stories. I do not know what
better form could be found for them. It is the soul of man that is
the hero of the eternal drama of the world; "the Universe exists
for the purposes of the soul." From the beginning of time, events,
circumstances, and adventures are unfolding themselves about the
human soul; it is weaving them about itself. Man enmeshes himself
as in a web in the results of his own thought and action; and by his
own action and thought he must make himself free. The Great Ones
of old time knew well that there is a "small old path that leads to
freedom": a path of action, of thought, of wisdom. They related
the Story of the Soul; leading it from the first freedom of Gwynfyd,
down into the depths of Abred and incarnation, to the gates of that
path of freedom, and then onward to the heights. They that had ears
to hear, heard; and found in the great stories the indication of the
path for themselves; as for the multitude, there was entertainment
for them; and the mere outward teaching of the sagas would be their
incitement to virtue, to courage, to a sound, generous, and magnanimous life.

The stories long survived the time when their real meaning had been
forgotten. Druidism, as a state religion, might not withstand the legions
and proscription of the Caesars; if it lived on, it was in secret. But
the druid-born stories that had been the amusement of the chieftains
in the evenings of winter; that were for inculcating the traditional
virtues in the young men and maidens — there would not cease to be
a need for them. The winter evenings were no shorter than of old;

the virtues taught by the new religion were of another order; the feast times would still be incomplete without bards and story-tellers; and these must have their old capital to draw upon: they must have the outward and visible sign, if not the inward and spiritual grace. Perhaps all the ancient stories we have, Celtic or Scandinavian, Greek or Persian or Indian, are but the retelling of the sacred Mystery tales, by bards who had forgotten their meaning: forgotten something of it, or most of it, or all of it. For nothing dies until it has lost its first virtue; if the religions of antiquity had been true to themselves, had remained uncorrupted, they would not have passed away. Does not history prove to us — this little fragment of history that we possess — that the history of religion is always the story of the waning of a Light, and its rekindling elsewhere when too dim for further utility?

The generations of story-tellers, then, would add a little to their traditional material here, or leave out some detail there; they would modify this or that incident to suit their own ideas or the views of their audience. In general they would tend to introduce personality where before there had been merely the vast and impersonal; sex in particular would offer them a wide field for " improving " upon the ancient models. Do but contrast the Irish, or the purely Welsh tales, with those Welsh tales that have come to us in a Normanized and be-troubadoured form. Contrast the story of Pwyll and Rhianon with that of Tristan and Esyllt. In the former, which is far the older, there is no " love interest "; in the latter, there is nothing else. Some one has claimed that " romantic love " is altogether a growth of Christian times; not true in one sense, for men have experienced youth at a certain stage of their lives for quite a number of ages; but the claim is true to a certain extent, of romantic love considered as a theme for fiction. It came in, at any rate, whenever fiction ceased to be a method of teaching by symbology the sacred truths of the Mysteries, and became a mere minister to entertainment.

So too the ancient masters of fiction — their names are lost to us — had little concern with character-painting. The story of the human soul unfolds itself in action, and again action: actions, events, sufferings, deeds and deaths and sacrifice; battle and ruin and victory: these are the language in which the thoughts, experiences, and growth of the soul express themselves. What character-painting there was, was done in sweeping lines and prismatic colors: " he was a man from

whom no one ever got any good"; "noble and excellent are the men
of whom this is spoken." Naturally; since the characters were but
symbols of characteristics: of virtues or vices; of subtle powers
within that may aid, or subtle lures and weaknesses that may over-
throw us.

That is to say, they did not seek to tell you things *about* the
soul — which is the method of philosophy; but to present in great
pictures that soul itself — which is the true method of art. So the
love story of Pwyll and Rhianon is simplicity itself: man comes in
contact with that inward and divine light which is to make a god of
him at last; how should you enlarge upon "love" in such a con-
nexion? She will take queenhood in the Island of the Mighty, in
Dyfed, sharing the throne of the man who has made conquests in the
Underworld; he will share his throne with her, will become as it
were her disciple; since she is the brightest and most beautiful vision
of his days. It is the revelation of the divine to the personal principle
in man; it is not, and does not pretend nor desire to be a love story.
Not the husks and externalities of life are recorded; but symbols
are given of the inward and eternal things. And if in certain of the
ancient mythologies — not in the Mabinogi — there are incidents which
offend our sense of decency, we should still remember that these were
never intended as the record of physical fact and action; they were
symbols of inward happenings, which perhaps could only find their
recording in that way.

The Red Book of Hergest, in which the Mabinogi appears, was
written in the twelfth century or thereabouts; but the stories themselves are admittedly prechristian in origin. Would they not have
lost much of their pristine significance during that time, and gathered
accretions from the troublous and uncertain ages? It is certain
that the Gods would have appeared in them originally; as the Gods
appear in the Greek and Irish stories, or in the sagas of the North.
It is certain that some of the characters in them, who appear now
as mere men, were Gods when the stories were first told; the Children of Don, Gwydion and his brothers, are cognate with the children
of Dana in Ireland, and were Gods as surely as were the latter.
Gods figure in all the old mythological tales: Gods, men, and demons; because in the battle of the world, the eternal warfare of
the Gwynfydolion, good is perpetually at war with evil: man is the

battlefield whereon the divine and the devilish are at conflict; and
we, our conscious selves, stand between the two hosts, and ally ourselves now with one, now with the other. Is not that, almost, or
quite, a truism? Will any one quarrel with it?

So in this attempt to retell the Mabinogi, the Gods had to be
restored. For the endeavor has not been to bring the stories up to
date, as down through the centuries so many have done with that other
Welsh saga, the Arthurian legend; the endeavor has not been to make
an acceptable modern novel of them, or to charge them with any criticism of life — twentieth century life; as Tennyson charged the Arthurian legend with criticism of nineteenth century life; or as Malory
charged it with criticism of the life of the Middle Ages. Malory and
Tennyson both attained wonderful results, no doubt, from the literary
standpoint; but I think that from the standpoint of a lover of ancient
Wales and ancient Welsh traditions and ideals, they both made a failure of it, on the whole. The atmosphere of our mountains calls for
some older glamor, some magic more gigantic and august: you must
have Gods and Warriors and great Druids, not curled and groomed
knightlings at their jousts and amours. Those treasure-laden pages in
Culhwch and Olwen, in which the list is given of Arthur's men —
there you have an indication of the great things that were in the ancient Celtic or preceltic mind: voices call there from peaks which have
since been wrapped in silence; in all Welsh and Welsh-inspired literature, I find nothing so Welsh as that. Tennyson indeed, occasionally
forgetting the nineteenth century and his purpose, which assuredly
he had a right to work out in his own way, did speak now and again
in a kindred language, or in one as truly echoing the ancient world.

But his purpose and standpoint were other than those of the old
bards who first told these stories; whose purpose and standpoint, be
the result what it may, it has been sought to use here. The life
that those old bards criticised belongs to no age, has not changed
since they wrote or sang: since it is the inner life of the soul struggling
towards freedom. It is proper to the days of prehistory, the age of
the Italo-Celtic unity and the flowering splendor of the Celtic empire;
it is proper to the time when our ancestors were defending their hills
against the Norman invaders; it is proper to our own time, and to
tomorrow. For to any of us, today, tomorrow, next year, it may
happen to behold from the heights of our own inward Gorsedd Arberth,

Rhianon mystically riding through the twilight and beauty of the valley; we may hear at any time the music of the Three Singers of Peace. We may at the moment of attainment lose through rashness or fear the Goddess we have so nearly won; we may be compelled to go forth seeking such another basket as Pwyll Pen Annwn sought and found; to us, as we watch upon the sacred hill, the Gods will come with their lures and wiles and machinations, striving against their own will as it were to draw us away: to defeat their own immediate, for the sake of their own ultimate ends; who would make us, too, divine; who would prepare us to wage their warfare with them, where they are camped out against chaos on the borders of space. For the ancients did not posit omniscience or omnipotence as qualities of those whom they called the Gods: they saw evil in the world, and were logical. I think the truest idea they had about them was, that the Gods were the great generals and battle-captains in the eternal war against evil: wiser and stronger a thousand times than we are, they yet stood in need of us as a general stands in need of his private soldiers. (Only the difference would be far wider than that between general and privates.) So the effort would have been, not to obtain help from the Gods, but to give help to them.

The Gods had to be introduced then; but our Welsh Gods have not been remembered as the Greek, Irish, or Scandinavian Gods have been. So one might have either taken the God-names that appear in Gaulish or Brythonic inscriptions of Roman and perhaps preroman days; or sought what was required in the great mass that exists of Welsh tradition, bardic verse, triads, and the writings collected by the ever-to-be-honored Iolo Morganwg and the bards of the School of Glamorgan. This latter is the course that has been followed. The names from the inscriptions lack that Welsh ring, that strange combination of the familiar and the infinite, the homely and the poetically wonderful, the intimate with the far and marvelous, which I think will mark our Welsh contribution to art and literature, when we shall have attained self-consciousness as a nation. Teutates, Tarannis, and the like, though they sound scholarly, and no doubt meant something at one time, if only to Romanized Gauls and Brythons — bring no pictures with them, breathe no subtle music, seem to represent no spiritual reality, as do the names of Apollo, or Angus Oge, or Balder the Beautiful. But turning to the triads, one found something differ-

ent. Hu Gadarn, sniffed at by the scholars and critics, has credentials
of his own for the intuition and imagination; Plenydd, Alawn and
Gwron — the Light-bringer, the Lord of Harmonies, the Heartener
of Heroes — they form so perfect a symbol of powers that lie latent
in ourselves and in the universe, that if they were invented by Iolo
Morganwg, or by Meurig Dafydd, or by Llewelyn Sion, one would
say that the invention was rather a discovery: that they were Gods and
Welsh Gods before those men were born; just as the blood circulated
before Harvey's time, and America was in the west of the world before
Columbus sailed. No matter whether such names are ancient, medieval, or comparatively modern; one would have been put to it to invent them oneself, if one had not found them ready to hand.

There is Tybie of the Fountain, for example. What? — make a
pagan nymph or Goddess of Saint Tybie ferch Brychan Brycheiniog,
canonized by the Celtic Church! But why invent a new name, when
the scent of the mint-beds of Llandybie, the brightness of the kingcups
and the sweet music of the waters have been clustering round the
old one during all these centuries? And one might well suspect that
she has but been restored to her rights. Once a sacred well, you may
say, always a sacred well; the church, recognizing the sweet influences of such places, adopted them from its druid predecessors; you
had but to make a saint of the old-time Goddess guardian, and the
sweet influences needed not to be wasted because the religion had
changed. Whether you call her Tybie ferch Brychan, or Tybie of
the Family of Hu, she is there, *she is there!*

So with all the God-names used in this story. None of them is
the invention of the present writer (though the epithets attached
to them often are); they all occur somewhere in the tangle of traditional literature that has come down in Wales. Of this it may be said,
that if any part of it first appeared in the thirteenth, or in the six-
teeth, or in the nineteenth century, it does not follow, as the critics
appear to think, that it originated then; it may have flowed on beneath the surface of written literature since Druid and even predruid
days; and indeed, much of it carries a stronger and sweeter odor of
antiquity than any of the data served to us as strictly historical by
the great scholars and archaeologists of modern times.

There are two methods of criticism: the analytical and the synthetic. The former is all the rage these days, at least in Wales. Its

end would seem to be a barren scholarship: one analyses the Good, the Beautiful, and the True into the dust-heap; one disproves everything, laying the axe of a merely intellectual research to the roots of the creative imagination. There is no finality in this tendency: the last word has not been spoken. Modern modes of thought, and our modern civilization, are not, as we too often suppose, the fruit and perfection of the ages, up to which all past human activity has led, as to a supreme goal. We shall react from it, and turn to synthetic methods. We shall take what material comes down to us, and make use of whatever in it is beautiful, appeals to the imagination, or shadows forth some spiritual truth; and of this we shall build that great imaginative literature which we are longing for and feeling after even now. The Irish, using the materials they have to hand, have laid the foundations of a great Irish drama, and have made the peculiar Irish note heard in the symphony of the literature of civilization. Our materials, somewhat more shadowy and disorganized it is true, we are at present mainly engaged in trying to analyse off the face of the earth. But to produce an imaginative literature we must fortify the imagination, not starve or stultify it; we must put our paints on the canvas, not perpetually submit them to the test tube and the crucible until there is no health nor color left in them.

This analytical rage is the reaction, natural enough, from old methods of syntheticism that lacked all discipline, were wholly uncritical and directed toward no goal; and which therefore spent themselves without ever producing anything in art or literature capable of passing the boundaries of our small nationality, and becoming a part of the art or literature of civilization. If the reaction from our present analyticism is not to carry us back to the old condition, some new element, some new knowledge, some new discipline, must come in. Wales has given just one work to world-literature; has produced just one work which by its innate vitality was bound to be translated sooner or later: the Mabinogion — we use the word as including the twelfth century romances translated by Lady Charlotte Guest. We have had many fine writers of the second rank: Dafydd ab Gwilym and Rhys Goch Tir Iarll; Morgan Llwyd o Wynedd; Goronwy and Ceiriog and Islwyn, to name a very few of them. Of these, Islwyn and Morgan Llwyd did indeed make some original contributions to thought, for which perhaps the literature of civilization may find a certain place.

The others, I think, will inspire Welsh poets to come who will speak directly to the world; will teach them their art, provide them with a treasure of music and color. But they wrote nothing that must inevitably be translated into other languages; they wrote nothing that will influence the world at first hand. It is just the music and color, which they used so well, that must be lost in translation, unless the translator is himself a poet equal to those whose work he may be translating.

Why then do the Romances stand in a class by themselves? Why are they for the world and all time; while the poetry of that age was, mainly, only for that age; and only for Wales — or indeed, only for Gwynedd, or Powys, or the South?

The answer is, because the Romances came down from a much older time; because when they were first written, they were still near enough in spirit to that older time to carry with them some of its force; and because in that older time there did exist such a discipline, such a knowledge, such a purpose as we stand in need of now. The knowledge is the knowledge of the spiritual laws of life; the purpose is the purpose of the human soul on its evolutionary journey; the discipline is that discipline which tends to subject the brain-mind and animal man to the domination of the divine part of man, the deathless and birthless soul.

So-called Realism concerns itself with but the froth and spume on the surface of life, the sordid play of the passions, the externalities that pass. Such Dead Sea Fruit has a great vogue in this age of slums and materialism; but we and civilization will evolve; the world will be cleaned up a little; men and nations will forgo their predatory habits; and we shall forsake this making of mud pies. Above all I would urge that there is no message for Wales in it; realism will never call forth the genius of a race that has always been nearest greatness when most leaning towards spiritual and imaginative ideals.

The true function of Romance, on the other hand — we need not say how sadly it has fallen away from it — is to proclaim indestructible truth in terms of the imagination: to use the symbols provided by the poetic or creative imagination for showing forth those truths which are permanent, because they lie at the heart of life, not on its surface; and which belong to no one age, but to all ages, because all eternity is the birthday of the soul.

Traces, shadows of these truths are to be found in the traditions
of almost every race under the sun; Welsh traditional literature is
peculiarly rich in them. Indeed, if Iolo Morganwg and his compeers
and predecessors really invented all that they claimed merely to have
collected and handed down, then let their names be written far above
any other names in our literary annals; for what they gave to the world
contains that which is original, permanent, and splendid: as Welsh
as Snowdon or the Cymraeg, it yet achieves being universal; if we but
understood it, it ranks with, or outranks the Mabinogi itself in value.
But this, not until we have applied to it a certain criterion; not until
we have fitted it into its place among the traditions of the whole
world; pruning and restoring it in the light of such traditions.

We owe it to Madame H. P. Blavatsky, the Foundress of the
Theosophical Movement of modern times, and to William Q. Judge
and Katherine Tingley, her successors in the Leadership of that Movement, that the criterion exists effective for this work: that there is
accessible a compendium, an explanation, a correlation and explicit
setting forth of those inward laws: the knowledge, the purpose, and
the discipline out of which all religions drew their origin, and which
are the heart of all true religion; which proclaim this to be the end
of all existence: that that which is now human should be made more
than human, divine. We may call this Druidism, we may call it Theosophy; it is also Christian and Buddhist; whatever name may be
applied to it, it is a trumpet-call to the Divine in each of us, the Grand
Hai Atton of the Immortals; it is the Dragon Warshout of the ages:
" Y Ddraig Goch a Ddyry — Gychwyn! " — *The Flamebright Dragon
has arisen* — the Dragon that of old was the symbol of spiritual wisdom, spiritual courage, mastery of the forces of the lower world —
Go forward!

.   .   .   .

I take this opportunity of acknowledging most gratefully the help
so kindly given by Mr. R. Machell, my fellow student of Theosophy
here at Point Loma, in making the splendid drawings with which the
book is illustrated.

CONTENTS

The Fates of the Princes
of Dyfed

Here are the Three Branches of the
Bringing in of it, namely:

The Sovereignty of Annwn

I N the old, antique, ancient times it happened to the Immortal Kindred to be taking counsel, and considering among themselves, in the House of Hu Gadarn in the Wyddfa Mountain in Wales. Hu had called them together, on account of a matter that was on his mind at that time. As to who Hu Gadarn was, should any one have heard no tidings about him, and about his power, and fame, and sovereignty over the Gods and the Cymry: he was the one that was supreme over both those races; he had led them out of the Summer Country into the Island of the Mighty, ages before; and tamed Nynnio and

Peibio, the Exalted Oxen, and with them accomplished the
ploughing of the whole island, and the destruction of the
Afangc of the Lake of Floods. Whenever it seemed fitting
to Hu Gadarn to be born among men, he would take no name
nor title but the name and title of the *Emperor Arthur;* and
from that alone it may be known what dignity he had.

With Hu the Mighty in the council were Math fab Mathonwy the Enchanter, and Tydain Tad Awen the Archdruid
of the Gods. Ceridwen Ren ferch Hu was there, the Queen
and Mother of the World. There also were the three Disciples of Math: Gofannon and Amaethon and Gwydion, the
three magnanimous Sons of Don. (Gofannon was the chief
of the smiths, and Amaethon of the husbandmen; while as
for Gwydion, he was unequaled, even among the Immortals,
for laughter, and for narrating stories; and no subtlety of
wisdom would ever be concealed from him.)   Their sister,
Arianrhod of the Silver Wheel, who declares fates and destinies; and Don Ren herself. The three Primitive Bards of
the Island of the Mighty, the divine Disciples of Tad Awen:
Plenydd Sunbright, and Alawn with the Harp, and Gwron
Gawr the Heartener of Heroes. Idris Gawr, the Marshal of
the Stars, and Einigan the Giant, and Nefydd Naf Neifion,
Prince of the Sea. Menw the Son of the Three Shouts, and
Mabon ab Modron, and Modron Ren herself, and Malen
Ruddgoch Ren, the War-red War Queen. None of them
were absent, so far as is known. They were a peerless tribe,
a family to be praised and lauded and honored; flaming-
bodied, even the least of them; august and beautiful. It
was they who preserved the beauty of Britain, and the valor,
and modesty, and truthfulness, and wisdom of the Race and
Kindred of the Cymry, in the ancient days.

What they were considering will be made known in the
length of the story, should any desire and have patience to

seek for it. The end of the council was this conversation taking place between them:

"As far as stags are concerned," said the Son of Mathonwy; "if one were needed for this work, I could put the guise of a stag on any one. The peculiarities of my wand would be enough for that."

"Who is there that would desire to have it put on him?" said Hu the Mighty.

"I know the road from Dyfed into the Underworld," said Gwydion ab Don. "It would be nothing but a day of pleasure to me, to have hounds pursuing me from dawn to dusk."

The Gods laughed. "Let it be so, Lord Brother," said Hu Gadarn.

That evening a splendid, many-antlered stag stood forth in the moonlight on the southern slope of the Wyddfa, and took his way southward, cantering lordlily. Before dawn he had covered the whole length of Wales from the north to the south, so speedy he was; and when the dew was at its brightest on the bracken, he was watching for hounds from a fern-brake in Glyn Cuch, by Llwyn Diarwyd in Dyfed.

N those days, Pwyll Prince of Dyfed had not his equal in beauty and prowess among the warlike sovereigns of the Island of the Mighty; and he held lordship in a country the most lovely in the world; heaven knows where may be its better, or whether more of excellence and delight could be crowded into it than is there already. As for his people, the Dimetians, there were none more kindly or valorous, either in the three Islands of the Mighty, or in the three islands near thereby, or in the island of Ireland. In the court of the Crowned King in London there was no one, unless it was the Crowned King himself, or Taliesin the Chief of Bards, or the great Druids of Ynys Mon, or Teyrnion Twrf Fliant, King of Gwent, that had more dignity than Pwyll had; indeed, the Princes of Dyfed had always been held to be among the three Supporting Pillars of Sovereignty of the Island of Britain.

Whatever may have happened to Pwyll before the day he went hunting in Glyn Cuch, nothing is known of it; that was the seed and beginning of all that is related concerning him. For that reason, no one would leave the story of that hunt unrelated, if he were for setting forth duly the History of the Fates of the Princes of Dyfed.

In the cold of the dawn and the youth of the day he rode out from Llwyn Diarwyd, and the hundred men of his teulu, and a hundred dogs followed him. Before the drying of the dew, they roused up in Glyn Cuch a splendid, many-antlered stag; as soon as he saw it, the desire of his life came on Pwyll to overtake it. Until dusk he had it in view; by mountain and meadow, by rushy field and ferny forest, it cantered on lordlily before him. It was well known that no four-footed creature in the Island of the Mighty, except Fflamwen Aden-Goleu the mare of Twrf Fliant, was equal in speed to Pwyll's mare Blodwen; indeed, those two were sisters, of the one sire and dam. The men of the teulu were the best riders in the world, so far as was known, and as for his hundred dogs, they were a hundred swift, unrivaled, harrying hunters. But there was no success for any of them against that stag; and that was a cause for great marveling with the chieftain. Dusk came over the trees, and a glow of gold and rose and saffron covered the western heaven; he saw the stag pass behind a shoulder of mountain, barely a bowshot in front of him. Impetuously he rode forward in pursuit; but when he came out into the valley beyond, there was no sign of it to be seen. In a little while he drew rein, finding nothing, and the dogs being at fault. He blew three resounding blasts upon his horn; but got no answer, beyond the shouting of mountain echoes.

It was on the shore of a long, dim lake he was, in a great valley; and the clear water lapping among the reeds, and on the pebbles at the mare's forehoofs. A few birds flew through the twilight, calling with shrill and mournful voices. Around him the dogs were running hither and yonder, confused, and whining uneasily; it was clear to him that neither

he nor they knew the place, or had seen it before during
their lives, or would know which way to take, if they desired
to be returning to Llwyn Diarwyd.

While the echoes from the horn were dying away among
the mountains beyond the lake, a sound came down from the
hillside behind him, that seemed to be barking, but was unlike
any barking he had heard until then. He turned, and suddenly the stag dashed out of the wood there, making towards the
water; then, seeing him, it swerved, and ran out before him
along the lake edge. He forgot everything but his desire to
catch it; away with him, and the dogs in front of him, in a
moment. As he rode, he heard the barking of the strange
dogs; and once there came to his ears the sound of a horn
unlike any hunting-horn in the Island of the Mighty; but
with his haste, and his eager desire to come up with the
stag, it was the same to him as if he had heard nothing.

He was nearing it now; it seemed to him that a shadowy
light was playing about its proud horns and beautiful body.
On his left hand was the lake, and the round, lone, boulder-
strewn mountains beyond it; on his right the darkening,
rushy fields rose up to the rim of the woodland. Suddenly
the pack that he had heard barking poured out from among
the trees there, and swept down after the stag. In the whole
world there was not the like of that pack in those days; much
less is there the like of it now. Clearly the dogs shone against
the dusk and purple of the edge of the forest. Their bodies
were wan and luminous like pearls, but whiter than any
pearl in the east or west of the world. Their right ears were
redder than deep roses, and sparkled and burned as if made
of ruby-stuff with the moon strangely and brilliantly shining
through it. As for their barking, there was a wild music and
sorrow in it; never had a sound so mournful been heard in
the three Islands of the Mighty.

Before they could reach the stag, Pwyll was in the midst of them, driving them back, and setting his own dogs upon it instead. It was standing at bay in the water; the Dimetian dogs not farther from it, the foremost of them, than they might have leaped; and the chieftain himself coming up as swiftly as he might. He saw its two eyes, and perceived clearly that there was no fear nor expectation of danger in them. He raised his hunting-spear, and was in the act of casting it; three of his dogs were in the act of leaping. But before the spear might be loosed from his hand, and before the dogs might leave the ground in their leaping, he heard a sound that suddenly stayed him and them: his own name called thrice from the border of the forest behind him. With that there was a shaking out of somber laughter over the water, and the stag rose up in the air, and ran shining through the dusky air, high above the lake, luminous against the far, wild, purply-darkening mountains beyond — and was lost.

Then Pwyll turned, and saw a man riding down out of the wood, whom even the blind would have known to be a mighty king. Without haste his grand, dun-colored charger bore him, splashing with its hoofs through the pool-starred, rush-grown field. Dark was the mantle blown back from his shoulders, like a storm-cloud trailed across the face of night. Set in his brooch were deeply glowing rubies and sapphires; in his hunting-cap a purple diamond, larger than a hen's egg, that burned and sparkled and twinkled through the gloom. He was stern and tall, slow of speech, and unlike any of the kings of the Island of the Mighty; for they were handsome, proud, bright-eyed, laughter-loving men, but he seemed as if great labor and sorrow were never apart from him. Yet a dignity akin to that of the Immortal Kindred was upon him, and it was to be seen that kings would obey when he commanded.

"Ha, chieftain!" he cried. "What breach of courtesy is this that you have committed?"

"The greeting of heaven and of man to you," said Pwyll. "No breach of courtesy in the world, so far as is known. Hunting my own stag have I been, in my own country."

"Hunting the stag in my country have you been," said the other; "and driving my dogs away from it."

It came into Pwyll's mind again that although he knew every field and mountain, and lake and stream, and vale and woodland within the boundaries of Dyfed, he had never seen the like of those mountains, nor heard so much as a rumor of that lake and valley until then. The place was neither in his own kingdom, nor in any known land beyond its borders.

"Ah, chieftain," said he, "a main breach of courtesy is this indeed. I will ride back quickly into Dyfed, and send what presents you may desire to requite you."

"No one that comes into this land may go out of it without doing service," said the king.

"As to that," said Pwyll, "if it please you, set a hundred well-armed men against me, in all courtesy, that I may make trial whether there is any going out of it or not. Less than fitting would it be to do otherwise. Whatever warfare I may wage against them, I will send the presents when I have come to my own court."

"Not so," said the king. "You have come to no land in the Island of the Mighty, nor in any of the four quarters of the world of men. Wherever the road may lie between this and Llwyn Diarwyd, take it you without hindrance, if there is any finding it for you."

It was clear to Pwyll that there was not; either for him or for his dogs.

' "The road is lost," said he. "What land is this into which I have wandered?"

"Annwn it is, in the Underworld. Arawn, King of Annwn am I."

Pwyll knew by that that he had left the world of men, and could not come to it again by any common traveling. He knew, too, that the one he was talking with was of the Race and Kindred of the Immortals.

" I will do the service gladly," said he. " Be it what it will, it will be an honor to me to undertake it."

" It will be the killing of Hafgan the son of Hunan, whose kingdom borders on my own," said the other. " There has been no peace in Annwn since he usurped the throne of it."

" This night I will go against him," said Pwyll. "And I will let no rest come on me until this is accomplished."

" Not so," said Arawn. " Hafgan will never be killed by any one, unless he thinks it is I who am killing him. My aspect you must wear when you go against him, and my sword you must strike with, or there will be no ridding him of life."

" Lord," said Pwyll; " put you the aspect upon me, as it may be in your power to; and give me the sword, to make trial whether I can use it or not." It was known to him without receiving news of it, that few could wield such a sword as Arawn's would be.

The king drew it from its sheath; a great, burning, beautiful brand, huger than any sword in the Island of the Mighty, or in Ireland, or in the whole world, so far as was known. Pwyll took it by the hilt as Arawn held it out to him; he was a strong man, and the best of all the swordsmen in Britain. But when he took that sword, it seemed to him that there was an arrogant, fierce, unsubduable spirit in it; it writhed and shook itself in his hand; a great flame and shouting broke from it; fiercely it struggled and tore itself away from him; and in a moment had returned of its own will to its sheath.

"No one could wield it, until he had been reigning in Annwn for at least a year and a day," said the king. "No one would be able to obtain success against Hafgan until after that time. And he would not obtain it either, if, on the field of conflict, he granted any request that Hafgan might make of him after the first blow was struck."

"Nothing will be granted him," said Pwyll. "If it please you to tell me, what will follow the killing of this man?"

"The best advantage in the world to the one that shall have killed him," said Arawn. "Whoever may obtain success in this will become one with the Immortal Kindred; first or last, he will become one with them. He will have a wife from the Country of the Immortals, and the Hill of the Immortals will be revealed for him."

While the king was speaking, a mist and a wild music were rising over the valley; and lake and woods and hills, and even Arawn himself, grew dimmer and dimmer before Pwyll's vision, beyond the dimness of the falling of night. Shadowy, opal-colored multitudes stole forth from the mists and mountains, moving and waving in their vague dances. He dismounted from white Blodwen, and went half dreaming towards the dun-colored charger. The dancers ebbed and flowed around him, filling the valley with the sound of their harps. At first they were faint and dim, far and stately; they might have been the forms of the hills and trees, flowing forth and rippling about the rim of the world. Their motion became faster; they drew nearer to him, taking on luminous, delicate forms, and the colors of all jewels; he could feel the cool, slumber-laden breezes from their waving arms on his face and in his hair; he could feel them drenching him with dews of peace and sleep and oblivion. A quiet rhythm of singing drifted from them; a whirl and wandering of music from their twinkling fingers on the strings. The sound lapped like calm lake water about his mind, until vision and memory faded from him, and he was unaware of the world and the sky.

Then the King of Annwn mounted Blodwen, and called Pwyll's dogs, and rode off to Dyfed by a little secret way across the mountains. There it is said that he reigned for a year and a day in the palace of Arberth, and none of the Dimetians ever so much as dreaming he was not their rightful lord. But as for Pwyll, a marvelous change came upon him. Instead of the blue cloak he had been wearing, it was the dark mantle of Arawn that was on him; for white Blodwen, and her splendid saddle, and her four-cornered saddle-cloth of purple with an apple of gold at each corner, he had the gemless saddle and the great, dun-colored charger. His face changed, and became dark and stern and brown-bearded; and his mien changed, and his carriage and bearing and stature; so that no one would have known it was Pwyll he was, and not Arawn. Then the dream-weaving multitude left him, and he awoke.

 HE last gleam of the sun had waned out of the west by that time. The moon shone pale yellow, like the primrose, on the lake and in the sky, and the stars were out in their billions; beyond a little splash and rippling from the leaping of fish, there would hardly be a sound in the whole valley. Unfamiliar now, to the chieftain, was the name of *Pwyll;* unfamiliar was Dyfed, and the whole of his kinghood there. Without hesitancy he rode forward towards the palace of Arawn, and took his place on the throne at the feast, as if he had never dwelt elsewhere during his whole life.

He reigned there for a year and a day without song, without story-telling, without the sound of harping or laughter. They say that Annwn would be a good country enough, if the sun shone there, or if the sea-wind blew in from the southwest, or if rain fell at any time on the hills. But the sunlight reaches no farther than to its borders; beyond them, it is not known if flowers bloom or birds sing. There are light and darkness there; but no blueness in the sky by day, or beauty of starlight at night-time. During the whole year, he was without delight or glory. No one knew that he was not Arawn; least of all did he know it himself. The people were fierce and silent and sullen, without any of the ardor and warlike gaiety natural to the Cymry at that time; small the pleasure or satisfaction of governing them. . . .

When the year and the day had passed, the great chieftains of Annwn came to him. " Lord," said they, " the truce is at an end." " Yes," said he; " we will go forward against Hafgan." The next day he led forth his teulu into the sunshine on the borders of Annwn, and camped by the ford in the river that flowed between Hafgan's kingdom and Arawn's.

The river was broad and shallow at that place, and singing over innumerable stones; and with many alders on either bank, and great oak-trees beyond the alders. The road ran down through the river between the trees; the sunlight dappled the shallow water there, gleaming down on it through the leafage. The two armies were on the plain facing each other, one on this side of the ford, one on that.

It came into the minds of the men of Hafgan's teulu at that time that it would be better for their lord and Arawn to fight alone, body against body; and whoso might be the winner, he should be the king. They had no quarrel, themselves, against Arawn or his men. They sent an embassy to the man that seemed to be Arawn with the message; it appeared to him, too, that there would be no better means for ending the warfare. As for his princes, they were willing to be ruled by him; although it was taking the whole of their pleasure out of the day.

At noon, therefore, he put the golden breastplate of the sovereignty of Annwn on his breast (it was adorned with magical designs, and with inscriptions in the coelbren character, of high potency and significance). He set the shield of Arawn on his left arm (it was of hide that had been steeped, for the sake of strength, in magical waters for a hundred years, and studded over firmly with nails of the burnished bronze of Annwn). He took Arawn's spear in his right hand (it was a keen, swift and peerless piercer). On his head he set Arawn's helmet (its two wings were the wings of an eagle; although dinted and without brightness, no defense could be better where there might be neither boasting nor cowardice). He hung the sheathed sword at his side, and went forward with his princes; they rode into the daylight on the borders of Annwn. The sun gleamed on the gold of the breastplate, and on the purple beauty of the diamond in the helm, and on the sunbright silk of his mantle, that was of the color of the softest moss on the floor of the forest. Never had they seen their king more regal of mien or proud and handsome of aspect than then.

A wonder of strange thinking drifted into his mind as he rode forward. Far and wandering music was made known to him, and a song more marvelous than any one in Annwn could sing; it grew stronger and nearer and sweeter, mingling with the sunlight and triumphing on the wind. It filled him, heart and mind and imagination, with beautiful, mysterious and heroic things: things half forgotten, such as it would be a glory to remember; as if one should know that there were favorable deities considering one from beyond the near mountains, who, waiting for their time, will make no sign now, nor stretch forth any hand; but will yet presently break forth upon the twilight gleaming.

Hafgan and his men were waiting on their side of the river; he and Pwyll would fight in the middle of the ford, with the shallow water playing about their feet. They strode forward into the stream; the one from this side, the other from that. Hafgan lifted his long spear, and hurled it out vigorously at the one that seemed to be Arawn. It flew hissing over Pwyll's shoulder, within a little of his right ear, and was driven into the bank a yard deep, quivering, harming nothing. Then the spear of Arawn leaped forth, trembling through its long length, raising up song, delighting in the free air and the sunlight and the battle. Easily it pierced through the ruby in the helmet of Hafgan, and smote the helmet itself from his head, so that it fell down and rolled in the water, and whatever witchcraft might have been in it, was lost. "Lord," said Pwyll, "reset it in its place, if it please you, before there shall come to be strife and violence between us."

With the whizzing of the two spears, the music he had been hearing — and it all intermingled with the rustling murmur of the young leaves on the alders, and the whisper in the swaying of the oak boughs, and the rippling of the water over the stones — became articulate and crowded with mysterious meanings; clearly he heard vocal song blown in upon him with the wind and drifting down with the water. Here now is the form that it took:

> *Was there never whisper wandered*
> *through your quiet hours and dreaming*
> *Of a land all lovely seeming*
> *with the wild white rose a-bloom,*
> *And the harebells bending heavy*
> *when the dews of June are gleaming,*
> *In the foxglove fields of Cemais,*
> *where the white waves boom?*

> *Came there ne'er at noon or night-time*
> *any wonder-rumor winging,*
> *How the southwest wind is singing*
> *over woodlands wrapt in dream,*
> *When the moon is o'er the mountains,*
> *and the fairy-folk go flinging*
> *Their wandering incantations*
> *down the dim-foamed stream?*

It's from Teifi side to Tywi side
the hills are filled with yearning
For their chieftain's swift returning
from the sun-forgotten strand;
And the light about the High Crown
in the King's town unburning
Till you turn, Pwyll Pen Annwn,
to your own loved land.

There came back into his mind the wild, lone valley and
the lake, and the dimly twinkling feet and waving arms of
them that wove sleep and oblivion for him with their dancing;
and the stag he had pursued since the dawn of morning, a
year and a day since, through lands more beautiful than any
in Annwn. He remembered the Island of the Mighty, and
the proud, heroic race that held it; faintly, indeed, he remembered them as yet; like one who has not wholly shaken himself free from a dream.

Hafgan stooped and picked up the helmet, and reset it
on his head; then they met in the midst of the ford. With
the first onrush of the one that was against him, there came
into Pwyll's memory the Warshout of the Golden Dragon,
the regal, loud, menacing, Warshout of the Island of the
Mighty; and he raised it so that it could be heard from one
end of Annwn to the other. Fierce, resolute and cunning
was the attack of Hafgan, but all his blows fell harmless
on Arawn's shield. He was not one that could gain success
against a king from the Island of the Mighty with the Dragon
Shout upon his lips.

Then Pwyll let the sword have its will. Eager it was
for the sunlight, and for the conflict, and for the striking of
great, griding blows, and for the opposition of strong, well-

worn shield and helmet. Not untame, not disobedient it was, to the desires he framed in his heart. High in the air it flashed in his hand; keen and dazzling was its sweeping fall. Whatever weapons Hafgan opposed to it, they were torn and crumpled and withered, they were smitten through and utterly brought to ruin. His shield was no better than a sere leaf; his sword no stronger than an elm twig in autumn; it flew from the hand of Hafgan, this half and that half divided lengthwise, and splashed in two deep pools far below them among the alders. At the same blow the son of Hunan fell. Then Pwyll knew clearly the whole fate that had fallen upon him. He remembered the rain-swept, green, beautiful ways of the Island of the Mighty, and the councils in the palace of the Crowned King in London; most of all he remembered his dear and native town, lime-washed Arberth in Dyfed, and all his state and kinghood there, and his warlike, dear and eager companions the Dimetians.

"Ha, chieftain," said Hafgan, " finish the work that you have begun. It would be ill to leave me between death and life."

But Pwyll remembered the warning of Arawn. "Not so," said he, " the one blow was enough; it would be an insult to the sword to think otherwise. Go you, if it please you, without my troubling your going."

"Strike in the name of heaven and man, unless you desire that I should recover."

"I desire it not; and therefore have I sheathed the sword."

"Evil fall upon the sword and the one that wielded it. Hereafter I shall come by no new body, on account of this." With that it was as if he were changed into a light wisp of cloud above the water; a wind came, and away with the cloud; and it is not known whether there was any new life or being for him from that out. Never a rumor of him was heard in Annwn, after; much less in the Island of the Mighty.

As for Pwyll, no sooner was Hafgan dead, than his own form and aspect came on him again; and there was Arawn on the bank waiting to greet him, leading Blodwen by the bridle.

"Go forward," said Arawn; "you shall not come to Arberth without meeting the reward of this."

"What reward will it be, if it please you to give me news of it?" said Pwyll.

"The Making Known to you of the Hill of the Immortals, and the Seeing a Marvel from the head of it," said the other.

Therewith Pwyll went forward, and the way was clear for him as far as Llwyn Diarwyd in Dyfed; there he came upon the men of his teulu, hunting, where Arawn had left them in the morning. It was a main marvel to them when he gave them the news of Annwn, and who it was that had been reigning in Dyfed during the year that had passed.

He had the name of *Pwyll Pen Annwn* from that out, beyond his old one of *Pwyll Pendefig Dyfed*. It is because it relates how he came by that new title, that this Bringing-in of the Story is called *The Sovereignty of Annwn*. It ends with his meeting his companions in Llwyn Diarwyd, and his setting forth with them to journey towards Arberth, which was his chief court at that time.

The Story of Pwyll and Rhianon
or
The Book of the Three Trials

Here is the First Branch of the Story of
Pwyll and Rhianon,
the First and Second Parts of it;
the whole Branch has the name of

The Coming of
Rhianon Ren ferch Hefeydd

I. THE MAKING-KNOWN OF GORSEDD ARBERTH, AND THE WONDERFUL RIDING OF RHIANON

ELL known to the chieftain as he rode forward towards Arberth, and the men of his teulu with him, were every wood and glade, and field and river, and hill and vale in the land; and if well known, they were dearly loved by him, and a gladness to his eyes when he saw them; long it was since he had seen their like. More pleasant was this journey to him, than any journey he had ever made.

Towards evening on the second day, the road they would take ran through a valley; as they came to the head of the valley, suddenly the place was unknown, and as if he had never seen it before. Where of old there had only been a rushy meadow in the middle of the valley, and through the meadow the road, and below that, on the left as one rides towards Arberth, a little, noisy river; now there was a high hill, and on the top of it what seemed to be a great throne of rock. A hedge ran between the road and the hill; at one place there was a break in the hedge, and a stile, and from the stile a grassy pathway up to the throne on the hilltop. A druid was coming down the path towards the road.

"What hill is this?" said Pwyll. Not one of them had heard so much as a sound or a rumor of it before that evening. "It would be well to ask the druid," said they. "If any one will know, he will."

"Soul," said the holy druid; "the hill is called Gorsedd Arberth; the Hill of the Immortals it is."

"For what reason has it been unknown hitherto?" said Pwyll. "For what reason has there been no revealing it until now?"

"For the reason of its peculiarities, truly. There will be no making it known at any time, unless one of the Cymry should have won victories in Annwn."

"What peculiarities are with it, beyond that one?" said Pwyll.

"This peculiarity," said the druid. "Whoever ascends it, and takes his place on the throne, will not come away without either seeing some marvel, or suffering blows and violence."

"Evil fall upon my beard," said Pwyll Pen Annwn, "unless I take my place there."

"Lord," said they; "it would be well to ride forward. Not fitting for a prince of your dignity to meet with blows and violence."

"Let them fall on whomsoever may deserve them," said Pwyll. "It would be an ill thing if wonders were for the seeing, and we without the seeing them."

With that they rode to the top of the hill, and dismounted, and Pwyll Pen Annwn took his place on the throne, and his men standing around him. They saw the road running on below them westward to where the sun was setting between the far hills. Eastward it ran down the valley into the dusk; the dark blossom of night was beginning to unfold over the sky there. As they watched the gloom and purple beauty of that deep bloom, there rose and glimmered a mist of light afar beneath the heart of it, that moved along the road slowly towards them. It came nearer and grew brighter; it was of pale blue and rose-color and violet; immortal music stole through the valley as it came.

Then they saw that it was a princess, riding on a proud, matchless, snow-white horse; light shone from her as she rode. Among all the golden-chained daughters of the Cymry, clear it was to them that there would be no one to compare with her, either for grace and beauty of aspect, or for majesty and queenly dignity of bearing. Of purple silk was her robe, bordered with the colors of the snowdrop and the primrose; it would have given light in a dark place. Very slowly trod her proud, arch-necked, long-maned, high-stepping palfrey. About her as she came the air quivered and glimmered into all the hues of the opal, the rose-pearl and the amethyst. Along the roadside bloomed forth hyacinths and daffodils of flame: mysterious daffodils and hyacinths and violets. Branches put out from invisible trees around her head, and on them apple-bloom and almond-bloom of star-fire. Always, around and in front and above and behind her, shone and winged and sang and quiveringly twinkled three bright, beautiful, wizard birds; now paler and more glamorous than three moons in winter, now richer than three clouds torn from the glory of the dawn. As they drew nearer, it was to be seen that the first of them was white, and the second blue, and the third hued like the rainbow of heaven. Whatever music might be heard there, came from those three; it was such that whoever heard it might listen for a thousand years, and at the end it would seem to him no more than an hour that he had been listening.

Pwyll bade one of his men go down and meet her on the road, and give her the courtesy of a prince of the Cymry, and the greeting of god and man, and ask her in what way the lord of the country she was traversing might serve her. He strode quickly down the hillside; with the slowness of her riding, it was apparent that he would come to the stile before she would. He came down to the road; as he was mounting the stile, she passed him. He leaped down, and followed her quickly, walking. She went no faster than at first; slowly, with high steps, her swan-white horse went forward. He began to run; the more he ran, the farther she was from him. He put out his whole speed pursuing her; and it was clear to them all that she never quickened her horse's pace. They saw him run and run until she was no more than a faint cloud of beauty on the horizon. Made one she was, at last, with the whole glow and loveliness of the sunset; the magic of her coming waned from the valley, and they heard no music beyond the rippling and laughter of the river below them. Then they rose up, and took horse, and went forward musing into Arberth. But Pwyll Pen Annwn knew there would be no peace for him, until he had heard tidings concerning that Princess of the Immortals.

The next day he rode out again, and his men with him, and they came to the Gorsedd at the same time as before. He had a swift horse saddled by the throne beside him, and the best and lordliest of all his horsemen waiting in the saddle for whatever might befall. No sooner had he taken his place on the throne, and looked eastward along the road and down the valley, than the twilight began to bloom in light and beauty there, ten times more wonderfully than on the day before. They saw the lady riding; if there had been light from her before, and marvelous grace with her, and glory of mien, ten times more were they shining from her now. The daffodils of pale and beautiful flame that bloomed beside the roadway; the flame-mists of forget-me-not; the unfolding of the colors of the opal and the turquoise, of the pearl and the amethyst and the diamond, were all ten times more luminous. And if her three birds had appeared like three moons, or like three clouds out of the dawn; now they were of such splendor that there is no likeness for them in the summer sky, or the sunlit sea, or the four quarters of the immense world.

While she was still a long way off, the horseman set forward, and away with him galloping down the hillside. It was clear to even the least of them that she was riding even more slowly than before. He leaped his horse over the stile; but she had passed the stile before he could leap it. He set spur to his horse, and pursued her; a very little way in front of him she appeared to be riding. With slow, proud, high steps her beautiful palfrey journeyed forward. As for the one that followed her, for all the speed his horse could put out, he came no nearer to her than at first; indeed, the faster he went, the farther she was from him. He made pursuit of her as long as he could see her; she never went more than slowly, yet was always dwindling and waning farther and

farther away from him. At the last she was one with the
sunset again, and he turned and rode back to Pwyll. And
ten times surer was the chieftain that there would be no
quietness of mind for him, without his having heard any
better tidings concerning the princess than he had heard
until then.

The next day they rode out again; when the sun was
brooding in a sky of flame over the head of the valley, Pwyll
Pen Annwn took his seat on Gorsedd Arberth, and turned
his back to the sunset, and his face towards the somber, empurpled budding-forth of night in the east. There in the
midst of the dusk, again arose that wonderment and many-
jeweled luminance; indeed and indeed now, sorrow upon me
if it was not as much as seventy times brighter and more
wonderful than before. He would trust no longer in any
horse but his own, or in any other rider than himself. Blodwen stood waiting by his side; well-saddled she was, and
the saddle-cloth of purple about her, with an apple of gold
at each corner, as was right and fitting for the saddle-cloth
of a king; well-equipped for riding was Pwyll Pen Annwn
himself. No sooner did the twilight-glamorous valley begin
to bloom in sprays of marvelous starry flowers; no sooner
did the low, sweet, melodious singing of the three birds begin
to sway and whirl and steal forth, and put dreams and delight
and bewildering enchantment on the winds and the hills and
the waters; no sooner was the roadway lined afar with mys-
tical daffodils and iris and lilac, bending and dancing on a
wind blown from no mortal land — than he leaped up from
the throne, and to horseback, and away with him in a thunder
of hoofs towards the stile.

At that time she seemed to be far off; more slowly than
ever, and with prouder steps, her gleaming, swan-white,
deathless palfrey bore her. As for Pwyll, the sods were

being knocked out of the turf by the pounding, galloping hoofs of Blodwen, and they were flying in the air about his head as he rode. At one bound he cleared three spear-lengths of the hillside, and the stile with them. As he cleared it, and came down into the road, there the lady was, magically having passed the stile before him. At full speed he followed her; slowly she went on, and slowly waned from him. In spite of his speed and vehemence and unappeasable eagerness to come up with her, and in spite of the unhurried dignity of her riding, at the last he saw her, far off, made one with the fading brightness in the west.

Seven times he rode out, and seven times saw her from the hilltop, and followed. Here is the truth now about this matter: however wonderful for beauty of soft flames and mysterious blossomings, and for spreading, swooning, sway-ing, glittering, enchanting, ambient glory of light and color and song her last coming had been, and however great and majestic and glorious the splendor and queenly dignity of herself, with each evening they were seventy times, or indeed more than that, greater and more excellent; till there would be no telling, and no recounting, and no finding a likeness for it, the last time; and were the best bard in the world setting forth the story, or even Gwydion ab Don himself, — for all his being gifted with the words of magic — it is likely that he would pass this by with no more than making mention of it.

Now here is what Pwyll did that seventh time of his pur-suing her, and he in amazement and exaltation at the things that were made known to his vision. Clear to him had it become that speed would never bring him up with her; not even if he had the speed of Henwas Adeiniawg in the ancient days, against whom no fourfooted beast could ever hope to run the distance of an acre, much less could it go beyond it.

Here is what he did then: he called out to her as she was riding into the sky-glow, far away, in the midst of vanishing, and beyond any ordinary hearing.

"Ah Princess," he cried, " evil fall upon my beard surely, unless it is doing you service I desire to be."

In a moment she had grown plainly visible to him; in a moment she was there, in all the wonder of her flamy, shadowy beauty, right before him on her white horse on the road.

" It would have been better if you had spoken to me before," she said. " These nine times have I ridden through the world and through Dyfed to get word with you; more often than that it would not have been permitted to me to come."

" For what reason do you desire speech with me, if it please you to make it known? "

" I am Rhianon the daughter of Hefeydd Hen," she said: " my father has many lordships in the Kingdom of the Immortals. It was desired of me that I should marry Gwawl the Son of Clud, the lord of an unknown region; but I had heard a sound of the fame of the Island of the Mighty, and it seemed better to me to take queenhood here. Not pleasing to me would be sovereignty in a realm without needs or sorrows. As for the queenhood I desire to take, it will be in Dyfed. Beyond that, there is no mortal who may wed with the Immortal Kindred, unless he has first won victories in the Great Deep of Annwn, beyond the confines of the world of men."

" I have won victories in Annwn, such as they were," said Pwyll. "As for Dyfed, and queenhood in it, they are mine to give you, if it is not beneath your dignity to take them from me. There never was a prince in this island, or sovereign wearer of the crown of London, that had such honor paid to him as this."

"I will make this known to you," she said: "an honor it is; and the crown of all advantages it will be to you, this choice that you are making of me. Here is what the end of it will be: to become one with the Princes of Beauty, with the Immortal Kin; and to have what star and mountain you will for your palaces, and to rule in realms of imperishable excellence, and to do service until the waning of the age of ages. That is what the end of it will be."

As she spoke, it seemed to him that the whole fate of the Cymry was revealed to him. "Whatever will be the end of it for you or for me, it is known to me for whom it will be an advantage until the end of time. Unto the Dimetians, and unto the whole Race and Kindred of the Cymry it will be that. Therefore, if it shall please you to ride with me, the throne shall not wait for you longer in Arberth than it may take us to come there."

"Not so"; she said. "Not until after a year and a day can I come to you. And you must know this," said she, "before you undertake this adventure. It would be difficult for any man to gain me; and even if I were gained, sorrow might easily come of it. He who gained me would never come to be my equal in dignity unless he were advised by me in all things, so that I might lead him as far as attaining immortality. The third time he might disobey me, he would lose me; and if he lost me, sorrow and long wanderings would be for him, and it is not known, even to the Immortals, whether he would come to me again."

"Let what may come, come," said Pwyll. "My will is to serve you, that you may bring what beauty and excellence you will into the Island of the Mighty."

With that she told him how he should gain her: he should bring a hundred men with him to her father's court at the end of the year and the day, and he would find the wedding-feast prepared. When she had said as much as that, it seemed to him that she gathered into herself the whole beauty of the blooms and birds that were about her, and that she shone for a moment more wonderfully than the dawn or the rainbow, or than the sunset over the sea when you are standing on the sands of Teifi, and the far hills of Ireland bloom and glimmer upon the forehead of the evening, more beautifully than whatever is most beautiful. Then the light waned until it was gone, and Pwyll and Blodwen were alone on the road. The sky was all softly glittering with stars, and no sound from them that might be heard; beyond the lonely calling of an owl from the woodland, or the calling of a corncrake from the fields below the road, and the call and murmur of the river over its stones, and a whispering and tremor in the oak-leaves, there was no music for the hearing in the world. He blew his horn, and his men came riding down to him from the head of Gorsedd Arberth, and together they rode back to the palace in the town. There he was in peace, so far as is known, for the greater part of the year and the day.

II. THE FIRST OF THE WEDDING-FEASTS AT THE COURT OF HEFEYDD, AND THE COMING OF GWAWL AB CLUD

HERE was an apple-tree covered with bloom in the courtyard of the palace at Arberth; one morning, when the king looked out, it was as if it were ensouled with three shining fountains of beauty and inspiration. Every leaf and bloom and young shoot was a-tremble with delight of the beauty that was being born in their midst; beyond that, the whole valley of Arberth was filled with delicate and melodious song. By reason of that, he knew that the three that were in the tree would be none other than Aden Lanach, Aden Lonach, and Aden Fwynach, the three Birds of Rhianon, the three Singers of Peace; and rose up, and called the hundred men of his teulu, and rode out with them, following the birds. By what secret ways they may have journeyed, is not known. They left Dyfed, and they left the Island of the Mighty; dry-shod, and without ships they passed. At the end of three days they came to the Court of Hefeydd Hen in the Kingdom of the Immortals; that was a year and a day after the parting of Pwyll from Rhianon on the roadside in Dyfed, when he made the promise to her that he would come.

Never had any one of them seen the equal of the palace of

Hefeydd, either for loftiness, or for beauty, or for immense, impregnable strength. There were seven wide, stone-paved ramparts; on the smallest of them, seven hosts, equal in size to the complete hosting of the men of the Island of the Mighty, might have waged wild, free, indiscriminate warfare, with ground for chariots, and room for archery, and no discomfort or crowding. On each of the ramparts was encamped a company of seven score and seven giants; the least of them wore the torque and breastplate of a king, and was of such strength that he would have made little of breaking the bole of a well-grown oak-tree across his knees. There were seven immense gates of granite; and seven watchdogs guarding them: seven lean, eager wolves would easily have been vanquished in the conflict by even the feeblest and puniest of those dogs. Between each of the gates there were seven flights of seven score stairs, the smallest step of them high-treading for a giant. On the seven towers — and the least of them as high as the Crag of Gwern Abwy in the ancient days — were seven spears raised, with seven sunbright beautiful banners of silk and linen, adorned with dragons of supreme beauty. Beautiful was the place, truly; and if beautiful, strong; and if strong, kindly and hospitable.

The dogs greeted the Dimetians with delight, leaping and fawning. The stairs were endowed with such magic by Hefeydd, that they seemed no more than level ground beneath their feet; as for the giant companies, they were eager for nothing at that time but the welcoming of guests. The granite stairways broke out into soft grass and blossom beneath their feet; everywhere there was harping and vocal song, and delightful mirth, and courteous greeting as they came into the hall.

If it had been proud and fair-seeming without, much better was it within. On the walls were the armor of Gods

and giants, and hangings of flame-colored satin and taffeta,
and the hangings adorned with the exploits of Hu Gadarn
and the noblest stories from of old. Covering the flagstones
of the floor were skins of the bear, the wolf, the lion, and the
beaver. The rafters afar in the roof were carven in the
forms of splendid dragons. As they came into the hall, they
all marveled at the beauty and dignity of Rhianon, and at
the lofty bearing of her and her people, and at the kindness
and courtesy of the welcome they had from them. Hefeydd
Hen himself rose from his throne to greet them; it was
apparent to them that not even the Crowned King of the
Island of the Mighty in the pride of his might, and he breaking battle in the east or the west of the world, or with the
princes of Greece and Spain and Asia having greeting, and
welcome, and courtesy, and honor from him at feast time,
would be the equal of Hefeydd Hen, or nearly the equal of
him; either for beauty, or for kindliness of aspect, or for
pride and glory of bearing. With courtesy and proud friendliness they returned his greeting; and it seemed to the Dimetians that they would never desire better companionship than
that of the Gods; and it seemed to the Gods that it would be
hard to come on guests so free, and high-minded, and courteous as the Dimetians.

That night they feasted there, at the wedding-feast Rhianon had prepared for Pwyll Pen Annwn and for herself.
Regal were the stories that were told; regal and magnificent
were the songs sung. On the dais at the head of the hall
sat Hefeydd Hen himself, and with him Pwyll and Rhianon;
according to the custom and precedent of the court, even
Hefeydd had less honor there than Pwyll had; it was as if
Pwyll, and not he, were the sovereign ruler of those domi-
nions. Below those three were thirteen long, beautiful, rich-
ly-furnished, well-adorned tables for the hundred that there

were of the Dimetians, and for a hundred bards, and a hundred princes, and three hundred high-born, golden-chained, well-speaking ladies of the court. The smallest and poorest of the plates and drinking-vessels were of pearl and costly enamel; delicate, well-cooked and nourishing was the worst of the food. While they were feasting, the Birds of Rhianon sang through the hall; it came into the minds of the Dimetians, that if it had been for nothing but the hearing of those birds, that feast would have been better and more desirable to them than any pleasure they had known during their lives.

Towards midnight they heard a great shouting of the giants from the ramparts, and a great barking of the dogs from the gates; and the shouting and barking died away into a silence unequaled before in the world, so far as was known.

"It would be well to be cautious," said Rhianon. "Fear of some danger has come upon me."

"Fear it not," said Pwyll; "there are the Dimetians."

"Some one will have overcome the giants and the watch-dogs," said she.

"That would be well," said Pwyll; "conflict has been the only pleasure that has been lacking to us." While they were talking that way, the gleam and beauty flared up in the jewel-work, till the whole hall was one blaze of light. Not a dragon carven on the rafters, but seemed to quiver into life and motion. The songs of Aden Lanach and Aden Lonach and Aden Fwynach rose and quickened and billowed forth, until the air reeled and trembled for excess of glory and sweetness. The cause of it was the door opening, and the coming in of a tall, handsome man; with every step of him forward towards the dais, the light and the music were multiplied.

"Soul, soul," whispered Rhianon, "here indeed is the peril."

"I see nothing of it," said Pwyll.

"Grant nothing that he may ask of you," said she.

But Pwyll was utterly caught up in the delight of the glory and song, till the whole life of him danced and exulted; beyond that, he never had been one to take thought for caution, when it came to the practice of generosity. "Soul, soul," he made answer; "unprincely would it be to refuse his requests."

"It will be the falling of all loss and sorrow," said she; but he was beyond heeding her. Barely had she said it, when the man was before the throne, and praying Pwyll to grant what he might be asking.

Tall he was, and more beautiful than the fairies, and radiant with strange, untroubled light; but his limbs were slender and his eyes bright with exultant dreaming, and he had not the aspect of the heroic kings of the Island of the Mighty with him. Lightly the chieftain answered him: "Whatever you may ask, I will grant it to you," said he. "Name you whatsoever you will, and you shall come by it. Unfitting and discourteous would be refusing, this night."

And the last word of that was not out from between his teeth, before the sorrow of the world descended upon him, so that even the darkest moment he had ever known, seemed to him to have been bright and joyful in comparison with this. The light waned in the hall, and the songs of Aden Lanach and her sisters ended strangely; or if they did not end, they became nothing to him but harshness and bitter sound. So far as he could see, there was no hue nor beauty left in the plates of pearl and amethyst, nor in the drinking-horns of polished diamond; the best of them might have been of ungarnished lead. The flowers of adornment had the appearance of withering, the food of wasting away; as for the Dimetians and the people of the court, it was clear to him that they had all fallen to remembering whatever sorrows they might formerly have known. In silence and sorrow they watched him.

"I am Gwawl the Son of Clud," said the man; "prince of the Land of Timeless Beauty. The request that I make of you is that you shall forgo the princess."

Slowly Pwyll answered him. "Marvelous is the request," said he. "Marvelous and terrible it is truly. For what reason is it made of me?"

"Not out of hatred for thee, but out of consideration for her have I made it. Warlike and kingly, I know, are all the princes of the Cymry. Princely is the dignity, without bounds the hospitality of the Island of Britain. Yet it would be unfitting for the princess to take queenhood there. Sorrow would come of it, were she wedded to any one subject to mortality."

"Whether sorrow would come, or joy, it was there that it was my will to reign," said Rhianon. "It was well known to me what would come."

"Soul," said Gwawl, "it was my will that you should be saved from sorrow." Then he turned to Pwyll again. "Not yet is the whole request spoken," he said.

"Speak you," said Pwyll, "if it please you."

"Soul," said Gwawl, "there is this for you to learn concerning the Immortal Kindred. One race of them have their troubling when any evil happens to men; they made choice of old to preside over the destinies of the world. Of that race are the Clan of Hu Gadarn, the Gods of the Cymry, and the Children of Dana in Alban and Ireland. And there is another race to whom it would be unknown if your mountains crumbled, and your world were burned, and your stars withered in the sky; of these are the Children of Clud, I and my people. And there is a third tribe, that has kinship with both races: the people of Hefeydd Hen, and the Lady Rhianon among them. Though she never left this fortress, she would have no peace here; and that by reason of the wars and sorrows and exultations of the men of the Island of the Mighty; much less would she have peace if she went hence, and took queenhood with you. Therefore my request is that you shall give the princess to me, that I may bring her beyond the shaking of her peace."

"According to the promise that was given, it must be," said Pwyll. "On her it was binding, as well as on me. Woe is me for the Brython."

"Never at any time have I desired unshaken peace," said Rhianon. "Peace shall I find where there is war, joy only where there is sorrow. On me indeed is the promise binding; yet in the Island of the Mighty it is my desire to be."

"The chieftain gave you to me," said Gwawl. "Neither with you nor with me was the making of this fate; neither with you nor with me will be the breaking of it."

"So great is my longing for the Island of the Mighty," said Rhianon, "that I will desire to know this from you, if there is any knowing it. If there is breaking the fate, how will it be broken?"

"I will tell you gladly," said Gwawl. "There would need to be an obtaining power over me, and a putting compulsion upon me; and all that by this chieftain. And it would need my going of my own will into the place where he might put the compulsion. But there will be no doing it," said he. "It has been foretold of me that I shall never fall into the power of any god; much less shall I get my compulsion from a mortal."

"What will be, will be," said she. "Not many would be better at breaking fates than Pwyll Pen Annwn. He put compulsion on the Princes of the Underworld."

"Of my own will I shall not suffer it, and therefore I shall save you from the Island of the Mighty. Whether there is life or death there, or war or peace, or feasting or fasting, or silence or song, it shall be nothing either to you or to me. Even the striving of your own race shall be forgotten."

"It shall be as it shall be," said she. "Is it your will now, that the feast should be broken?"

"Not so," he said. "Let it go forward."

"Lord," she answered; "I made it for Pwyll Pen Annwn."

"Yes," said Gwawl; "it would be less than courtesy in me to remain here. No one would desire to take anything from the dignity of such a prince as he is. I will come again whenever it may please you."

"At the end of a year and a day the feast shall be prepared for you and for me," said she.

"I will come then," said the other; and went towards the door.

"Lord Gwawl," said Pwyll, going down and accompanying him; "high and princely indeed is your courtesy. Better than this is unknown among the enthroned ones of the Island of the Mighty."

"And yours also," said Gwawl. "It pities me that the fate should be mournful for you." With that he went his way.

Then they went forward with the feasting; but there was no desire with any of them either for food or drink, for story-telling or for conversation, for harping or for vocal song. In a little while they went to rest.

In the morning the Dimetians rode forth, and Pwyll at the head of them. Rhianon said to him:

"Let not sorrow overcome you. If there is any breaking the fate, it will be broken, and no one will be better gifted for breaking it than you. As for the instrument of breaking it, that would be the Basket of Gwaeddfyd Newynog, if there were any obtaining it."

"I will go forward in search of it," said Pwyll. "Is it known to you where it might be obtained?"

"I can not tell you," said she. "Whether it is known to me or not known, of no avail the basket would be to you, unless you yourself found it in the length and the breadth of the world. And I will give you this warning," she said. "Lose no chance of doing service, wherever you may find it; and if you should see sorrow, pass not by until the sorrow be lightened."

"This counsel will I heed, although I heeded not the other," said he. "And beyond that, I will gain the basket. Am I bidden to the wedding-feast of Gwawl?"

"You are bidden," said she. "Nowhere but at that feast might the fate be broken." With that Pwyll and the Dimetians rode forward.

"Indeed and indeed," said Rhianon; "in my deed to my own queenhood," said she, "sorrow upon me if I come not into the Island of the Mighty yet."

As for the Dimetians, they went forth wandering through unknown and immortal regions; wandering they were for the best part of the year and the day; and neither news nor rumor of the Basket of Gwaeddfyd Newynog, nor of Gwaeddfyd Newynog himself, overtaking their hearing during the whole of that time. Whenever they came upon sorrow, they lightened it; wherever they found the opportunity of service, they did not pass until the service was done. They traversed mountains, and green valleys full of flowers; often the flowers would be gifted with human utterance, and discoursed with them; but knew nothing concerning the Basket. They traversed cornlands, and fruitlands where the trees bore fruitage of pearls; and wild, goblin-haunted regions, where the rocks and bushes would turn as they came into armies of opposing demons. Many warfares they waged, until their raiment was worn and tattered, and their swords dinted and old, and the glow gone from their breastplates and helmets, for the most part. But they met none that might obtain success against men from the Island of the Mighty, and at the end they were no fewer in number than they had been at the beginning: one hundred men, the flower of the hosting of the Dimetians, and Pwyll their lord at the head of them.

Here now is the Second Branch of the
Story of Pwyll and Rhianon, although the
First has not yet come to its End

The Name of this one is:

The Basket of Gwaeddfyd Newynog,
and
Gwaeddfyd Newynog himself

I. THE ANGER OF PENDARAN DYFED, AND THE PUTTING OF FIRING IN THE BASKET

THE year and the day were over, all but three days; and still they had heard no rumor of the thing they were seeking. With their long wanderings in the east and the west, and the strange, glamorous nature of the world they were traversing, there was no such thing for them as to know were they near or far from the court of Hefeydd, or what way they should take to come to it; and they were due there in no more than three days' time. This is where they were that evening: in the midst of a wide, sandy plain, with here and there sparse reeds on the brink of a pool, and here and there the round tump, knee-high, and its meager bearding of dry rushes, hardly enough to put a whistle on the passing wind. Far on the right the land rose; from sand it became green, low-lying, pleasant country, as they could see from the head of any eminence; and beyond, a line of forest-clad mountains, ruddy-purple now against the sunset. On their left, all was flat; marsh or dry sand, and gleaming stretches of scarlet and yellow where there were waters. The road ran by a house half in ruins, in a garden where once there would have been flowers of a thousand colors, and all the herbs that

Ceridwen needs for her enchantments; now there was little there but rank grass, and the nettle and the burdock, the wild chicory and the mullein, and a little, indeed, of the blue forget-me-not, run wild, and passing from blossom into seed. As for the house, the white lime was half washed from it by rain, and the fern-thatch half broken in; the whole appearance of desolation was over it. An old man was sitting beside the doorway ; his clothing was little better than rags, and his hair and beard untrimmed, and his aspect no less bitter than miserable.

"Greeting of the god and the man to you kindly," said Pwyll Pen Annwn. "Is there news with you concerning the Basket of Gwaeddfyd Newynog, or concerning Gwaeddfyd Newynog himself?"

"If I knew anything, it is doubtful whether I would tell you. Shall I have no peace to consider my sorrows, without listening for rumors on the winds of the world?"

"As for the sorrow, it might well get its lightening with us."

"It would be better for you to do that, than to be troubling the peaceable with these foolish inquiries."

"Lord," said the Dimetians, "there are no more than three days. It would be better to go forward in search of the basket."

"Not so," said he; "we will heed the counsel of the Princess. If there is sorrow here, we will not pass till it is lightened."

"Sorrow there is, and three heavy parts of it," said the old man. "See you yonder line of mountains in the east?"

"We see it."

"I can get no firing that will comfort me, except the fallen beechwood from the forest on their slopes. Hereto-

fore I was able to travel thither, and fill a basket with the
firing; and that would be enough to satisfy me from one
January to another. But now I am old, and bent double,
and a prey to weakness and coughing, and the thought of
journeying is hateful to me, and undoubtedly I shall perish
of the cold. If any one desired to lighten the first part of
my sorrow, he would obtain the firing for me; he would not
idle here, and trouble me with vain questions and inquiries."

"We will obtain it for you gladly," said Pwyll. "With
the dawn of the morning, there shall be a going out after it."

In the morning they rose up early. "Lord," said Pendaran Dyfed (he was Pwyll's penteulu; there was no one
among the Dimetians either stronger or more impatient than
he): "is it permitted to me to go for the firing?"

"It is permitted to you gladly," said Pwyll. The old man
came out of the house. "Ah, it is you that will go, Pendaran
Dyfed," said he. "Take you this basket with you, and let
it be filled to the brim; less than that would be no lightening
for my burdens." It was a flat straw basket; the firing it
would hold would hardly burn for an hour. "Filled to the
brim shall it be," said Pendaran. "It will be easy to accomplish that." Thereupon he went forward.

He crossed the plain swiftly, and the rolling land of
bracken and heather; blue was the sky above his head,
sweet-scented the bog-myrtle by the slow peat-dark streams;
delicately poised the tufts of the bog-cotton in the hollows.
Before the dewdrop was gone from the bloom of the hare-
bell, where it might have shade from a brake-frond, he had
come to the rising of the ground, and the fern-land running
up in a wide, green, beautiful bay between two arms of the
forest. Bright were the acres of fern, delicately bending
before the wind; brightly gleaming was the golden green

of the beech-tops; hardly could he see the gentle blue and purple of the mountains beyond them. Through that bay of bracken the path led towards the heart of the wood, where the firing would be to be gathered.

He had traversed as much as half of it, when there fell an unknown delight and glory upon the morning. The beeches seemed to be fountains of green fire; through their trembling leafage, sprays of some arcane, quickening flame seemed to be playing. There was a stillness of winds, and yet a quivering of the fern as if with delight; the whole air became brighter than the diamond. As he looked and marveled and exulted, he saw a man coming down towards him out of the forest; never had he known the like of such exultation, and delight, and glory as thrilled inward from his two eyes, and over his whole being, when he caught sight of him.

The man was white-haired and white-bearded, yet it was to be seen that there was such strength in him as would be with few, even of the proudest breakers of battle. A sheathed sword was beneath his cloak; a helmet of bright silver on his head; on his left arm was a little shield of such pure, clear, white brightness as will not be found on snow or foam, though the sun be shining on them. His face was complete in beauty and majesty, so that there will be no likeness for it in the length and breadth of the world; but the kind friendliness of his aspect was equal to its majesty and beauty.

" The greeting of heaven to you, Pendaran bach," said he, speaking to that great, warlike champion as if he were a child. " The greeting of heaven to you, Pendaran dear."

" Lord," said Pendaran, laughing with delight to get such words from the like of the one that was speaking to him, " the greeting of the god and the man to you, courteously and reverently; and a thousand times better to you than to

me, and more than a thousand times. Who shall I say that
it is then, if it please you to tell me?"

"Whoever it is, would you take counsel from him?" said
the old man.

"And proud and glad would I be to take it," said Pendaran; for he knew the aspect of a god when he might see
one.

"It is this, then," said the other. "Heed no advice you
may obtain in the forest. As for the basket, it would be
unfitting to be over-heedful whether it were full or not.
When it may seem to you that you have gathered as much
as should fill it, go back with it to Pwyll Pen Annwn. It
would be better that he should have the looking into it, and
the examining whether it be full or half full. And there
is this saying also," said he: "*Common with the impatient
is their meeting with misfortune.*"

"That is true," said Pendaran; "and a hundred thanks
to you. Will there be peculiarities with the forest then?"

"There will be few things without peculiarities," said
the other. "The forest is the Forest of Celyddon; it is a
main privilege for even the mightiest to go up into it, and
of those that go, there will not be many that obtain the firing.
As to that last, whoever kindles it will get more than the
warming of his limbs; no smallness of soul and no ungenerosity will remain with him. And there is the basket too,"
he said; "that also will have peculiarities."

"Indeed will it?" said Pendaran. "Is it permitted to
me to obtain tidings of them?" But in the midst of his
speaking, the old man was gone. At one moment he was
there, in his whiteness and kindly dignity; at the next, there
was nothing but a hawthorn in the glory of its bloom where
he had been standing. "There was no bloom on it before

his coming, whatever," said Pendaran. " In my deed to
Himself," said he; " Hu Benadur Byd was that one. Hu
Gadarn he would have been, if there are eyes with me for
the seeing."

Then he made this song in honor of Hu, and sang it as
he went up towards the forest:

> *I saw the forest beeches yield*
> > *and fountain forth in feathery flame*
> *Their secret glory unrevealed,*
> > *and lo, from out the fire sprays came*
> *The Master of the Shining Shield,*
> > *Heart of the World-heart's Oriflame.*
>
> *I saw the trembling leagues of fern*
> > *and the huge beech-trees bow them down,*
> *And a thousand dark green rushes turn,*
> > *and bend their tufted blossom brown,*
> *And the whole woodland bloom and burn*
> > *to yield him golden robe and crown.*
>
> *And as I passed the marshy mead,*
> > *I heard a little, peat-dark stream*
> *Grow vocal; and indeed, indeed,*
> > *a song that had the opal's gleam*
> *Went tinkling down from reed to reed,*
> > *till the whole world was wrapped in dream.*
>
> *Because of Him, such wild delight*
> > *hath filled the ousel's bill with tune;*
> *The cuckoo's far and wandering flight*
> > *with such lone merriment is strewn,*
> *And the thrush makes the wood's edge bright*
> > *beyond the cloudless light of noon.*

And still from out the purple hills
I hear Him roving through the sky;
And still the wondering wildwood thrills,
His footsteps drop such melody
To ripple forth in music rills
on all the winds that wander by.

O Mightiest of the Mighty Ones,
and Smallest of Small Things that be,
Commensurate with stars and suns,
and the plumed splendors of the sea,
Who through the Atom burns and runs,
bide Thou and shine at heart in me!

— for the exultation of the morning had taken hold upon him, and the beauty of the world was multiplied before his vision with every step of his going. Never had he known the sun to have such an appearance of gleaming on all the tremulous leaves of the forest. Like fountains of delicate green, golden-tinged flame, the great beeches rose before him; never had he understood till then their secret aloofness, the haughty exultation of their pure dreaming. He passed the first of them, where their boughs swept low along the ground; he came to the great spaces of the forest, where the lowest branches would be as much as a bowshot, almost, from the earth; a place pillared with innumerable gray, un-branching tree-boles, the roadways of the squirrel; a quiet, shady region of the music of the ringdove and the black-bird. Many an old limb of a tree was strewn among the crisp, brown leaves of the forest floor; but he would take only the best wood, and none that was moss-grown, none that had turned blue-green with age and decay, none that had softness of rot in it. Delightful to him was the singing of the birds; delightful the green gloom, and the play and

dappling of sunlight and shadow through the leafage far
overhead. On and on he went; and as he finished one poem,
would turn to the framing of another; with many liquid
consonances and sweet assonances of melodious sound he
framed them, for it was beneath the dignity of a warrior,
in those days, to leave any poem unmade, of which he might
have the making. Beautifully they sang themselves through
his mind, imitating the crooning of the wood-dove, the music
of the ousel, the far, sweet shouting of the cuckoo; reflecting
the rich greenness, and the shining of the sunlight on the
leaves. He had more success with poetry than with getting
wood there; for what there was, was blue-green through and
through for the most part, and he would not take it. So
he went forward from one wood to another; crossing glades
and valleys and stretches of heatherland; mounting always
towards the mountains, and gathering firing here and there
as he went. Certainly, whatever he might have put in it, the
basket was less than full; but Pendaran was not heeding it,
or heeding it little. Here there would be rushes to consider,
and the sweet breath of the bog-myrtle; here there would be
the small growth of the bilberry on the forest floor, or the
darting of a lizard among the sunlit pebbles and mosses; and
all these things were a delight to him. How should he heed
what firing he might have taken from the gloom of this wood
or that, from the borders of this glade, from the sward there
between the beeches and the heather? There had not been
much for the taking, in any place. At noon he came to a
green drive in the midwood, narrow and ferny, where the
trees might branch low, and the thrush find sunbright leafage for his verse-chanting, and still sunbright leafage rising
above him, a mountain, not solid, of quivering, gleaming
greenness. There at last he found much good firing strewn
over the ground; the sight of it brought the basket to his

mind. He opened it and saw that it was half full; and with
that fell to considering better the filling of it. He would
return with it to Pwyll when he should have gathered enough;
there was Hu Gadarn's counsel to be thought of. He began
picking up the wood, following the drive eastward; and
indeed, soon again heeding more the framing of a poem, than
giving any scrutiny to Hu Gadarn's counsel. He came to a
bend in the drive, and stooped down there after the best
firing he had seen; with his rising up from that, and his
face turned in the new direction, what had been concealed
before was made known to him.

Before him the lane cut straight through the wood, so
that there was a narrow revealing of the mountains, sun-
dusky, sun-purpled, beyond unseen valleys afar, between the
two high banks of beech-leafage. There not ten paces from
him, and as if waiting his coming, a woodman was standing
in the middle of the drive: a man huger than any of the
Dimetians, with a club in his hand studded with iron, and
an ax at his belt that few could have wielded, even in those
days.

"The courteous greeting of the god and the man to you,"
said Pendaran pleasantly.

"The greeting of the forest, such greeting as it is, to you
also," said the other.

"Pleasant is the place, truly," said Pendaran. "More
delightful to me than harping is the singing of yonder bird."

"Yes," said the woodman. Suddenly he raised his club,
and swung it, and smote with it vigorously at Pendaran,
knocking the helmet from his head, and coming near to
destroying him, but for swiftness in turning aside. With
that the sky was clouded over, and great drops of rain began
to fall. The poem he had been framing fled out of Pen-

daran's mind, and the impatience of his nature rose up.

"Discourtesy dims the sunlight," said he; "I marvel that it should be found in such a place as this."

"Discourteous is the place for thieves and pilferers," said the woodman. "Often they meet with their death here."

Whatever delight and pleasantness of mind had been with Pendaran during the morning, so much the more bitter was the anger that rose in his soul then, faster than the oncoming of the ninth wave of the Atlantic when it beats upon the Headland of Gannion, and a wind from the north driving it furiously. Like the foam of it clouding the world, and hissing and bitterly whipping the precipice; and like the weight of it caught and hurled, and thunderously booming on the face of the rock, and whirled and churned and shattered, and whitening and pouring in froth and spume; so was his mind impelled by vehement, raging anger against the woodman, and the beauty of the world and song hidden from him, and the whole of his memories and purpose broken and confused and driven. His sword was out from its sheath in a moment, and he leaping to the attack. "Detestably discourteous is thy hospitality," he cried. "Unknown to me until now has been the like of this arrogant opposition."

They fought, and the rain drove and beat upon their fighting, and the green turf became mire under their feet, and the wind howled over the trees and made billows of the tossing tree-tops. Never had Pendaran met the equal of that warfare; for long and long there was no shadow of advantage for his obtaining; and he with the swift, sharp, slant rain driven always in his face. By the time the gray world was darkening, it seemed to him as if his strength were gone. A great blow from the club fell; he took it upon his shield, that was shattered by it; he himself was driven back staggering amongst the low boughs and leafage. "Thou art a puny pilferer," said the woodman. "It is permitted to thee, out of contempt and generosity, to return to the one that sent thee with what thou hast already in the basket." Pendaran laughed; his anger rose till it drove all hurt and weariness from his limbs. "When the basket is full I will return," said he. "When thou art slain and the basket is full it will be time to consider returning." Like a dragon through the firmament he sprang forward again to the attack. If there had been ten men such as the woodman opposing him, or more than ten, it would have been hard for them to have resisted him at that time. Swifter was his sword than the swoop of the falcon; he divided the club from the end to the handle; he shore it away from the hand of the woodman, so that the two halves of it fell out into the forest, leaving a broken stump alone in the hand that held it. Shameful was the course that his anger compelled him to; he forget the courtesy of war, not waiting while his enemy might draw the ax from his girdle. Without pausing the sword swept forth again, and the head of the woodman fell from his body. With that a loud, harsh laugh rang out through the rain and grayness, and the bodiless head was converted into a raven, and flapped off, croaking and laughing harshly, and mocking at him, through the dripping leaves into the tree-tops.

"I will have the basket full," cried Pendaran. "By the splendor of the Clan of Hu Gadarn, I will not leave the forest until it is full to the brim." The laughter of the dark bird, quickening anger, and the sobbing of wind and rain, were the only answers for him. Then it came into his mind how he had broken the laws of courteous warfare, and done what was unfitting in a warrior of the Island of the Mighty; and the memory of it was bitterness with him during the whole night, and the stubborn hardening of his thoughts. He would fill the basket, although all good and evil might oppose him. He would not meet with the shame of returning with it less than full.

All night long he went wandering through the rain beneath the trees, getting what firing he might, sound or rotten; at dawn the basket was half full, and no more than that. Then blind bitterness took him, and complete forgetfulness of all bright and desirable things. " Evil fall upon my beard, truly," he cried, " if there is no magic in this hateful basket. Half full has it been since the noon of yesterday."

"And half full it will remain, while the ignorant are filling it," said a voice from behind him. He turned; there was a dwarf sitting at the root of a tree there; everything about him was of the color of the bare earth, but there was white motion in his eyes like the motion of a weasel in its hole under a bank. Pendaran drew his sword, and turned on him angrily.

" If thou art here for the sake of fighting — " said he.

" Fight thou the wind above the trees," said the dwarf; " it is for the sake of helping and good service I am here."

" That is well," said Pendaran.

" Half full will the basket remain, until compulsion be put upon it," said the dwarf. " Nothing but force would overcome its peculiarities."

"Give me news of them," said Pendaran.

"Yes, will I," said the dwarf. " Yes, yes," said he pleasantly. " No one would fill that basket with mere labor and gentleness," he said. " Force and compulsion must it have."

" It should have them gladly, if the means of giving them were known. Nothing but evil have I received from it."

" Trample on it," said the dwarf. " Overcome its pride by trampling. It is no old cocklewoman's pannier from the sands between the Tywi and the Llwchwr. No one would

get it full without violently treading down the stuff he may
have put into it."

" By heaven I will do that," said Pendaran. He set his
left foot on the firing in the basket where it lay open on the
ground, and trod it down violently.

" With both feet must it be," said the dwarf. " Otherwise its pride would not be conquered." Pendaran did as he
was counseled. No sooner was the right foot of him beside
the left in the basket, than the dawn and the dwarf and the
forest were suddenly blotted out from him. It was as if
he were at the bottom of a deep well, so marvelously had the
sides of the basket shot up into the air above his head.

Far above, against a brightening of sky and leafage, he
saw the face of the dwarf peering down at him over the
edge. "Ah," said that one, meditatively, " it is a pity that
so little thought should have been taken for the peculiarities
of the basket. Too impetuous you were, truly. It would
have been better to have waited till the whole secret had been
made known. There are many that make this trial of treading down, but few escape without their enveloping in the
basket, and their being made the slaves of the owner of it
from that out. Neither his fault nor mine will it be. And
there is this saying also," he said: " *Common with the impatient will be their meeting with misfortune.*"

II. THE OVER-EAGERNESS OF CEREDIG CWMTEIFI AFTER KNOWLEDGE, AND THE PUTTING OF BULRUSH-HEADS IN THE BASKET

ITH the first whitening of the eastern sky, Pwyll Pen Annwn rose up; and it was a wonder to him that Pendaran Dyfed should not have returned, and no more than the two days left to them, and the two parts of the old man's sorrow still to be lightened. "It would be well not to wait for him," he thought. Thereupon he greeted the old man, and asked for news of the second part, and whether there would be need to wait for Pendaran before setting forward to lighten it.

"There would not be need," said the other; "many would have shown more eagerness in their generosity. See you yonder low, faint gleaming in the west?"

"I see it."

"The gleaming is from a sea," said he, "that only ships of the Immortals traverse. No more than a stone's throw from the high-tide mark there, there is a marsh of bulrushes. Now if I sleep on any bed not made of the down from the flowers of those rushes, I am afflicted with evil dreams and the destruction of my peace. Heretofore I was able to journey thither once every year, and to fill a basket with the rush-heads; and that would be enough for me from winter solstice to winter solstice. But now heaven knows I am over old, bent double and troubled with coughing; if I journey as far as from the house to the road, there will be a giddiness in my head and a misery in my feet; and for lack of the rushes I am deprived of my natural rest, and have no clearness of vision. If any one desired to lighten my sorrow, instead of waiting here he would go forth after the rushes."

"Lord," said Ceredig Call Cwmteifi (no one among the Dimetians was more eager after knowledge, and learning, and information than he was), "is it permitted to me to get the rushes?"

"Gladly it is permitted to you," said Pwyll.

"Is it you that will go, Ceredig Call?" said the old man. "Well, well, I will give you the basket," said he. With that he went into the house; and between the time of his. going in, and the time of his coming out with the basket, Pendaran had held conversation with the dwarf in the forest, and had had his enveloping and making captive in the basket, and his bringing down magically across the plain.

"Look you now, Ceredig Cwmteifi," said the old man; "brim full must this basket be, or I shall never have the ending of my sorrow with it."

"Brim full you shall have it," said Ceredig; and set forward towards the west, walking.

His shadow was still thrown out far along the ground before him, when he had crossed the plain, and the pale, sun-rich wave-rippled sand stretched before him down to the gleaming of the sea. Delicately the sunlight sparkled on the green and dark-blue and purple of the ocean; lazily the little shore-waves ran in and curved and whitened and spread themselves in a wide sheen of silver. Northward, the plain extended to the foot of a high gorse-grown hill running seaward; the sands of the bay ended under the hill, and beyond them the waves whitened on the dark rocks incessantly. First southward, and then northward, Ceredig turned, looking for signs of the bulrush marsh where he was to get the bedding; to the north, at about half a mile from him, and where it would not be more than a stone's throw beyond the high-tide mark, in the shelter of the promontory, he saw it. While he was looking, and indeed, as soon as his eyes lighted on the rushes, it seemed to him that a subtle music rose up from the sea, and that the light and brightness of the sky were extraordinarily multiplied, and that the sand and the far rocks and the headland began to glow like the shining of the sun through jewels. He turned towards the sea, and there was an old man in the guise of an archdruid walking up from it towards him, where a moment before there had been no one. The jeweled moon upon his breast shone beautifully; from the diamond acorn in his scepter a spirit of singing seemed to flow out over the world. In his deep, clearshining eyes there was a look of such vision as nothing could be concealed from, of such memory as might contain the whole of the stored-up secret wisdom of the world. A white bird that was walking on the sand rose not on the wing as he came to her. "In my deed," said Ceredig, "fortunate is this meeting. Not unknown to me is the aspect of the Immortals."

"The greeting of heaven to you, Ceredig Call Cwmteifi," said the Druid.

"The greeting of heaven and man to you, Lord Druid," said Ceredig. "Who shall I say that it is, then?" said he.

"Whoever it is, would you take counsel from him?" said the Druid.

"With pride and delight I would take it," said Ceredig.
"It will be this," said the Druid. "Many come down
to the Marsh of Celyddon, seeking the rushes that give clear
vision during sleep; but few succeed in obtaining them. That
will be by reason of one thing and another," said he. "They
will be apt to take what advice may be offered them, after
they have come to the marsh; and to be over-curious as to
the peculiarities of the rushes; and to concern themselves
unduly as to whether the basket is full or not full. It would
be better to gather the rushes quickly, and trouble with
nothing but gathering them and returning, and to leave the
examination as to fulness for Pwyll Pen Annwn. And there
will be the courtesy of gift-giving to consider also," said he.
"The new cloak will be the good gift, not the worn one; the
whole fruit, not that which may be bitten into. And beyond
that, there will be this saying to muse upon and remember:
*Common with the over-eager after knowledge will be their
coming by deception.*"

"A hundred thanks to you, and more than a hundred, for
the counsel," said Ceredig Call. "Undoubtedly it is the
honor of the world to me, to get advice and counsel from
one of such dignity."

In the middle of his speaking, the Druid was gone; and
no knowing in the world what might have been the manner
of his going. "It would have been Tad Awen himself," said
Ceredig; "it would have been the Instructor of the Bards
of the Immortals that was counseling me." He went forward along the sands towards the bulrush-bed, chanting these
verses in honor of Tydain Tad Awen:

> *A hand to the skies,*
> *And a hand to the golden horn;*
> *And a lifting of songs that shall rise*

Round the citadel turrets of morn,
To the House of the East, for Tad Awen,
From whose singing all singing is born.

The croon of the sea,
And the call of a sea-bird fair,—
The glittering waves in their glee,
And the daughter of ocean and air —
And, a sudden, a God on the sea sands,
And the Master of Mysteries there.

Yea, He that took thought
In his trance, on the measureless deep,
Saw the glimmering galaxies wrought,
And the Universe shaken from sleep
By the sound that went kindling the silence,
More swift than heaven's lightning may leap.

About him of old
Came Gods to the gates of his school;
Came Plenydd, flame-mantled in gold,
Ere the sun had delight in his rule,
Ere he scattered noon-gems on the sea-wave,
Or dawn-scarlet and gold on the pool.

Came Alawn, a child,
And his little, bright harp in his hand,
To learn song that should ring through the wild,
That should bloom o'er the wilderness sand,
That should keep the stars moving in slow dance;
That should hearten the mountains to stand.

And, a blemishless boy,
Young Gwron, the third of them, came,
And the heart of him glory and joy,

And the robe and the form of him, flame;
And he learnt to be heart of all heroes,
And the hellions of Abred to tame.

Thee, Lord of the Breath
That runs kindling the winds of the world,
That goes raising up music in death,
And where darkness and death are unfurled
Maketh laughter, and vision, and huge hope,
E'en when souls on the death-winds are whirled—

That was wisdom of old,
And the brilliant enkindling of minds
The dreams of the sea to behold,
And the wisdom at heart in the winds,
And the fathomless lore of the mountains,
And what song-spell the firmament binds —

Thee, Tydain, I saw
In the sunlight come up from the bay;
And the world in a glory of awe,
And all trembling the wild waters lay,
Though thou cam'st not in dragon nor god-guise,
Aflame from the bloom of the day;

They knew, as I knew
The druid-hid glory of a God —
The white robe embroidered in blue,
And what shone from the gem in thy rod —
They knew, as I knew too, what godhood
The brink of the wilderness trod.

Hast thou counseled the sand
With some secret enfolded of old?
Is some wonder-revealing at hand,

That it throbs so of topaz and gold?
That it beats so with life to the footsole,
That it glows so with light to behold?

Didst thou plot with the sea,
That, where waters were moving, mine eyes
See sapphire and amethyst, see
Waves beryline, opaline, rise,
A great flood of flame of all jewels
Burn blue to the bloom of the skies?

And as for the heaven,
Is its madness of gladness from thee?
Was its turkis-stone loveliness given,
And its soul sapphirean, to be
For adornment of rapture at hearing
Thy voice on the verge of the sea?

Yea, a hand to the skies,
And a hand to the golden horn,
And a lifting of song that shall rise
To the gates of the palace of morn,
For high love of thee, Tydain Tad Awen,
From whose singing all singing is born!

The rushes were full of whisperings when he came to
them; such whisperings as seemed to him to hold the whole
secrecy of magic, and wonderful, dim, undreamed-of things
that would be known only to a few among the druids. It was
a place of many pools, of black waters, of jewel-green and
golden mosses, unstable and treacherous for the footsole.
Never had it been given to Ceredig to see such bulrushes
as were growing there, either for height, or for beauty of
growth and color, or for excellent length and soft brown-

ness of heads. But always between his feet and the coming
near to them, between his hands and the gathering them, there
was the black bog-water too wide to be leaped, even might
there be firm ground to light down on beyond; too perilous,
by reason of its hungry, all-swallowing mud, either for wad-
ing or swimming. Indeed, he made trial of it; he was not
one to fear adventuring; nor was he one to give up life
needlessly, when nothing might be gained by losing it. He
made trial, and that more than once, of the water; but it
was as if the mud laid hold of his feet; it was a marvel that
he could draw himself away from it, and come off without
meeting destruction. After that he took himself to search-
ing for dry land from which he might gather the rushes. At
the end of a while he came on the opening of a path that
had the appearance of leading in towards the heart of the
marsh, and took it. There were flagstones laid down so
that one might stride or leap from one to the other of them,
and on either side, the bright, unstable mosses or the bog-
water, and beyond, and where there was no reaching them,
the rushes.

It was a world of tall, whispering reeds that was about
him, and no seeing the hills beyond and above them, and no
hearing even the voice of the sea, by reason of the rumor
they were keeping, the incessant mystery of the whispering
that trembled about the pools and ran along the still water-
ways. The farther he went into the marshland, the more
it took the nature of music; rippling, quiet, mysterious,
subtly alluring, full of the whole dream and wonder of the
world. It took hold of his soul; he had no thought but for
going on and on; at the heart and center of the bulrush
region he would come to the source of it.

The rushes opened out before him on this side and that;
he was at the beginning of a winding water that might lead

to the place he desired to reach, and to the harper whose
strings and fingers made such a mystery and melody of the
marsh. It was impossible for him to doubt that it would be
harping. There in the water at his feet was a coracle; the
thing he had been needing since he came to the bulrush-bed.
He got into the coracle, and paddled it along the edge of
the waters, cutting rushes here and there with his sword, and
putting the heads of them in the basket. Before he had half
filled it he came to a winding of the water, and saw that the
rushes beyond were ten times more beautiful than those he
had been gathering. Dark was the water before him, bordered with the motionless emerald lines where the rushes
were glassed on its surface. There was a trembling of the
water, and a light shaking of the reeds, and a soft gust of
music was blown towards him. "It would be foolish not
to go forward," he said. He threw the rushes he had gathered into the water, and went on slowly, gathering new ones
where they were most beautiful. At the next winding of the
water, it was the same; in the stretch beyond there were
better rushes, more excellent murmurings of song. "At the
end of this stretch I shall come on the cause of the music,"
he said. It seemed to him that he would have gathered more
than the fill of the basket since he emptied it; but when he
looked, it was no more than half full. He remembered the
counsels of Tydain, and emptied it again; and went on,
delighting in the quiet loneliness of the marshland, delighting
in the sunlight on the green, tall rushes, in the still or rippling
lines of emerald thrown out on the water from the banks;
delighting in the music that drifted and whispered down to
him across the water.

He passed seven windings of the water-way, and at every
turn emptied the basket, by reason of the greater size and
beauty of the rushes beyond; and going forward, gathered

and put more in it than he had emptied out. At every turn he was drawn on by the greater nearness of the music, and the better sweetness and more alluring nature of it. At the seventh turn he came out into a little lake, and a sunny island in the midst of it; and the cause of the music was made known to him.

There was a maiden sitting on an old tree-stump on the island, her white fingers twinkling and wandering over the strings of a harp, bringing out of them such music as he had never attained the hearing of during his whole life. Her hair was darker and softer and browner than the bulrush-heads; her eyes were like the sunlight playing through clear water, when one ray may be brightening the dark peat at the bottom; her raiment was brighter, and of a fairer green, than the reflection of the rushes on the surface of the pools. About her small, proud, beautiful head was a crown of gold, and an emerald stone gleaming in the front of it, of greater beauty and brilliance than any diamond. She played on, watching Ceredig as her slender fingers wandered over the strings; but no words coming from her, beyond the low, soft, melodious crooning of magical tunes. As for him, he was under the enchantment of the music, and without power of utterance until it should cease. The coracle touched the brink of the island, and he stepped out from it and stood before her. Then her hands fell from the harpstrings, and she laughed; her laughter was like the sound of a little stream in its deep course on the mountain, when the gorse and heather have grown out from either bank, hiding it, and there will be no getting sight of the gleam of its waters from above.

" The greeting of heaven and of man to you, Ceredig Call Cwmteifi," she said. " The welcome of the world to you, to the Marshland of Celyddon."

" The greeting of heaven and of man to you, Lady of the

Marshland," said he; "and better to you than to me. It is you that strew magic through the enchanted region?"

"Magic there is, but it was made before I was. More excellent is the secrecy of these reeds and rushes than anything that has been made known to you hitherto."

"Ah me!" said he. "Oh that one might know what is concealed!"

"A mystery it is, hard to become acquainted with. There is glamor in it, and wonder, and the whole of the shadowy beauty of the world."

"It would be better to me, learning it, than winning victories in the east and the west."

"The impatient could not come by this. Neither giftedness nor good fortune would be equal to it in value."

"I would abide here in patience for the learning."

"Not so, but Pwyll Pen Annwn would have need of you. Both the Gods and the holy druids covet this learning."

"Whether he had need of me or not, until the dawn of the morning I would stay."

She laughed. "Easy it is to obtain, and yet not easy. No one would obtain it, without making use of the rush-heads he may have gathered."

With his eager covetousness after knowledge, and the enchantment of laughter and music and conversation that she put upon him, he made little of the end for which the rushes had been gathered. The counsels of Tad Awen drifted from his mind, and he forgot the whole courtesy of gift-giving. It seemed to him that one would lose no dignity, giving away the worn cloak, or the fruit that had been partly eaten. "I will do that," said he, "if you will direct me."

"It would be well to rest, then," she said. "It would be well to lie down on the turf here, and let your head be on the rushes for a pillow, and the two eyes of you closed."

"A hundred thanks to you, and more than a hundred," said he, and followed her counsel. Then she began her playing again; if the music she had been getting from the harp before was wild and sweet, the music she got from it now was overpowering in the subtlety and mysterious delicacy of its excellence, and laden with the whole wonder of the wind above the trees or among the reeds, of the quiet wind of twilight, when the world is betaking itself to dream. No sooner were his eyes closed than vision upon vision, as it seemed to him, of astounding secrecy, of glamorous splendor, was revealed to him. World upon inward world gave up its beauty to his gaze. The sun went down and the moon rose; and still her twinkling, wandering fingers traveled over the strings, loading the air with beauty and mystery. Unknown to Ceredig was the passing of time. At the first whitening of dawn it seemed to him that whatever he desired to see had been revealed to him; last of all, he was made aware of the secret, marvelous peculiarity of the manner of filling the basket. Then the music ceased with her, and he rose up.

" Is it made known to you? " said she.

" In my deed, it is made known. Deeper than the sea is that which I owe to you. Wonderful is the power of the rushes and the music; wonderful are the peculiarities of this little basket. Clearly I know the reason of its not being filled."

"Ah," she said, " have you learned that? "

" By the splendor of the Family of Hu Gadarn, I have learned it. It is the Basket of Gwaeddfyd Newynog; Pwyll Pen Annwn would have obtained no news of it, unless you had made it known to me. Swiftly shall it have its being filled now."

With that he set it, open, on the ground, and put the right

foot of him on the rushes in it, and the left foot beside the right. No sooner had he put it there, and the two feet of him inside the basket, than whatever had happened to Pendaran, happened to him also. There he was, as if it were at the bottom of a well; and there was the maiden, far above him, looking down over the brink.

"Ah," she said, "common, with the over-eager after knowledge, is their coming by deception. It would have been better to have waited until the peculiarities of the basket had been fully made known. There are many that go forth to fill it; but the greater part of them will fail, and will come by enclosure, and envelopment, heaven knows, and by being enslaved by the owner of the basket, if they learn no more than this secret of treading it down."

"Ah, Ceredig Cwmteifi," said Pendaran Dyfed; "Has the same fate overtaken you, that overtook me yesterday?"

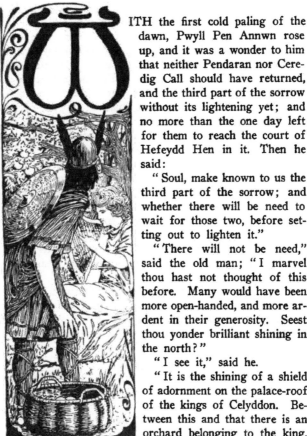

ITH the first cold paling of the dawn, Pwyll Pen Annwn rose up, and it was a wonder to him that neither Pendaran nor Ceredig Call should have returned, and the third part of the sorrow without its lightening yet; and no more than the one day left for them to reach the court of Hefeydd Hen in it. Then he said:

"Soul, make known to us the third part of the sorrow; and whether there will be need to wait for those two, before setting out to lighten it."

"There will not be need," said the old man; "I marvel thou hast not thought of this before. Many would have been more open-handed, and more ardent in their generosity. Seest thou yonder brilliant shining in the north?"

"I see it," said he.

"It is the shining of a shield of adornment on the palace-roof of the kings of Celyddon. Between this and that there is an orchard belonging to the king, and seven score and seven sweet apple-trees in it, equal in age, height, size, beauty, and flavor. So great are the infirmities of my nature, that unless I shall have to eat one of those apples at dawn, and another at night, food and drink become no better than filth and poison to me, and there will be a heaviness on my chest, and an evil taste in my mouth, and a vomiting at the changes of the moon. Heretofore I was able to go out after the apples, and I was permitted to gather as much as a basketful of the windfalls in the orchard, and that would be enough for me from the first day of January to the last day of December. Unless the apples are brought to me, undoubtedly I shall pine away during the remainder of my life; and of this I shall die. It is a pity that ever I was born. Common with the offenseless are sorrow and tribulation, and to be despised and persecuted, and to have no lightening of their burdens. If there were any one here with generosity with him, he would go out after the apples."

"Lord," said Einion Arth Cennen at that, "is it permitted to me to go after them?"

"Not so," said Pwyll. "The one that was pledged to the lightening of sorrows, let him lighten them. I myself will get the apples."

"Lord," said they, "it would be unfitting. And beyond the breaking of custom and precedent, and regal dignity, there is the court of Hefeydd Hen to be considered, and the arriving there this night. There will be no time for you to undertake this adventure."

Then the old man said:

"Lord, it would be beneath your dignity to get the apples. Let Arth Cennen go; it is not fitting that I should be waited on by a sovereign ruler."

"If thou desirest apples, get the basket; and indeed, whether thou desirest them or not. I myself will obtain those

apples, if there is any obtaining them in the world. They
will restore to thee the vigor of thy limbs; and furthermore,
they will be a medicine for thee against complaining and
ingratitude. It is a miserable thing when there is ill-natured
impatience under misfortune."

Thereupon Gwaeddfyd went into the house after the basket; and between that and the time when he came out with
it, Ceredig Cwmteifi had had his enveloping, and his enclos-
ing, and his being made captive in the basket, as far away
as the marshland of Celyddon; and his being borne by magic
across the plain.

Pwyll was in the saddle, and Blodwen impatient to be
gone, when the old man came out to him with the basket.
"If there were no more than a few apples in it" — said he.
"Be thou silent, further," said Pwyll; "and it will be the
better. Brim full shall the basket be; less than that would
not cure thee." With that he rode forward.

Gray and heavy was the sky; the wind rose fiercely from
the sea, driving the immense clouds; rain came with the
wind, beating against him furiously as he rode; the plain
became a marsh, and it was hard for Blodwen to put a hoof
anywhere without slipping. He left the plain, and rode over
many bare ridges, brown with peat and burnt gorse; and
the dark, gray, streaming sky low over all of them. From
the top of such a ridge he saw the walls of the orchard;
there was a valley flowing down from before him, not deep;
and the walls along the ridge beyond; between him and them,
the width of the valley, and the waters everywhere over the
close turf, and more perpetually falling; and the stretches
of bracken broken and beaten down, and the sprawling stems
of the bramble tossed and battered, crimson and shining in
their wetness. Before he had come to the edge of the ridge,
and the beginning of going downward, suddenly it seemed

as if the whole of the waters of space were falling, driving against the earth, an illimitable gray deluge between the turf and the low sky, fiercely swift, bitter and irresistible in opposition, beating down the fern and the bramble; and through the driving and whirling, and uprising from the smitten and sodden ground of it, and that as high as the mare's shoulders, suddenly a wet, tremulous gleam shot up and towered before him, cream-white and silvery; and there, in a little lulling and steadying of the rain, stood one that had the stature of the pine and the poplar, shedding sheen on the watery air about him from his white beard and from his helmet of silver, from his eyes and from his mantle, from the shield of intense starry whiteness on his left arm, and from the whitely flaming sword that was drawn in his right hand. Handsome he was, with stern, sublime majesty of mien and aspect, of visage and bearing; a menacing, terrible severity of beauty; a lofty radiance through the innumerable raindrops, and the wind driving the light of him hither and yonder on the falling waters of the atmosphere, making liquid lightnings on the slant, and drive, and perpetually pervading wateriness of the rain.

"The greeting and courtesy of heaven and of man to you," shouted Pwyll Pen Annwn. There was not a word from the Other, but only the menace of the beautiful drawn sword, the stern aloofness of the countenance. "There will be passing," shouted Pwyll; "even if Hu Gadarn be opposing it." With that he drew his sword, and leaped down from horseback, prepared and eager for combat. A great wind came howling and lamenting up from the sea, and a terrible swift impetuosity of rain advancing upon him as he ran forward, so that there was no seeing through the nature of it, no making way through it for the legs of man. When the fury of it had passed, there was no one waiting for him.

He went back to Blodwen where she stood, head down,
and the waters streaming and steaming from her body, and
led her down the hill towards the gates of the orchard; not
riding, by reason of the slipperiness of the world. As he
went, supporting her gently, he framed these verses of a song
in the face of the rain, as best he could, and sang them:

> *It's delight that hides in the storm-winds blinding,*
> *   It's wild mirth rides through the rain-swept sky;*
> *Where will be peace and ease for the finding?*
> *   Where the blinding battle goes thundering by.*
> *   Winds of the world, shout loud and high!*
> *Sweet wild rain on the east wind driven!*
> *Come storm-riding, you Lords of Heaven,*
> *   I shall not turn from you, no, not I!*
>
> *When the word was given for the lightening sorrow,*
> *   Ye left not heaven to make smooth the way,*
> *Nor the barrier rocks of the world rift thorough —*
> *   Should wild March borrow the skies of May?*
> *   Hu with the Shield, it's proud's this day,*
> *This wild, wet morn on the wind-loud plain,*
> *That saw thy glory gleam through the rain,*
> *   Thy whiteness shine through a world of gray.*

When he had sung as much as that — such singing as
it was, with all that wateriness against him — he was drawing towards the bottom of the valley; it was all a shallow
stretch of hissing, rain-pitted water at that time. Again
a driving down of rain impenetrable by the eyesight; and
again, through that, a certain gleaming and wavering brightness, and beauty shed over the floor of the vale; and when
the rain had quieted a little, there stood one in the guise of
a Druid above the waters. He had the stature of a well-

grown silver birch-tree; there were flickerings of magical blue embroidery about his white robes, that seemed rather of woven light than of linen, and were motionless on the wind, and not made wet with the rain. Sternly beautiful was his face; an aspect of intense, all-penetrating, all-remembering vision shone from his eyes. He stretched out his scepter, barring the path before Pen Annwn; as he did so, a marvel of brightness flashed forth from the acorn of diamond in it, and the rain ceased about them, and the wind was stilled, and there was quietness there suddenly.

"The greeting of heaven and man to the Archdruid of earth and sky," said Pwyll. "Not without recognizing the majesty of Tydain Tad Awen am I."

"And you also; wherefore come you?"

"To get apples from the orchard have I come. This basket full to the brim will I be obtaining."

"Perilous is the quest. Many go up into the Orchard of Celyddon, but few attain the bringing away of apples. Many set forth with that basket, but few go back with it in their hands. If you desire safety, it would be better to return."

"Return I will, truly," said Pwyll; "as soon as the basket may be filled with apples. I will tell you," said he. "The filling of this basket will be the doing of a service; and without doing whatever service I may find to do, I should not come by the thing I am seeking; and without that thing, no compulsion would be put upon Gwawl the son of Clud; and if no compulsion were put on him, there would be no breaking the fate of the daughter of Hefeydd Hen; and without breaking it, she would never come into the Island of the Mighty; and if she did not come there, the whole Race and Kindred of the Cymry, the sons and the golden-chained daughters of Ynys Wen, would be without the best help and glory that might come to them. Therefore undoubtedly I will fill the basket, if there is any filling it; if the gods are opposing, it would be less than fitting for me to turn aside for them."

"Now listen you to this concerning the basket. Whosoever may undertake the filling of it, he never will succeed unless he can come by learning its peculiarities; and even if he learns them, it is a marvel if he should escape being enveloped in it, and being made captive, and the slave of the owner of the basket from that out. Pendaran Dyfed met that fate, and Ceredig Call Cwmteifi also. Go back, unless you are heedless of this peril."

"I will make this demand of the Immortals, and of you that are Chief Druid among them," said Pwyll. "I will not ask them for peace, nor for cessation from opposing; neither for life, if they desire mine, nor for protection against peril. But I will be so bold as to ask them what may be the peculiarities of the basket, and the manner of filling it."

"If you desire to know that, I will tell you a little of it, and not more than a little. No one will enter into the Orchard of Celyddon without meeting opposition and insult, blows and violence. And he would have to overcome these cheerfully, and to go forward without vexation, or repining, or querulousness of spirit. There are seven score and seven trees in the orchard, equal in age, height, size, beauty, and flavor. He would have to pick up all the apples that may have fallen from every one of them, and to do that fasting, in spite of the whole hunger of the world consuming him. Beyond that, if he were merry and wise, and heedless and heedful, not less than polite, and not more than courteous, it might happen to him to learn the manner of filling the basket."

When the last word of that was out of his mouth, he was gone; the whole light of him had vanished, and the wind was howling and driving through the valley again, and the rain beating down against Pwyll as it had been before. He went forward till he came to the gate of the orchard.

Said Pwyll Pen Annwn: "Is there a porter?"

"There is; for what reason hast thou come to the gates of the Orchard of Celyddon?"

"Seeking apples, good soul; seeking apples have I come, truly."

"Unwholesome is the place for thieves and pilferers. Unless thou desirest miserable death, quickly go back to the one that sent thee."

The king laughed. "O man," said he, "open thou the portal. Undoubtedly I desire whatever may come to me."

The gate swung open, and behind it stood a porter with a great club of beechwood in his hand, and an ax at his girdle such as few would have wielded, even in those days. Sullenly angry was his aspect; he was greater both in stature and in girth than even the greatest of the Dimetians. "It is death that will come to thee," he said, lifting his club.

Pwyll's sword was in his hand in a moment, and he leaping aside from the falling of the club, and rushing forward with laughter, and with raising up the ennobling Dragon Shout of the Island of the Mighty. In a little while he took the end of the club with the edge of the sword, and swept through the vast, well-seasoned, iron-studded length of it, and made two clubs of it, equal in weight, from the end to the handle, and scattered the two of them, the one in the orchard, the other in the valley behind him.

"It would be well to take the ax," said Pwyll; "the club was worthless."

"Courtesy is not lacking in you," said the porter, and drew the ax. In a little while there was an end to the fighting there.

"It is I that am slain," said the porter. "As for you,

you will go forward, if you desire peril. For the sake of
your courtesy I will tell you this," said he: "there is one
in the orchard that knows the manner of filling the basket;
but it would not be possible to learn it from her, if you ac-
ceded to her requests and invitations; she has the power to
put enchantments, and a heavy spell, on any one that may
accede to them. And heed you this, in the name of man,"
he said: "the basket has peculiarities with it, and it happens
to many to become enveloped in it, and to come by loss and
shame. Evil will fall on the one that takes no more thought
and consideration for this basket, than he would for the pannier of a cocklewoman on the shore where the Llwchwr falls
into the sea."

With that, it happened to him to perish in the guise of
a man, and he rose up in the air in aspect like a starling, and
took refuge among the apple-trees, chattering through the
rain. "Ah," said Pwyll, "counsel will be from this one and
that one. There will be many races among the Immortals."

He left Blodwen by the gate there, and went in, and fell
to picking up the apples. Never had he seen the like of them
during his life, either for size, or for beauty, or for the desirable emanations of them, kindling hunger in whomsoever
might behold. There were ten fallen apples under the first
tree; and by the time he had picked them up, and put them
in the basket, he had never desired anything so much as food;
and if food, apples; his whole body was consumed and torn
with a great raging, devouring hunger. At the second tree,
his hunger was multiplied upon him; it was doubtful to him
whether, after a while, there would be enough apples in the
world to appease it. Quickly he passed from tree to tree,
ravenously desiring apples. There were six circles of the
trees, one within the other; he went taking circle after circle,
inward towards the heart of the orchard. At the last tree

of the third circle the rain ceased suddenly; between the picking up of two apples the clouds were blown from the sky, and the sun shone forth, making known to him the full beauty of the trees. Not one of them was less in size than a full-grown oak; not one of them without its innumerable apples, mellow golden and of the color of the ruby-hearted rose; not one of them without its glory and softness of bloom, like white clouds in the east of the sky with the faintest pinkness of sunset on them. As he went forward, they budded perpetually, and the bloom fell about him like soft snow silently, and the young green apples ripened, spreading the alluring delightfulness of their scent over the world. The sight and the perfume of them were the ruin of his peace, the intense multiplying of his hunger. "There will be magic in all this," thought he; "it would be beneath dignity to pay heed to it." So he passed his four circles, and would have put as many as a thousand apples in the basket; but it was no more than half full for all of them. "It will be the peculiarities of the basket," he said. "Only the circumspect, and the watchful, and the judicious, would obtain learning the secret of filling it."

Slowly the silence of the orchard grew into a quiet, dream-laden delightfulness of harp-music. It would have been between the fourth and the fifth circles that he became aware of it; its whole burden was that he should rest and listen; that he should satisfy his hunger with the fruit, and no desire would come to him again from that out. The sight of the apples was the kindling of longing in him; their scent was its making burn furiously; but it was ten times more difficult to withstand the allurement of the music, than to withstand the golden beauty and emanation of perfume. "Well, well," he thought, "in my time I have heard the Birds of Rhianon singing." With that there rose on his

hearing a faint, far wonder of bird-music, as if it were from
beyond the rim of the world; and he knew the voices of the
Singers of Peace. "True it is," said he, "that the harping
is dull and harsh in its comparison." So he took the last two
circles quickly, and came to the lawn that was in the middle
of the orchard: a region of multitudinous blossoms, a market-
place for the bees, laden with the scent and glamor of the
daffodil. Then he looked up, and was aware of the source
of the harping.

At midmost of the lawn was a little hill, and on it, the
tree of all trees, the most beautiful of them all. But that
which was more beautiful even than the tree was the maiden
that sat in the shade of it on the hillside, and her long, foam-
white fingers twinkling and wandering over the strings of a
golden harp. Except Rhianon, he had never seen any one
with such beauty as she had. Redder were her lips than the
brightest redness of the apples; more delicate was her skin
than the pinkness and whiteness of the bloom. Her robes
were greener and fairer than the beauty of the young fruit,
or the greenness and brightness of the new-budding leaves.
As for her two eyes, they sparkled like the sunlight in the
raindrops not yet fallen from the leafage; as for her long,
shining, beautiful hair, it was nine times blacker than the
starling's wing. He came through the daffodils and lilies-
of-the-valley towards her; but she made no cessation of
harping until he was picking up apples from beneath her
own tree.

"The greeting of heaven and of man to you, kindly and
courteously, Pwyll Pen Annwn," said she at last.

"The greeting of heaven and of man to you, courteously
and kindly," said he, going on with the picking up of apples.

"It pities me that you should be hungry, and all this
fruit ripe for the eating," she said.

"A hundred thanks to you, and more than a hundred. But it would be unfitting to eat them," he said; picking up the last of the apples.

"Wherefore would it be unfitting? It would not be unfitting to receive the hospitality of a queen."

"And queenly indeed is the hospitality," said he. "But there is fitness to be thought of, and moderation, and the subjection of bodily desires. It would be little better than gluttony in me, to be consuming these apples."

"Soul, soul," she said, "there are also the peculiarities of the basket. Without eating apples, there would be no manner of learning the art and secret of filling it."

"Kindly," said he, "is that thought also. Delightful to me was ever the conversation of the considerate. But there is Pendaran Dyfed —"

"What man is that?" said the lady.

"And beyond Pendaran, there is Ceredig Cwmteifi," said Pwyll. "It would be the pity of my life to bring inconvenience and crowding on those two men."

"What happened to them?" said the lady.

"Have you heard nothing of their fate?" said Pwyll. "It is a marvel to me that you should not know anything concerning them. The best of the Dimetians were Pendaran and Ceredig."

"I have heard nothing," she said. "Would it please you to tell me?"

"And they having their fame, and their renown, and their glory, and their praises, and their honor sung by the bards; and that from the top of Pengwaed in Cornwall to the bottom of Dinsol in the North, and unto Esgair Oerfel in Ireland," said Pwyll. "And not a word of it more than their deserts."

"And what befell them?" said she. "Where will they be now?"

"In the basket," said he. "Enveloped in the basket, according to its peculiarities; and the magic of it holding them."

She laughed. "I have heard a rumor of such a basket as that," she said. "How did they come by their enveloping?"

"How do men come by their enveloping in it?" said he. "There was Pendaran Dyfed," he said. "No one could look upon Pendaran without loving him, by reason of his boldness and his generosity, and the glory of his mien, and the handsomeness of his aspect, and the kingly dignity of his bearing; and yet all that without lack of gaiety, or consideration, or courteous kindliness. It was he that went out to the Forest of Celyddon to get firing in the basket."

"Did he get the firing?" said the lady.

"And there was Ceredig Call," said Pwyll. "If there had been one man to be named with Pendaran Dyfed, it was Ceredig Call Cwmteifi; and he no less good as bard than as warrior; the best man in conflict or council, in the hall or on the hill, in friendship or in foray. I asseverate to you now," said he, "that there would be no accusing Ceredig of anything, unless it might be that he would be over-eager for acquiring knowledge, and learning, and information about this matter and that. It was he that went out to the Marshlands of Celyddon to get rushes, and —"

"Ah," said she, "he was not the man."

"As to his not being the man," said Pwyll, "I declare to you, and affirm it, and make it strong with asseverations, that there was no better man among the Dimetians; and if not among them, then not in the whole of the Island of the Mighty, nor in the three islands near thereto, nor in the island of Ireland; and much less in the rest of the world.

I marvel that it should be said that Ceredig was not the man!"

"Peace, peace!" she said, growing weary of the praises of Ceredig. "Whoever makes trial of filling the Basket of Gwaeddfyd Newynog, by treading down the stuff he may have put in it, if he be not the right man—"

"Be it requited to you a hundred times, and even more," said Pwyll, "for your courtesy in making this known. It would be unfitting for me to abide here longer."

As he went, he heard her quiet laughter and harping, but it had no enchantment for him; hunger and weariness had left him by that time. "Yes," he said; "we will make a trial of this treading down. It may be indeed that Ceredig Cwmteifi was not the man." He rode forward swiftly until he came to the house of Gwaeddfyd Newynog on the plain.

Said Gwaeddfyd: "Give me the basket."

"Not until it is full will I give it to you." With that he put the basket on the ground, and made ready for treading down the apples.

"In my deed it would be perilous to do that," said Gwaeddfyd. "Half full, it will be enough for me."

"Be you silent further," said Pwyll. "Full to the brim shall it be, or there will be no virtue in the apples. There must be an end to this querulous impatience under misfortune." Thereupon he put his left foot upon the apples, and as he did so, Pendaran leaped out from the basket, and stood at his left hand. Then he put the right foot beside the left; with his putting it there, Ceredig Call Cwmteifi came forth, and stood at his right. As for the basket, it was undoubtedly full of apples, and three of them more than it would hold, falling down and rolling in the road.

"I will take them into the house," said Gwaeddfyd.

They went into the house with him, and he emptied the

apples out on the sleeping-bench, lacking a better place for them. "Yes," he said; "the third part of my sorrow is gone, and the third part of my ignobility. My youth will return because of this, and the ancient sapience of my mind, and the warm kindling of my soul. If you desire apples, take you as many as half of them, or more than half, for a reward."

"I do not desire them," said Pwyll Pen Annwn. "They are for your own healing."

"The basket is yet full," said Ceredig Call. "There will be rushes in it."

Gwaeddfyd emptied out the rushes; there were enough of them to make bedding for ten men such as he. "That is well," he said. "Hereafter my dreams will not be troubled; knowledge will be revealed to me in clear vision. The second part of my sorrow and ignobility has departed. If it please you, take as many as half of the rushes for a reward."

"It would not please me to take them," said Ceredig; "the rushes are for your own peace and healing."

Then Pendaran Dyfed said: "The basket is yet full, and it is in my mind that there will be firing in it."

"Firing there is, and the best of firing," said Gwaeddfyd Newynog, emptying it out; "and that will be the end of the whole enchantment that was put upon me. Take you half of the firing, in the name of gratitude and good will."

"Not so," said Pendaran; "the firing is for you."

"As ye will have neither apples, nor rushes, nor firing from the forest for a reward," said Gwaeddfyd, "take you the basket; undoubtedly it is the one ye were seeking. And I will make known to you its peculiarities," he said. "There will be no means in the world of filling it, except by treading down the stuff that may have been put in it; and if any one should undertake this treading, unless he be the rightful chieftain, in his rightful place, and unless the time be the right time, he will come by being enveloped in it, and he will be the slave of the owner of the basket from that out. And now go forward, and may success, and victory, and delight, and advantage attend you."

So they rode away to the southward, and by the time the sun was at his setting, they saw the palace of Hefeydd Hen rise up before them in its strength and beauty beyond the plain. Before the rising of the moon, and when the world was dark, they had taken their places in the orchard without any one having seen them. Then Pwyll bade them wait, until they should hear him blow upon his warhorn the hai atton of the gathering of the men of Dyfed, and he himself went forward towards the hall.

Here is the likeness of him when he went forward: no more than driving on his twenty-five years he was; and his long, white cloak was about him, fastened with a brooch of gold over his breast; and the golden torque of his kinghood was round his neck, and the two acorns of it alone were of the value of fifty kine. His forehead was smooth, and the hair and the beard of him blacker than coal, and his limbs stronger than whatever may be strongest, and his heart eager for battle or for peace, whichever might be awaiting him. With proud, long strides he went forward towards the first and lowest of the seven gates of the high-reared, giant-guarded, immense, impregnable fortress of Hefeydd Hen in the Country of the Immortals. With his going, the Second Branch of the Story of Pwyll and Rhianon comes to its end.

As for this, it is going back to the First Branch, called

The Coming of Rhianon Ren ferch Hefeydd

III. THE SECOND WEDDING-FEAST IN THE COURT OF HEFEYDD, AND THE ENCHANTMENT OF THE STORY OF THE SONS OF CLEDDYF CYFWLCH

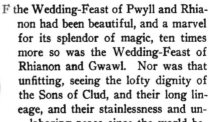

F the Wedding-Feast of Pwyll and Rhianon had been beautiful, and a marvel for its splendor of magic, ten times more so was the Wedding-Feast of Rhianon and Gwawl. Nor was that unfitting, seeing the lofty dignity of the Sons of Clud, and their long lineage, and their stainlessness and unlaboring peace since the world began. Hefeydd Hen had his place on the dais, and Gwawl and the Princess beside him; according to usage and precedent, Gwawl had greater honor even than Hefeydd the Ancient himself. Below them was a great company of the Immortals, Hefeydd's warriors and bards, and the ladies of his court; and many also of the Gods of the Family of Clud, the people of Gwawl. Fair, tall and beautiful they were; their conversation was as pleasing as song, and their song better than any that may be heard from the wind beside the river, or from the wind above the forest, or from the waters of the world, or from the winged gorsedd of the woodland. If there had been richness of music, and pomp and luster and high magniloquence of story-telling, and keen, quick wittiness of conversation at the first feast; ten times more magical were the songs now, and the stories were ten times more marvelous — and they telling of the wonderful priceless things of the world, from the bottom of the Great Deep to the top of Infinity; and being decorated, and adorned about, and interwoven, heaven knows, with cunningly contrived consonances and assonances, with flows of excellent melody and sweet sound. As for the conversation, it was such that the wisest man in the world would have desired to listen to it; and if he had listened at all, he would never have come away of his own will until it was ended.

At that time Taliesin the Chief of Bards (his forehead shone like the morning star) had made journey to the court of Hefydd Hen; wandering the world and the waters he was at that time in Prydwen, Arthur's ship of glass, in quest of learning. The bards of Hefeydd and Gwawl had sung their songs and related their stories; at last they besought Taliesin to set forth one of the heroic tales of the Island of the Mighty, having heard of his renown. Thereupon he began to make known to them the story of Bwlch and Cyfwlch and Sefwlch, the three sons of Cleddyf Cyfwlch, the three grandsons of Cleddyf Difwlch; three warlike princes of the Island of the Mighty, in the ancient times, were they. It would be hard to hear the equal of that story anywhere; only a bard of the dignity of Taliesin — and heaven knows there never was another of such dignity — could attain relating it in a fitting manner. Before the twenty words were out between his teeth, no one in the hall, except Rhianon, had any thought for anything but for the deeds and weapons and wonderful peculiarities of those three men, and for their journeyings to and fro, questing adventure, between this world and that. As for Gwawl, it was a year and a day

since he had known the light and beauty of his own land,
and he was worn with sorrow and exertion, through camping
during that time in the Country of the Immortals.   But
Taliesin had such power in relating stories, that Gwawl had
never come by comfort equal to listening to him; all dismay
and lack of ease were gone while he might be harkening to
the rising and falling, and the quivering and the gathering,
and the crooning and the crying, and the raging and the
triumphing, and the majestic intoning of Taliesin's voice.
While he heard it he might be at peace, and consoling his
soul with innumerable sunlit clouds of dream.   As for Rhianon, whatever magic there was in the story-telling, it had
little power to hinder her from wondering concerning Pwyll
Pen Annwn, and would his soul be great enough to bring
him past the dangers he would have to meet.   It is well
known what those dangers were.   They were the seven
companies of giants on the seven battlements, the least of
them able to snap an oak of nine hundred years across his
knee; and beyond the giants, the seven watchdogs at the
seven gates, and the smallest and feeblest of them all equal
in the conflict to seven full-grown, fierce, flesh-desiring,
battle-eager wolves — and indeed, more than equal to them.
What with considering these things, and cogitating, and
musing upon. them, and concluding that the soul of Pwyll
would be great enough for them, little heed would she pay
to the three shields of the sons of Cleddyf Cyfwlch, that were
three gleaming glitterers; and little would she bother with
their three spears, that were three pointed piercers; nor even
with their three swords themselves, even though they were,
as is well known, three marvelous, great griding gashers —
Gles, Glessic, and Gleisad.

From one thing to another Taliesin took them, filling the
hall with bewildering glory.   He was barely touching upon

their three dogs, Call, and Cuall, and Cafall, when there rose up a sound of furious barking outside. Twice it rose during the story of Call the Hound of Bwlch, and twice in the story of Cuall the Hound of Cyfwlch, and twice in the story of Cafall the Hound of Sefwlch, and once at the end; each time it waned slowly into a long, whining wail, and died away. At last it broke in upon his peace as he was telling the story, causing him to forget what would follow when all that was known concerning those three hounds should have been related.

" What barking was that? " said he.

" If there was barking, it would have been the voices of the dogs of the Sons of Cleddyf Cyfwlch," said the courtiers. " Call and Cuall and Cafall it would have been that we heard, by reason of the magic of the story-telling."

" I heard barking, but it was not from those three dogs," said Taliesin.

" It would have been Pwyll Pen Annwn against the seven watchdogs," said Rhianon. " Every one of them will have been slain before now."

(And Pwyll it was; and the war he waged with them was equal to three years of his life passing for each one of them, and he three times seven years older at the end than at the beginning of it. No one but Rhianon had heard the fierceness of the barking, and the leaping of the dogs through the air, and the impact of their bodies on the shield of Pwyll Pen Annwn, and the sweep of his sword as he slew them.)

" Not so, princess," said Gwawl; " it will have been no more than the story-telling. It would be easy for a bard of such dignity to cause this. Lord Radiant Forehead," said he; " go you forward with the story, if it shall please the princess to be heeding you."

"Greatly will it please me," said Rhianon. With that, Taliesin went forward.

He filled the hall with the warfare of those three men; when they went out against Caer Sidi amongst the stars, and had the three thousand defenders of Caer Sidi against them, and fought from the dawn until the noon, and by noon had made three piles of the slain, and in each of the piles not less than a thousand men. By reason of the noise of that warfare, no one but Rhianon heard clearly the raising seven times of a single warshout from the battlements, and seven times the roaring of the warshout of a whole host opposing it; and the roaring dying away, and losing itself in the end in the single warshout that was raised at first. But when silence came on that shout the seventh time, it broke in on Taliesin's peace again.

"What shouting was that from the battlements?" said he.

"We heard nothing, except what was in the story," said the courtiers.

"It was Pwyll Pen Annwn against the giants," said Rhianon, giving them such warning as was their due in courtesy, according to the custom of the Gods and the Cymry. "The Dragon Warshout of the Island of the Mighty he was raising."

"Not so, truly," said Gwawl. "It would have been no more than the magic of the story. Go you forward with the telling of it," said he; "if it please you, and if it please the princess."

"Lord Radiant Forehead," said she; "it pleases me, and more than pleases me."

With that he went forward again, and made account of the armories of Caer Ochren, and the assailment of them by the sons of Cleddyf Cyfwlch, and the breaking down of the lofty towers, and the toppling of the stones from the heights, the sinking of the jeweled pennons. There came a grand clamor from the battlements, a hollow clashing and ringing, and the smiting of bronze and iron on the flagstones, as if vessels of iron were falling in a furious storm and turbulence from heaven; but by reason of the glamor of the story-telling, no one but Rhianon heard it clearly; and not until it was dying away did it break upon Taliesin's peace, and shake the power of the story in his mind.

"Evil fall upon me," he said, "if there was no sound of fighting."

"Noise of fighting there was, by reason of the magic of the story," said they. "Marvelous truly is the power of the Chief Bard of the Island of the Mighty."

Then Rhianon made it known to them again. "It was Pwyll Pen Annwn on the battlements," said she; "sweeping the swords and shields and helmets from the giants he was, and making seven piles of each of them upon the flag-stones. Marvelous is the triumphing power of this sovereign ruler of the Dimetians."

(And Pwyll Pen Annwn it was; each pile that he made was the equal of a year from his life; so that he was three times seven years older at the end than at the beginning of it. But no one would believe Rhianon, because of the story, and their intense desire to hear what was yet untold of it; and Gwawl believed her less than any of them.)

Taliesin went forward then, and finished the story; and there came sound upon sound through it as if rocks were being hurled from the peak of Cadair Idris, and were dashing from crag to crag, and thundering and booming along the slopes, and crashing into the lake in the valley below, and driving the waters of it afar over the mountains: but no one heard more than a faint rumor of it, except Rhianon. Then at last the story came to its end; and in its very finishing, there rose a sound as if Cadair Idris himself had fallen, the whole mountain of him, into the lake; and by reason of the story being at its end, they heard that.

"It will be Pwyll Pen Annwn, and he flinging the chieftains of the giants over the battlements into the moat," said Rhianon. "Lord Gwawl," said she; "it is unlikely that I shall go hence with you."

"It will be no more than the tempest, and the blowing down of trees," said Gwawl. "Lord Radiant Forehead," said he; "it would be the delight of my life, and the consolation of my soul, were you to make known to us another of the stories of the Island of the Mighty."

But before the Penbardd could get the first word of it between his teeth, they heard a low knocking at the door. When it was opened, they beheld an old, white-bearded beggarman, and he in a ragged cloak, and his back bent double, and his face lined with old age, with care, and sickness. "I have been through the fierce storm," said he; "I have journeyed without ceasing for a year and a day. Without doubt it would be better to let me in."

Said Taliesin: "If he comes in, let him make clear the reason for the noises."

"Was there barking of the dogs at the gates?" said the porter. "I marvel that you should have had such protection, that you came past them unharmed."

"There will be few in these worlds, that do not know there was barking. I came past when it was ended, and the dogs did not harm me. It would be unfitting for me to relate to you the reason for the barking."

"Is there news with you concerning the raising up of warshouts?" said the porter. "Was there shouting to be heard?"

"As for shouting, I marvel if there will be any one in the Island of the Mighty now, and sleep visiting his eyelids, on account of it. The deaf would have been aware of it, from the Island of Ireland to Greece in the East."

"What protection had you against the giants?" said the porter. "Of their own will, they would not have allowed any one to pass."

"I came by when the shouting was ended, and they did me no injury. It would be unfitting for me to tell you more."

With the end of the story-telling, sorrow and anxiety and longing for his own land came upon Gwawl; and they oppressed him much more when he heard the beggar speaking. Impatiently always, and with sighs, he would listen to the voice of a mortal — for, although of the race of the Cymry, no one could call Taliesin mortal; with the life of him extending throughout the ages, and his being able to come and go between the worlds as he might please.

"Let him come in," said Gwawl. "So that there may be an end of this wrangling, let him have whatsoever he will. Except the hand of Rhianon my bride, or freedom to enter my own land, I grant him his request."

"It is a small thing that is requested," said the beggar-man. "The fill of this basket, of the food from the feast."

"Fill it to the brim for him, and let him be silent," said Gwawl. "Let no complaint of niggardliness come from him."

With that Taliesin began another story, and one of the serving-men took the basket, and put what food from the first table might not be required into it. Food for ten strong, hungry men he put in it, but at the end it was no more than half full. Then he took it to the beggar.

"It is not full," said he. "The word of the chieftain was that it should be filled to the brim."

Like a keen, bitter wind of mid January, the words of the beggar, the voice of a mortal, swept across the mind of Gwawl; and he endeavoring at the time to lose his thoughts and longings in the tale Taliesin was telling. " What trouble is on him? " he said.

" Food for ten strong, hungry men have I put in the basket, and the first table is cleared," said the serving-man. " It seemed to me that he would be contented with that."

" Woe is me," said the beggar. " It would be the sorrow of my life if the promise should be unfulfilled, and the basket less than full."

" Fill it, and let him go," said Gwawl. " Oh that there might be peace in the court! "

They cleared the second table without appeasing the hunger of the basket. They cleared the third and fourth, the fifth and the sixth, the seventh and the eighth, the ninth and the tenth, the eleventh and the twelfth and the thirteenth; they left nothing but what was needed by the princes for the satisfying of hunger. When they brought the basket to the beggar, indeed, half full it was, and no more than that.

" Were it not for the beauty of the story-telling, I would make an outcry concerning this. Undoubtedly the word of the chieftain was that it should be filled."

Bitterly the mortal voice broke in on Gwawl's peace again, driving away the whole delight of the story. " What trouble is on him? " said he, sighing. " For the sake of heaven, grant him his request."

" We have cleared the thirteen tables of whatever food is unneeded," said they. " It appeared to us that he might well be contented."

" Fill the basket, fill the basket and let him go," said Gwawl, the sorrow of the world oppressing him. Then they went and gathered all the food in the hall; gladly the princes gave up whatever might be before them, and no thought taken for hunger, or the desires of the appetite. At the end, the basket was no nearer to fulness than before.

"The word of the chieftain is unkept," said the beggar. "Hungry I came in here, hungry I shall go away. The sorrow of my life is this." More keenly laden even than before with the unbearable misery of the world, his speech went drifting and wandering like the sea-mist through the musings of Gwawl; and Taliesin himself without the art that could make them endurable to him.

"Woe is me that he should remain here until we are withered with the infection of mortality, and until we look with loathing on our own forms. Fill you the basket, and let him go."

"There is no more food in the palace," said they; "and yet the basket is no more than half full."

Then Gwawl betook himself to considering in what way he might be released from his sorrow. "Soul, soul," said he; "will nothing requite you for the loss of the food?"

"Nothing will requite me for it," said he. "Neither sovereignty, nor riches, nor extravagant praise from yonder bard."

"The basket will have peculiarities," said Rhianon. "It would be unwise to let him go, without learning what news there may be concerning them. It would have been full, but for peculiarities."

"What peculiarity is with the basket?" said Gwawl. "Is the manner of filling it known?"

"It is known," said the other. "Its peculiarity is that if its mind is set against being filled, there will be no filling it, unless there be treading down the stuff that has been put in it."

Then Gwawl said to the chief serving-man: "Tread you it down, if it please you."

"Ah, for the sake of heaven, not so, truly!" said the beggar. "It would be the peril of his life were he to do that."

"Wherefore would it be the peril?"

"Are there no peculiarities with the basket? Is no consideration to be paid it? Is it no better than the pannier of an old cocklewoman, from the shores of Penclawdd in Gwyr? So reckless you are!"

"O man of sorrowful conversation, make known to us the whole of it."

"Heed you this, then," said he. "Whoever makes trial of filling this basket by treading it down, unless he be the rightful chieftain, and unless the place that he holds is his by right, and according to desert, and no usurpation nor defraudment; and unless the time be the right time, and the best of time for him; he will never attain filling the basket; and not only will he never attain filling it, but it will be a marvel if he himself shall escape without meeting hurt, and harm, and misfortune, and injury and disaster."

"It is I that must tread it down," said Gwawl. "Clearly I forsee that it is I that must do it."

Thereupon he rose up; and as he rose Rhianon said to him: "Lord Gwawl, is there any breaking the fate that was put upon me at the wedding-feast, when Pwyll Pen Annwn lost me? Is there any permitting me to go hence in peace to the Island of the Mighty?"

"Of my own will, there is no permitting you. Unless compulsion is put upon me, and that before the ending of this feast, and by the chieftain that was here formerly, it never will be broken."

"Broken will it be, and compulsion will be put upon you,

and I shall go forth with Pwyll Pen Annwn tomorrow."

They rose up from the tables as he went down from the dais, out of respect and courtesy. He went down towards the beggar, and towards the hearth in the center of the hall. The men of the court ranged themselves against the wall at his left; the men of the Family of Clud ranged themselves against the wall on his right.

"Lord Gwawl," said the beggar; "is it of your own will that you tread down the food in the basket?"

"It is of my own will, out of desire that you may have what you need, and go. Unbearable to me is the presence of a mortal."

"Tread you it down then," said the other. "And may better befall you."

With that he put the basket on the floor, bulging open with its half-fulness. Gwawl set his left foot on the food, and trod it down, but the basket was no fuller. "With both feet must the treading be," said the beggar, "or it will never get its filling."

Thereupon Gwawl set the right foot beside the left on the food.

And still the basket was no more than half full; indeed and indeed now, evil upon the least and the best of us, if it was any fuller than that. Half full it was after the treading; half full, and no more. But if the fate of Pendaran Dyfed, and the fate of Ceredig Call Cwmteifi be remembered, the fate of Gwawl ab Clud will be known. Whatever may have been the stature of him before, inside that little, bag-shaped basket he was now, by reason of the magic, and power of illusion and phantasy, and strange peculiarities, and devouring nature of it; and it knowing that not he, but Pwyll Pen Annwn, was the rightful chieftain at that wedding-feast, and the rightful husband of the Daughter of Hefeydd. It was

closed upon him, and lifted with him, and thrown over the
shoulder of the beggar. As for that one, he was on his feet,
and the war-horn at his lips; and for all his age and weakness, it was the grand hai atton of the men of Dyfed, the
gathering call of the Dimetians in the Island of the Mighty,
that he blazed and sounded, and regally drove out echoing
through the horn. Before the Immortals, the Children of
the Family of Clud, or the people of Hefeydd Hen, had flung
their surprise from them, there was Pwyll Pen Annwn in his
dignity before them; they perceived that the beggar was no
other than Pwyll. Old he seemed, indeed, as if fifty years,
and not one year, had passed since he went forth on his
wanderings; yet they saw that there was peril for them in
his majesty of mien, and in the light in his eyes, and in the
drawn sword in his hand. If they had sought to overcome
him, before they might have reached him the Dimetians with
their war-worn, terrible swords were in the hall.

"Lord Gwawl," said Rhianon; "the compulsion has been
put upon you. Pwyll Pen Annwn did it."

"Yes," said he; "and therefore the fate is broken. Let
there be peace in the hall, and let the chieftain take his rightful place at the wedding-feast."

Pwyll set down the basket, and opened it; and Gwawl ab
Clud came forth. "Lord Gwawl," said Pwyll; "what gifts
will requite you for this discourtesy? By my will, your
dignity shall not be lessened."

"Nothing will requite me, but journeying with you into
the Island of the Mighty, and dwelling there from this out.
I shall have no delight in timeless beauty and peace hereafter,
but in serving, and doing deeds, and devising plans for the
benefit of the Race and Kindred of the Cymry."

"It shall be granted to you gladly," said they. "It will
be an honor to us."

" And beyond that, I desire your taking back the gift of your youth and vigor from me, that you lost while you were conquering the watchdogs, and while you were sweeping the armor from the giants, and making piles of it on the battlements, and while you were raising the Warshout of the Island of the Mighty, and while you were driving the giants over the battlements, so that they fell into the moat. It is a marvel to me, and a cause for delight and admiration, that any one should have accomplished this."

With that Pwyll was restored to his youth; even younger and stronger Gwawl made him, than he had been before.

Then the feast went forward until its ending, in peace, and in merriment, and in splendid song, and in listening to the stories of Taliesin Benbardd, until the dawn of the morning. Ten times more and better was the food that was taken out of the basket of Gwaeddfyd Newynog, than that which had been put into it. The men of the Family of Clud wondered at the strength and heroic bearing of the men of the Island of the Mighty; and the men of the Island of the Mighty wondered at the grace and beauty and dignity, and excellence of conversation of the Family of Clud; and as for the Gods, the people of Hefeydd Hen, they had equal delight in those that were from above them, and those that were from below.

The next day they departed; the Family of Clud for their own land, and the Dimetians under Pwyll and Rhianon, and Gwawl ab Clud with them, for the Island of the Mighty. After three days they came to Dyfed, and to Arberth; and it seemed to Gwawl that he had never seen a fairer region, nor a better city. With their coming there, the First Branch of the Story of Pwyll and Rhianon has its end. As for Taliesin the Chief of Bards, it is not known whither he may have journeyed, at that time.

It is the Third Branch of it that will be related now,
and the Name of this one is:

The Coming of Ab Cilcoed, and the Three Trials of Pwyll Pen Annwn

IN the seven cantrefs of Dyfed there was little but delight, and prosperity, and advantage for every one, during the year after Rhianon's coming there. Indeed, it was well known that she was without her equal, or nearly her equal, either for beauty or for wisdom, for nobility or for kindness, in the Three Islands of the Mighty, or in the Three Islands near thereto, or in the Island of Ireland, or in the length and width of the whole world, so far as was known; wonderful was her renown, and her glory, and the songs that were made in her praise; and none of it equal to her deserts. Complete was Pwyll in delight and favor and well-being. As for the Dimetians, she never abated her proud, sweet friendliness towards them. Unless it were Madog Crintach, or Deiniol Drwg, or Catwg Gwaeth, or Gwylltyn Gwaethaf Oll (they were men of the east that had

come into Dyfed when they were children for fosterage, and
had remained there, and acquired wealth; little good was
spoken of them), there were none that were without help
from her, and profit by her counsels. Never had her countenance shown less than delight, and glory, and radiant gaiety
of aspect since the day the queenhood was bestowed upon her.

A year passed, and on the morning after it, it was clear
to Pwyll Pen Annwn that there was sternness on the queen,
and a certain gravity of mind. He asked her what would be
the cause of it.

" If there is gravity," said she, " it is on account of Llwyd
the son of Cilcoed from the region of Uffern. Were there
any one that could keep him out of Dyfed this day, the land
would be safe from him for another year. But he will be
making trial to get in, and that between noon and sunset;
and it will not be easy to prevent him."

" What would the one do, that would spoil the trial for
him? " said Pwyll.

" He would ride as far as Gorsedd Arberth, and take his
place on the throne there; and let no one else come near the
throne till the sun was gone from the sky," said she. " He
would maintain silence from the time of his setting out until
the time of his returning, and heed nothing that might be
said to him, either on the Gorsedd or on the way."

" As much as that I will do gladly," said Pwyll. " If
there is any spoiling his trial, I will spoil it."

With that, he had them saddle Blodwen, and bring her
into the courtyard. He looked at every nail in the four shoes
on her four hoofs, and there was not one either loose or
wanting. He examined every strap and fastening of the
saddle, and the whole of the purple saddle-cloth, and the
apples of gold at its four corners; there was nothing about
them that was less than perfect. He went forward, taking

the road towards the Gorsedd. Hardly had he ridden half
the distance, when the shoe of the right forehoof was
gone from the mare. He dismounted and tied her by the
roadside: walking quickly, he would come before noon to the
place where he desired to be. While he was tying Blodwen,
he heard the clink of hammer on anvil from beyond the bend
of the road. "It would be better to have her shod," he
thought; not considering that he had known of no smithy
there until then. He untied her, and led her forward. On
the left of the road, when he had passed the bend, he saw the
smithy; it had no appearance of newness with it. It was a
wonder that he should have passed the place not three days
since, and taken no note of it.

There was a yoke of oxen standing in front of the forge,
and with them a tall, white-bearded Ploughman — ploughman or not, clearly he had the dignity of kings and druids
with him. Then Pwyll remembered the morning when he
rode out after apples to the Orchard of Celyddon, and the
beating of the rain upon him, and a white, running glimmer
through the rain. There was no knowing why such memories
should be taking his mind, at that time; he had seen no
ploughman at Celyddon, so far as was known to him.

He heard conversation between the Ploughman and the
one that was in the smithy; like this it was:

"Is the fire white in its heart with you?" said the Ploughman. "Is the iron of the right color, neither so bright as to
be white, nor so dull as to be black or brown or gray?"

"White is the fire, and red is the metal," said the other.
"There is nothing lacking, so far as is known."

"Well, well," said the Ploughman; "it is the day for
the trial." He turned as he spoke, catching the eyes of Pwyll
for a moment before he went on his way, driving the oxen.
Never had it chanced to the chieftain of the Dimetians to

know anything equal to the sad majesty of his gaze, as if all the sorrow in a thousand dark stars were known to him; as if he had been waiting for something desired and hoped for since the Shouting of the Name. He gave Pwyll no word of greeting, but turned again, and went on down the road, singing strangely and quietly to the oxen.

The Smith came out from the forge, and took the bridle from the king's hand without either of them speaking. He was a tall, handsome, black-haired, blue-eyed, fair-skinned man, and no better known to Pwyll than the Ploughman had been. It would be some king, perhaps, out of the north or out of Lloegr, and he doing smith-service for one of the Immortals; there would be nothing strange in that. There was an oak of a hundred limbs on the other side of the road; Pwyll took his stand by the bank at its foot, waiting; and his mind running out to Gorsedd Arberth, and to the peril of Dyfed from Llwyd ab Cilcoed. Who this Llwyd might be, he had not heard; the fullest tidings he had of him, was that he came from the regions of Uffern. It would have been unfitting for him to have made inquiries of Rhianon; and she with the concern only that he should go forward and hold the Gorsedd.

The sound of the hammer on the anvil called him from his musings; barely had the seven blows been struck, when it became clear to him that the Smith was knocking out a music unlike anything he had heard during his life. The sound grew and was multiplied wonderfully upon him; it took strange rhythms, and raised up innumerable echoes along the rim of the world, like far thunder rolling among the mountains, or the boom of the billows on the cliffs, or the roaring of all the flooded torrents of the wilds. The sparks flew faster and faster; wandering showers of them playing and quivering through the sun-flecked leafage, driving out across

the road, and falling about him on this side and on that.
It might have been with the twentieth blow, that it happened
to a spark to fall into his right eye; instead of pain and burning, it became sharp, swift vision with him for an instant
into the illimitable secrecy of things. For an instant he saw
that, the like of which not many will have to see, while their
bodies and mortality may still be encumbering them.

It was as if a wind blew out of the immortal regions,
sweeping away the road and the tree and the little white-
washed smithy; sweeping away the sunlight and the blueness
of the sky, and the Dimetian hills, and the glory of the morning; and sowing over leagues upon leagues a great confusion
of darkness, a whirling red glare; in the midst of it, what
seemed to be the crimson and fiery sun, when he goes down
amid heaped cloudbanks of purple; and by that again, One
that had the stature of the poplar, the splendor of the sunset
and the dawn. But before there was so much as telling
what colors might be in his raiment, the whole glow and
vision was caught up in a whirl of smoke, and blown away;
and there was the smithy again, and the Smith, and the anvil,
as they had been before. It was a cause of marveling with
Pwyll Pen Annwn.

"Soul," said the Smith; "not many will attain entering
into this smithy. To please the Ploughman of these Islands
it is permitted to you."

Then Pwyll knew that it was Hu Gadarn was the Ploughman he had seen on the road; and with him the Exalted
Oxen, Nynnio and Peibio, that had been kings of the world
before they were changed into ploughing-beasts for their
querulous and battle-eager pride. He made no answer, at
that time. "Although I was warned against conversation,"
thought he, "it would not have been the conversation of the
Immortals." Keen was his desire to learn what forge it was,

and who was the Smith that was swinging the hammer in it.

"Did you not learn that?" said the other, hearing the question without language having been put to it. "It is a marvel to me that a man should come to Pen Gannion, and be without knowledge or recognition of the place. Behold now the splendor of it," said he.

With that he smote, not sparks, but one great brilliance of flame out of the iron; and with its waning, road and sky and tree and smithy were gone again, and the aspect of a mortal fell from the Smith, and he stood revealed in all his grand stature and beauty, towering over the king, in the glare and gloom of a huge, unearthly region. Pwyll knew then that it would be Gofannon the King-Smith that he was; that Son of Don, on whose anvils on the Headland of Gannion swords are forged for the Immortals, for their warfare with the demon races. Glorious he was, beyond the finding of any likeness for him; shadowy light and bright darkness played about his form and his visage, grape-purple and of the color of the deepest roses. There was a spear in his hand that seemed to have flame running and rippling through it; its head glowed and shone until it was the greatest light in the world. What had seemed, in Pwyll's first glimpse of vision, to be the setting sun amidst clouds, was made known now for an anvil of intense glory. A hall of innumerable forges extended on all sides, filled with shadowy and gigantic toilers, and with the sound of innumerable titanic hammers, beating upon such anvils as might be used for the shaping of mountains. All was lurid gloom, immense darkness and sudden glare; as for roof or walls, there was no sign of either of them; only blackness, and sudden ruddy startings up of flame afar, or sudden deepening and blooming out of crimson glory over a vastness wider than the sky. It seemed to Pwyll that if two armies had been in that hall, neither of them less in number than the army of the king of London, when hosting is made of the whole of the men of the Island of the Mighty; and both of them eager for battle, and vehemently desirous of winning fame and renown and glory out of the ones that were opposed to them; and either skilfully led, with proud, experienced sovereign rulers at the head of them, and such guides as might be the best in the world, and no less good in an unknown land than in the lands in which they were born; it seemed to him that they might wander for a thousand years, seeking, and never finding their opponents; that they might pass each other near at hand, and be unaware of it; passing, and attaining no end nor goal for their wanderings; so vast it was; and so great the fume, and tumult, and confusion, and bewilderment of momentary crimson-breasted clouds, and dark firmaments unkindled by a star; and again, of fountains of sparks arising, more countless, as it seemed to him, than the multitudes of stars in the Castle of Gwydion, in the Milky Way.

Said Gofannon: "What gift will you take from the Forge of the Immortals? No one goes from the Headland of Gannion," said he, "without labor accomplished for him; much less if it is by the favor of Hu Gadarn that he came in."

From close at Pwyll's hand, a whinny came through the gloom. He turned, and reached out, and took Blodwen by the bridle, and led her forward into the glare of the anvil, and pointed to her shoeless hoof.

Gofannon laughed. "Here is one come to Pen Gannion for the shoeing of a mare," he cried. "Here is one that is going against Llwyd ab Cilcoed, and no desire on him for such a weapon as might win him success."

The laughter of millions of giants rang out and swayed and rocked through the hall. "Let the gifts be shown to him, that he may make a wiser choosing," said Gofannon.

He saw the giants moving through the gloom; suddenly in the midst of them sprang into light a thousand spears, equal in glory to the spear of Gofannon himself. The sight of them drove the feeling of mortality from Pwyll's limbs. Out of the thousand, one shone pre-eminent; it was clear that that one, if there were a foe before it anywhere in the world, would not rest in the hand that might be holding it, but would strain, and writhe, and struggle, and loose itself irresistibly, and make pursuit of its aim through the night and the day, and have no peace nor satisfaction until he were slain, and itself returned to the hand of its master. "Ah heaven," thought Pwyll; "Llwyd would have little power, whoever he may be, against the man that had a spear like that one."

"Is it spears you desire?" said Gofannon.

Once more Blodwen whinnied, and the king's mind went back to the behests and desires of Rhianon, and the watching on Gorsedd Arberth from noon to sunset, and the maintaining of silence both going and returning. He pointed down at the right forehoof, that was shoeless; and shook his head against accepting spears.

"Let the shields be made known to him," said Gofannon.

With that, the middle air was brilliant beyond noonlight with what seemed to be the flashing forth of a thousand suns. When he looked at their bright glory, strength and piercing vision flowed into him through his eyes, and he was filled with the whole joy and magnanimity of the world. It was a marvel that even Gods should have been able to look at those shields; yet Pwyll beheld them without winking an eyelid. One of them rose up, and beamed so proudly forth that the rest grew pale.

"Let trial be made of that one," cried Gofannon ab Don.

The spears came flying from every part of the firmament;

like the roar of a burning pine forest was the noise of their
passage through the air. Wherever they flew, the Shield
took them, and quenched them, and splintered them in pieces.
The clamor of their smiting on it made the sound of the
hammers on the anvils seem quietness and peace. Then
boulders hurtled through the air; no more than nine of them,
heaped together, would have been needed to make a mountain equal to the Wyddfa. , They crashed upon the Shield,
and fell; at the end there was neither dint nor scratch on its
beautiful surface. "By heaven," thought Pwyll, "if one
had a shield such as that one —"

"Is it the shield you will take?" said the King-Smith.
"It would be the protection of Dyfed from Llwyd ab Cilcoed —"

The words were between his tongue and his teeth to take
it, and give praise and gratitude for it; when he felt Blodwen
nuzzling and caressing his hand again. He shook his head
against the Shield, and pointed to the right forehoof, the
shoeless one. Yet, "In my deed, true it is that little could
be done against such a weapon," thought he.

"There is no end to his ambitions," said Gofannon. "He
will have neither spear nor shield, though the Gods covet
them. Make the swords known to him."

They did so; and whatever might be thought of the
spears or the shields, however excellent they were, and beyond human imagining; compared with the swords they
seemed little better than the wooden toys of a child. It was
as if the whole herd of the lightnings of heaven were let
loose in the upper air; indeed, if they had been, their glory
would have been contemptible beside the glory of those
swords. The sight of them kindled in Pwyll's mind, and
caused such ardor and loftiness of soul to flame up in him,
that it seemed to him that he would have attained suddenly

the stature of the well-grown poplar, the firmness of the mountains. "Make trial of the swords," said Gofannon ab Don. Then they uplifted the shields again, and those that had the swords smote with them upon the shields; and the shields, in spite of the wonders that they were, were easily destroyed. Pwyll marveled; he took no thought for the requests of Rhianon; he forgot Gorsedd Arberth; it was the same to him as if he had heard no rumor of the son of Cilcoed from the time his life began.

"Is it a sword you desire?" said Gofannon.

"By heaven, it is a sword," said Pwyll. "They never had their equals under the stars."

"Let a sword be forged for him," cried the son of Don. "Let a new sword be forged swiftly for this prince of the Cymry of lofty desires. It is unfitting that an old and outworn weapon should be foisted upon him." He robed himself in shadow as he spoke. Then Pwyll heard a great stir, and the whole tumult grew into the sound of one hammer smiting on one unseen anvil. Eagerly he waited; this would be a weapon for him against Llwyd ab Cilcoed; Rhianon would glory in this. Against Llwyd? Indeed, against all the demons; the Island of the Mighty at least should be made free from evil now. It was fitting that since one of the Immortals had taken queenhood there, the man that was reigning at her side should have a blade from Pen Gannion, to work her will with it throughout the world. This was a marvelous honor that Hu Gadarn was doing him; it would be as much as choosing him for champion of the Immortal Kindred. Thunder upon thunder upon thunder of the hammer on the anvil; sunset upon sunset upon sunset where the glory of the upleaping flame reddened on the vastness between the floor and the rafter beams. The Gods had seen to it that when he held the Gorsedd, he should be fittingly armed to meet Abred let loose, the whole multitude of the following of Cythraul. . . . Thunder upon thunder upon ringing, clanging, resounding, booming, far-rolling thunder . . . and now silence, and the waning of the red glow on the upper and middle air. Suddenly a sword flashed forth there, held in some vast shadowy hand. He remembered the thousand swords that had been revealed to him; contemptible they seemed, and unworthy of notice, and such as would betray their wielder upon the field of conflict, in comparison with this one.

It flew forth, as if of its own will, until Gofannon was holding it. He lifted it suddenly, and swung it against the anvil that was before him; and he himself in a half darkness, not clearly visible. A million lightnings broke loose and fled and quivered into the far gloom. The sword was shivered into ten million fragments, and was strewn like hailstones over the immensity of the floor.

"A miserable weapon, truly," cried the King-Smith. "It would be an insult to offer the like of it to this warlike prince of the kindred of the Cymry. Let a better smith take better steel, and let a weapon be forged that may be called a sword, and that will be worthy of the man that will swing it in battle."

Again the clang of the hammer, a grand music as if of bells, not without ringing, martial, vibrant sweetness. Such a sword as the last one would have been equal to all victories; it might have overcome Gods and Dragons without boasting. As for this one that was being forged now, the thought of it was wild delight, a tumult of flaming glory in his heart and in his imagination. Peal after peal of the ringing clangor; what hammer was this that could so fill the world with unearthly music? What anvil that could strew such beauty over the dark void of the air? At last it was forged, this

new sword also; and flamed forth upon wings as the first
had done, and Gofannon caught it by the hilt as it flew. He
smote the anvil with it, and clove the iron anvil in two. Then
he put the point of it on the flagstones, and set his foot on the
blade, and exerted his strength against it three times, and
broke it contemptuously. "Ah," he said; " it was better than
the other; but it was a paltry, miserable weapon. Only myself will be equal to forging a sword for this haughty sovereign of the Cymry."

Then he stood forth in such glory that it seemed to Pwyll
he had not seen him at all, but only some shadowy vagueness
of him, until then. There is no poplar in the world, or pine-
tree in the heart of its forest, or sheltered between mountains where no wind can bend it, that would be the equal, or
nearly the equal of him in stature. A dark blue mantle was
on him, fastened over his heart with a brooch, the size of
a shield, of living opal, sapphire and amethyst; the mantle
had the appearance of the firmament on a night of stars,
but the lights overstrewn on it were lovelier than the stars
of a cloudless midnight in August, when no moon may be
shining. He flung back the mantle over his shoulders, revealing the beauty of his being. Evil upon the world, if his
very corporeal frame were not of purple and rose-dark fires,
of gloom and glow and glory and mystery. Such beauty
dawned upon his face, and upon the coal-black, purple-
shadowed bloom and luster of his hair, as may not be seen
among the mountains, at sunrise or at sunset, at dark midnight or at bright noon.

Then it seemed as if the whole darkness of the world had
died. As far as Pwyll could see, from the north to the south
before him the whole hall burned up into a bright, beautiful rose, an intense vortex of flame; and in the midst of it,
an anvil vaster than the mountains; vaster, heaven knows,

than huge, five-peaked Pumlumon, or the god-sheltering
Wyddfa, or Cadair Idris of the Druid of the Stars.   Beside
it stood the King-Smith radiant, fire visibly rippling through
his bare arms and his breast.   On the anvil there was that
which glowed in the glow, and was brighter and more intense
than the flame; beating on it, a hammer that might well have
crushed the world in its falling.   The sound of every blow
that fell was the equal of all music, the dispelling of all sorrow, the rousing up, in the heart of whomsoever might attain
hearing it, of the whole heroism of the world.   Not one
thought was in Pwyll's mind as he watched the forging, as he
watched the sword take shape, as he saw the immortal King-
Smith hold it up gloriously in the air.   It was a hard gap of
brightness in the intense glow that filled the hall; it was a
long gleam of sudden and surprising light.   No one but a
God could have dared to touch it; but it seemed to Pwyll
that it would not be too great for him.

"As for making trial of it, let the boulders be thrown,"
said Gofannon.   Again the great granite masses came hurt-
ling through the air, and a marvel such as this was to be
seen: the sword take one of them after the other, and
sweep through it easily.   Then the King-Smith turned with
it towards the great anvil, and clove that, so that it fell out
in two equal pieces to the left and the right.   Then he put
the point on the flagstone at his feet, and bent the blade, and
trod on it, and exerted his strength seven times; it flew out,
straight and gleaming again, the moment he lifted his foot;
no power in the world could injure it.   "It is a sword of the
right forging," he said.   "No one could accuse it of any
fault.   The one that has a right to it, let him take it;
nothing would prevent its flying to its rightful lord."   Not
until then had there been sternness or sorrow in his voice.
He let loose the sword.   The hall rocked and trembled; its

glory of fires died. Great wonder-lightnings of wings burst
from the sword-blade, flashing out from end to end of the
darkness. Was it Hu or some other God that shone for a
moment, severe of aspect, in the far, somber gloom? Away
with the sword, winging and singing terribly through the air,
towards that stern momentary figure; and sword and God
were lost in darkness, more swiftly than the lightning reaches
its home.

Then Pwyll remembered the counsels of Rhianon, and
his loss and heedlessness were made clear to him. The immensity of the hall was gone; the unearthly gloom and brilliance had become sunlight and shadow; the clamor of immortal hammers gave place to the beating of the last nail
into the horseshoe, and to the rustling of a soft wind in
the leaves and branches of the oak. . . . His loss and heedlessness were made clear to him. . . . He looked up at the
sun; its was within a few minutes of its noon.

" Ah," said the Smith — and no likeness of godhood on
him then — " it is a pity, truly, for any one to enter Pen
Gannion without advice. Time will stand still for the man
that is silent there; there is no peril for the one without
desire. But often hours are squandered as soon as the lips
may be framed for speech; and often there will be the desiring the Sword of the Gods, and the claiming it, by those who
have no right to more than to be on Gorsedd Arberth before
noon."

" True it is," said Pwyll. " Upon me let the sorrow
fall." He rode forward towards the Gorsedd sorrowfully,
as swiftly as he might.

He came to the stile at the foot of the hill a little after
it was noon. A small cloud was blown across the heavens
on to the hilltop, hiding the throne for a moment before it
passed on and darkened the whole sky. As he made his way

up the hill, he met a man coming down; it was Madog Crintach from the east of the world. If there was a hard curmudgeon of a man in the Island of the Mighty in those days,
it was that Madog; and it was for that reason that the name
of Crintach was given him.

Pwyll watched on the Gorsedd until dusk; but it was in
his mind that little good would come of the watching. The
whole green land of Dyfed, as he looked out over it, had an
aspect unlike any that he had seen on it before; even the
bees that sought the blossoms on the hilltop, had a certain
sound of mourning and heaviness in the music of their wings.
He saw no marvel, and met with no blows or violence. In
the evening he returned to Arberth. He heard no singing as
he passed through the town; no joyful barking greeted him
at the gates of the palace. When he went into the feasting-
hall with the courtiers and the guests, he saw that a third
part of the light and music there was gone. Aden Lonach,
indeed, and Aden Fwynach, were shedding their delicate
splendor from among the rafters; but there was no sign of
Aden Lanach, the eldest of those three lovely ones, the
white one of the Singers of Peace. In silence and a strange
gloom, the feast went on to its ending.

"Soul," said Pwyll to Rhianon, "because of me this sorrow hath fallen."

"It is known," said she, "both to you and to me." Then
she said: "Useless would be reproaches and finding fault.
It would have been better to have desired to be on the
Gorsedd."   •

"What evil will have come of this?"

"Llwyd ab Cilcoed has come in; it will be hard to preserve the Dimetians from molestation by him. Already has
he been empowered to steal Aden Lanach, and there will be
no recovering her, except by your son and mine, when he

is grown a man. There was one upon the throne on Gorsedd Arberth at noon, of a shriveled, twisted and sidelong nature; and he escaped not without blows and violence; and he had them from Llwyd ab Cilcoed, whose coming into Dyfed he brought about by his being upon the Gorsedd."

"It was the Crintach from the east of the world," said Pwyll. "It would have been better to have driven him forth when he was a child —"

"It would not have been better," said she; "even though the like of him should be the cause of evil. It would have been ungenerosity, and inhospitable unkindness, and the bringing in of a niggardly spirit among the princes of the Cymry, and the corruption of the virtue of the sovereign rulers of this island."

"That is true," said he. "Is there nothing that I can do to requite you for this evil?"

"There is nothing," she said; "until the time may come for doing it."

II. THE HOSTING OF THE ARMIES OF MALEN RUDDGOCH REN

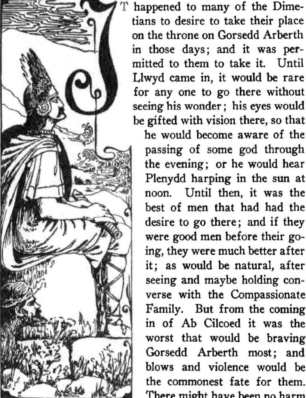

T happened to many of the Dimetians to desire to take their place on the throne on Gorsedd Arberth in those days; and it was permitted to them to take it. Until Llwyd came in, it would be rare for any one to go there without seeing his wonder; his eyes would be gifted with vision there, so that he would become aware of the passing of some god through the evening; or he would hear Plenydd harping in the sun at noon. Until then, it was the best of men that had had the desire to go there; and if they were good men before their going, they were much better after it; as would be natural, after seeing and maybe holding converse with the Compassionate Family. But from the coming in of Ab Cilcoed it was the worst that would be braving Gorsedd Arberth most; and blows and violence would be the commonest fate for them. There might have been no harm

in that, but that, as the story relates, whoever encountered
the blows and violence, no one would get good from him after.
It was the souring and embittering of minds. They had gone
up for the sake of the wonder, considering they had a right to
see whatever another might have seen; and envy took them
that they should be held of less account. So there grew up
sorrow and ill will, little known theretofore among the kindred of the Cymry; and none knowing that behind it were
the quiet workings and incitements of Ab Cilcoed, except
Rhianon; and she opposing him as well as she could. Indeed,
Pwyll too knew a little of it; and there is no telling what
Gwawl ab Clud may have known.

A year and a day passed; and again there was anxious
gravity to be seen with the princess. "Soul," said Pwyll,
"for the sake of heaven and man, what will be the cause of
the gravity? Nothing could be more desirable to me than to
lighten this."

"Gravity there is," said she. "It is the day on which the
son of Cilcoed has his power, and that will be the reason for
it. It is the day he will be seeking to bring his men into
Dyfed. If Madog or Deiniol, or Catwg or Gwylltyn, should
be on the throne on Gorsedd Arberth between noon and sunset this day, undoubtedly it would be the empowering Llwyd
to bring in his armies."

"Ah," said Pwyll; "I will hold the throne."

He rode forward through the gray morning, and came
to the Valley of Gorsedd Arberth without meeting any one.
In the field below the road at the head of the valley there
was a man ploughing; Pwyll heard voices there, and turning
his head, saw the Ploughman, and a woman talking with him.
It seemed to him that they were very proud and kingly of
mien, for a countryman and his wife; but he paid little heed
to them, his mind being full of watching on the Gorsedd, and

of a certain joy that he would be able to do something against
Ab Cilcoed that day, after his failure a year before. But he
heard this much from them as he passed:

"It would be an evil thing if there should be success with
us, where none may be desired," said the woman.

"True is that," said the Ploughman; "but this is the day,
and there is no escaping it. Let the trial be made, if the men
and the horses are in readiness; there would be no attainment nor advantage without it."

"Everything is in readiness," said she. "What has been
designed shall be accomplished, and may good come of it."

"Yes, yes," said he. "Good will come; at long last
good will come."

Pwyll rode on and took his place on the throne an hour
before noon. By midday he saw smoke rising on the edge
of the sky eastward, first in one place, then in many. As he
watched, slowly the smoke columns became more numerous,
and rose from places nearer and nearer. Far off he could see
herds driven down into the road from the mountains, and
taking their way then towards the Gorsedd and towards Arberth. Carts and wagons began to gather there, too, with
country people, women and children; and little crowds of
people on foot; and all hurrying westward. There came a
horseman thundering along the road at full gallop; as he
passed the stile, he looked up, and saw who it was that was on
the throne. He reined in his horse quickly and dismounted,
and ran swiftly up the hillside.

"Lord," said he; "the greatest host in the world has
come up out of Morganwg, and the eastern commotes are
laid waste by them."

Would this be the way that Llwyd was bringing his hosts
into Dyfed? Pwyll made no answer, nor stirred out of the
throne. He waved the man away, pointing towards Arberth.

" The Dimetians are not hosted," said the man; and wonder in his voice as he said it. Again Pwyll pointed towards the city, and motioned to him that he should go.

He turned, and went grumbling. " I will take the news to Pendaran, since there is no help for us with the rightful chieftain. Or I will take it to Catwg and Deiniol; by heaven, there are still men that will not abhor fighting. An evil thing, truly, is this marrying with the unhuman clans." He mounted at the stile, and rode forward towards Arberth. Pwyll saw him turn, and look back towards himself where he was throned, and hatred and open disloyalty on his face. During his life he had not heard, until then, of any disloyalty towards a sovereign ruler in the whole of the Islands of the Mighty.

The countrymen and their herds began to pass, a long stream of them; the women and children to take refuge in the city, the men to join the hosting of the Dimetians that would be going forward. It was long before any of them chanced to look up towards the throne on the hill; at last, when the road was crowded, and no gaps between this group and that, it happened to a horseman to look up, and to stop the ones that rode with him; and to them all to raise a great shout when they saw Pwyll. He did not stir; he remembered that he was to heed nothing. Nine of them broke from the crowd, and came hurrying up the hillside; the whole multitude stopping and watching. " Lord," said the nine; " it is an army out of Morganwg; and no pleasure in the world with them but to burn, and raid, and work injury, and harry, and destroy."

" And not the guise nor seeming of mortals with them," said one. " Stern and proud and terrible as the Gods they are; and seven cities there burnt to the ground with them." .

. They related it to him in confusion; it had never hap-

pened to him to behold fear on the faces of any of his people
before; not even on the least and least noble of them. They
besought him to go with them; there would be no true hosting except by the king. He made them no answer; considering within himself that they would be children of Illusion
and Phantasy, and persuading himself of it; since the Cymry
were unacquainted with the nature of fear, at that time. But
he saw the great crowd below watching; clear it was that
wonder and sorrow were growing upon them. When had it
happened that a prince of the Cymry had been reluctant at
the hour of the hosting, or had given no answer to those who
might desire to be led? The nine went back, and he saw them
give the news of his silence to the people. A little girl broke
out into wailing; one of the women turned on her, fiercely,
it might be said, and shook her till there was little breath in
her body. The whole crowd began to move forward again;
the men with an aspect of sullenness on them; the women
wailing or quarreling among themselves. Never had he either
seen or heard the like of this among the Dimetians; and
yet. . . . The memory of it afflicted his mind all day, like
flies about the kine in the meadow, on the hottest morning
in July.

They passed, and the road became empty again; and now
he could see the army that was coming against Dyfed. The
valley began to fill with such a host that he had never seen
nor dreamed of the like of it since his life began. Thousands
of chariots, bright and lofty, long-scythed, made of brass,
came streaming along the road; innumerable warriors covered the hillsides; proud battle-bards in advance, with loud-
stringed, ringing, martial harps, and with noble and exalted
utterance of vocal song, and that thunderous with the desire
for war. It was a strange guise for the men of Llwyd,
thought he. The gray sky was beginning to bloom into pale

primrose in the west, when the foremost of them came to the
foot of Gorsedd Arberth. He saw a queen at their head,
of unparalleled warlike dignity. She rode in a chariot that
seemed to be quickened with immortal flame; and for scythes,
long sprays of scarlet and golden flame budding and shooting
from the axles of its wheels. Somberly majestic, darkly com-
manding was her aspect; the head of her long, potent, living
spear was a darkly glowing carmine flame. About her proud,
dark, unbending brow the wan air quivered into radiance like
a fierce, empurpled sunset after storm. Her car stopped at
the foot of the Gorsedd. She turned towards the standard-
bearer that rode at her right, and pointed with her spear towards the hilltop. He leaped down from his horse, and shook
out the folds of his beautiful flag, and vaulted lightly over
the stile, and came swiftly striding up the hill.

It had never happened to Pwyll to behold so bright and
splendid a banner as the one he was bearing. The dragon
on it was flame-red, and much more than flame-red in color;
it was brighter and prouder and more vehement than all the
flame in the world. It seemed to be rather a living, curving,
rearing, beautiful Winged One, than any semblance painted
upon silk. Proud were its arching, glinting, wavering neck,
its sweeping, lambent wings, its long, lithe, well-poised, terrible tail; as for its eyes, they gleamed and were living; they
gave light upon light. The whole hillside glowed with ruddy
and golden and scarlet glory from it. Whoever might look
upon it would be filled with heroic strength, and with pure,
unsullied manhood, and with the intense desire to have hosts
out before him, and to be opposing multitudes single-handed,
and to be reaping the flower of the warriors of the world.

As for Pwyll himself, at the sight of it his soul strained
towards the field of conflict. Nothing would have brought
him joy, or pleasure, or any delight in the world, except to

ride out without aid against that whole vast army. "An evil pleasure were this," he thought; and took his gaze away from the banner. He remembered clearly, with that, the behests and desires of Rhianon, and to be holding the hill against Ab Cilcoed until the sun went from the sky.

" The greeting of heaven and of man to you, Pwyll Pen Annwn," said the herald. He was a tall man, fair-haired, glorious of face and form; his voice was such that whoever might hear it, would take delight in him, and would desire his companionship, so cheerful and pleasant it was. He got no more answer, than as if he had spoken to the wind.

" It is the War-red War-Queen against the Island of the Mighty," he said. " Courteously she greets you, desiring conflict at your hands. From Cent to Gwent, and between Gwent and Dyfed, she has met no such warfare as would please her; and it would be a cause of reproach and sorrow with her, and the bringing about of pining away, if she were to leave this island without tasting fighting."

Pwyll looked out westward in silence. The clouds were wan and primrose-colored there; the sun would be near his setting behind them; but they were concealing whether he had yet set or not set. " It will be better to wait," thought Pwyll. " Subtle are the devices of this Ab Cilcoed," thought he.

"I marvel that there should be silence," said the herald. " The queen has heard of the fame of the Dimetians; and that their king was not one to choose peace when war might be offered. She sends you the privilege of battle-breaking princes." (No one might claim that privilege for himself, by reason of modesty; if he claimed it he would be unworthy of it.) " Come you down into the roadway, and she will set her champions against you, one after the other, until such time as the way may be clear for her to go forward. As for

the hosting of the Dimetians, she herself will send forward
heralds to hasten it."

"It is all a trick of Llwyd ab Cilcoed," thought Pwyll.
"Exceedingly skilful is he truly, in devising plans, and in
proffering temptations, and they the most desirable in the
world. Clearly he will not be able to pass, while I may remain here upon the throne." Talking to him was not more
profitable than talking to the wind would have been, at that
time.

"Discourteous is this," said the herald; "in my deed to
God, discourteous it is truly. I marvel that the like of it
should be found among the Cymry." He turned, and went
quickly down towards the road.

Then Pwyll saw the queen call the bannerman upon her
left; and he, too, dismounted, and shook out the folds of his
flag, and began to make his way towards the top of the hill.
A great sadness came over Pwyll at that. North and east
and south, he saw the far farms and white, quiet homesteads
charred and ruined, or bursting up into a red brilliance of
flame. Fields where the young wheat had been greener than
the beryl stone; where it had rippled in long, whitening waves
under the wind in the morning, he saw now trampled down
and wholly laid waste. Like bees at the honey-taking, like
wasps in the fruit season when their nests may be invaded,
the remembrance of the shame and anger of the country people when they passed from before him in the morning, and
he without having heeded them, swarmed enangered about
his mind, bitterly stinging, the cause of grief. Then his eyes
were taken with the herald's flag, so that he could see nothing
else. Sorrow, and disgust, and hatred, and loathing flowed
into his heart at the sight of the heavy burning menace of the
dragon on it. Blood-red it was; with sluggish, world-encum-
bering coils; the like of it had never been exposed upon the

free winds of the Island of the Mighty. On the black cloth of
the banner its despicable eyes gleamed and glanced cruelly,
its length and bulk quivered; its long, merciless jaws were
slavered with a foam of smoke and blood and flame. Whoever might look on it would be smitten with fear and grief,
and with mourning for all that might have fallen in war,
of those that had been dear to him since the world began.
Looking at it, it seemed to Pwyll marvelous that any one
should be found to take pleasure in warfare. The memory
of the burning farms and the waste of the land afflicted him;
a sadness hard to be endured. Most of all he thought of the
sorrow of widows, and their desolation, and of the Dimetians
unhosted, and of the shame and anger of the people that went
from him unanswered in the morning.

Fiercely proud, and with vehement anger the herald strode
towards him. He was a tall, dark man; of huge limbs, of
features shapeless and brutal; no one would desire either his
friendship or his love. As to his voice, it would be the
frightening of maidens, and the sorrow of little children to
hear the like of it; even the best word in the world from him
would be ill hearing. It was a marvel to Pwyll that such a
one should ever have been sent upon an embassy, even by the
men of Uffern and their princes.

"Come down," said the herald; "come down, if the
woman in the city yonder has not ruined you. If there were
an unspoilt man here, he would not wait for the second message."

Pwyll made no answer, and desired to make none. "Insult is better than courtesy, from the like of him," thought he.

"Will you stir and come down before you hear it?" said
the herald. "Even for the timorous and the cowardly, it
will be a worse message than the first."

Pwyll looked out towards the west; the sun was still hidden behind clouds; if not gone down, very near the going. " I will run no risks," he thought. " There are the behests of Rhianon to consider."

" Here is the message then," said the herald. " The queen will lay Dyfed waste, and leave nothing alive within your borders, between the Tywi and the Teifi and the sea. As for you, she will stay while you mount, and speed forth, and ride to the head of the valley; and after, it will be well if you are able to escape from her hunting."

" Rhianon spoke truly," thought Pwyll. " It is not easy to withstand these subtle devices. If night would only come, to give me sure news of the sun's setting — "

" Blows will be better than words, when it comes to awakening the craven." He struck Pwyll on the forehead with the flag-spear, so that blood flowed; and worse than the blood-flowing was the flapping of the folds of the flag in his face. The touch of them filled him with sudden sickness and loathing, so that the sweat broke from him, and his whole frame trembled. It passed, and a cold wind blew down upon him, body and soul; the air was alive with whisperings and threatenings of evil; the whole hostility of unfathomed Abred seemed to have gathered there. Even Blodwen ran to him, shivering and whinnying in her terror; and she tugged at his cloak with her teeth; for the first time since she was foaled, the desire for flight overtook her. Before his own vision the picture of Arberth rose up, and a longing for it; indeed, a longing for the whole of the rest of the world; it seemed clean and lacking corruption, lacking some cold, corrupting evil that crowded about him there on Gorsedd Arberth. " Little this Ab Cilcoed knows concerning the customs of the Cymry, and precedent among kings, and the courtesies of war," thought he; stroking Blodwen's neck, to put courage into her. "Our place is here, thine and mine," he thought; and without words she understood him.

"Wilt thou go, fool?" cried the herald. Pwyll was as far as ever from stirring or making answer. Then the other turned, and went back swiftly to the queen; and Pwyll saw the third of her warriors sent forth by her, and ascending the hillside towards the throne.

"Pwyll Pen Annwn," said that one: "time it is for you to be considering prudent wisdom."

Pwyll made no answer.

"Over-strong are the enchantments; no one would prevent the coming in of the armies. The message that is sent to you is this: Escape you quickly while you may."

Pwyll made no answer.

"Since you heed not that message, heed this secret one of my own," said the other: "out of regard for your fame is this spoken — Neither by watching here, nor by indiscriminate warfare in the roadway, will there be keeping out yonder armies; yet there might be saving Dyfed, were the counsel that I shall give you to be followed."

Pwyll made no answer.

"The hosts will go forward as soon as I shall have returned to them. But if there were a warrior here that had trust in the strength of his limbs, and in the firmness of his soul, and in his magnanimity and heroic might, he would go down and meet them in the road, and call for the one who is the chief of his enemies; and if he made combat with that one and slew him, it might well be that the whole army would obey him afterwards. It would not be impossible for you to accomplish that."

"Go back to the one that sent you," said Pwyll. "Well known to me are the machinations of Ab Cilcoed. The army cannot go forward beyond this."

" Unwise is this. Out of friendship and esteem the counsel is given. It will be seen whether the army can go forward or not."

With that he turned, and made his way down the hillside. Pwyll looked westward; surely the sun would be at his setting, or even well past it, by now. It was impossible to see, by reason of the gathering of clouds there. " It might be as he said," thought he; " undoubtedly these enchantments are powerful. Furthermore it would be the best service for the Immortals, were one to destroy this prince out of Uffern." He called Blodwen, and took the bridle in his hand as he watched. " There may be praise and renown and glory for thee and for me, out of this," he said; " even if the watching has been in vain." He saw the one that had counseled him speak to the queen; and saw her turn, and give orders to her captains. He heard the battle-trumpets sound, and saw the host move forward. He watched eagerly until it was certain that they were moving, until the foremost of them had passed. Then he said: " Indeed, I made little of the warnings of Rhianon; I spoke to the herald, and that will have empowered them ·to do this." Exultation and delight filled him, that now he should be striking blows, and not suffering contumely in silence. To horseback with him, and away in a thunder of hoofs down the western slope of the hill. " By heaven," he thought, " fighting may serve, even if the spells and wisdom of Rhianon were not strong enough." He laughed out loud, and proudly raised his warshout. " Fighting is a thousand times a better diversion than watching," thought he. " It will not be said that the Dimetians were without a victorious protector."

" Oh man," cried the queen, " what unwisdom has taken you? For what reason have you left the throne on Gorsedd Arberth?"

"For the sake of fighting have I left it," said he. "That I may save this land from you, and from your guiles and machinations and enchantments. Not easily shall any one out of Uffern make his entry into Dyfed with armies. Let the son of Cilcoed come forward, and as many as he may desire with him."

She pointed with her spear to the head of the Gorsedd. "Yes," she said; "he has come."

Pwyll looked up. There was a man standing before the throne there, and his two arms raised towards the sky. A black cloud blown up out of the east came down over the Gorsedd, hiding the throne and the one that held it; then it blew out over the whole heaven, covering Dyfed from the sky. Westward, before its oncoming, there was a little cloudless space on the sky-edge; there Pwyll saw the last gleam of the sun's rim, as it went down over the brink of the world.

"It is the army of Llwyd ab Cilcoed," said the queen. It seemed to Pwyll Pen Annwn that he had never known the nature of sorrow until then.

"Who art thou, O princess, that hast made this trial of me?"

"I am Malen Ruddgoch Ren," she said. "All warfare among men is entrusted to me by the Immortals."

"For what reason is Dyfed harried by thy hosts? For what reason are the homesteads burned? Might not the trial have been made of me, and disgrace and dishonor imposed, without working this injury against the Dimetians?"

"It was dreams and enchantment," said she. "The homesteads are not burned; the herds have not been harried. None of the Dimetians have fled before me. I have other needs for my men, than to be harrying the people of this island. Dreams and imaginings have troubled thee."

With that she turned to her host, lifting her spear, and a great, sad call was blown from her trumpets, and men and horses and battle-cars, they all rose up into the air, and were carried in a streaming pomp of scarlet and golden cloud over the mountains westward. Pwyll knew that a second time trial had been made of him by the Gods, and that the second time he had failed to carry out the behests of the Daughter of Hefeydd.

He rode up to the head of the Gorsedd, seeking the man that had brought in the armies of Llwyd; but could find no one. Then he went back sorrowfully into Arberth.

In the feast that night, there was silence and lack of ease with every one; even the song of the Birds of Rhianon, the two that were remaining of them, was without joy. In the midst of it there came a clap of thunder, and a shaking of the casements, and a sudden waning of the light of the torches. When they burned up again, it was clear to every one that half the delight of his life had left him. There were no magical birds among the rafters. Aden Fwynach had fallen down into the lap of Rhianon; but make what search they might, there was no sign of Aden Lonach the Beautiful to be found anywhere. In sorrow the feasting came to an end.

"I knew that it would not have been easy to succeed," said Rhianon. "The desire of his life had overtaken Deiniol Drwg, to take his place upon the Gorsedd before sunset; and he came up behind the throne at noonday, and concealed himself there; and as soon as you went down to the War-Queen, he came forward, and met with heavy blows and violence, and empowered Ab Cilcoed to bring in his host. Deiniol Drwg he will be indeed, from this out."

"Is there any requiting you? Is there any taking steps against Llwyd?"

"No," she said. "But the third chance will be given you."

"For what reason did Malen come? For what reason are the Immortals conspiring?"

"Undoubtedly they are conspiring to bring about good," she said. "I shall never hear you speak such evil, as to accuse the Immortal Kindred."

"That is true," said Pwyll. "On me alone is the blame."

From that out there were plots and hatred being raised against Rhianon, and a growth of grumbling and unmanly ill will, such as never had been known among the Cymry, between the Tywi and the Teifi and the sea. The queen, they whispered, was no more than of the soulless races of the woods and the mountains, and her spells were luring Pwyll away from his kinghood, even from his humanity. There was no finding the source of such rumors, and no one with the daring to speak them aloud; much less could any one be found who would raise up armies against her. Yet before the year was out, it was clear to every one that there would be few faithful left in Dyfed, and few retaining the magnanimous manhood of the Cymry; beyond, indeed, those hundred chief warriors that had been with Pwyll Pen Annwn in the Country of the Immortals.

III. THE MACHINATIONS OF CERIDWEN FERCH HU,
AND THE FALLING OF THE SORROW OF THE
DIMETIANS

YEAR and a day after the Hosting of the Armies of Malen Ruddgoch Ren in the Valley of Gorsedd Arberth, the son of Pwyll and Rhianon was born. It was easy to see that he was of a line of kings and Gods, even then. Beautiful was the long, golden hair of him, new-born baby as he was; beautiful were his proud, June-blue, tearless eyes. There was not a more princely-aspected child living; even in the Isle of the Mighty; even in those days. As for a name for him, Rhianon gave him the name of Pryderi. She took her own fillet of golden braid, and fastened it for a belt about his flaxen swaddling-clothes; she took a thread of gold, and threaded her own golden ring on it, and tied it round his neck for the torque of his sovereignty. She had had the ring inscribed in the coelbren characters with this inscription: *Bydd i ti ddychwelyd;* There shall be a returning for thee. She called Pwyll to her. "Is it your desire to requite the Dimetians?" said she.

"It is known to you that it is my desire, and more than my desire."

"It may be accomplished, though not easily. If any one were to guard Gorsedd Arberth this day, Llwyd ab Cilcoed would lose a great part of his power."

"It will be the sorrow of my life to leave you. So bitter is the enmity of the Dimetians towards you, that it is not known whether they would not rise and harm you, if I were not here for your protection."

"I know that their enmity is bitter; I know well how they have been deceived. Yet Pendaran Dyfed and Gwawl ab Clud and the teulu will be enough protection for me. As for you, rise not up from the throne on the Gorsedd until the dawn of morning, or there will be no staying the falling of many sorrows."

"It is the third time," said he, sighing. "If I were not to obey you now, I should lose you. Better with me would be losing life."

They brought Blodwen to him, saddled, and he rode forward sorrowfully through the rain; his mind full of anxiety concerning the hatred of the Dimetians, and the peril of Rhianon and Pryderi; and of wonder that there should be need for watching on such a day as that. He came to the head of the Valley of Gorsedd Arberth. On the left side of the road there was a little, white-washed cottage there; it drifted in through his musings that he would have seen no cottage there before. Passing, he had a glimpse of a great cauldron steaming over the fire in the cottage, and a wrinkled crone leaning over and stirring it; and of an old countryman that was standing and talking with her. The crone might have been as old as the Owl of Cwm Cawlwyd; three forests might have grown and died since she was born. As for the countryman, Pwyll would have seen him somewhere, he

thought; but it was not known to him where or when. He
heeded them little as he rode forward.

He came to the head of the hill, and dismounted; that
was an hour before noon. At first he was for leaving the
mare to graze where she would, as before; then, for send-
ing her back to Arberth, and being wholly alone on the hill.
"Blodwen fach," said he; "it will be best for thee to seek
the stable." She put down her white nose sadly, nuzzling
his hands. He lifted her beautiful head, and kissed her between the eyes: "Yes, yes," he said; "it will be better for
thee to leave me now." He remembered how he had mounted
her the year before, to ride down against the host he thought
was Llwyd's. She stood there in sorrow for a moment; but
it had never happened to her to disobey him. She neighed,
and went down towards the road, and he saw her gallop off
through the rain towards Arberth. It was hard for him not
to be filled with mourning when she disappeared; it was
hard for the tears to remain without falling from his eyes.

He took his place on the throne, and as he did so, his
mind went back to the two that were in the cottage; and his
thoughts were filled with spoken words that it seemed to him
he would have heard from them; though he had been without knowing, at the time, that he had heard anything. As
for what the words were, they were these: *The trial will be
tonight,* said the one. *Shamrock, mistletoe, vervain and
nettles; they will all be needed in the Cauldron, if there is no
failing.* And again, in answer to that: *Shamrock, mistletoe,
vervain and nettles; nettles and nettles, nettles and nettles;
nothing has been forgotten that may be needed.* And again:
When will it be ready? — and: *By midnight it will be ready;
much more will it be ready by dawn.* Until noon there was
no driving that conversation out of his mind.

The slow, soft rain was falling, and gray mists came

down over the mountains, and filled the valley; by noon they were in a ring about him, and no seeing for his eyes beyond the level ground on the hilltop. It would have been an hour after midday, or more than that, when suddenly he heard a footstep, and Ceredig Call Cwmteifi stepped out of the mist. One moment, and Pwyll was alone; the next, and there was Ceredig standing before him. No sound of hoofbeats had come up from the road; there had been no sound, until that last footstep, of any one ascending the hill.

"Lord," said Ceredig — if Ceredig it was — "Pendaran Dyfed sent me. Barely would you have been a mile beyond the gates of the city, when the men of Arberth rose up against the queen. Beyond that, Madog and Deiniol and Catwg and Gwylltyn have come in with an army, and the men of thy teulu are at great labor defending the palace. It will be the worst of evils if you do not return."

Pwyll remembered the unfathomable machinations of the Immortal Kindred, and did not stir or seem to heed. In a little while the other went as silently and suddenly as he had come.

An hour passed, or maybe more than an hour, and the southwest wind rose riotously, and drove away the mists; the slant, cold rain fell beating and driving against Pwyll, stinging his face; and no cessation from it. He heard a call from the road, and saw a man dismount there, and vault over the stile, and come hurrying up the hillside. Einion Arth Cennen he was, or had the guise of Einion; than whom, except Pendaran himself, and Ceredig Cwmteifi, there would be hardly a better man in the teulu. Full of sorrow and anxiety was his face as he came.

If the first news had been bad, the second was much worse. Over fifty of the teulu, he said, had been slain, and Pendaran Dyfed with them; it was Rhianon herself that had sent him, praying her lord would return. Pwyll looked at him, and saw that his mantle was not wet, and his helmet barely spotted with the rain. "Ah," he thought; "subtle are the devices of the Immortals in the hour of making trial."

"I must hasten back," said Einion; "no one can be spared. Woe is me for the princess, on account of this silence and reluctance in returning." Pwyll watched him go, without having stirred to heed, or breathed to answer him; but his grief and anxiety were not without their increasing, with what he had heard.

An hour would have passed after that again, when he heard the beating of eager hoofs along the road, and saw a horseman riding furiously from the head of the valley. "It will be Meurig Mwyn of Bronwydd," he thought, "or one of the Immortals in the guise of Meurig." (Few among the men of the teulu were better than Meurig.) In a little while he was at the hilltop. Although Ceredig had stepped so suddenly out of the mist, and although the mantle of Einion had been unmarked with rain, there was no doubt of the riding that this man had made, and no doubt that he had passed through as much rain as would have fallen between that and Arberth. Beyond that, he opened his cloak, and beneath it sheltering was a bird that had the whole likeness of the last left of the Singers of Peace.

"The queen sent her for a token," said Meurig (if Meurig it was). Then he gave Pwyll the message. Rhianon had sent him; at the time of his leaving Arberth, there were no more than a score of the teulu left alive. They had made a truce with the Dimetians until he should return with news concerning Pwyll. For here is what the Dimetians were saying: that the king had been enspelled by Rhianon, and was lost, by that time, in some dim region out of the world. "Unless you come back now," said he; "undoubtedly they will destroy the queen." The twenty that remained for her protection, he said, would never last until nightfall, against the thousands that opposed them.

Bad was the news indeed; but here is what was worse: the one that had the guise of Aden Fwynach (or it might have been Aden Fwynach herself; there was no knowing at that time) flew to the back of the throne, and perched there, and raised up such a music of lamentation as it had never fallen on Pwyll to hear until then; as he listened to it, the entire sorrow of the world drifted down bitterly and drearily upon his mind. All that he had been hearing, it seemed to him, might well be true. There were the machinations of the Immortals indeed, and the promise he had given to Rhianon; and yet, here was word from herself bidding him forsake the watching, and come. And all this concerning the uprising of the people was no more than what was to be looked for; when he came away in the morning, he had known the peril of it. Then, " By heaven," thought he, " she too is of the Immortal Kindred; she would not fear the Dimetians." He turned his eyes and mind away from the messenger, and got a little peace binding his soul down to the watching. It was not long before the man that had been speaking to him went his way. But the bird stayed there, and did not cease from her singing; and if ever he might forget the watching for a moment, or his complete trust in the power of the queen, the song flowed in upon him like the spring-tide in the estuary, and the froth and the foam of it grief and anxiety, sorrow and doubt and weariness of spirit.

At the end of another hour, or a little more than that, he saw ten men riding along the road from Arberth; he heard their laughter as they came. Madog and Deiniol, Catwg and Gwylltyn were there; and the six that were with them, although Dimetians, had become but little better than themselves. Before they reached the hilltop, the bird flew from the throne; he saw one of them loose an arrow at her, but the arrow missed its mark.

"Lord," said one of the Dimetians, "if you desire to save the life of the woman you made queen, it will be well for you to return quickly with us."

Pwyll made him no answer.

"Lord," said another of them, "it is said that the enchantress has put spells upon you; if it be true that she has, the Dimetians will destroy her to avenge you. We have come here to learn whether it is true or not."

Pwyll made him no answer.

Then Deiniol Drwg said: "You see how it is with him. The spells are on him, or he would answer."

"If the spells are on him now," said Gwylltyn Gwaethaf Oll, "they will not always be on him. If ye will take my counsel, his head should be carried with us into Arberth; then would he never have vengeance upon us for the loss of his wife."

"Let a better trial be made to arouse him," said one of the Dimetians — it was Yniol Ystwyth, and he was a man that would never do anything unless a thousand had done it before him. "The like of killing one's own lord has not been heard of among the people of this island."

Catwg Gwaeth laughed. "Yes, yes," he said; "I will make the trial." He threw back his cloak, revealing that which was beneath it. "Lord," said he; "if it is in your power to break the spells, save the life of this child."

Pwyll Pen Annwn did not bow his head; he did not cover his face with his hands. Proud was his aspect, and he gazing out over the valley, without appearance of hearing or heeding them. There should be no failure with him this time. But there was no hindering his vision from what it saw. The

child had the guise of his son Pryderi; no one that had seen
it would not have known. There was the golden fillet bound
about its swaddling-clothes, Rhianon's fillet; there was the
golden thread round its neck, and Rhianon's ring tied to it.
There was the beauty of golden hair, and the eyes with sea-
blueness in them. It stretched out its baby arms to him,
laughing and fearless; would he not know his son by that?
How was he not to believe that which he saw? He knew
well how they hated him, and how they hated the queen; he
knew their nature. . . .

He heard the baby laughter turn into one sharp, wailing
cry. The whole sorrow of the world was multiplied upon
him; more bitterly piercing was the sound than anything he
had known during his life. It took nothing from his grief
that he remembered the machinations of the Immortals making trial of him. He heard clearly the laughter of Catwg,
and Gwylltyn, and Deiniol; he heard Yniol and the Dimetians groan. But there should be no failing from him, this
third time.

"And now," said Gwylltyn, "where the child is gone, it
would be folly not to send its father also."

Six of them answered: "He was our lord at one time."

He did not turn or bow his head; his eyes did not quiver
from their gazing out over the valley. The bitterness of the
trial would be over for him. He would desire no better meeting with the Margan that greets the dead, than to come to
her from obeying the behests of Rhianon. Proudly he looked
forth, not heeding them, expecting the stroke of liberation;
were he free, and his sword drawn, they would none of them
long be living men. Without turning he saw Gwylltyn draw,
and rush towards him . . . and Madog strike up Gwylltyn's
blade with his own at the moment of its falling.

"Stop," said the Crintach; "stop you now, and consider

caution. There is Teyrnion Twrf Fliant, and there is the Crowned King in London. Even the King of Tara in Ireland was his friend. Not one of us would escape, if harm befell him."

" Whoever it might be he was," said Catwg, " it would be desirable to destroy him, if it were not for caution. It will be easier for us to defend ourselves against him, than against the whole of the Island of the Mighty and Ireland."

" That is true," said they; " it will be better to leave him." Pwyll heard their hoof-beats along the road, and their laughter and quarreling as they went. Then the bird Aden Fwynach — if it were she indeed — flew back to her perch, and began her singing again; it was ten times more mournful than at first. Like slowly-drifting snowflakes in the dusk, her cold, piercing, grievous notes floated in upon his soul. Sorrow grew and grew upon him, as the day grew wan towards evening. He had obeyed indeed; there was no accusing him of weakness or faltering. But it was unknown to him whether he had done well to obey, or whether he had done worse than ill. Doubt came down on him, drop by drop, note by note with the chill, lonely music. There was Pryderi; there was the fate of Rhianon herself; there was the whole sorrow that would fall on the Dimetians. Would it not have been better, and would it not have been better to have disobeyed? Dusk fell; dimly he could see what seemed to be the slain form of the child where they had thrown it. He did not rise; he did not stir from the throne.

The gray, wet gloom deepened; the wanness of evening ebbed into darkness. Swift and cold and slanting the raindrops beat upon him; shrill and desolate was the wailing of the wind; dark was the night, rainswept, with never the gleam of a star. Beyond this gloom were the Immortals; he had obeyed them; it should not be said that he accused

them. Let them raise up truth and phantasy against him,
which they would; what should be stable in the Islands of
the Mighty, unless the Bright Ones could find princes upon
whom to depend? Phantasy, indeed, it might all have been
— the three warriors, and then Madog and his men . . .
and the cry of the child Pryderi. Only, less painful in his
heart would have been the poisoned steel, than the memory
of the baby laughter, the sudden wailing cry. He could hear
it in the notes of Aden Fwynach, more bitter, more poignant,
more coldly mournful always. Seven times he drove her
from the throne; but she only circled above his head, screaming, and returned. It appeared to him that it would not have
been phantasy; that it would none of it have been phantasy.
His son would have been slain before his eyes. His kingship
had withered away; the wars that were waiting him would be
joyless, and his own land out before him for destroying. And
ah, Rhianon, Rhianon!

In Pen Gannion he had prepared this; and when the
armies of Malen were hosted in the valley there: who should
be accused, except himself? As for the queen, wisdom and
compassion would wane from the Island of the Mighty;
from such a world as this, she could but proudly pass to her
own realm. So grief rose about his being, like the tides of
the sea about a rock on the shore; like the tides of a gray
sea, about the rocks of a barren, sunless shore. What hope
he had had that all might have been trial and illusion, was
covered away from his vision, as the sea-wave hides the sky
from the drowning. Now he would be half angry that he
should have made such a promise to Rhianon, leaving her
on the day her son was born; now he would be half angry
that he should have been bound to keep it, holding himself
away in peace on the hilltop when such wars were raging
in the city. Darker was his mind than the night; more bitter

his hopelessness than the bitter wind. Through the rain and the riot of wind and the storm of his thoughts, the slow, ghostly bird-music fell about him, wan, piercing, bitterly grievous.

A sound of galloping came up from the road, and of chariot wheels; they stopped at the foot of the hill. Some one with a lantern came hurrying towards him; it was Gwawl ab Clud, or had the guise of Gwawl. "Lord," said he; "the princess is here, and the Dimetians of Madog are making pursuit of her. She entreats you that you will not abandon her to her foes."

He started from the throne, almost, when those words were out on the air of the night. But . . . remembrance gleamed up palely in his mind. He had promised; he had been warned; the Immortals already had made marvelous trials of him. With a groan he stayed himself; indeed to God he would bide there until the dawn.

"Lord," said Gwawl (if it was Gwawl); "listen to the galloping of the horses of the pursuers."

From far off along the road, already he could hear dimly the beating of innumerable hoofs, that grew louder and louder and nearer always.

"Lord," said Gwawl, very quietly, and the slow tears falling from the two eyes of him; "for the sake of the Daughter of Hefeydd Hen, and the warfare you waged when you won her from me."

He knew Gwawl; he knew there was no one loftier of soul than he was. He could not doubt that it was he was speaking. Yet he maintained his silence; he did not stir from the throne.

Then Gwawl turned, and bowed his head, and mourned; Pwyll heard the sobs shaking him. "Better if she had gone with me at first," said Gwawl; "this world is not fit for the

Immortals. Ah Rhianon, Rhianon," he mourned; "you the
pride and jewel of the Gods; did I not foretell that sorrow
would come? It would have been better if you had taken the
queenhood I desired that you should take; it is not I that
would have been deaf when you called." So Pwyll heard
him mourning as he departed, as he made his way back to
the one that was waiting in the chariot in the road. Well
known to Pwyll was the son of Clud; well honored by him
was his royal and lofty soul. It was not possible that the
messenger should have been any one but Gwawl; it was not
possible that Gwawl should have spoken falsely or without
wisdom. . . . He sat there as he had sat since noon, un-
stirring, proud of mien, his gaze fixed on the darkness beyond
the valley.

Then he heard the voice of Rhianon herself; it was impossible to doubt that it was she who was speaking. The
words came up to him from the road; but even then he did
not stir. "Bring you me to him," she was saying; "it will
be better for me to die if he will not help me." Two men
came, carrying lanterns, and supporting the queen between
them. In the little glare of the lanterns he saw her; her face
whiter than ivory; and she kneeling before him. He felt
her arms about his knees, and heard her prayers and beseech-
ings; it was impossible for him to doubt that she was his
own wife.

"Lord," she said; "I could not foresee this when I sent
you forth to watch this morning. The harm was done before
this; watching would have no power to prevent it. Llwyd
ab Cilcoed is stronger than the Gods. My immortality is
gone since the child was born; if you do not come with me
there will be no saving either you or me."

The tears fell from his eyes faster than the mist-drops
from the poplar leaves in autumn. "Ah, that this grief

should have fallen on you!" he said. "Ah, that the child
Pryderi should have been slain!"

With that her wailing rose on the night; he felt the dropping of her innumerable tears. "He is slain, and ah, he is
slain!" she cried; "the little frame that was prepared for
a God! The blue eyes and the golden hair! I could not foresee, and ah, I could not foresee!" she cried. "All my magic
is withered since the morning."

He had lifted her from the ground, and stood supporting
her. Indeed some change and loss of divinity had befallen
her, who wrung from him pity now, where before she had
had his reverence.

"Come," she said, "swift must be our going; it is
possible that I may yet bring you to the Country of the
Immortals."

They went down the hillside together, the men following
them. "Take you your place in the chariot," said he; "I
myself will wait here for the Dimetians."

"It would be foolishness," said Gwawl ab Clud. "Not
scores they will be, but thousands."

"That will be the better," said Pwyll.

Then the queen said: "If you desired to requite me for
what has befallen through Llwyd, you would come in the
chariot." With that he took his place beside her. Sorrow
and shame were heavy upon him as he took it.

The wind died down and the rain stopped as they moved
forward. It happened to him to turn, and look back towards
Gorsedd Arberth. The moon had risen dimly, and was shining through a thin place of clouds above the throne. He
saw a shadow rise, and heard the rush of wings; it swept
out darkening on the wan moonlight, and was lost beyond
the hills towards Arberth. Doubt came upon him, like a
sudden cold wind.

"What shadow was that?" said he.

"It was Llwyd ab Cilcoed passing towards the palace," said the one at his side. The chariot was moving more swiftly than anything can move without wings; it was unknown to Pwyll whether it was along the roadway or through the air they were moving.

"For what reason will he be passing there?" said he. "All the injury in the world he has already worked us; it will not be possible for him to do more."

"It will be possible," said she. "Passing towards the stealing of Pryderi he is. He will be free to steal him while the watchers are asleep." There was no sound or trace of wailing in her voice; but loftiness; but the age of the world; but lone, illimitable wisdom.

He turned towards her. The sorrow in his mind was driven forth by wonder and confusion. Unknown now, unfamiliar to him wholly, was the veiled August One at his side.

"Pryderi is slain," said he. "There will be no watchers . . . ?"

"Not so," she answered. "The teulu under Pendaran were watching in the palace, and their hundred wives were guarding the cradle of Pryderi. But sleep came upon every eye in Dyfed, as soon as there was a rising up from watching on the throne on yonder hill."

"Sleep came not upon Rhianon; sleep never would have come upon Rhianon."

"Rhianon is not there," she said. "In the Wyddfa with Hu Gadarn is her place this night."

There is no wind that blows in March that can move as swiftly as that chariot was moving.

"For the sake of the whole race and kindred of the Cymry, turn the chariot towards Arberth."

"There is going forward, but never going back. It would be impossible to turn the chariot."

Before him he could see the backs of the horses, rippling and glimmering wanly in the darkness. Their long manes, as they tossed their heads or strained them forward, were faintly shining like the midnight wave. Huger they were than the hugest stallions. No sound of hoof-beats rose from their passaging.

"Who art thou, princess, that hast made this trial of me?"

A strange light shone from her; she stood in the chariot, extreme in her radiant majesty. The trees of the woodland would not have concealed her; she could not have hidden among the mountains; grander was her beauty than the gleam of the sunset from among thunder-clouds. At one moment she seemed more ancient than the forest; at another, younger than the apple-bloom in April, than the young sedge by the streamside in the early spring. As for the chariot, Pwyll could see then that it was moving through the play-ground of the lightnings.

"I am Ceridwen, the Daughter of Hu," she said. "I and Ceridwen, foster-mother of the Immortals, and queen of all the green things in the world."

With that, name and memory and all strength and thought ebbed from him; in a dreamless slumber he passed with her to her own palace in the heart of the world.

IV. THE COUNCILS OF THE IMMORTALS, AND THE DECLARATION OF THE FATES OF THE PRINCES OF DYFED

THAT night the Gods were gathered again in the palace of Hu Gadarn in the Wyddfa. Considering the Fates of the Princes of Dyfed they were: the fate of Pwyll Pen Annwn, and the fate of Pryderi fab Pwyll, and the fate of Rhianon Ren the daughter of Hefeydd.

"Difficult it is, this raising up of Immortals," said Hu the Mighty. "Difficult it is, this raising up of auxiliar godhood out of the ranks of men. Declare what success you had, Lord Brother, when you made the trial of him in the Forge of Pen Gannion."

"Such success as it was," said Gofannon ab Don. "Sorrowful success. He withstood the temptation of the spears, although they were proud, peerless, pointed piercers. He withstood the temptation of the shields, although there would be few among ourselves that would not desire them. But the swords were more desirable than he could withstand. He chose a sword from Pen Gannion, rather than to be watching on the Gorsedd."

"What will be written on the web, on account of this?" said Hu the Mighty. "Let the Lady of the Silver Wheel, Arianrhod Ren, Don's daughter, declare the fate."

Arianrhod Ren stood forth, and turned her Wheel in the heavens. The threads are the deeds and meditations of men, and the spun web is their destiny.

"It is failure," she said. "Undoubtedly the desiring of such a gift would be the hindering of immortality."

The Gods sighed, and betook themselves to silence, and to their musings, while Arianrhod considered that which had been spun. "But it would not be irrevocable," said she, when it had become clear to her. "Another trial of him would be made."

"Another trial would be made, and it was made," said Hu Gadarn. "What success was with you, Malen Ren, when you hosted your armies in the valley?"

"It is known," said she. "He withstood pride, when the privilege of the Great Battlebreakers was offered to him. He withstood fear, when I poured it upon him from all the quarters of the world. But I caused it to seem to him that watching was in vain, and that he might save the land by prowess, when the wisdom of the one that sent him had failed. Very subtly I labored to accomplish this, and when I had accomplished it, he came down from the Gorsedd."

"Let the Wheel be turned," said the Mighty One; "and let the fate be made known."

Arianrhod turned her Wheel. "It is failure," said she. "It is a gulf between him and immortality."

"Make known to the Immortals whether it would be irrevocable or not irrevocable," said the Mighty One. "Make it known, Arianrhod Ren, if it please you."

She turned her Wheel in the heavens, and read the writing on the web. " Three trials for the Cymro," said she. " There would be a third trial for Pwyll Pen Annwn; though hard it would be for him to obtain success in it."

Thereupon Ceridwen came into the hall, and with her Gwydion the son of Don, the Initiator. The Gods rose up, and gave them the greeting of heaven and man; and had the two greetings from them in return.

" Let it be known from what labor or from what happenings you come," said Hu the Mighty.

" From the third trial of Pwyll Pen Annwn we come," said Ceridwen. " The third trial is accomplished."

" Make known what success was with you," said the Mighty One. " Eagerly the Gods desire to know this."

" Woe is me, on account of the success," said she. " Here is what happened to me," she said. " I tried him not by pride, but by pity. I used spells that heretofore have been unacquainted with failure, and he withstood them. Then I took the last spell of all, according to fate, and law, and custom, and precedent, and necessity; and exercised the whole of my power. I went to him in the guise of Rhianon Ren; few but the Immortals would not have been deceived. His vision became less than clear. His purpose became less than all-dominant. His heart became less than unshakable. Sorrow and tears overtook him. He came down from the Gorsedd; he quitted the throne of watching."

The Gods shook their heads sadly and slowly, musing within themselves. " Woe is me, on account of the success," they murmured.

" Let the Lady of the Doniaid declare the fate," said Hu the Mighty.

Arianrhod turned her Wheel.

"The Immortals shed not tears," said she. "This also is failure."

"It is known to me already that the Cauldron was prepared for him," said Hu Gadarn. "It is known to me already that he would have been in the Cauldron. Relate to us, Ceridwen, whatever may have befallen."

(Very wonderful is Pair Dadeni, the Cauldron of Ceridwen Ren ferch Hu. Whosoever may be put into it, if he be dead, he will return to life; and whatever name he may have had before, he will have a new name after.)

"The Cauldron was prepared," said Ceridwen. "Shamrock and mistletoe, vervain and nettles: nothing was lacking that should have been boiling in it. I brought him through the air from Gorsedd Arberth to the House of the Cauldron; sleep and oblivion were on him while I brought him. As for what befell then, it would be well for Gwydion ab Don to relate it."

Thereupon arose Gwydion the son of Don, the Initiator. It was he that initiated Brython, and Eurwys and Euron, and Euron and Modron; indeed, Five Battalions of the Mighty Wise. He had the aspect of a bard, and of such a one that, if he were singing, the winds of heaven would grow calm and listen to his verses; and if he were relating a story, it might well happen to the imperial stars themselves that they would lean down from their thrones to heed him, and that for as much as a thousand ages, if he desired it; and in oblivion of their splendor until the story should have been told. He had an alder wand in his hand, studded with nails of Welsh gold; with that he would be working wonders whenever it pleased him.

"Nine regal and handsome youths were watching beside the Cauldron," said he; "and I myself was the tenth at the head of them. As soon as Pwyll Pen Annwn rose up

from the throne on Gorsedd Arberth, the liquid boiled over
and was wasted, and there was no saving it. I kept the three
Drops of Wisdom; but it was clear to me that they would
not be for Pwyll.   Then I filled the vessel again, and put in
it what herbs there were, so that it should be ready for the
chieftain, when the Queen of the World might bring him. If
it should please the Mighty One, let him direct for whom the
drops shall be."

" Of those who have need of them among the Cymry of
the Island of the Mighty," said Hu Gadarn, " who will be the
best man, and the one that is nearest to deserving them? "

" There is Teyrnion Twrf Fliant," said Ceridwen.   " It
would be hard to find his equal, even if one had the vision of
Drem the son of Dremidyd."

(When the gnat arose in the morning with the sun, Drem
could see it from Gelliwic in Cornwall as far off as Pen Blathaon in North Britain.)

"Arianrhod Ren," said Hu Gadarn; " make known, if it
please you, the deserts of the king of Gwent."

Thereupon Arianrhod threaded upon her wheel the deeds
and meditations of Teyrnion Twrf Fliant, king of Gwent
Iscoed, and turned the wheel and span. " Undoubtedly he
will deserve the Three Drops," said she.

" Let them be taken to Caerlleon on Usk," said the
Mighty One; " let them be dropped upon the lips of the King
Twrf Fliant while he is asleep."

(As to what came of that dropping, it will be made clear
in the Story of Rhianon and Pryderi fab Pwyll.)

" What herbs were in the Cauldron, when the chieftain
was bathed in it? " said Hu Gadarn.

" Vervain and nettles," said Gwydion.   " There were no
herbs gathered, beyond those two."

" Let the Lady of the Doniaid declare the fate," said Hu.

Arianrhod turned her Wheel. "Vervain of oblivion; nettles of sorrow," said she; "sorrow and oblivion will the fate be. It is not given him to become one of us."

The Gods sighed. "It is not given him," they said.

"As for the Queen, the Daughter of Hefeydd Hen," said the Mighty One, "let it not concern her; it is not she that will be without consolation and reward. She shall have her mountain palace here in Wales; either Moel Siabod in its majesty, or one of the peaks of Yr Eifl, or a mountain by the Tywi in the land she has loved. It shall be requited to her; she shall sway the Brython; in all things she shall be the equal of the Gods of the Cymry throughout these islands. She shall forget the one for whom she toiled and suffered; his destinies shall be nothing to her from this out."

The Immortals nodded. "Less would be unfitting," they said.

Then Rhianon rose up. Her body was slumbering in the palace at Arberth at that time; but she herself was with the Gods in the Wyddfa at council.

"It shall not be so," she said. "O Mighty One, I marvel at this. O Clan of Hu Gadarn, is it thus that you would obtain new gods from among men? I will not suffer this man to be forgotten. By Ceugant and the Lonely One that dwells in it, Pwyll Pen Annwn shall be Immortal yet."

"As much as that we could not ask from you," said Hu. "The Gods, truly, are not without consideration and gratitude. It is your due that you should have the Dragon Kinship of these Islands, godhood and honor among the Gods of the Cymry. It would be unfitting if we were to ask more from the one that came from afar to help us, or if we were to grant her less. All that the Gods could ask of you, you have accomplished, and even more. Take you the reward that is offered."

"No," said she; "I will take much more. What I will take will be Immortality for Pwyll Pen Annwn, even if it be not until the head and end of a hundred ages. Were the price of what is offered me," said she, "that he should be forgotten, and should forfeit godhood, I would take lives of oblivion instead. I will not suffer that your whole effort to raise up immortality in him shall be wasted. You shall have two Gods from this labor of mine; Pwyll Pen Annwn and Pryderi fab Pwyll. Beyond that, I shall remain upon earth for the protection of the Dimetians."

"Pwyll Pen Annwn gave them over to Ab Cilcoed. Neither you nor any of us could drive him out."

"I could hold the land for my lord Pwyll," said she. "I could prevent the triumph of Ab Cilcoed in a thousand ways; and undoubtedly I will prevent it."

"Let the Daughter of Don Ren turn the Wheel," said the Mighty One. "Let the fate of the Princess be made known."

Arianrhod turned the Wheel.

"It is known what fate has been offered," said she. "If she will accept it, there is this for her: no one shall hold more honor among us than she will. As for her son Pryderi, no harm will overtake him; he shall be fostered by the best of the Cymry. Even it might be that what came to Pwyll Pen Annwn, will come to him also; and it might be that he would succeed where his father failed, and that he will become immortal.

"But if such a fate as that be not accepted, there is this other. Her son they shall accuse her of slaying; it is known already that Ab Cilcoed has stolen him; and there will be no defending her against this charge. For years and years she shall do penance for it, sitting from dawn to sunset at the

palace gate at Arberth, making known to any that may ask
on what accusation she is condemned to do penance there.
She shall have no consolation from the Three Singers of
Peace. She shall have no news of Pryderi until he is a
grown man; and even then it is not known whether she will
have news of him. It is not known whether she will ever
have news of Pwyll Pen Annwn. Hardly will it be given her
to make any stand against her enemies; hardly will it be
given her to protect her friends from them. Blind she will
be also. And thus it will remain with her, unless Pryderi or
Pwyll should save her, until she shall choose to forgo that
fate, and take the fate Hu Gadarn offered her.

"Yet if she should undertake this, truly, it may be that
Pwyll Pen Annwn will be saved by her. It may be that he
will come into the Cauldron again, and find the four herbs
there; even that he will obtain his immortality in the end.
But it is not known; it will be in accordance with what deeds
and meditations I may get from him for the spinning from
this out. If there should be any imperfection from him, there
will be no saving him."

"It pities us, Rhianon," said the Gods. "It pities us that
you should suffer such a fate as this."

"It pities you?" said she. "Never was it unforeknown
to me. I came down out of my father's kingdom for the
sake of Pwyll Pen Annwn, and for the sake of the Cymry
of the Island of the Mighty, and for the sake of raising up
new godhood, as is known to you. I see little evil in this. If
the fate were worse, I would take it; and I would not forgo
it, while it might still be possible to awaken godhood in this
chieftain. Are your hosts so triumphant on the borders of
space, that there is no need for new warriors? Pwyll Pen
Annwn would be the best of auxiliars; on the day of conflict he would be equal to an army. I know how lofty is his

soul — he the impetuous as a fire in a chimney. Undoubtedly
I will take this fate."

Hu the Mighty rose up from his throne. "Let it be so,"
said he.

Then Gwydion arose. He was mantled about in a glamor
of gold and green; unstable, jewel-luminous mists floated
about him; his hair had the magnificence of the peacock
above his head. "Lady," said he; "as for me, if there is
any bringing Pwyll Pen Annwn to the Cauldron, I will accomplish it; it will be an honor to me to do this."

Then the Primitive Bards came down from their shining
thrones; in flaming, wavering, wonderful beauty they came,
and bowed themselves down before the Lady Rhianon: Plenydd, Alawn and Gwron. "If the Prince, the Son of Don
Ren, should succeed in this," said they, "and adversity should
still befall Pwyll Pen Annwn, we will not rest day or night
until we have requited him; and we will labor for him, and
be beside him, as far as it may be permitted to us; and this
we will do also for Pryderi fab Pwyll."

Then said Hu the Mighty: "Listen now, you Immortals. If it should happen to Pwyll Pen Annwn to succeed
at last, this promise is made to him: much greater shall be
his throne and his pomp among us here, than it would have
been if he had come among us now. And much greater shall
be the throne and the pomp of the Princess also."

   .   .   .   .   .   .

The dawn came, and Rhianon returned to her sleeping
body in the palace of Arberth, and awoke. Aden Fwynach
had disappeared; Pryderi had been stolen. The whole fate
that Arianrhod had foretold for her, came upon her. The
eyesight waned from her beautiful eyes; her beautiful hair
became white. Day by day she took her place at dawn at the
palace gate, doing her penance. When they had accused her

of destroying the child, she had been at no pains to answer them. Year after year went by. Day by day the teulu waited upon her, and protected her, and she instructed them in the secrets of wisdom. There was nothing so beautiful in beautiful Dyfed, as the old, blind, beautiful queen that sat at the gate in her majesty and mournful dignity. Day by day, Three came down that she did not see and had no news of: Plenydd, Alawn and Gwron; surely they were the most beautiful, the most beloved of all the Immortals. Night after night in her sleep she saw Arianrhod Ren clothed in the glory of her godhood.

"Ah, darling, darling of the Clan of Hu," said Arianrhod; "are you willing yet to take the better fate?"

"I have taken it," said Rhianon. "It is sorrow now, and blindness, and long waiting; and to save Pwyll Pen Annwn in the end."

That is the end of the first part of the Fates of the Princes of Dyfed; namely, the Story of Pwyll and Rhianon. On account of its relating what befell Pwyll on Gorsedd Arberth it is also called *The Book of the Three Trials of Pwyll.*

The Story of Rhianon and Pryderi, or
The Book of the Three
Unusual Arts of Pryderi fab Pwyll

This is the First Branch of the Story of
Rhianon and Pryderi, Namely:

The Mare and the Foal of Teyrnion Twrf Fliant

I. THE DROPPING OF THE THREE DROPS OF WISDOM ON THE LIPS OF TEYRNION

T will be known already that Teyrnion Twrf Fliant was King of Gwent Iscoed in those days; he had not his better in the Three Islands of the Mighty, and it is doubtful whether he had his equal. Pwyll himself had received fosterage from him, and had learned from him many sciences, such as the constructing of poems and the courtesies of war, the nine huntings and the laws of Dyfnwal Moelmud, the nine manly sports, and the rightful governing of kingdoms. So great was his fame for wisdom and loftiness of soul, that no king would send his sons for fosterage anywhere, at that time, except to Caerlleon on Usk; among the foster-sons of Teyrnion were princes from Spain and Persia, from Alban and Llychlyn, from Cornwall and Corsica, from India the Less and India the Greater. Not one of them would ever become less than a pillar of equitable sovereignty, a warlike dragon on the field of conflict.

In the king's stable at Caerlleon there was one of the Priceless Things of the Island of the Mighty: the most peerless and beautiful mare in the entire world. She was of one sire and dam with Blodwen the mare of Pwyll; but many would be thinking that she was a better steed even than Blodwen. The winds of heaven could never come up with her, when she had a mind to leave them behind. Ten men could not hold her back, if she desired to be going forward. Never in her whole life had she needed the word of command from her lord; by reason of her love for him, it was easy for her to perceive his will without language passing his teeth. Beyond that, whoever might be riding her would receive no wound in battle; and wherever she might set her shell-formed hoofs, if it was on the rolling stone on the mountain-side, it became stedfast beneath her; if it was on the greenest place in the quagmire, it became as firm when she touched it as the best road in the world. She had the name of Fflam-wen Aden Goleu with her; and such pre-eminence among horses as her lord had among kings.

With every Eve of May, she had a foal as beautiful as herself. It was well known that honor had come to the whole island, whenever such a foal had been kept unharmed until full-grown. No king in Britain but would have given the best of his possessions for one, if Teyrnion had been a man to sell what he might give away as a free gift. The Crowned King of London, indeed, and the High King of Tara in Ireland, had had such gifts from him; also Taliesin the Chief of Bards, and the Archdruid of Ynys Fon, and Paris King of France. But now for two years there had been no foal for any one; and that was a main sorrow for the whole of the Island of the Mighty. One would be born in the night, but by the dawn of the morning it would have been stolen from the stable.

The Story of Rhianon and Pryderi begins on the night
when Pwyll was overcome by the machinations of Ceridwen,
and when the Gods gathered to get news what fate would
be allotted to him, from the Wheel of the Daughter of Don.
The night after that, the third foal would be stolen from
the stables of the king of Caerlleon, if there were no preventing the theft. Here is what happened when the first two
were taken: —

The first year there had been no fear of thievery on any
one, and no guards set in the stable, beyond the seven grooms
of Fflamwen; they were the best grooms in the world at that
time, so far as was known — as was fitting for a mare of
such dignity. Sleep had overtaken them all, and in the morning the foal was gone. " Next year there must be watching,"
said Twrf Fliant.

When May Eve came, he set his foster-sons to keep guard:
twenty proud, wakeful, magnanimous princes they were, all
of them eager to serve him. It is related that any one of
them might easily have gone nine days and nine nights without cessation from warfare, or from watchfulness, or from
merriment and heroic games. They had their place in the
stable with the mare; beyond them, nine great druids had
come from Mon, out of friendship for Teyrnion, to make the
nine pacings of magic, and to chant imponderable potent
spells in the stableyard; for it was clear to every one that the
stealing would be more by enchantment than by common
thiefcraft.

When midnight came, marvelous music rose, and made
conflict with the chanting of the druids, till one by one they
forgot their spells, and fell to nodding and dreaming, as if
they had learned no secrets during their whole lives. The
music drifted in through the walls of the stables. " Here are
the enchantments," said the princes. They raised the best

shouting they could; few could have raised a better or a louder. But their very shouting was turned into a melody, the most overpowering in the world. Ten of them fell asleep where they stood.

The rest gathered about the mare and the foal, raising laughter for the sake of wakefulness, and pressing their sword-points into the palms of their hands. Beautiful clouds came floating down; glamorous legions leaned out of them, putting forth such song as would lure the tempest into quietude. *Between earth and sky,* they sang, *there would be empires richer than the ruby, islands to shame the heart of the opal, where sickness and old age never came. Would not the heroes wend there, inheriting beauty and peace?* Five were found to make answer with the slashing of swords; but five were taken with desire for what was promised, and had a wealth of sweet dreams until the morning, but much bitterness of spirit after.

When the glamor waned, the little foal was still unharmed; and the five princes were still waking. Great was their delight, deeming the spells overcome; but Fflamwen Aden Goleu was no less uneasy in her mind than she had been at first. While they were exulting over their victory, it was a raising of warshouts that they heard, and the whole city filled with innumerable invading hosts. Shouting and wailing rang from street to street; with the war-cries of the Gwyddel Ffichti from Ireland, and the men of Gwent unhosted to meet them. They looked at each other in doubt; it was made to appear to them all that Teyrnion had been at war with the Gwyddel Ffichti, and Caerlleon under siege. They were in doubt whether they should leave their watching, to meet this greater danger. They heard men leaping down into the stable-yard, the battering of axes on the door, shouting and confusion on all sides. Clearly the yard was full;

the five of them would be against a whole host, and there was
no resisting the allurement of that. They left the stall and
ran towards the door; they unbarred the door and flung it
open; delightful would be fighting, after all that over-sweet-
ness of spells. With the lighting of their eyes upon the night
and upon the stars, silence fell. Wan shadows melted and
vanished; nothing moved through the moonlight in the empty
yard. There was no sound anywhere, beyond far-off barking and crowing. They looked at each other troubledly; without speaking they hurried back towards the stall. Fflamwen
Aden Goleu turned her head towards them as they came up
to her; they saw the slow dropping of tears from her eyes.
The beautiful foal they had left at her side was gone.

A year passed after that, all but a day, and while Pwyll
Pen Annwn was watching on Gorsedd Arberth, and withstanding the machinations of Ceridwen, Teyrnion Twrf Fliant was holding council with his druids and foster-sons concerning the watching of Fflamwen Aden Goleu the next
night. " Indeed now, evil fall on me," said he, " if there shall
be any guard there beyond myself."

" Lord," said they, " it is not fitting that a sovereign
ruler should undertake such work as this. Let us watch in
the stable."

" Not so," said he. " There shall be watching, and I will
be the one to watch."

" It would be the peril of his life for any one to go alone
against enchantments. Let us go with you," said the foster-
sons.

" Indeed, no," said Teyrnion. " None shall go with me,
and none shall be within call."

That night, as he lay on his sleeping-bench of ivory, he
was wakened by the touch of a drop of water falling on his
lips; and leaped to his feet, for such warlike vigor thrilled

through him, soul and limbs, as he had not known even in his best days of prime and battle-breaking, before Pwyll came to him for fosterage.

"What will it be?" said he. "One of the Immortals will be here."

The most wonderful laughter in the world rippled out through the hall. "Ah, sleep on, sleep on, Twrf Fliant," said the Laugher. "It will be no more than the Art of War in the midst of Peace."

Teyrnion lay down again; he knew the voice of a God, and had no concern beyond being obedient. Hardly was he asleep, when the second drop touched his lips; what ran through his veins then, as his eyes opened, was such calmness as might bide untroubled in the valley when the mountains went to war.

"What will it be, O Laugher of the Beauty of the World?" said he. "What will it be this time, O Gwydion of the Multitudinous Enchantments?"

Again the laughter was peopling the hall with running, merry ripples of quiet music. "Sleep on, sleep on, Twrf Fliant dear," said the God-voice through the darkness. "It will be nothing but the Art of Peace in the midst of War."

Teyrnion obeyed, and it was not a minute or two before he slept. Again a drop falling on his lips awoke him; and now what came to him was such vision, that he felt it would but be the trouble of looking, for him to see the secrecies of the universe, and the Gods laboring in their sky-halls or in the mountains, or in their unseen palaces on the trackless wave. This time there was no hindering Teyrnion from mingling his own laughter with the divine laughter that rocked and rippled about him.

"What will it be, Lord Gwydion?" said he. "In the name of heaven and man, what will it be?"

"Ah Teyrnion, Teyrnion bach, it will be no cause for losing sleep," said the Other. "Tonight is for sleep, and tomorrow night for watching," said he. "It will be no more in the world than the Spell of the Wood, the Field and the Mountain. It will only be the Spell of the Three Places in Wales, that contains all compulsion in it, and the mastery of invisible things."

Teyrnion knew then that the Gods had given him the three Drops of Wisdom out of the Cauldron of Ceridwen, that change mortality into immortality, human life into God-life. He turned without disquiet or exultation upon the sleeping-bench, and nothing broke his slumber until dawn. Whoever saw him the next day, was aware that there would be the breaking of enchantments in the stable that night.

II. THE MARE AND THE FOAL OF TEYRNION TWRF FLIANT, AND THE FINDING OF GWRI GWALLT EURYN

THAT morning he sent his foster-sons to Garth Maelor for a day and a night, to hunt in the Vale with the King of Glamorgan. As soon as they were gone, he hosted the whole of his armies, and set them on the shore of the Hafren at Aber-rhymni, "To watch," said he, "against an invasion out of Ireland." Then he rode back swiftly into Caerlleon; no one remained in the city with him, beyond old men, women and children. "This will be well," said he. "This will be entirely convenient and fitting. I shall have peace now for the watching."

Early in the evening he went into the stable, and took his place beside the mare. She turned her head towards him as he came in, and as soon as she saw who it was, laughed within herself. "There 'll be an end of the enchantment now," thought she. As for the foal, its hoofs were more delicate than the sea-shell; it was perfectly formed, beautiful-eyed, firm of limb; not one hair on its body was black or gray, or dun or chestnut, or brown or ruddy; not one was less white than the mountain snow, or the April cloud, or the foam on the wave, or the petal of the lily, or the reflection on the waters of Safaddon from the wings and the breast of the swan.

"You will be one to hurry the winds," said Teyrnion, stroking it. "Unless you should come by a better, you shall have the name of Gyrru'r Gwyntoedd from me." "Yes, yes," thought the mare, reflecting in her mind. "Gyrru'r Gwyntoedd will be the name for him."

The king watched, pacing up and down, or pausing to fondle Fflamwen and the foal, and to communicate to them the thoughts he might have in his mind. A deep contentment was with the mare, such as she had not known on a May Eve for three years; the silence was hardly broken at all with the motion of her beautiful hoofs. The foal was as gentle and fearless with the king, as if he had already ridden it through many battles.

With midnight, it was as if the petals of a crimson rose were falling and drifting unseen through the air. Slowly the silence grew into such music, that it seemed as if the dreaming moon and stars were leaning down over Gwent, and stroking from their silver harpstrings low, slow, melodious, indolent notes, that floated over woods and palaces as softly as the drifting of thistledown on the breeze, or the falling of snow-flakes in spring, when no wind may be blowing. Song came in through the windows, a marvel of quietness and dream:

> Rest, King of Gwentland, rest,
> Under the lonely moon!
> Deeds are a wandering tune,
> Dreaming is best.

Dream you, and dream!
What are men's ways and wars,
Horses and battle-cars?
— Foam on a wandering stream,
Foam on a noisy stream.
Let them alone, and dream
Under the stars!

— The place was filled with a million invisible spinners, weaving around him silvery webs of sleep and dim peace.

Ah, let your strivings cease!
Beauty alone hath blooms
Here in our moon-pale peace.
Here are no deaths nor dooms,
Nor any warfare looms;
Only White Beauty blooms
In our White Peace!

— The music rose and wavered and swooned and withered on the air; mysterious blossoms did indeed bloom and glimmer up everywhere; white, wax-like flowers with such an odor of dream and honey to them, that a warlike army in the moment of victory would have been lulled into slumber and silence by no more than a single breath of it. Swords would have fallen to the ground, from their sweeping through the air towards the cleaving of helmets. Arms would have dropt limp, that were in the midst of hurling spears. Eyelids would have fallen over eyes grown weary, that a moment before had been blazing with battle-anger. Throats would have become silent, while half of the war-shout remained unuttered. Sleep would have overtaken the mighty, the eager, the wakeful, the raging; but sleep could not overtake the King Twrf Fliant.

Dream, King of Gwentland, dream!
Dream while the dream hours flow.
Kings and their deeds and all,
These are but leaves that fall
And wither, and where they go
None but the four. winds know.
You, King of Gwentland, dream
While the dream hours flow!

Fflamwen Aden Goleu looked into the king's eyes, and he into hers. It seemed to her that she had never beheld any one less for sleep and dreams than he was. " In my deed," thought she; " here will be the end of this enchantment."

The stable grew fuller and heavier with blooms and scent and music. The white, wonder-flowers began to move and wave with the music, glimmering like the opal as they moved, and growing and changing, till they lost their flower form, and were guised like the Children of Beauty, the Family of Gwyn the son of Nudd. There were hosts and hosts of them, circles upon circles upward. Their wings were of all the hues of the iris, the rose, the peacock. Of the soft luster of mother-o'-pearl were their cloudlike, gossamer garments. For the hair of their heads, they had plumage like night intermingled with dawn. Untroubled were their brows; their eyes mild, somber, glorious, fathomless with antique innumerable dreams. Softer was their song than the wind of twilight among the reeds of Teifi; than the call of far waters from the valley when the moon is shining at midnight in August; more drowsy it was than the monody of bees amidst the lime blooms on a cloudless noon in July. In slow and slumber-weaving dances, they swayed and waved and drifted around him. Downward and nearer they came;

tremulant, murmurous; sighing song, softer than dream, breathing through their circles. He stood beside the foal and waited. He could feel the breath of them on his face; it was sweeter than the scent of pansies. His head dropped; he fell a-nodding, nodding; his eyelids covered his eyes. "Heigh ho," thought Fflamwen, sighing; "will it be loss again, and no end to it at all?"

One arm of him was about her neck; he leaned his head against her neck, as if he were sleeping. She turned quietly to the stall again, laughing to herself. His head dropped nodding, nodding; the long breaths of the sleeping came from him. Soft fingers brushed against his eyelids; delicate arms came winding about his limbs. The low singing trembled up into laughter; silvery laughter of victory quivered up to the rafters. But it broke off suddenly into a quick gasp; he had flung forth an arm, and seized the prince of the singers, and dragged him down till he was kneeling before him on the stable floor.

With that a sigh passed through the whole cloud of them, and they were gone. The light and shadow from the lantern fell on the manger, the hayrack and the rafters; it was as if there had never been enchantments in the world.

"And now," said Teyrnion; "it would be well for me to end your days."

"Not so," said the other. "Were I to remain alive, I should not oppose you further."

"I do not know," said Teyrnion. "Intensely discordant, to me, was the sound of the song you were singing."

"It was the song we were willed to sing," said the other. "Whosoever may have mastered us, we sing what he wills us to sing."

"Such singing as you raised might well merit death," said Teyrnion. "Who willed you to terrify the mare?"

"Your enemy and hers. If I were to remain alive, I should serve you, and sing in accordance with your desires, and with your commands, and indeed, with the thoughts that you may never have spoken; and this we should do, both I and all those multitudes that were here, from this out."

"Let song be raised with your people now, then," said Teyrnion. "And if the singing be good, and in accordance with my desires, and even with the thoughts I may never have spoken, I shall take thought, and give it consideration, and formulate my plans and designs concerning you. But if it be less than that, I will avenge the mare for her terrifying."

With that the other began his singing; there was keen delight and wakeful vehemence in the most slumber-heavy note he sang. The song was taken up by the whole of his host; although they were unseen, they multiplied their harmonies over Gwent Iscoed, till the notes fell, from Henffordd to Aberrhymni, like the first rain after a drought, like the warshout of a friendly host drawing near on the ears of the hopeless, the besieged; or like the battle-music of harps to warriors grown fretful in a long peace. Hearing such a song, and the immortal triumph and vigor of it, no one would remain sad; the quarrelsome would become peaceful; even the mischievously stupid would cease from doing harm.

"Well, well," said Teyrnion, "it shall be pardoned you on account of this singing. Few would accuse it of discordance or hateful sound. And now," said he, "by my will, and by the Wood, the Field and the Mountain, go you forward, and sing the like of it wherever there may be evil in the Universe."

He heard them go; he knew there would be no breaking the Spell of the Three Places. "Two of the Drops have

benefited me," said he.   No harm in the world had come to
the foal.

The song died away at last into a silence broken by no far
barking, by no crowing of cocks, by the calling of no owls
from the woodland.   Slowly the king paced up and down;
Fflamwen betook herself to her oats peacefully, or to nuzzling
and caressing her foal.   Presently it seemed to him that the
deep peace of the night without was stealing into far-off
noises; he stood still and listened long.   It would be the
tramping of warward hosts; it would be hoofs pounding
afar, warshouts raised, the screaming of the creels of impatient chariots.   Slowly the whole noise of battle was driven
in upon him; it would be two hosts at war, and between that
and Aberrhymni; and they would be drawing nearer.   They
were to be heard now outside the walls of Caerlleon; now
within the town itself.   He could hear the voice of Gwron
Gwent his penteulu, and his own warshout raised; and the
warshout of the men of Ireland opposing it.   He heard the
crash of falling houses, the wailing of women and children;
through the window he saw the glare of burning.   Nearer and
nearer the warfare would be drawing; the stableyard itself
was becoming thronged with the anger of armies.   Clashing
of steel, rolling of fierce wheels, creels creaking, thunder of
hoofs and screaming of wounded steeds, sharp cries and lamentation, and the surging roar of two great warshouts —
nothing but the stable walls divided him from it.   " Teyrnion! Teyrnion!" cried the Gwyddel Ffichti; " where is the
King Twrf Fliant?   Never before this night was it said that
he feared the men of Ireland on the field of conflict."   " Teyrnion! Teyrnion!" shouted his own men; " Where, in the
name of heaven and man, is the King Twrf Fliant?   Never
before was it said that he was absent when the armies of
Gwent were hosted at Caerlleon."   So the battle raged about

him, made known to his ears, but not to his vision. Suddenly
in the press and fury of the tumult, the walls of the stable
fell, leaving the roof supported on the four corner-beams that
upheld the rafters. He looked forth; about him was only
mad battle surging and screaming, louder than a storm in
the forest branches, wilder than the tempest on the raging
sea.

They stood there under the roof, the three of them, and
the two hosts not noting them; not noting, in their ardor,
the falling of the walls of wattle and clay. Gyrru'r Gwyntoedd held his head high, fearless, eagerly watching; delightful to him were the things he saw. Fflamwen herself was
no more than half remembering the enchantments; half she
was quivering with desire to be out beyond there, and the
weight of her lord on her back. Twrf Fliant looked out on
the proud, innumerable, war-scarred warriors of Ireland, and
on the huge, heroic, princely chieftain that led them. He
looked out on his own men; he saw that there would be no
reproaching them; he saw the heroic deeds of Gwron Gwent
at their head. It was difficult for him to withstand pride
at their regal aspect, their invincible demeanor; at their
having succeeded in deceiving the courteous men that were
against them, and in coming out few against many, according to the ambition of the men of the Island of the Mighty
and of Ireland. In peace he stood there while the warfare
raged and clamored. Swords swept cleaving helmets; spears
whizzed hissing through the air; scythed chariots rolled forward, reaping. Fflamwen neighed and stamped impatiently;
she was unused to remaining at peace when war might be
going forward before her eyes. The king laid a hand on her
neck; she remembered, and hung her head. It was apparent
to her that her lord heeded it as little as he would have heeded
a fly buzzing among the rafters, or a wisp of straw falling

from the stall. "Indeed and indeed now," thought she, "although I myself might grow foolish and querulous, and might forget what I desired to remember, and sleep where I desired to wake, it would be otherwise with my lord, Twrf Fliant. Sorrow take me," thought she, heeding her oats again, "unless I see this night the end of all this weary old enchantment."

Suddenly with a shout the battle turned towards them; it was apparent that the two hosts had seen them at last. Then the men of Gwent were overcome; they were borne down before the onrush of the Gwyddel Ffichti, and the whole inimical host surged towards Teyrnion. The Prince of Ireland ran in upon him with sword on high. "There will be death where there is no yielding," cried he.

"There will be no yielding," said Teyrnion. "Yet many would consider courtesy."

"That is true," said the other. "The time is given you to draw the sword, and if it needs sharpening, to sharpen it also."

("The Gods help them better!" thought Fflamwen. "Few would attain cheating the King Twrf Fliant.")

"Ah no, good soul," said Teyrnion. "No doubt the sword will be rusted into its scabbard."

"Death it is then," said the other. "Death it is bound to be." While his blade was in the midst of its falling, Teyrnion regally made answer.

"Nor that either," said he. "Peace it will be."

A sigh passed through those warlike hosts; they ebbed away like the ninth wave after its falling. There was the quiet stable, and the light of the lantern over the manger and the walls. The sword that had been raised for destruction fell with a clang on the flags of the floor. Fflamwen Aden Goleu stood with her nose in the manger, quietly munching her oats, laughing within herself. "Dear, the prowess of this man!" thought she. "The splendor of his soul and all!" There was the one that had the guise of the Prince of Ireland, bound in chains at the king's feet.

"Yes, yes," said Teyrnion, thoughtfully; "in deep peace you will be, undoubtedly, from this out. Nothing will disturb your quietude hereafter."

"For the sake of heaven and man," said the other, "lay not that fate upon us. Destruction would be better."

"For what reason would destruction be better? Wherefore should I not lay upon you this merciful fate? I am not one to desire revenge."

"We are the children of war," said the other. "We should pine away forever, unless we had violent confusion and warlike strife to sustain us."

"Who sent you here?" said the king.

"Your enemy and the mare's," said the other.

"If I laid not peace upon you, it might be that you would come troubling the mare again. A mare would desire peace on such a night as this."

"Without your will we should do nothing and trouble no one from this out. Let there be destruction for us, but not peace."

"Well, well," said Teyrnion, "you might do no harm, and still have violence to sustain you." With upraised arms he stood, majestic, druidlike. "By my will," said he, "and by the Wood, the Field, and the Mountain, go forward, and make your war on the one that sent you here. And be you at peace with what is best, and at war with what is worst from this out, in all the four quarters of the world."

That fate was on them then, from that out. The king went forward with his watching.

It would not be more than a minute before the sun would
be over the rim of the world, and an end to all danger of
enchantments. Suddenly the mare whinnied, and there was
a crash at the window above her head. A great talon broke
in and clutched at the foal; the least of its claws would be
as big as the body of a well-grown man. Gyrru'r Gwyntoedd
looked up at it curiously, unafraid. The king was on the
manger in a moment, vigorously harrying and slashing at it
with his sword. He wounded it so that it dropped what it
was holding into the manger; he drove at it with vehemence,
and gave it no peace. For all its size, and its strength, and
its hardness like steel, and its tearing, wounding, angry claws,
it could obtain no advantage against him. When the seven
terrific blows had been dealt to it, and the seven deep wounds
given, it was snatched back through the window. Teyrnion
leaped down to the stable floor. The sun had risen, and the
enchantments were at an end. Gyrru'r Gwyntoedd the foal
of Fflamwen was as safe as if there never had been magical
plots and thievery in the world.

As for what the talon had dropped into the manger when
the king wounded it: it was a beautiful and princely child,
the best in the world, so far as Twrf Fliant had seen. His
age would be no more than three nights, if as much. His
swaddling-clothes were of white fine silk and linen; his eyes
were better than the sky on a June day for blueness. His
hair was long and beautifully golden. Round his neck was a
golden thread, and a gold ring threaded on it; on the ring
was this inscription in the coelbren characters: *Bydd i ti
ddychwelyd.* About his middle was a fillet of woven gold
of Arabia. It was apparent from the first that he would be
the descendant of kings and Gods. From the moment he
set eyes on him Teyrnion loved him.

When the world was waking he took the child to the

queen. "We have no son of our own," said he. "Yes,"
said she; "this child shall be our son."

They gave him the name of Gwri Gwallt Euryn, until
he should find the name his own mother had given him, or
come by a better name for himself. As for a naming-gift,
he had the best naming-gift in the world from Teyrnion.
Any one would know that that would be Gyrru'r Gwyntoedd,
the foal of Fflamwen Aden Goleu. With the naming of
Gwri Gwallt Euryn, and the giving to him of Gyrru'r Gwyntoedd for a naming-gift, the first branch of the Story of
Rhianon and Pryderi comes to its end.

The Story of Dienw'r Anffodion

Here are the Two Branches of

The Story of Dienw'r Anffodion

(Although they are not part of
The Story of Rhianon and Pryderi, it will
be better to relate them here)

I. THE MISFORTUNES OF THE ONE WITHOUT A NAME, AND THE MERRIMENT OF GWYDION AB DON

DURING the years in which Gwri Gwallt Euryn was growing up from babe to boy — and, dear knows, the fairest and most fearless of boys, and the one of most courteous disposition, and the equal at thirteen to another of eighteen — there was a man from the Island of the Mighty wandering the world, that was more unfortunate than any one in the east or the west at that time, almost. It was not known to him, nor to any other, from what land he had come at first, nor from what town. He was unacquainted with the nature of rest, or peace, or delight, or receiving kindness. If he went upon any adventure, or undertook any enterprise, it would end in sorrow and blame for him, in sorrow and blame, and scorn and reviling, and bitterness. The army for which he fought would meet with defeat; although none were stronger or more heroic, the defeat would be attributed to him; whoever might fail or show cowardice, he would receive the blame

for it. As for his journeyings, the story relates that he had
been in Europe and in Africa and in the Islands of Corsica,
reaping disaster, and in Caer Brythwch and Brythach and
Ferthach. Also he had been in Tara, in the court of the
High King of Ireland as a serving-man; and in the court
of the Island of the Mighty, doing service for the Crowned
King of London; and in the court of the Princes of Greece
in the East. He had neither name nor known lineage; for
that reason, and on account of his misfortunes, he was called
Dienw'r Anffodion. There is this to be said about him also:
it had never happened to him to boast or to lie; though he
had known all sorrow, he had known no fear; he had never
kept for himself that which he might have given to another,
and whatever adversity or false accusation might be out
against him, never had he been less than kind and magnanimous, and courteous and firm-souled, and valiant and kingly.

This branch of it begins at the time Gwri was thirteen
years old. Dienw'r Anffodion was journeying through Arfon, making his way towards Ynys Mon and Ireland; and
never had he been so luckless as he was then. By reason of
his misfortunes, he could find little welcome, and less employ-
ment anywhere; and he was such a one that idleness was
worse to him than hunger. It was long since he had passed
by any habitation, or seen the face of man. Three days
before, he had shot an old, lean rabbit on the mountain, and
had seen neither bird nor beast to shoot at since. Although
it was the beginning of autumn, the fields bore no mush-
rooms for him, nor the thorn berries; there was no finding
so much as a whortleberry on the low bushes on the floor of
the forest. The flesh of the rabbit had lasted him three days;
by that morning there was no more left of it than the right
hind leg, and the best that could be said for that was that
it was cold and dry and lean and withered.

He had risen from the heather at dawn, after a night of rain, and was keeping the meat he had until midday. The sun shone from a blue sky; the great mountains rose in their beauty on either side of the road. He was without shoes, much more was he without horse; and weaker and wearier than ever he had been; beyond that, there was little hope remaining with him, by reason of innumerable failures. He had bruised his left foot the day before against a rock, and was lame with it; as for his clothes, they were little better than a beggar's rags, at that time.

Going forward, he became aware of sweet and marvelous harping, and of a song that filled the valleys with wonder. He might have been hearing it for some time before he became aware of it. It rose up, and stole over the green slopes, and grew loud, and leaped up from crag to crag, and from cliff to cliff, ringing and echoing; it made the morning wholly magical and beautiful, and set the raindrops on the bracken quivering and gleaming, and brought a hundred long-eared furry ones lopping from their burrows to listen. An old, gray wolf sauntered down into the road, and stood still, and sniffed, and paid no heed to him as he passed. A young eagle out of Eryri came sailing down and lighted on a near rock without fear of him. A herd of mountain goats above stood still within bowshot of him, all of them enchained and set dreaming by the music. As for himself, such a spell and delight came on him, that he had no thought of arrow or bow.

Soon he came to the one that was harping and singing; having left the road, and ascended the mountain-side on his right, that he might come to him. It was a youth of great beauty and nobility of demeanor that was floating out all that glamor on the morning; he rose up and slung his harp over his shoulder and came down towards Dienw when he saw him. As soon as the music stopped the wolf was gone in a moment

with a growl; and away with the eagle towards the sky, and
the goats to the inaccessible crags, and the rabbits to their
burrows.

He was hardly more than a boy, yet had the blue robe of
an institutional bard on him, fastened with a bard's brooch
of gold. He was tall, but not over-tall; it was clear that few
would not follow when he led, or would refuse to obey when
he commanded. His laughter had the ripple of harp-music,
and it was merrier than anything in the world. His hair was
long and black; his two eyes bluer than the sea, more spark-
ling than the June sunlight on the wave-crest; it was apparent that little would be hidden from them, that they might
have the desire to see. In his right hand was a wand of
alderwood, studded with nails of Welsh gold; almost any
one would have known there was subtle power in it.

" The greeting of the god and the man to you pleasantly
and kindly," said he, laughing. It was the best greeting
Dienw had had, so far as was known to him, during his life.

" The greeting of the god and the man to you pleasantly,"
said he; " and better to you than to me, and more copious.
More delightful to me than anything I have known was the
sound of the harping and the song, and it would be pleasant
to me to remember the name of the one that made it."

" The name will be Goreu the son of Ser," said the bard
— and clear it was, indeed, that he would be of starry lineage.
" It was foretold to me that I should meet the man I desire
to meet in Arfon before noon this day; and I raise the music
so that, if he should hear it from afar, he may be drawn to
seeking the reason of it. It might well be that you yourself
are that man."

" Who will he be, and for what reason do you desire to
meet him?" said Dienw. " No one would pass, truly, without seeking out the one that raised that music."

"I will tell you," said Goreu. "It is a man to do service is required, and a marvelous adventure that is to be embarked upon by him."

"As for that," said Dienw, "weary I am with seeking service to do, and adventures to embark upon."

"Well, well, I will make this known to you further," said Goreu, "so that it may be seen whether you are the man or not. The six chief chieftains of the Island of the Mighty, and Taliesin Benbardd at the head of them, desire to go upon a quest into the west of the world; but it is of such a nature that it would be unfitting for less than seven to go, and it is hard to find the seventh."

"For what reason is it hard to find him, among all the princes of the Cymry?"

"Owing to the peculiarities of the quest. There is danger of pride and ambition in the one that may go on it; and if there were pride or ambition, there would be failure. The man that I am seeking will have been divested of these things by thirteen years of misfortune, and no rumor of delight or praise or pleasure during the whole of that time. The princes of the Cymry are too fortunate."

"It will be a marvel if this should be for me," said Dienw. "Yet true it is that during thirteen years I have not known delight, or heard praise, or taken part in pleasure. It may be said also that I have seen misfortunes, such as they were."

"What name is with you?" said Goreu.

"Never the rumor of one," said the other. "Dienw'r Anffodion is the best there is to call me."

(The meaning of that is: The Nameless One with the Misfortunes.)

"In my deed to God," said Goreu, "it may well be that you are the man. I will expound it to you further," said he. "Owing to the perilous nature of this adventure, the man that undertakes it must be encumbered neither by name nor lineage; and it would be the peril of his life if he were burdened with the memories of more than thirteen years."

"Soul, soul," said Dienw; "here is the truth, if you desire to listen to it. It is thirteen years since I awoke at the dawn of a bleak rain-swept morning on the mountain-side, without tidings who I was or whence I came; and from that time to this I have been reaping misfortunes. All that may have befallen me before, is unknown."

"Undoubtedly it is you that I came here seeking. If the conditions are not too difficult for you, it will be permitted to you to undertake this adventure."

"Give me news of them," said Dienw. "If they are difficult, it will be the better."

"They will be these," said Goreu: "that, having set forth, you will not turn back; and that, until I leave you, you will not forbear to accompany me."

"I will accept them," said Dienw, "whether they may prove to be difficult or easy."

"Pledge you the faith of your life and the honor of the Cymry to it."

"I pledge them to you gladly," said he. "By the faith of my life, and by the honor of the men of the Island of the Mighty, who neither boast nor lie, I will not turn back from this quest, and I will not leave you until you may leave me."

"That is well," said Goreu. "We will go forward."

They went down into the valley, and took the road towards Mon, and journeyed on until noon. There was no more talk between them concerning the adventure that was to be undertaken. It had never happened to Dienw, so far as he knew, to be as light-hearted as he was then. He made little of his past sorrow and wanderings; he had no thought but for the hopefulness of the quest, and the delight of the morning, and the brightness of the one that accompanied him. As for Goreu, not for a moment was he silent with his songs and stories, his laughter and diverting conversation; it was better to Dienw, listening to him, than food or rest or the cure of lameness. At noon he broke off in the midst of a story suddenly —

"The hunger of the world has overcome me," said he. "Are there provisions with you in the wallet?"

"Such provisions as they are," said Dienw. He opened the wallet and brought out what it contained.

"Miserable food is this for such a one as I am. Is there no more than this rabbit's leg?"

"There is no more."

"Ah me," said Goreu sorrowfully, "detestable to me is hunger, truly; detestable is the insufficiency of food upon a journey! Utterly sorrowful is this!"

"Take you the whole of it, such as it is," said Dienw. "Common with me has been the knowledge of hunger."

"Yes," said Goreu; "that will be better." With that he ate the food.

From that time the whole of his sorrow came back to Dienw; drifting back into his mind it came, and over his limbs; more of it with every step of his going forward.

"Now that I have partaken of food," said Goreu, "I am refreshed, and sorrow and weariness have forsaken me, and I am filled with the desire for music."

He took the harp from his shoulder and prepared to play it, and play it he did as they journeyed forward. But there was no likeness in his music to the music he had made in the morning. Quick and merry it was indeed; but the merriment with a certain ruthless bitterness at the heart of it. . . . The quicker it grew the less joy had Dienw from it, and the more he was made aware of his old failures and misfortunes.

Now and again a fox would rise from his covert and slink away, smitten with uneasiness of mind; or a hare would start up from her couch and skim down the valley in terror. The music quickened and quickened; and with its quickening Goreu fab Ser quickened his pace. "Ah," he said, " weariness has gone from me. I cannot abide sloth and dawdling when I have been refreshed with food."

They left the road and took to the mountains; more lithe and surefooted was Goreu than the mountain goats of Arfon; no rock nor bog could hinder his swiftness, nor the mad, swift impetuosity of his harping. For all the heaviness of mind and limbs that oppressed him, the music took possession of Dienw, and as it were dragged and jerked him forward, stumbling often, and with much cutting of feet. Whatever misfortunes overtook him, it was nothing to Goreu but the occasion for talking augustly of the power and beauty of his music, or of his own peculiarities; or for raising faster, wilder harpings. He reeled out jig after jig, of such a nature that it was a wonder that the mountains maintained their stillness, and wild, tumultuous war-tunes, that might well have compelled them to quit their peace. The more whirling was the jig, the less desire the one that heard it had for dancing; the more warlike the battle-tune, the more he desired quietness and rest. But quietness and rest were not for him; only breathless giddiness and aching of limbs. Early in the afternoon, the silver streak of the Menai between its trees gleamed near at hand below them; and in a little while they came to the shore and to the house of the ferryman.

Goreu fab Ser greeted the ferryman pleasantly. " The hunger of the world is upon me," said he. " Is there any food in the cottage? "

" Such as it is," said the ferryman; " such as it is, and little enough of it." He went into the cottage, and brought

out half an oatcake and a small piece of cheese, and it was
Goreu that took them from him.

"Better for one to have his fill, than for two to go hungry," said he. "There is not enough for the two of us."
He ate it, offering none to Dienw. "Do you grudge me the
food?" said he.

"No," said the other. "I am accustomed to hunger."

"It will be the better for you," said Goreu. There was
neither merriment nor mockery in his voice; indeed, there
might have been compassion in it.

The ferryman had launched his coracle, and the three of
them went into it, and began the crossing. As soon as he
was in the boat, Goreu became merrier and wilder than he
had been during the whole day; yet on his countenance no
lack of augustness. It was as if he had never seen a coracle
before, or made the crossing of any stream or strait. He
went from gay talk and singing, to leaning back and loud
laughter; there was no little wave or ripple but caused him
laughter. It would have been more profitable for the ferryman to have warned the wind of heaven, than to have warned
him; it was impossible for Goreu to remain without motion
for a moment. As soon as they were in the middle of the
Menai, here is what he did — a perilous thing for a man in
a coracle. His eye caught the leaping of a fish out in the
water to the right of the boat. "Ah, in the name of man,
look you out yonder!" cried he; "it will be the oldest salmon in the waters of the world." He was upon his feet in a
moment, and the right foot of him on the edge of the coracle.
With that, it turned over, and the three of them were in the
water.

"On me is the sorrow of all my race!" cried Goreu.
"Never have I feared anything so much as death by drowning. If there were any one here better than a cowardly

boaster, he would quit his extreme selfishness, and take some thought for saving me from the fury of the waves." Indeed, even weeping he was, and that with such mournful august-ness as a God might use, who lamented the destruction of a constellation of stars. "This is a marvel to me," thought Dienw. "I am here, truly," he cried out; "it is not fated that you should drown." He held him up in the water, and began swimming with him towards Mon. It was harder swimming than any he had known during his life. Not for an instant was Goreu still or silent. Struggling and striking at Dienw he was, until they came to shore; and beyond that, filling the world with his complaints, and his wailings, and his lamentations, and his framing of insult. As for the ferry-man, he had swum back quietly with his boat towards Arfon. There is no righting a coracle, and entering it, from the breast of the sea.

"It will be better to rest here," said Dienw, when he had dragged his companion beyond the reach of the waves. It seemed to him that the last of his strength was gone.

"It would be the unwisdom of the world to rest," cried Goreu, leaping up to his feet. "The sun is gone, and the sky clouded, and there will be a storm beating up from Ireland. Now that I have been half killed with drowning, it would be the death of me to be caught in that storm. I marvel that this selfishness should be. Ah me," he cried, "if I had with me one not given to lies and boasting, he would not seek to destroy me! Ah me, that men will pledge the faith of the Cymry, and break their word!" It was as if he were a God wailing for the treachery that caused the ruin of a world.

"You have no need for sorrow," said the other; "I will go with you." He rose up painfully. "Were he to go upon a voyage, it might go ill with him," thought he; "he has little knowledge of the sea."

With that they went forward through the sacred woods of Mon. From that time, every word that Goreu spoke was solemnly bitter and insulting. " It is the pity of my life that there was no one in the water with me, that knew the art of swimming," he said. " I was nigh my death by drowning, on account of your clumsiness, and your desire to save your own life. Henceforth it will never be the same with me. By reason of this, I shall be taken with loathsome coughing every first day of January, and it will not leave me until June; and I shall be lame in my two legs whensoever it rains. If I had been traveling with a man whose old lives had not been evil, there would have been no overturning the coracle."

They journeyed forward among the great oaks, and suddenly Goreu burst out augustly weeping. " What trouble will be on you now? " said the other.

" Trouble enough, and never was there greater on any man," said he. He flung his harp down upon the ground. " I cannot so much as carry it farther," he said, " so weak and worn am I after the drowning." There was no sign of weakness on him; it had been hard for Dienw to keep pace with him. "Ah me that there is no one here with me, who reveres the Gods and the holy bards! It is the disgrace of his life for one of us, to lose the harp of his bardhood. Many would have offered to carry it for me before this!"

No one would readily refuse the request of a bard, in those days. Courteously Dienw picked up the harp, though not without marveling. " I will carry it for you gladly," said he.

They went forward. If Dienw had been weary in the morning, ten times more so was he now; there was no strength nor vigor left in his limbs, nor reasonable thought in his mind. There was a catch in his breath, a powerful aching in his body, and a giddiness in his head; and as for

the harp, for all its lightness at the time he took it up, before
he had traveled more than the twenty steps with it, it became
heavier than anything he had happened to carry in his life.
It seemed to him that if he had been at the top of his strength,
and with the whole might of his young and warlike days in
him, he could hardly have borne it without staggering. But
still Goreu hurried on, and Dienw might have no peace nor
rest with him, nor quietness of mind, nor escape from insult.

"Were there any one here with the least skill, he would
lighten the road for me with playing," said Goreu. "It is an
ill thing for such a one as I am to be journeying without
music, and too weary and sick to raise it for himself."

"The strings will be wet from the Menai," said Dienw.
"If they were dry, I would make a trial of it."

"It is the nature of the braggart and the coward to lie
and make excuses," said Goreu. "Many would have made
the trial without accusing the harp."

"It would be the most priceless of the Wonderful Gifts
of these Islands," said Dienw, "if it would give music after
swimming the Menai."

"If I had the strength to argue with you, I would argue,"
said Goreu. "I am such a one that my health fails me,
and my heart grows sad at the best of times, if there is no
music. Few will be so lofty and delicate of soul. It is a
shameful thing for a man to be selfish. Never will I travel
with the selfish hereafter." All this he spoke with extreme
augustness of demeanor.

Dienw laughed to himself as he took the harp from his
shoulder, and felt the strings. They were all wet and loose
from the Menai; no one would have dreamed of playing
them. "I will make the trial," said he, "if it will please
you."

As soon as he struck the first string, it was clear to him

that there was more music in that harp, than in any harp he
had ever attained seeing, and that all the wetness of the
Menai could not quench nor injure it. Majestic music he
struck from it, that rolled out, and set delight and magic on
the sacred oaks and the brambles, and put the bracken quivering with joy to hear it, and lifted his own soul beyond the
reach of its sorrow, and his body out of all its weariness.
He played on; marvelous were the tunes he got from it.
Even the gray thunder-clouds were driven from the sky, and
the sun was made to shine more brightly than he had shone
during the whole summer. Suddenly he felt his arm seized,
and his fingers dragged away from the strings. In the
manner of a God or an Archdruid conjuring the powers of
evil from the world, Goreu adjured him:

" For the sake of this island, Mon the Mother of Wales;
and for the sake of the Gods that dwell here, and of the
Three Orders of the Holy Druids, give me the harp!" he
cried. "Woe is me that I should have fallen to hearing such
evil and sorrowful sound! Unless I play myself to appease
them, without if or were-it-not, the Immortals will be destroying the world in revenge for this."

Dienw gave him the harp; although he marveled, he had
no desire to display discourtesy; and Goreu was an institutional bard of the Gorsedd of the Island of the Mighty.
" Now shall you hear music," said Goreu fab Ser.

Therewith he began to strike the strings fiercely and
violently, until the world was filled, and crowded, and over-
borne with discord, and jangling, harsh dissonance, a fan-
tastic clamor of grunting and squealing, a desolation and
confusion of abominable sound. Half the leaves on the oaks
turned brown and withered; the brake grew sere with terror
throughout Mon; the birds of the forest took wing towards
Ireland, and in the whole of Mon and Arfon there was no

milk in the dairies but curdled and turned sour. The harp
screamed, and screamed louder; and while the high strings
screamed, the low ones gibbered and chattered and mumbled
and snarled. Like the cut of a leathern whip-thong, the
screaming rose and rose and afflicted the hearing of the
world; piercing, keen, piercing. Then there rose up a long,
mournful roaring from afar; it was the rising and utter
terror of the Four Princely Waves: the Wave of Fannau,
the Wave of Alban, the Wave of Werddon, and the long,
proud, foam-crested, ocean-traveling, ship-destroying Wave
of Gwalia of the Warlike Hosts. Darkness covered the sky,
to hide the sun and the blueness, and preserve them against
the pain of that miserable harping. Clearly there was enough
magic in it to destroy the world, to disfoundation it and batter
it down. The horror and sickness of the entire universe came
upon Dienw'r Anffodion. It seemed to him that death was
around him, encompassing and prepared for him; and that
death itself would give him no refuge from cacophony.

"Ah," cried Goreu, stopping at last, "I am such a one
that music is better than rest or food or slumber for me.
The sweetness of this exquisite harping has cured me of half
my sorrow. Did it not seem to you that there was the power
of magic in it?"

"Indeed, it did seem so," said Dienw.

They came to the edge of the forest, and the greatest oak
in the world was growing there. "Ah," cried Goreu, "in
the name of heaven and man, it is the tree that bears mistletoe. It would be equal to losing the whole of the privileges
of my bardhood, were I to pass that mistletoe without gathering it." He went up to the tree, and took his sickle from his
belt; but was not tall enough to reach the mistletoe. "Come
you," said Dienw; "I will gather it for you, if it is your
desire." "Fool, fool!" cried Goreu, "if you were to touch

it, you would defile it; if you were so much as to handle the sickle, it would be the corruption of the whole of my bard-hood. No one but a druid or a bard may touch the mistletoe. Woe is me!" he cried, "was it to receive insult such as this, that I was made a Druid and a Serpent, and a companion to the Dragon of the World? The anger of the Three Orders will be potent against you on account of this."

"Whether it will be against me or not, it is my desire to help you to obtain the mistletoe," said Dienw. "Unless I were to cut it, it is not clear to me how it might be obtained."

"How evil a thing is pride!" said Goreu. "If there were one here without pride, and fit to go upon the adventure, he would have offered to kneel down before the tree, that I might have stood upon his shoulders to cut the mistletoe."

"That also will I do for you," said Dienw.

He knelt down, and Goreu stood on his shoulders, and cut the mistletoe. As soon as it was cut, Goreu fell down where he was standing, and lay groaning on the ground.

"Go you forward, if you desire to," said he. "Go you forward, and leave me here to perish, and let your pledge be broken. Owing to your clumsiness and ill will I am half slain, and I am not able to rise, much less to journey forward."

"I will not go forward without you," said the other. "If there is any house near by where you may obtain a cure, I will bring you to it on my shoulders. Being a bard, you will know what houses there may be on this island."

("I have strength enough for this," thought he.)

"There is the house of Henwrach the daughter of Hen," said Goreu. "If the dead went to her, she would bring them to life, and would charge little for it."

"I will bring you thither," said Dienw.

Goreu picked up the mistletoe, and the other gathered together what strength he had, and lifted him up on to his shoulders, and went forward staggering and stumbling, half blind, and the blood issuing from his mouth and nostrils. They left the forest; it was darkening with evening, and the keen rain was beginning to drive and slant against them. The road led through open country of gorse and heather; there was not so much as a single rock or tree to be seen anywhere, much less a house with a roof to it, where they might shelter and obtain the cure. On and on Dienw staggered; and Goreu on his shoulders never ceasing from his insults and abuse, and all of them delivered majestically. He struck his foot on a sharp stone, and his knees at last were giving way beneath him. Suddenly Goreu leaped down lightly from his shoulders. "Ah," he said; "this is the house of Henwrach ferch Hen; it is here that we shall shelter for the night."

II. THE FOUR HERBS THAT WERE IN THE CAUL-DRON OF REGENERATION, AND THE NAMING OF MANAWYDDAN SON OF THE BOUNDLESS

OREU FAB SER took him by the arm, and held him up from falling. On the side of the road, and not ten paces from them, stood a little cottage, and the light from a fire of peat and chaff shining through the doorway. "Come you, dear soul," said Goreu; "there will be little misfortune remaining." He led him towards the door of the cottage.

As they came to the door, Goreu said:

"If there is wisdom with you, desire drink from her."

"Soul," said Dienw, "desire it you, that you may be cured by it."

"Not so," said Goreu; "it is not I that will need curing."

They went into the cottage; there was an ancient, withered crone there, stirring a smoke-blackened, battered cauldron that hung over the fire. It seemed to Dienw that she would be older even than the Owl of Cwm Caw-lwyd, that saw three forests grow up and die, and three cities built and wasted where the forests grew; so wrinkled she was, and so bent double; and so beyond memory or understanding the secret potency of the charm she was crooning.

"The greeting of heaven and of man to you," said Dienw.

"Since you have come, you have come," she said.

"Is there food with you for the two of us?" said he.

"There is not food."

"Is it permitted to us to shelter here?"

"Grudgingly it is permitted."

With that he sat down.

As for Goreu, there was no appearance of mockery or of harshness of spirit, or of having received injury on him. Without speaking he went up to the cauldron, and threw the mistletoe he had gathered into it. "It is the fourth of them," said he; and she got no greeting from him beyond that. She gave him no word of answer; and he took his place in silence beside Dienw on the sleeping-bench.

At the end of a while, an old man rose up out of the shadows, and came into the firelight; it could not be concealed that he would have done many deeds in his time, and gained all wisdom, and suffered all sorrow. Both Goreu and Dienw rose up, and greeted him courteously; but little greeting had either of them from him in return.

"Daughter," he said; "will the Four Herbs be at the end of their boiling?"

"At the end of it," said she; and went on with her crooning. "Nettles and shamrock, vervain and mistletoe," she crooned; "shamrock and mistletoe, shamrock and mistletoe." Then Dienw turned to the bard.

"For what will the nettles be?" said he.

"For sorrow," said the other, quietly; but Dienw was not understanding him.

"'And for what will the vervain be, if it please you to tell me?"

"For wiping out the sorrow it will be," said Goreu. " For sleep, and for wiping out the sorrow."

" And the shamrock, if it be fitting for me to ask?"

" The shamrock is for me," said the crone, turning towards him suddenly.

" And the mistletoe?" said he; " if it be permitted to you to answer."

" Will there never be an end to his questions and his idle chattering?" said she; and went back to her crooning and stirring. " The mistletoe is for me," said the countryman; " inquire not into it." It appeared to Dienw that there would be a secret meaning in their words, and a deeper wisdom than it had been given to him to hear until then; but what the meaning or the wisdom might be, there was no knowing for him, at that time. With the fumes of the cauldron, and the crooning of charms, and his own weariness and hunger, a dream and a vagueness came over his mind; sometimes the two eyelids fell over his eyes, and the three that were with him seemed to be arrayed in fiery beauty and splendor; but as soon as he might raise the eyelids to look at them, they were no other than they had been at first.

" There is dry fern in the corner of the cottage," said the crone. " It would be bedding for him, if he desired to sleep." He heard her speaking, but her words had little meaning for him. Thereupon the bard rose up, and fetched three armfuls of the fern, and laid them on the sleeping-bench for him.

" Be not gluttonous after sloth and slumber," whispered Goreu. " Remember first the counsels that I gave you as we came into the cottage."

" What counsels were they, in the name of man?"

" Require drink of the crone; it would be the pity of your life to sleep without drinking."

" Soul," said Dienw to the crone, " is there drink with you? "

" There is drink," said she.

" I ask it from you," said he, " for the sake of the kindness of the Cymry."

" You shall have it," said she.

She rose up, and took an old goat's horn, rimmed and tipped with iron, and dipped it in the cauldron, and hobbled across the floor to him with it. He looked into it; the drink that was in it was brown and earth-colored, and the whole bitterness of his days fell upon him as he looked. " This will not be the drink that I desire," said he. She threw the drink out on the floor, and hobbled back to her place by the cauldron.

" Soul," said he, after a little while, " for the sake of the kind courtesy of the Cymry, let me have drink if there is any with you."

She rose up without answering, and took a drinking-cup of silver from the wall, and dipped it in the cauldron, and brought it to him, hobbling painfully across the floor. He looked into it; the drink was dark blue, and there rose a fume from it laden with drowsiness and oblivion. He knew that if he drank it he would be freed from all the memories of his sorrow, and from all the memories of his striving, and from all the magnanimity of his soul.

" Soul," said he courteously and kindly, " this will not be the drink that I require." She threw it out upon the floor, and hobbled back to her place.

" Soul," he said to her again, after a little while; " if I might obtain drink from you, I should not break your peace further."

She rose up, and took a cup of unpolished emerald, and dipped it in the cauldron, and hobbled over to him with it, with much complaining and grumbling. He looked into it, and his vision was crowded with the dancing of the Family of Beauty, and his hearing with the music of the Children of the Air; and it was clear to him that after drinking it he would attain such beauty and peace as are given to those two races. "Soul, soul," he said, "evil be upon me if this is the drink that I am requiring from you." "There is no end to thy desires and thy discontent," she said; and threw the drink out upon the floor, and hobbled back to her place.

After a little while he spoke to her again. "Soul," he said, "there will be no peace either for you or for me until I have obtained drink from you."

"What will be, will be," she said, and rose up. Then she took a drinking-vessel of clear, carved and polished crystal from a shelf among the shadows; it shone whiter than the moon as she brought it to the cauldron. She dipped it in the cauldron, and brought it to him. He looked into the drink, and it was clearer than the mountain-springs of Eryri; it was clearer than the air of mid-heaven in August, when the sun is at his zenith, and there is no cloud or shadow within the borders of the sky.

"The grace, and courtesy, and gratitude of the world and of this island to you," said he. "Without if or were-it-not, this will be the drink."

No sooner were his lips wet with it, than the whole cottage was filled and blazing for him with the light of a thousand dawns; from a peasant's cottage, it became the hall of a palace-place of the Immortal Kindred.

"No longer are you concealed from me," he said. "Hail to you, Ceridwen Ren, Queen of the World!"

"Sleep!" she said; and with her saying it, he sank back in his place on the sleeping-bench, and was asleep.

．　　　．　　　．　　　．　　　．　　　．

He awoke with the dawn; he was lying on three armfuls of dry bracken on a flat rock, in a little hollow among the heather. The sun was shining, and the grass and the heather were bediamonded with raindrops; he himself was dry, and without hunger or weariness. By his side stood Goreu the son of the Stars, as if he had awakened a little before him, and was waiting for his companion to awaken to begin the journey.

"The greeting of heaven and of man to you, Manawyddan, son of the Boundless," said Goreu.

"That is true," said the other; "Manawyddan, son of the Boundless will be the name I have attained. Where is the Palace of Ceridwen Ren?" said he.

"What palace is that?" said Goreu.

"The palace in which we sheltered during the night," said Manawyddan.

"We lay here," said Goreu. "We have made no journeying since the evening."

"Although that be true, we sheltered in the palace," said Manawyddan. "Here is what happened to me," said he. "As soon as I had obtained drink from the crone, sleep fell upon me; and although I was asleep, I had more vision than ever I had in waking. This is what I saw: you yourself were grown flaming-bodied and beautiful beyond the dawn, and with golden mists and green glamors about you. The old crone was revealed to me as Ceridwen in all her ancient beauty and mystery. As to the Countryman, it is known to me who he was: he was the Tamer of Nynnio and Peibio; he was the dragger of Afanc from the Lake of Floods; he was the Ploughman of the Island of the Mighty, the Lord of the White Shield; he was the Forefather of the Gods and the Cymry; he was Hu Gadarn himself. There is no means known of describing his majestic glory, or his beauty, or his radiance of kingly mien.

"As for the Cauldron, it was alive; it was undoubtedly the Cauldron of Regeneration; beauty and light and magic beyond telling were streaming from it. It was wrought of polished bronze, and adorned with the stories of the Gods, and inlaid with the brightest of the turquoise stones of Asia, and with blue enamel without peer, bluer than the Western Sea, when the sky of June is at its bluest. The steam that arose from it was pale purple and green, luminous, and more lovely than the rainbow; a sound as if the stars and the sea and the mountains were singing arose from the boiling of its waters.

"Then there came nine beautiful and deathless youths, and took up my body, and laid it in the Cauldron. The heat of it was for healing and immortal vigor in my limbs; the fumes of it became a passing of oblivion, and a clear wisdom in my mind. It was revealed to me that I was heretofore Pwyll Pen Annwn; the whole of my kingship and my trials in Dyfed were made known to my memory. I remembered the wisdom, and the sorrows, and the compassion of Rhianon Ren the daughter of Hefeydd, who came to me from the Country of the Immortals; and it was revealed to me that at last it would be permitted to me to return to her. From namelessness I attained the name of Manawyddan, son of the Boundless. After attaining it, sleep without vision came upon me."

"That is true," said the other; "all has been as you saw

it in the vision. If any man will accompany me upon a journey without complaining, rarely will he fail to attain a name at the end of it."

" Although I saw Hu the Mighty and Ceridwen distinctly, and recognized them, it was not given to me to see more than the glow and glamor that encompassed you. It was not given to me to know which of the Princes of the Immortals you are. Not yet will I have seen you in your own guise, nor held converse with you."

" Indeed, indeed now," said the Bard, " it would not be well for me to wear such a guise as this among mortals."

While the words were between his tongue and his teeth, the aspect of him was changed suddenly, and he had the stature of the pine and the poplar, and the flaming body of the Immortals, radiant with the hues of the rainbow and the peacock. It would be difficult for more beauty to be revealed anywhere, than was revealed to Manawyddan then.

" I am Gwydion the son of Don Ren," he said; " I am the Prince of Wisdom and Laughter. It is I who lead men always to the Cauldron of Regeneration, when the time has come for the inception of their immortality. Much laughter and mockery I make of them, while I am leading them there."

"And now, look you yonder, Manawyddan dear," said he; and led him out of the hollow to the top of the hill. They saw six men coming towards them over the heather, at about a mile away. " They are the six chief Chieftains of the Island of the Mighty," said Gwydion. " The one that rides there at the head of them, and his forehead shining like the morning star, is Taliesin the Chief of Bards. It is they who will go with you upon a quest into the west of the world; until that quest is accomplished, it is not allotted to you to return to Dyfed in the South."

"It is true," said Manawyddan. "I undertook to go upon the quest, and I will not turn aside from it."

With that Gwydion became one with the sunlight and the glory of the morning. Manawyddan went forward to meet the six. His beggar's rags had been taken from him during the night, and he was clothed now like a king. He knew that the time would come for his returning to Arberth, and that he would see Rhianon when the quest was accomplished. He went forward without sorrow; and as he went, chanted these words of the hymn:

> *I have been enchanted*
> *By Don's son, by Gwydion;*
> *Purity I had from him,*
> *The Purifier of Brython —*
> *The Purifier of Brython,*
> *And Eurwys, and Euron,*
> *Of Euron and Modron,*
> *Of Euron and Modron —*
> *Of Five Battalions of the Wise*
> *The Gods had set their spells on.*

— As for that hymn, it was Taliesin Benbardd himself that made it originally; he sang it when he had been in the Cauldron of Ceridwen, and was reborn the son of Ceridwen, and from Gwion Bach became Taliesin.

With Manawyddan's chanting it, and with his going forward to meet the six chief Chieftains, and with his meeting them, and their going forward together, the Story of Dienw'r Anffodion comes to its end.

The Story of Rhianon and Pryderi

Here is the Second Branch of the Story of
Rhianon and Pryderi, namely:

The Three Unusual Arts of Teyrnion
and Gwri Gwallt Euryn,
and the
Freeing of the Birds of Rhianon

I. THE ART OF WAR IN THE MIDST OF PEACE, AND THE FREEING OF ADEN LANACH

HEN Gwri Gwallt Euryn was at the end of his eighteen years, and driving on his nineteen — and he equal, at the time, to a man of ten-and-twenty — he set forward on his journeyings. Here is what caused him to go: he desired news, if there were any obtaining it, concerning the Talon that had dropped him into the manger of Fflamwen Aden Goleu; and news concerning whence the Talon might have stolen him originally; and more than all, news as to who

might be his parents. It was not the King Twrf Fliant that
would hinder him, or seek to hinder him, from such a journeying and quest as that.

Teyrnion had taught him Three Unusual Arts, beyond
all it would be customary, in those days, for a prince to learn
from his foster-parents. At learning them, Gwri was the
best pupil Twrf Fliant ever had; indeed, maybe he was the
only one; it is not known. He had no equal among the king's
foster-sons either at poetry or at war, at games or at the
relating of stories; also he was the wittiest of them all, and
the blithest and the most handsome, and the delight of every
one that was acquainted with him. No one had ever heard
the rumor of false speech from him, nor the rumor of discourtesy, nor the naming of his own deeds and attainments;
again, at no time had he entered upon battle or contest, without seeing to it that the opposer had the advantages of place
and number at the onset, according to the courtesies of war,
and the usage of the men of the Island of the Mighty. All
these arts and sciences Twrf Fliant taught his foster-sons,
and none but learned them well. But beyond them were
these Three Unusual Arts that he taught Gwri, who was
more a son than a foster-son to him. They were the arts
Twrf Fliant himself had acquired when the Three Drops
of Wisdom were dropped on his lips during sleep. The first
of them was the Art of War in the midst of Peace; the
second was the Art of Peace in the midst of War, and the
third was the Spell of the Wood, the Field and the Mountain.
"With the three arts," said Teyrnion, "it will be a wonder to me if you do not obtain success in whatsoever adventure you may undertake."

So Gwri rode forward, leaving the wind behind him
whenever he had a mind to; for the horse he was riding was
no other than Gyrru'r Gwyntoedd the Wind-driver, the foal

of Fflamwen Aden Goleu, and there was pre-eminence in all
that race of horses. He traversed Europe and Africa and
the Islands of Corsica; he was in Llotor and Ffotor, in Caer
Se and As Se, in India the Greater and India the Less. At
the end of two years he came to Dyffryn Llwchwr in Ystrad
Tywi, and rode forward until the fall of evening.

At that time he was passing through a field in a green
valley; a place of rushes and cuckoo-flower, of forget-me-not
and mint and marsh-marigold, and hidden waters murmurous amidst the grass and mint-beds. Mysteriously beautiful
it was in the evening; it seemed to him that the Immortals,
unseen, might well be watching him. Suddenly he drew
rein, and fell to listening, hearing the magical croon and
tinkling of a song. Here is what he heard:

> *Whoever drinks at the Secret Well,*
> *All that he seeks shall be made full clear,*
> *For the Stars and Gods set a druid spell*
> *Of old on the Well at Llandybie.*
>
> *Murmur of bees in the marshland flowers,*
> *The linnet's song in the linden trees —*
> *Who were the lone, supernal powers*
> *Breathed the wealth of the Wise in these?*
>
> *What the wind whispers, who shall tell?*
> *Or read the dreams of the mountain mere?*
> *But the Stars and Gods set a bardic spell*
> *Of old on the Well at Llandybie.*
>
> *Out of the vast, and all alone,*
> *Kings come riding a-quest at eve,*
> *Whence they came at the first, unknown —*
> *But whoso drinketh, no more shall grieve.*

For there's wondrous sight in the Secret Well,
And all things hidden were made full clear
When the Starry Gods set a druid spell
Of old on the Well at Llandybie.

He looked down, and saw a little runlet amidst the delicate ferns and rushes; it became clearer to him than anything, almost, that it would be magical in its nature, and that he would obtain no success at anything, unless he obtained success at drinking water from its fountain. Therewith he dismounted, and went seeking the source of the runlet; long it seemed impossible to find it; but the more impossible it seemed, the less would he give up the search. Now it would appear that there was no stream there at all; again, he would hear it rippling and whispering invisibly; again he would catch a glimpse of the gleam of its waters. "By the Three Places in Wales," he said (they were the Wood, the Field, and the Mountain), "find the fountain undoubtedly I will." He looked down; there it was before his feet, and the evening star glassed in it.

It was a clear, round pool, spring-filled perpetually; and dimly the yellow sand and pebbles could be seen dancing in the diamond water as it bubbled up out of the ground. He kneeled down, and scooped up water in his hands, and drank. Barely had it touched his lips, when it was made known to him indeed how magical the water was. A breath of wind, all a-tremble and murmurous with the spirit of song, came stealing and whispering through the valley; when he lifted his head, he beheld the hills all other than they had been. Rainbow-colored palaces glimmered up through the gloom and beauty of them; they were all dwellings of arcane, immaculate fire. In his delight and wonder he spoke out loud: "Wonderful, truly, is the water!" he said.

"Wonderful it is, without doubt," said one, answering him. It was a voice that had the sound in it of a far wind among the pine-tops, or of the hum and undertone of falling waters afar on a night in August. He saw a maiden standing by the water's edge on the other side of the pool. In the dusk of twilight a certain glow and dark radiance shone from her, as if she were the heart of all the purple of the evening. The gentle wind rippled through her darkly glowing hair, and swayed her pale green, gold-embroidered mantle; her two eyes were darker than the night sky, and more liquidly glimmering than her own fountain when it may be glassing the multitudinous stars. He rose up, and gave her such greeting as a prince of the Cymry would give to a Goddess; for it was not concealed from him that she would be of the Family of Hu.

"Make known to me who it is that you are," said she, "and what you may be questing; for it is a main privilege for any one to drink from this fountain."

Then he said: "I am Gwri Gwallt Euryn, the foster-son of Teyrnion Twrf Fliant; as for my questing, it is for news concerning a Talon that dropped me in the king's manger at Caerlleon; and for news concerning the parents from whom the Talon stole me."

"Many would perform service in return for the water," said she. "Tydain Tad Awen, the Lord of the Fountain, would expect it."

"Without doubt I will perform it," said Gwri. "Name you whatsoever you will."

"In these waters," she said, "there is the clearing away of uncertainty, and the discovery of inaccessible antique things. It might well be that, having drunk, and thereafter doing the service, you would obtain news both of the Talon, and of the ones from whom it stole you."

"Whether I shall obtain it or not, I will do the service; and that out of courtesy and the desire to requite you for the water."

"Here is what it will be, then," said Tybie of the Fountain: "it will be finding the Birds of Rhianon, that were stolen away from her before your body would have been made. I will make known to you the story of them," said she. "My kinswoman Rhianon ferch Hefeydd had three birds, three daughters of magic, three Singers of Beauty and Peace. It was their custom to come to the fountain at dawn to quench their thirst, and when they had quenched it they would sing, and it would be hard to come by better singing, even among the Immortals. It was the pity of her life that they were stolen; and it was the pity of my life also."

"It will be an honor to me to find them," said Gwri.

"If you will find them," said Tybie, "ride not forward without advice and counsel. It will be better for you to rest here until the dawn; and with the dawn to ride forward. And no one would have success in finding Aden Lanach, the eldest of the birds, unless he had a feather from her wing to guide him; for that reason, it will be well for you to take this feather, and set it in the horse's mane, between the two ears; and in whatever direction the wind may bend the feather, in that direction travel forward. If you part with the horse, part not with the feather also; and when you have found the bird it fell from, return here, and drop the feather in the fountain. You will know her by this: her singing is awakenment, and the passing of sloth into valor.

"Beyond that, it would be unwise to travel on this quest without taking the fill of your drinking-horn of the water from the fountain; it is good for the moistening of eyelids, when there may be need for more than common vision; and three drops of it will put a wonderful excellence in tools, should there be any labor requiring tools for its rightful doing. Also whatever substance may be desired, it will often be found that the water will be equal to it, and even better; for all these reasons, it will be better to take the water. And success attend you," said she, "according to merits and deserts."

She had given him the feather while she was counseling him; there were no means of telling it from the feather of an old white hen. At the end of the counseling, she stepped out over the water in the air, and became a trembling purple dimness, and sank down beneath the stars that shone up from the pool. Gwri filled his drinking-horn, and lay down. Through his sleep he heard the murmur of innumerable unseen waters, weaving magical wisdom into his dreams with song.

He rose up in the youth of the day, and rode forward, having set the feather between the two ears of Gyrru'r Gwyntoedd, as Tybie of the Fountain had directed him. It must be said that the place had changed again, and was without the spiritual beauty of the night before. Beautiful, indeed, were the green hills; and they well-wooded, pleasant places where the linnet sings; but the stars and fires in them were no longer visible, and there was no seeing within them the houses of those Youthful Ones whose prime and youthful May-time is equal to the age of the world. Beautiful, too, were the waters; sweetly rippling was their music in the light and gaiety of morning; but they were bereft of articulate Welsh, where last evening they had spoken and sung. Beautiful were the gold marsh-marigolds, splendid in the dawn; sweet-scented were the mint-beds, beautiful the blue forget-me-not and the pale purple of the cuckoo-flower. But in the midst of all that bloom and beauty, the Fountain of Tybie was not made known to him; it was as if it had never been anywhere, except in his dreams. But he knew what water it was that filled his drinking-horn. The feather bent forward, blown by a wind from some immortal region; it is all a magical country, is that. Gwri rode forward, singing.

In the dusk of evening he came to a branching of ways, and for a moment the feather stood upright, doubtful of its direction. The road on the left ran down a little, and then across a valley-floor of bogland; the setting sun was a flame of gold on the broad pools there, and on the river where it broadened into a ford. Beyond, the world was encumbered and strewn with immense uncouth mountains, somber in the evening, looming up to a rose and primrose and daffodil sky. As for the other road, it would turn off, after a mile or more of straightness, as he could see, into the heart of a great gloomy, marshy wilderness of mountains, ridge upon ridge and shoulder on shoulder of them; wild slopes and morasses and precipices, half dusk-hidden, dark purple, night coming over them. The wind rose up whispering again, and the feather bent down over the left ear of the Wind-driver. Gwri turned, and took the road into the valley. Not long before he was on the brink of the ford.

As soon as the foremost hoof of Gyrru'r Gwyntoedd was wet with ford water, the whole world began to drift and wander, and to become uncertain, and all solid things to flow and scatter, and be driven like foam upon the cataract, like froth caught in the whirlpool. When he turned his head, there was no seeing, any longer, the bank he had left; looking forward, there was no seeing the bank to which he desired to come. It was as if all the waters of the world were foaming about him, or the shadow of all the waters, in a kind of dream and incertitude, with a murmur from infinitely far like the gathering of a shadowy multitude, or the clamor of dim battles, or the roaring of a ghostly wind among oaktrees beyond the borders of the world. It was impossible for him to find meaning or reality anywhere; it was a bewilderment of cloudy waters, of unreal sound, that waxed for awhile; and then waned, until there was an end of the rising of a smoke of foam from the falling of the hoofs of the Wind-driver, and all sound had grown fainter than the dying of a wind. It was to be known by that that the far bank had been reached; but still the world was no better than dimness and a wandering spray. " If ever there were need for more than common vision — " thought Gwri, and took the lid from his drinking-horn. As soon as the end of his finger, wet with the water of the fountain, had touched his two eyelids, foam and mist and uncertainty rolled away and perished. It was clear to him in a moment that he had left the confines of the Island of the Mighty, and indeed, the whole of the regions of the man-inhabited world.

Behind him was the welter and confusion of a foaming torrent without sound, cloudy and impassable, beyond which no vision might travel. Before him was somnolent marsh-land, gleaming on its pools with the deep gold of the sun; an abode of silence, and again silence, and it appeared to him that no sound would have been heard there since of old the Shouting of the Threefold Name. The boom of the bittern, the bleating of the snipe, would never be wafted there from beyond the ford. If the stag were belling in the uplands in October, or if the wolves were howling when the snow lay deep, it would be the same in that marshland as if there were no live creatures in the world. No wind stirred the tufts on the rushes, nor rippled the pale blue or daffodil brightness of the pools. In front, and the wall of the valley before him, what had seemed to be a range of mountains, now was revealed for a caer, its vastness a boundary for the border of the world. No sound came there; no sound. Were there an army of the Family of Hu Gadarn, or a horde of demons out of nether Abred and Annwn gathered; and they to go forth impetuous as a fire in a chimney, and to charge against the caer, it was doubtful, with Gwri, whether either would come as far as the portals of it, or whether they would be smitten with sleep unbreakable as they drove forward, and fall like long grass before the scythe of the mower in June, or like the yellow leaves of late autumn before the swift running of the wingless, footless wind.

There he chose three round stones out of the ford, the size of the largest apple in the orchards of the world; "They will be needed," thought he; and put them in his wallet. He left the Wind-driver to graze beside the river if he desired to; but parted not with the feather when he parted with the horse. Impatient was that one at being left, and eagerly desirous of accompanying his lord; but "it would be unfitting for you to come," said Gwri; "there is natural obedience for you to remember." Such counsel as that would be enough for Gyrru'r Gwyntoedd at any time. Then Gwri went forward towards the gates of the caer.

Never had he seen the equal of that place since he was born; and might never see the equal of it again in the length and width of the world. As far as could be seen on either hand, the walls extended; no light shone from window or casement anywhere. The walls were so thick at the portals, that no horse could have leaped the length of their thickness. The doors were of solid granite on their hinges; the stems of the ivy that had grown over them were greater in girth than the arms of any man. Three giants leaned against the doors, slumbering; the nature of their clothes or their armor was not to be known, on account of the growth of their hair and their beards.

"There would be no obtaining entry here," said Gwri,

"without strategy." He took the first of the three stones from his wallet, and dropped three drops of the water of the fountain on it, and chanted the spell for raising War in the midst of Peace.

"What will be required?" said the stone.

"Tumult, dear," said he; "tumult and buffetings."

He threw it down at the feet of the giants, and immediately it began its work according to his commands. While it was leaping up, and smiting the three of them vigorously, and raising the Dragon Warshout with unexampled vehemence, he went forward, skirting the wall northward in quest of the second door.

It was even vaster than the first when he came to it; the stems of the ivy that had grown over it had the girth of the body of a warrior, and the three giants that leaned against it, sleeping, were three times huger than the others. "There would be no obtaining entry without strategy," thought he; "and even with strategy many would fail to obtain it."

He took the second stone from the wallet, and poured seven drops of the water on it, chanting the same spell; no sooner had he chanted it than the stone became gifted with articulate utterance.

"What will be required of me, lord?" said the stone.

"The raising up of tumult, dear," said Gwri. "The raising up of tumult, and the dealing of impetuous belaborings." Hardly was it out of his hands, when it rose up to its work even more violently than the first had done.

Far vaster was the third door, when he came to it, than the second. The stems of the ivy that had grown over it were equal in girth to the trunk of an oak of three hundred years, and it was all intertwined with the beards of the three giants that slumbered there. As for those three, they would have been the encumberment of a world, so huge they were.

" There must be obtaining entry here," said Gwri, " whether with strategy or without it." Thereupon he took the third stone, and poured thirteen large drops on it, and chanted the spell. ·

" What will be required, master? " said the stone. " What will be required, in heaven's name? "

" Shouting, dear," said Gwri. " Tumultous shouting, in heaven's name, and the raising up of such confusion as few armies of a thousand men might raise, without grievous exertion; and beyond that, the delivering of well-aimed, stinging blows upon the bodies of yonder giants." The stone rose to its work, and Gwri stood by and watched it.

By that time, the first stone had attained awakening the giants at the first door. Slowly it became apparent to them that they were being belabored, and the affliction of it became more and more oppressive to them, until it seemed that the whole host of the Gods and the Cymry were upon them in the darkness. They fell to roaring and pounding upon the door, desiring admittance and shelter; but had no success at attaining either. " Woe is me! " they roared; " the ruin of the world is here! Alas for the coming of the Gods and the Cymry! " There was no shaking the door, nor rousing up the porter. It appeared to them that there might be entry by the second gate, and they fled towards it in confusion.

By the time they came there, the second stone had awakened the second three giants, and had begun to afflict them with a grievous fear of the ruin of the world, and of the onslaught of the Gods and the Cymry. The six of them pounded upon the door uproariously, but there was no breaking it down, and no rousing up the porter. They fled wailing towards the third door, and the stones oppressed them as they ran.

By the time they came there, the giants of the third door

were awakening; the third stone was belaboring them, and giving them no peace, and filling them with the terror of the Gods and the Cymry. The nine of them fell to pounding upon the door and howling to the porter. So great was their weight and their vigor, that at long last the door shook.

"For what reason is there knocking?" cried the porter. "It is no more than two-and-twenty years since Llwyd ab Cilcoed came here with the bird, and broke the slumber of the chieftains. Will there never be peace?"

"Open thou the portals before we are slain," they roared. "The hosts of the Gods and the Cymry are come against Caer Hun."

Above all the tumult, Gwri heard the creaking and rattle of drawn bolts, and the grumbling of the porter from within. "It is a miserable thing that there should be no time for rest and slumber," said the porter; "the portliness of our forms will be wasted with watching." Thirteen bolts there were; but before the tenth of them was drawn, with the pounding and pressing of the nine giants, the door fell inward, broken from its hinges. They surged in over the threshold, stumbling and falling over the door and the ivy stems. But the stones worked upon them vigorously; even then they might have no peace for slumber. They rose up and fled in confusion; some to the right hand and some to the left; and the stones pursuing them. The sound of their flight died away afar, as Gwri strode forward swiftly towards the hall. Through antique blackness, through soundlessness unbroken since the worlds were made, he journeyed; such was the vision that he had obtained with moistening his eyelids with the water, that he came there at last, without once having stumbled or turned aside.

Dim light fluttered and flickered there, like the flickering of a little flame among the wood-ashes, when the fire is near

its death. Vaster was the hall than would have been needed
for a battlefield for two hosts of ten thousand men. On all
the walls and pillars hung swords and spears and shields;
they were tarnished and rusted with disuse; no one would
have worn or wielded them since the Shouting of the Threefold Name. The smallest of the swords would have had the
length of a pine trunk, if the pine were taken from the borders of the forest. A scythed chariot and its horses might
have stood on the expanse of the least of the shields. A dead
fire was on the hearth, and a cauldron of giants over the
ashes. Round the walls without sleeping benches, and at the
bases of the immeasurable pillars, lay slumbering a race of
giants plunged in antique stupor, the limbs of them, huger
than beech-boughs, tossed and sprawling over the floor.

As for what it was that gave light in the hall, and the
one thing that had motion or thought there; here is what it
was: there was a leaden cage hung high over the throne of
the king on the dais, and in it a crowned bird of the color of
the sunlight on the snowflake, lovelier than any bird in the
forests of the world. It was the bird that gave the light.
Pale and beautiful she gleamed in the dimness. There was
no aspect of well-being with her; but sorrow, and disquiet
of mind, and forlorn unattainment of rest or peace or contentment. Ruffled were her pure feathers; she was fluttering endlessly; her faery wings were worn with beating
against the bars of the cage. More sorrowful she seemed
to him, than anything he had ever attained seeing. Clear it
was to him in a moment that she would be Aden Lanach,
the one he had come there to free.

He went forward towards the dais, musing on what
means he should use for freeing her. " It will be by raising
up War in the midst of Peace," said he; " such peace as it
is." Then he chanted that spell again. Barely were the last

words of it passing between his lips and his teeth, when he heard commotion and shouting afar, and their rapidly drawing nearer. " It will be the ten giants from the gates," he thought; " the nine sentinels, and the porter the tenth; and the three stones untiringly pursuing them." That was the truth; the stones had made pursuit of the giants three times round the caer within its walls, and were guiding them now into the hall.

In they came, roaring and blundering, and in great fear of their oppressors, and imploring protection from the chieftain sleeping on his throne. Him also the three stones betook themselves to belaboring, delivering fierce, well-aimed, stinging blows upon his head and upon his body. Beyond that, the ten from the gates came to him, and bellowed into his two ears the news they had concerning the Gods and the Cymry. It would have been easier for them to have awakened the mountains.

The three stones took thought within themselves. " We must increase our vigor," thought they; " there will be need of raising up commotion in this hall, although heretofore we may have maintained orderly quietness." Thereupon they rose up against the ten again, and if they had afflicted them grievously before, ten times more grievously they began to afflict them then. Three times they drove them round the hall, and mingled their own shouting of the Dragon War-shout with the bellowings of extreme terror they got from the giants. Gwri watched them, not without hopeful anticipation. During the first circuit of the hall they attained raising such tumultuous din, that the armor on the walls was shaken down, and fell clanging and rattling on the floor. " Not good, where there might be better," cried he; " redouble your exertions." They obeyed him, and at the second circuit raised such a din that the great pillars were visibly shaken. "It is better," he shouted; "but there must be a best. Redouble your exertions, in the name of heaven!" They obeyed him, and at the third circuit put forth their power, and raised ten times the clamor that they had raised before. So loud was the shouting of the stones, and the bellowing of the giants, and the thunder and pounding of their feet on the flagstones, that three of the pillars were brought down with it. "This indeed is tumult," shouted . Gwri, praising them; "this indeed is praiseworthy din and confusion!" The fall of the pillars made dust of the flagstones, and caused a trembling of the mountains over a great part of the world; it happened to the third of them to fall on the head of the chieftain of the giants. Then the stones forsook their persecution, and the ten from the gates fell asleep, being freed from it.

The chieftain of the giants lifted his hand to his forehead slowly; slowly he raised the eyelids that had fallen over his eyes.

"It is a fly buzzing in the rafters," murmured he; "it is a fly causing dust to fall from amidst the rafters. Evil upon the miserable fly that has broken my rest and peace! Let the seven harpstrings of slumber have their striking!"

With that a great, solemn harpnote boomed out from behind him on the dais, unconquerable slumber in the sound of it. Gwri leaped towards it; there was a harp there, the three sides of which were equal in size to three full-grown beech trunks from the depths of the forest. Before the note could come to its fulness, his sword had swept through the seven strings. Their snapping rang and shrieked and clamored from end to end of the hall, and voices laden with keen, intense wailing, detestably shrill and screaming, fled out and fled out from every broken end. " Broken, broken, broken! " they screamed; " woe is me, I am snapped! "

Gwri sat down at the base of a pillar facing the Chieftain, and listened to their piercing grief, considering that it would attain its end at last, even should there be waiting. "Here is the end of sleep forever!" they screamed; "here is the end of the delight of Caer Hun!" Although the noise they raised may not have been more than three times louder than the best noise raised by the stones and giants, yet it was ten times more terrifying, or even thirteen times, by reason of its piercing nature. There was no peace in the hall with them, until the last of the giants was on his feet, awakened and amazed, and moaning with bewilderment and vexation.

"Let the seven harpstrings of slumber be sounded! Ah, for the sake of heaven, let them be sounded!"

The master of the harp went to his work confusedly; but the best he could get from the strings was keener and keener shrieking, wailing ever more piercing and dismal, and no news but that sleep would be unknown in Caer Hun from that out. The giants bowed their heads in their hands, and lamented with tears for the breaking of their peace.

Then Gwri rose up, and stood before the throne. "For what reason is this unseemly lamentation?" said he.

"There is an end of sleeping in the hall of Caer Hun," said the chieftain of the giants. "Without it, there will be no diversion for us henceforward. Undoubtedly we shall pine away through grief and sleeplessness, and it will be the death of us. Woe is me for this rude destruction of our sleep!"

"Woe is me," moaned the giants, "for this rude destruction of our sleep."

"Dear help you!" said Gwri kindly; "there is a better diversion than sleeping."

" Undoubtedly this will be without truth. What power hast thou in the raising up of diversions? Sleeping have we been since the worlds were formed."

"As for power, I have Three Unusual Arts of extreme power. Easily could I show you a better diversion than this slothful sleep."

" Make it known to us! Make it known to us, in the name of heaven and man! Make known to us what diversion it will be! "

" Eating it will be," said Gwri. " It will be the preparation of delicious food, and the cooking of it in cauldrons, and the devouring of it. It will be a thousand times a better diversion for you than wasting the ages in brutish slumber and oblivion."

The giants glanced at each other wonderingly, and fell to confused cogitation. "We heard a rumor of it, before the old sleep of the worlds," said they. " It is a long time since we have forgotten this art."

" I will show you," said Gwri. Thereupon he went to the hearth and kindled a fire. 'He shook out three drops from his horn into the cauldron, and immediately it was filled to the brim with clear water. Then he picked up the wing of a dead bat that had been shaken down from the roof by the shouting, and threw that in also. As soon as it was in the cauldron, the water began to boil. Slothfully and sorrowfully the giants watched him.

He took the horn again, and looked into it: " Is there pepper with you? " said he to the horn; " pepper will be required." He shook it over the cauldron and pepper poured forth from it, stronger than any in the world; the power of it spread from the door to the dais, and from the floor to the rafterbeams. The wailing of the harpstrings died away. The giants looked at each other with slowly kindling delight.

"*Ah!*" they murmured; "*Ah! Ah!*" In a little while Gwri took the cauldron from the fire, and set it before the chieftain.

Since the worlds were formed, the senses of the giants had known no delight equal to the delight of the smell that arose from the cooked meat in the cauldron. An aspect of cheerfulness spread over their countenances. Few of them would have desired to sleep, even if sleep had been granted them.

"Let every one come to the cauldron," said Gwri, "and take out of it as much as he may require, and use it according to the desire that shall overtake him." Thrice nine men at a time, they did so; beginning with their princes. It became the strongest desire in the world on every one of them, to consume and devour greedily whatsoever he might have taken.

Beyond doubt, the food was hot, well peppered and of strong flavor. As they consumed it, their hunger grew, and they eagerly desired more. The more they desired, the more they devoured, and the more their sloth was lifted from them. "Marvelous indeed is this diversion!" they said; "many times is it better than foolish sleeping." Heat and liveliness, and the desire for exertion took possession of them, so active was the power of the pepper in the food. From heavy lamentations they were taken with cumbersome laughter and merriment; for the sake of gaiety they fell to snatching the food the one from the other, and even to the delivering of buffets where none might be looked for. So from merriment the shadow of anger would be blown across their souls, a thing unknown to them until then — the buffeted being undesirous of receiving blows. Eagerly, and with uncouth asseverations, with restraintless noise and unseemly vehemence, they clamored after the food and devoured it; and clamoring and devouring they were until the dawn of the morning.

With the first brightening of dawn, the cauldron was empty;
and they had long since forgotten that there was such a thing
as sleeping in the world, or ever had been. Beyond that,
Aden Lanach was at peace at last in her cage, and had left
the beating of her wings, and was watching what should
befall, not without astonishment and the awakening of hope.

"Wherefore is the cauldron emptied of food? Let it be
filled again; let it be filled again quickly, lest pining away
should overtake us! Let the cauldron be filled again with
food, lest we perish of hunger, and of the lack of this excellent diversion!"

"Miserable is this greed and gluttony!" said Gwri.
"The cauldron will never be refilled."

They began to raise up their lamentations again; now
there was a sound of bitterness and anger about it, where
before there had been only heaviness and loutish grief.

"Wherefore do you lament?" said Gwri. "For what
reason is this unseemly clamor of grief? It is a marvel to
me, truly, that this should be."

"Alas!" they said, "the cauldron is empty. We lack diversion, and are likely to perish."

"Dear help you better!" said he, cheerfully. "A far
better diversion is known to me, than this gluttonous consuming of food."

"Undoubtedly this is untrue. What power or knowledge
hast thou for the raising up of diversions? Consuming food
we have been since the making of the worlds. No other diversion hath been devised than this."

"As for power and knowledge, I have Three Unusual
Arts of extreme power and knowledge. For what purpose
were the weapons on the walls?"

"It is unknown to us," said they, bewildered. "For
adornment they were, so far as is known."

"Stupid are ye, truly. Useless they would be for adornment. For diversion, and for entertaining amusement they were."

They marveled. "Make it known to us, in heaven's name!" they said. "If there be any truth in this, make known to us for what diversion they were."

"For fighting they were," said Gwri. "For satisfying the ears with excellent din, and for the exertion of strength and violence, and for the laying on of sharp, stinging and well-directed blows. A thousand times a better diversion will it be for you, than the exercise of contemptible gluttony in the matter of devouring food."

A murmur of wonderment and deep cogitation went through them. "We heard a rumor of it indeed, before the falling of the night of the worlds."

"I will make it known to you," said Gwri. He went to two of the swords where they lay, and dropped water on the blades. "It is raising of strife that is required of you," he whispered to them. Then he called to the chieftain and to one of the princes. "Take them in your hands in this way," said he.

As soon as those two had hold of the swords, here is what happened:

"Ah ha!" said the chieftain; "thou buffetedst me!"

"Evil upon thee!" said the other; "thou accusest me falsely!"

Therewith they began to smite at each other with extreme vigor, as if they had been accustomed to fighting since the Crying of the Name. "Ah! Ah!" murmured the others; "mighty and regal indeed is this diversion! Were it but permitted to us also to engage in this!"

"Cheerfully it is permitted to you!" said Gwri, encouraging them. "Let every man pick up one of the long ones

and one of the round ones, and use them according to the
desire that shall take him, and according to the precedent of
the prince and the chieftain."

Eagerly they did so, and as soon as the weapons were in
their hands they became acquainted with the use of them, and
forgot all diversions except fighting. Delight in battle took
their hearts, and they roared with laughter and fell to smiting. Roaring and smiting they swept down from the dais,
making conflict in confusion, every man against every man,
without order or science, or the natural courtesy of war.

Then there rose up a sound through the hall, that easily
soared above the noise of the fighting. It was Aden Lanach
in her cage; song had returned to her. A wild war-song it
was, and rang and surged and billowed out gloriously, impetuous, tumultuous, millions of notes pursuing each other
in a supreme intoxication of battle-music, surging and swaying and leaping among the pillars. The warfare of the
giants was whirled by it into a wild, quick ecstasy of fighting.
Stately it grew then, slow and majestic, warlike still; and
according to its majesty and stern marching sweep, so they
were loosened and quelled from their tumult, and took courteous rank and order, until their fighting became of equal
dignity with the warfare of the men of the Island of the
Mighty. She sang, and her song was awakenment, and the
passing of sloth and brutishness into valor.

She sang, and the leaden bars of her cage melted, and
fell down upon the floor. She rose up through the air, and
beamed and glowed and lightened ambiently among the
heights of the pillars, pouring forth her marvels of melody,
flooding the hall with music hardly to be equaled in the
world. Hearing it, the loutish nature of the giants was continually changed, and they grew in speed and strength and
heroic courtesy and beauty. Then far off in the lofty vast-

ness of the hall, there shone forth a glory and a marvelous
dawn. Gazing, Gwri beheld the beauty and splendor of a
Prince of the Immortals. He saw that Bright One hold forth
his arm above the giants, and they came to peace swiftly. He
saw Him lead them forth. Then there was silence in Caer
Hun again, except for the singing of Aden Lanach.

Brighter than the star of evening, on the fairest evening
of July, she passed onward, leading him; sweeping and shedding beauty through the darkness. A breath of wind, sweet
from many mountains, full of the scent of heather and bogland, blew in upon his face. He came out from the mountain,
through the mouth of a great cavern; and knew that he was
within the confines of the Island of the Mighty again. The
sun shone over a marshland, that was other than the marshland from which he had passed into Caer Hun. The wind
swayed the rushes, and rippled the surface of the pools. He
heard the booming of the bittern, the bleating of the snipe
afar; he heard the lark chanting in the morning, from her
pathless playground in the sky. He saw the ford, and heard
the music of its waters; he saw the Wind-driver grazing
beside it, waiting for him. Where had been the immensity
of the caer, now there were only trackless mountains.

Aden Lanach rose up into the bloom and blueness of the
heavens, and he heard her trailing song far away over the
mountains. He rode forward, and came that evening to the
Fountain of Tybie at Llandybie.

II. THE ART OF PEACE IN THE MIDST OF WAR, AND THE FREEING OF ADEN LONACH

THE Well was hidden from him when he came there, as it had been at his first coming, and again in the morning, when he rode forth to seek the freeing of Aden Lanach. He took the feather from between the Wind-driver's ears, and cast it on the air; it drifted a little on the wind and then fell. Where it lighted, the ground began to glimmer, silken and shadowy, around it; and he beheld the Well of Wonder, and the hills on all sides plumed and luminous. Beyond the water, a dark, beautiful radiance, stood the Immortal Maiden; but she had little kindliness or favor in her aspect at that time.

" Greeting of the god and the man to you, courteously," said he.

" And you also, wherefore come you? "

" Aden Lanach is free," said Gwri Gwallt Euryn.

" Yes is she free," said Tybie. " But it was Pryderi fab Pwyll that freed her."

Gwri marveled. " If it please you," said he, " give me news of this king's son."

"He was stolen in the night out of his cradle, before he was a day old," said she. "The one that stole him, stole the three birds also; and it was decreed that no one should free them unless Pryderi freed them when he should have grown up to be a man. From the time of the stealing until now, sorrow, and doing penance, and a mournful fate have been upon my kinswoman, his mother."

Gwri marveled again. "For what reason do you marvel?" said Tybie of the Fountain.

"For this reason," he said. "During all these years it has not been given to Pryderi to find Aden Lanach, although it was fated that he should find her at last. But now that another has gone upon the quest, he has freed her. Considering I was, whether it would not be better for me to go in quest of Aden Lonach also, if it were permitted to me."

"There is no saying that it might not be better," said she; "and therefore it will be permitted to you. This feather from her breast will be granted to you for a guide; set you it upon the wind in the morning, and go forward following it. And it will be permitted to you also to take water in your horn from the fountain, for the sake of vision when it may be required, and for putting excellence in tools. Beyond that, there will be these counsels for you, given freely: Go not forth warlikely, and forsake not peace out of desire for strife, nor quietness where there may be blustering; for it is the nature of Aden Lonach to abhor senseless tumult. Her singing is a coolness upon all aching, and the passing of desire into peace. And neglect not this labor, if you desire to requite me; even though there will be no success for you in it, and no obtaining reward for any one but Pryderi."

"Evil upon me if I neglect it," said he. Before the words

were out on the air, she was made one again with the beauty and glamor of the evening.

In the morning he set the feather on the wind, and rode forward following it. It might have been the mere feather of a woodpigeon when he loosed it; but blowing forward, it took on more magical aspect, and glistened in the sunlight, and glowed dimly where there was shadow. By mountain pass and clovered valley, by meadowsweet mead and wood-anemone hedgerow, it drifted and eddied glimmering before him. At noon he passed Caer Hun, but the feather neither paused nor turned there; and from noon till sunset he was journeying on upward into the heart of a wilderness of mountains.

When the western sky began to bloom out in roses and daffodils, he was high above the world, and taking a grassy way that might have been traveled by seven sheep abreast; the bracken on either side was as high as the Wind-driver's knees. Before him the track dipped and wandered continually, so that no more than thirty paces of it would ever be visible at a time. Westward, and he to ride down into it, lay an unseen upland valley, whence, wind-borne, came the sound of pouring and pondering waters; beyond, new dim peaks and shoulders glowed in opal and silver and violet, and above them a sky all fading gold and roses and primrose and lilac glory. He rode down into the valley, and, as the feather directed him, followed the torrent upwards, and the windings and wanderings of the valley. As the dusk came down over the mountains, he came to where the valley widened, and saw, beyond the stream, and about as far away from it as three casts of a spear by the best of spearmen, an immense rock towering up into the heavens; it is unknown whether or not it would have been the loftiest in the world, and no less in height than the Crag of Gwern Abwy in

the ancient days, from which the Eagle of Gwern Abwy was
accustomed, for the sake of sharpening his beak, to peck at
the stars in the evening. Opposite to that, the track branched,
one way following the course of the torrent up into the mountains, the other crossing it, and running by the foot of the
rock. A breath of wind whirled the feather to the left; a
little flame of dim blue and purple, it hung in the air over the
stream, and then drifted over to the other side.

"There must be leaping this stream," thought Gwri. Indeed, the breadth of it would be easy for Gyrru'r Gwyntoedd,
and not such as to cause boastful thought in his mind, much
less the desire for braggart speech; though it might have
been impossible for one of a less gifted race of horses.
"Crossing here," thought Gwri, "I shall undoubtedly have
need of the moistening of eyelids." The more he considered,
the less was there gainsaying that. He dipped his right forefinger in the horn, and fastened the horn, and set it back
in his girdle again. As he was lifting his finger to his eyelids, the Wind-driver rose up in his leaping like a swallow in
the air.

The world changed, and the great foam of innumerable
unearthly waters swayed and churned and glimmered about
him bewilderingly, with far uncertain sounds, and the passing of a hundred thousand dreams too swiftly for any of
them to be seen or known. It seemed to him that he would
have been poised in that dim place of unrealities for it might
have been as long as seven ages, whence he had come unknown to him, and unknown the nature of his quest. At
long last there was a touching of his eyelids, and a moistening of them; at that moment the hoofs of the Wind-driver
were on the solid earth again, and all bewilderment vanished.
It was the water from Llandybie that moistened his eyelids,
and his own finger that brought it to them; it will be known

already that his hand started on that journey at the moment
the Wind-driver rose in the air. With the touching of the
hoofs on the ground, and the torrent cleared, and the eyelids
moistened, and the bewilderment vanished, it was clear to
him that he had left the Island of the Mighty again, and was
beyond the confines of the world.

Behind him was the roaring of the torrent, black and impassable; and no piercing it for the vision of man. Before
him, for leagues and leagues towards the purple darkness
on the edge of the world, a great plain extended, and over it
afar through the twilight, the roar of shadowy hosts with-
drawing from war. He saw their huge encampment on the
world-edge, their dwellings that rose against the sky, and
were loftier that the mountains, and more innumerable than
the innumerable stars. What had appeared, from beyond
the torrent, to be a vast rock, was revealed now as a caer,
vaster than any in the entire world, and loftier; beyond
doubt it would have had its building at the time when the sky
and the mountains were made. It seemed to him that if
armies were besieging it, the least of whose warlike captains
could crumble the mountains in his fingers, there would be
no knowing whether they would succeed in taking it by storm
or not.

He paused on the edge of the plain for consideration and
the making of plans. "Rightly spoke the Lady of the Fountain," thought he; "it is peace that would be needed in such
a place as that." Indeed, a rumor of incessant tumult, of
gigantic shouting, was borne out to him from the heart of
the caer, in spite of its vastness and the vast thickness of its
walls. He dismounted, and hid what arms he had under a
ledge of rock beside the river; then, leaving the Wind-driver
to his peaceable grazing, followed the feather to the portal
of the caer. There it rested on the door-clapper, and stirred

not until he had fastened it in the brooch on his breast. "Clearly there must be knocking," said he; and knocked.

Cried Gwri, " Is there a porter? "

" There is. Wherefore, O Immortals, is this clamor of knocking? Since the Crying of the Name, truly, ye have besieged Caer Drais; and during that time we have given ye what warfare ye desired between dawn and dusk daily, and even more than according to your deserts. It is unfitting that ye should break in upon our diversion by night."

" Neither an Immortal is knocking, nor any one bearing arms. A wandering craftsman with his craft it is, from the Island of the Mighty."

" I will tell you," said the porter. " During the daytime we make war upon a numberless company of Immortals; and during the night, for the sake of pleasurable diversion, we make war among ourselves. There will be no need for a craftsman, and it would be death for him to enter."

" If ye delight in making war, there will be extreme need for such a craftsman as I am. It would be better to obtain news of the nature of the craft."

" Give me news of it quickly, lest evil happen to thee. Death will overtake the craftsman surely, that cometh here with a useless craft."

" Three Unusual Crafts are with me, and the least of them so little useless, that it would be needed by any chieftain, whether in wartime or in times of peace."

" What will the first of them be, in the name of heaven and man? "

" Cooking," said Gwri, considering that it would be an easy art for him to practise, with the knowledge he had gained of it in Caer Hun. Then he expounded the nature of the cooking, according to the insight he had obtained from moistening his eyelids. " If the head of an old toad-stool

were thrown into the pot," said he, " at the end of this cooking it would be a nourishing meal for fifty men, or for a
hundred, or indeed for a thousand if they desired it; and it
would seem to every one that he had never consumed such
delicate, wholesome and well-flavored food during his life."

" There might be need for such an art as that," said the
porter, musingly. " What will the second be? "

"A better one than the first," said Gwri; "and a more
useful to the warward. Sharpening weapons it will be."
Then he made clear to the porter the unusual nature of the
sharpening. " Were this art to be exercised upon an old
hen's feather out of the fowl-house," said he, " it would work
upon the feather, and imbue it with peculiarities and virtues
and magnanimity unknown to it hitherto, and warlike designs
and desires such as few would look for in it; and it would
succeed in sharpening it into a sword equal to the swords of
the Gods and the Cymry; and the sword should be either
bluer than the sky, or paler than the lightning, or of the hue
of the invisible air of heaven; and it would have an edge to
wound the wind, and cause blood to flow."

" There might well be need of such an art as that," said
the porter. " Make known the nature of the third."

" It will be song, in the name of heaven," said Gwri, remembering the power of Glanach at raising it, and considering that Llonach would be the equal of her sister. " Such
song it will be," said he, " that if it were sung to an army
of grasshoppers in August, they would readily go against
giants; and they would obtain such power and strength and
heroic courage and magical prowess out of the singing, that
it would be amazing if they did not overcome them."

"Ah," said the porter, " there might well be need of such
an art as that." Then he mused and considered within him-

self. " Evil upon me," said he, " if, in consideration of these
three arts, thou shalt not be admitted into the hall."

With that he opened the portal, and Gwri went forward
into the hall.

There was such a fury of tumult there, as had never been
made known before to the hearing of man. In the vastness
and lurid gloom before him he beheld the warfare of giants;
a wild, extreme, insensate warfare, of such a nature that the
fighting he had raised in Caer Hun seemed quiet peace in
its comparison. There were seven vast fires on seven insati-
able hearths, the least of them equal to a conflagration in the
forest. The flames of them leaped up towards the rafters,
higher than the flight of the eagle at dawn. Between each
of the fires there was an ample battleground for a thousand
giants, without peril of singeing hair or scorching limb. The
flames roared and waxed and crackled with the waxing of
the tumult, the shouting, the bellowing of meaningless war-
cries, the thud and thunder of clubs, the crashing of axes,
the rending of breaking shields. The clubs would have
crushed the mountains; the battle-axes would have cloven
the skyward crags. A thousand giants were wielding them;
fierce was their strife. They hacked and hewed and mutually pounded, without cessation from roaring and ferocity.
They had no delight but in wounding each other grievously,
and in receiving grievous and hideous wounds. If any were
slain, they would not remain slain; but rose up swiftly and
went forward with the fighting.

Gwri traversed the hall without any one perceiving him,
and came at long last to the open space before the dais.
" Yes," said he; " undoubtedly it is the place." For here is
what he saw there: the Chieftain of Caer Drais throned
upon the dais, and high above his head a strong cage of iron,
and in it a bird equal in beauty to Aden Lanach, or even

more beautiful than she. She was of the color of the blue forget-me-not in the marshland; her head was sunk beneath her wing; it was clear that she would have been songless and plunged in torpor during the passing of many years. Few would have been without grief, beholding her beauty and the ignominy that had been put upon her.

"I marvel that Pryderi should not come," thought Gwri. "It would be amazing if yonder bird should be other than Aden Lonach." Then he fell to considering what art he should use for setting her free. "Peace must be attained first," thought he.

It may be a marvel to many that no greeting should have been spoken between the Chieftain of Caer Drais and Gwri, although the one of them was throned on the dais, and the other standing before the throne; and indeed, that Gwri should have stood there musing, unheeded and unseen. Here is the reason for it: huger was the chieftain than any other giant in the hall; and if he exceeded them in bulk and stature, much more did he exceed them in ill-favoredness of aspect. If he had ceased a moment from his roaring, and from his laying about him in the air with his club, the whole of the tumult would have waned; and therefore he never did cease from it, nor rose from his throne; but leaned forward there, and gazed upon the giants, and roared and laid about him, and maintained the fighting in that way. The louder he roared, and the faster he laid about him, the higher leaped the crimson flames from the fires, and the louder and more perilous waxed the warfare of his men.

"Is there a silentiary?" shouted Gwri. It was such a shout as might have been heard, on a day in July and the south wind blowing, from the top of Pengwaed in Cornwall to the bottom of Dinsol in the north; but in that hall, even he himself obtained no hearing it. "I myself will perform

the office," thought he. Thereupon he went to the pillar that was opposite the throne, and sprinkled it with water from his horn, and smote upon it three times after the manner of silentiaries in the courts of kings. In place of demanding silence, he chanted the spell of Peace in the midst of War. Such was the power of the water, and the smiting, and the chanted spell, that the chieftain ceased his roaring, and the fires burned low among the ashes, and silence trembled down over the whole hall.

"Woe is me!" said the chieftain, "there is a silentiary in the hall."

Then he beheld Gwri, and smote at him with his club, but Gwri stepped aside from it, and beyond his reach.

"Alas!" wailed the thousand giants, "there is a silentiary!"—and fell to bitter mourning.

"Why stand ye there idle when the hall is in peril?" said the chieftain. "Let the silentiary be slain swiftly, according to custom and precedent." It had ever been the usage in Caer Drais to extirpate silentiaries. "Let him be slain, in the name of heaven, lest fearful silence overtake us."

"As for silence," shouted Gwri; "although ye may have been dwelling in pitiful silence hitherto, there is an art with me that might well be the means of bringing noise and confusion into the hall. It would be the sorrow of your lives, if you should be without gaining knowledge of this."

Sadly the chieftain answered him. "Since the dawn of the worlds," said he, "we have striven against silence, and raised up such tumult as we might out of fear that it would overcome us at last. Owing to this fear there is little joy for us. Beyond doubt the quietness thou hast found here, and the lack of spirited confusion thou hast complained of, will be signs that our strength is waning. Woe is me, in an age or two there will be silence."

The giants sighed. More mournful was this thought to them than any thought in the world. It seemed to them that in the ancient times they would have given no man cause to complain of their quietness.

" Undoubtedly silence will overtake you," said Gwri, "unless ye fortify yourselves against it, and renew your strength. The art that is with me would be the means of freeing you from this fear."

" Make known what art it is, in heaven's name," said the chieftain.

" Cooking it is," said Gwri. " The preparation of nourishing and delectable food, and the boiling of it in cauldrons, and thereafter the setting it before you tastefully for the devouring. It would be of such a nature as to be the maintenance of your strength against waning, and the renewal of it perpetually, and indeed the increasing of it a thousandfold. The food would be in unlimited quantities, and of such natural excellence that little of it would become much; and that the more of it there might be devoured, the greater would be the capacity for devouring; and the greater the capacity for devouring, the mightier would be the power of the lungs for shouting, and the strength of the arms for smiting; so that by the exercise of this art, in a little while there might well come to be warfare, and strife, and noise, and arrogant confusion here; and all this would be at but little cost to yourselves."

" During ten thousand years we have tasted no food, lest silence should overcome us while we were consuming it. Undoubtedly thou art right; we are weakening now for lack of nourishment, or there would have been no cause for thy complaints. At what cost to us would be this providing of food? "

"At the cost of firing under the cauldron, and of water from the well, and of the head of an old toadstool out of the barn."

"Let them be brought to him," said the chieftain, and went back to his roaring, and the giants to their raising up strife. Gwri set the cauldron on the fire, and filled it with the water, and flung in the toadstool. The water boiled, and the tumult waxed, and the giants became even more restraintless than before.

"Their minds are overcrowded with the desire for fighting," thought Gwri. "Distraction will be needed, and the diversion of their thoughts." With that he took his drinking-horn, and made known to it what would be required. By that time the chieftain had recovered his rage.

"What filth and poison art thou putting into the pot?" he shouted.

"Pepper," said Gwri. "Peace be with thee, pepper it is for the flavoring."

"Give me thy pepper-box; let me hold it in my hand and examine it, lest thou cheatest us."

Gwri gave him the horn; it had no appearance in the world beyond that of an old, battered pepper-box. As soon as the chieftain had opened it, the whole hall became filled with the odor of pepper, so that the giants were overtaken with violent sternutation, until the weapons dropped out of their hands. "Ah!" they murmured; "invigorating is this!"

"Pepper it is, truly," said the chieftain. "Rewards and gratitude thou shalt have; and thou shalt even escape with thy life, if there is such flavor as this in the feast."

"Such flavor there will be, and even better," said Gwri. With that the chieftain flung back the pepper-box to him, and fell to roaring and laying about him again. Gwri went forward with the cooking.

The power of the pepper ebbed, and the giants renewed their fighting, not less vigorous than at first. " Somnolence is needed," thought Gwri, and considered how he might obtain it. Then he took his horn again, and made known to it what would be required.

" Dost thou put more pepper in the cauldron? " roared the chieftain.

" I put it not," said Gwri; " more desirable even than pepper is this. Wholesome and pleasant herbs are here; excellent both for flavoring and for nourishment: the leek, the garlic and the onion."

The drops that he shook out of the horn acquired the aspect of those herbs as they fell, and immediately an overpowering and somnolent odor arose from the cooking, soothing the fury of the giants. "Ah!" they murmured; "Ah! ah! the equal of this hath been unknown to us heretofore." So pervading was the power of leeks and onions through the hall, that there was little vigor in the fighting between that and the time the feast was prepared.

" The cooking is finished," said Gwri. " Draw forward the tables."

They did so. The food he set before them was enough for them all, and more than enough; and it was clear to every one of them that he had never tasted the equal of it during his life, either for flavor or for nourishing excellence. They feasted until midnight and drank until dawn; and then there was borne away from the tables enough for three more copious feasts for them, without stint or picking of bones. At midnight the household bard of Caer Drais (such bards as they had there — their office was to stand beside the chieftain upon the dais, and to howl execrations for his encouragement while the fighting went forward) — looked up at the cage. "Lord," said he; "there is danger. The sneezing hath shaken the bars of the cage, and the cessation from warfare hath caused the bird to move her wings."

"Trouble me not during the feast," said the chieftain, "Never have I known such delight as this."

With·dawn they finished their feasting, and fell to warfare again; but sluggishly, on account of repletion and heaviness after food; and raised barely such tumult as would have kept sleep from the eyelids of every man between the Island of the Mighty and Greece in the east. "Although there is peril for silentiaries," said Gwri; "the office must be performed."

Thereupon he went to the pillar again, and sprinkled seven drops from his horn on it, and smote it seven times, chanting the Spell. At the seventh smiting and the last word, the chieftain forsook his roaring, and the giants their warfare, and the fires burned low, and peace drifted down over the hall like snowflakes when no wind may be blowing.

"Woe is me for my birth and pre-existences!" sighed the chieftain. "There is a silentiary in the hall, and we are under peril of peace."

"Is there no gratitude with ye?" said Gwri. "Is there no desire for martial conflict? Will ye continue forever at this playful imitation of war?"

The chieftain sighed. "Discouraging is this," he said. "We raised the best tumult we could, and it did not please thee. Then we devoured food, and renewed our strength, and even increased it a thousandfold; and thereafter returned to the fighting, and put forth our whole vigor, and thou art not yet satisfied. Undoubtedly old age and weakening are overcoming us, or thou wouldst have had no cause for complaint. Silence we shall succumb to, woe is me!"

"It is weapons that ye need, and not strength," said Gwri.
"It is a certain slothful quietness of disposition, owing to
the use of childish weapons, that troubles ye. Although ye
may have been accustomed to peace hitherto, I could exercise such an art in your midst, as might well make ye acquainted with the nature of delectable strife."

"What art is it, in the name of heaven?"

"Sword-sharpening it is," said Gwri. "The preparation
and making keen of such implements as will cause this
playing with clubs and axes to seem dull, miserable, and
peaceful."

"Will they do that?" said the chieftain. "Will they
confirm us in warfare?"

"In such warfare as is waged by the Gods and the Cymry," said Gwri. "Keen, swift and pleasurable warfare, and
no menace of an end to it. Look you now," said he.
"Swords I can provide you with, that shall husband your
strength in fighting, so that ye shall have more delight out of
it in a day than ye have obtained heretofore in a year, and
with less waste of exertion; and if any of you should be
overtaken with slumber, the pricking of the swords would
awaken him, so excellent are they; and I can put the blue
sharpening on them, or the lightning-colored, or the sharpening of the hue of the invisible air; and they should have an
edge to wound the wind of heaven. And all this would be
at but little cost to you."

"Marvelous is this indeed," said the chieftain. "Delightful to our hearing is this excellent news. At what cost
to us would it be?"

"At the cost of the wear of the grindstone," said Gwri;
"and of the fetching of feathers from the fowl-house to be
sharpened into swords."

"Let the feathers and the grindstone be set before him."

They did so. Three old tail-feathers from the fowl-house they gave him; a black, and a brown, and a gray one.

"Which of the three sharpenings dost thou desire on the first sword?" said Gwri.

"The blue sharpening."

Thereupon he took the black feather, and dropped three drops out of the horn upon the grindstone.

"Dost thou put pepper on the grindstone?" said the chieftain.

"Not so," said Gwri; "oil it is." He held up the horn, and it had no likeness to anything in the world but to an oil-vessel, nor the water in it to anything but oil. "I marvel at this," said the chieftain; and for marveling, half forgot his roaring and his laying about him with the club.

Gwri began to turn the stone, holding the feather to it, and chanting the spell of Peace in the midst of War. The feather grew and hardened; a stridulent scream of sharpening rose up, and sparks flew innumerably into the air. More and more swiftly he turned the grindstone. The scream increased, and swayed from this note to that; now as keen as the war-cry of the falcon when she sees the heron in the air; now as low and deep and filled with murmurings as the undertone of the cataract heard from afar. It took some semblance of music; a thing unknown in Caer Drais since the worlds were made. The giants forgot their warfare, and fell to watching and listening and marveling. Aden Lonach stirred in her cage, and lifted her right wing.

"Ah," said Gwri, "here is the sword."

In his hand it gleamed, a great griding gasher, a war-like weapon, and the whole bloom and beauty of the June sky at noonday shining from it. It had been given to none of them to wield such a weapon as that; distaste for clubs and

battle-axes seized them at the sight of it. It seemed to them
that if they might obtain a thousand of its like, fighting would
become a bliss to them such as they had never dreamed of,
and that they would pursue the Immortals along the borders
of space. "Ah!" they murmured; "a bright, beaming marvel is this."

"What peculiarities are with it?" said the chieftain.

"It would cut through the bole of an oaktree nine hundred winters old, at a hand's breadth from the ground where
it was thickest," said Gwri. "It would do that at one sweeping stroke, and then not be at the end of its powers, nor
consider it a matter for boasting."

Indeed, it was such a sword as might easily have accomplished as much as that.

"Would it do that?" said the chieftain. "Would it
wound the invisible wind? Thou gavest me news of wounding the wind, and of causing blood to flow."

"It would not," said Gwri. "Swords that have the blue
sharpening have not attained that art." Then he took the
brown feather. "What sharpening wilt thou have on the
second sword?" said he.

"The lightning-colored," said the chieftain.

Thereupon Gwri took the horn, and dropped seven drops
on the grindstone, and chanted the spell of Peace in the
midst of War, and began sharpening the brown feather.
More marvelously it grew under the screaming stridulence
of the grindstone even than the black feather had grown.
Louder and keener and fiercer was the sound of the turning
and the whizzing and wearing of the steel, and in turn it
would be sinking to hollower far gurglings and more slumberous undertones. Rising and falling, and surging and
swaying, and rippling and trilling, and swelling and whirling and triumphing, nearer and nearer it came to having the

semblance of music with it, and that the most martial and heroic music in the world, and not less courteous than martial. If any one had looked up at Aden Lonach at that time, here is what he would have seen with her: a lifting and spreading of her two wings, and a folding of them again, and a raising of her proud and gentle crowned head.

"Ah," said Gwri; "here is the sword."

Splendidly it gleamed in his hand, one long, flashing excellence of the color of the lightning of heaven. Its glance, its beam, its pure brightness, sent a ripple of delight and purification through the minds of the giants. They looked down at their weapons with repugnance; one by one they dropped them silently, desiring a more courteous warfare than they had known before. They remembered the warfare of the Gods, and hungered to wage the like of it, or none at all. "Ah! Ah!" they murmured; "wonderful and beautiful, truly, is the sword."

"Wonderful and beautiful it is," said the chieftain. Then he said: "What peculiarities are with it?"

"It would cut through the mote upon the sunbeam," said Gwri, taking pains to enumerate its gifts with precision. "Upon the downward sweep it would cleave through the mote lightly, and divide it in such a manner that the one half should be neither greater nor less than the other. Or it would shave the beard from a midget in the air upon an evening in August beside the stream in the valley; and that without causing wound or scratch or effusion of blood, or even knowledge in the shaved one that his beard had been shaven."

"Would it do that indeed?" said the chieftain.

"It would," said Gwri; "and would consider it no cause for boasting. No granite in the mountains of the world could withstand the edge of this sword, if it had a mind for cleaving things."

(No one that beheld it could have doubted that the sword was equal to this, and more than equal to it).

"Would it wound the wind?" said the chieftain. "Indeed, would it cause blood to flow from the invisible wind of heaven?"

"Ah, no," said Gwri. "Swords that have the lightning-colored sharpening have not attained that art."

The chieftain sighed. "Although the swords that thou hast made are good swords, and although little accusation could be brought against them, it is none other than the Wind-wounder that we desire."

"Thou shalt have it," said Gwri; and went again to his sharpening.

He took his horn, and poured the whole of the water in it on to the grindstone; and in place of the third feather from the fowl-house, took the feather of Aden Lonach that he had had from Tybie of the Fountain: "It will need the best of feathers for this work," thought he. No sooner had the tip of it touched the stone, than instead of stridulence and screaming, sweet, keen song rose up from it, keener and sweeter than the mountain lark's pennillion that he strews over the skies in the morning — a million times keener and sweeter. The sparks fled forth from the meeting of steel and stone, and rose up to the rafters, and were whirled hither and yonder, and played among the rafters in a fountain of many-colored flames; with the jewels in the mines of the world, or with the flowers of May upon the mountains, there would be no equaling them in glory or in beauty of hue. The giants drew near and watched him; as they beheld the sword grow, and the flame of the sparks kindle and gleam and lighten, they marveled in their delight, and murmured gently, and

forgot fighting and brutality, and desired beauty and peace.
The cage of Aden Lonach was enveloped in splendor, so that
no one was able to behold what light began to glow from it,
and to be resplendent, and to impart to the iron bars the
nature of the daffodil clouds of the dawn; no one was able
to behold the lightnings and glories irradiant through the
sky-beautiful wings and feathers of Llonach herself. Loud
and sweet and wonderful rose the song of the steel sword and
the stone; even the murmur of delight was quieted in the
giants. The music beat upon the roof like sea-spray in the
caves; the whole hall grew dizzy with the loud, keen, gleaming ecstasy of it; and still it grew keener and keener and
shriller and shriller and sweeter and sweeter.

"Ah!" said Gwri; "at last, here is a Sword."

It was as much as thirteen times as beautiful as either of
the others, and indeed, more than that. The gleam of the
sunlight on the shore-wave, on the curling, glittering breast
of it when it glitters and sparkles before the forming of foam,
would be dull and without beauty in its comparison. It was
neither blue like the noon, nor yellow and pale like the lightning of heaven. It seemed less a sword of steel or bronze,
than an intense gap of hard brightness in the midst of the
invisible air; more invisible, but for brightness, than the air
itself. *"Ah!"* murmured the giants; *"Ah! Ah!"* It seemed
to them all that they had never experienced delight until
then; if they remembered their old-time warfare, they remembered it with disgust, and shame, and repugnance.

"Marvelous it is, and beautiful beyond beauty," said the
chieftain. "Make known its peculiarities, if it please you."

"It is a Wind-wounder," said Gwri. "Beyond doubt,
its edge would wound the wind."

"Would it cause blood to flow from it?" said the chieftain.

"Without if or were-it-not," said Gwri. "Faster than the fall of the dewdrop from the blade of reed-grass in the morning, when the dew of June is at its heaviest."

"In the name of heaven, make trial of it," said the chieftain. "Never have I desired anything so much as to see this marvel."

"I will show thee," said Gwri. "And I will make known the third of my Three Arts likewise."

"What art is that?" said the chieftain.

"Song," said Gwri. "Song such as should cause grasshoppers to go against giants, and to overcome them."

With that he leaped up lightly upon the grindstone, and swept the sword circling through the air. The whole hall lightened and flashed at every sweep of it. Then he raised up the chant of Peace in the midst of War, loudly, so that every one should hear and be enspelled by it. Seven times the sword circled; there was no seeing its passage, but only the likeness of the sun of heaven resplendent above his head. Nearer and nearer flew the point to the cage where Llonach the Bird of Rhianon was imprisoned, where she fluttered and preened her wings, desiring to remember the art of song. At the seventh sweep of the sword, and the third raising of the chant, here is what happened; with extreme truth this is recorded. Diamond drops began to fall out of the air, diamond-colored blood out of the invisible wind, more swiftly than the fall of the dewdrop from the blade of reed-grass in the morning, when the dew of June is at its heaviest.

Then suddenly it was as if the full moon were to take wings, and to fly up into the midst of the sky against the blackness of the darkest night in the year. It was Aden Lonach upon the wing. With the rising of her delicate, transcendent splendor, song filled the caer, such as if it willed would have imposed sleep on an army of restless hellions;

or if it willed would have raised up an army of grasshoppers on the driest day in August to wage impetuous warfare against the giants of the ancient world, and a marvel if they did not overcome the giants. It was Llonach the Bird of Rhianon; it was she upon the wing, raising song. The sword had sundered the bars of her cage; the spell had brought her memory of her ancient skill in music. Her singing was a coolness for all aching, and the passing of desire and ferocity into peace.

She raised the song; she multiplied it marvelously; the notes of it, and their swaying and pouring and crooning, and their bewilderment of sweet, keen ecstasy, entered into the nature of the giants. From ill-favored they became fair; from uncouth and furious, noble of aspect and bearing. They became acquainted with delight, and peace, and wisdom. They heard the breaking of the gates of their caer without sorrow. Without fear they beheld the Princely Immortals enter. They saw the Immortals shine at the end of the hall, like the glory of a daffodil dawn, a daffodil and foxglove dawn above the mountains. They lifted their arms and sang, hailing the beautiful Immortals. The Immortals called them forth; they went out from the hall, following them. As they went, Gwri heard this verse from the giants:

We that have warred since, a slumbering clod,
This wild world woke to the Spoken Flame,
And felt in her heart the dreams of God,
And heard in her dream the Chanted Name,
We have felt the flame of a keener fire
Than kindleth ire in the wrath-ensouled;
We have heard the songs of the Dragon Choir,
And how shall we dwell where we dwelled of old?

And he heard this verse from the Immortals:

Sleep must wane, and the weltering world
Hither and yon be whirled in war;
And life be laved in the foam up-hurled
From passionate Abred's storm-tossed shore;
But always strife shall be merged in peace,
And the storm in calm, and the dawn grow gold;
A flame, a song — and the tumults cease,
And how shall ye dwell where ye dwelled of old?

And he heard this verse from the giants again, answering them:

How should we come to our warfare's goal,
Unknown of old, until night was drawn
Into this wonder of time made whole,
This peace in the daffodil heart of dawn?
We that have warred since the Chanted Name
Rolled in flame through the Primal Cold,
We have felt the breath of the quickening flame,
And how should we dwell where we dwelled of old?

III. THE QUEST OF ADEN FWYNACH THE THIRD BIRD, AND THE OPPOSITION OF THE HOSTS OF BARGOD Y BYD

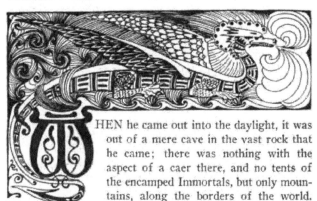

HEN he came out into the daylight, it was out of a mere cave in the vast rock that he came; there was nothing with the aspect of a caer there, and no tents of the encamped Immortals, but only mountains, along the borders of the world. He mounted Gyrru'r Gwyntoedd, and rode forward until he came to the Field of Llandybie.

It was evening when he came there, and the Well was under no spell of concealment from him. He dropped the sword, the Wind-wounder, into the Well; it turned into a blue feather and floated there, not different from what it had been at first. As soon as it touched the surface of the water, Tybie of the Fountain rose up before him.

"I marvel that you should come here," said she. "Aden Lonach is made free without your having freed her."

"Princess," said he; "not with the two that are freed, but with the one that is bound is my concern. For the sake of bringing success to Pryderi, will it be permitted to me to go in quest of Aden Fwynach?"

"Out of courtesy it will be permitted to you, and for no

better reason than that," said she. " There will be no success attainable for you."

" If it please you, give me news concerning this bird."

" There are better colors on her wings than in the rainbow, and her singing is more magical than any other sound in the world. On account of her pre-eminence, neither Glanach nor Llonach will allow themselves to be compared with Mwynach. Her music is the passing of the heart from its bondage, the fulfilment of the ultimate concerns of the soul. No one would obtain success at freeing her, except Pryderi fab Pwyll; and even he would not obtain it, unless he were master of the third of the Three Unusual Arts of the Gods and Druids."

" Yes, indeed," said Gwri. " It is known to me that he would need the Spell of the Three Places."

" What Three Places are they? " said she.

" Three Places in Wales, and the power of the Gods that dwell in them," said Gwri.

" You have not named them," said she.

" Rarely are they named," said he. " The first is the Wood of Mon, and the second is this Field — "

" Water from the Fountain I give you, and this feather that Aden Fwynach dropped here." It was like a little cloud out of the sunset for brightness and beauty. " Put you the feather on the wind in the morning, and go forward where it may lead you. And heed you this counsel," said she. " Let neither peace nor war turn you from this quest. And partake not of food nor drink, and give no ear to song nor story, in the place where you may hear lies spoken; for it is the nature of Aden Fwynach to abhor falsehood, and it would lead to spells being put upon you, as they were put upon her also on the day when you were born."

With that she was taken into the viewlessness again.

In the cold of the dawn and the youth of the day he rose up and went forward by ways unknown, following the feather. By mid-morning he passed the ford, and the marshland and mountains of Caer Hun; but turned not to the leftward. At noon he rode by the head of the valley where Caer Drais from of old had been besieged by the Immortals. But the feather had no mind for crossing the torrent there, and he rode on towards the east and upward, into the lonely places of the mountains.

The torrent grew smaller and smaller as he drew nearer to its source; from pouring and pondering over mossy rocks, it was now but rippling over pebbly shallows, and now no more than tinkling and whispering down the peaty softness of the mountain side. There all path came to an end, and only the wild, sweet breast of the mountain rose and rose above and before him. "Gyrru'r Gwyntoedd," said he, "there will be no traveling farther for you." "Whatever may please you," thought the Wind-driver; "there is good grazing here." There was no concealing thought, the one from the other, between those two. The feather still drifted and glimmered upward, and made no pretense of crossing the runlet; long he followed it, climbing the steep. At the very eye and birthplace of the waters, a place greener than the emerald and lovely with rush-tufts and forget-me-not blossom, a sudden gust carried it to the left, and it was clear there would be passing from the Island of the Mighty again. "Not without the moistening of eyelids," thought Gwri.

The foam and bewilderment of the world rose above him; innumerable swift dreams drove by like snowflakes on the wind. He heard the sound of rushing armies invisible above his head, a storm and torrent of swift loud hoofs and chariot wheels, a thunder and a grievous cry. It might have been the passing of ten ages before he felt the touch of his forefinger on his eyelids, and the moistening of them with the water of the Well. His feet were on firm ground again, and the Island of the Mighty was gone; but now there was no sudden vanishing of the mists, no cessation of bewilderment. What had been dim confusion took certitude and definition; the tumult of phantom armies came dropping down into a grim clamorous reality. He beheld the whirling smoke above him, filled with the rush and onsweep of the mighty; the cry that had been far and uncertain, became the hoarse roar of a warlike multitude. They gathered and circled, and drove downward and inward upon him. Gigantic chariots whirled and reeled and vanished; their scythes were of pale and subtle flame that leaped and flickered outward, licking the mists. Kneeling charioteers leaned forward, holding the reins; they were of stern, immortal beauty, dark flame upon their brows for hair. The warriors in the chariots leaned upon their immense spears of ashwood; their eyes far and flaming with visions of war, their lips apart, their throats strained with shouting. They gathered, whirling and circling, and drove on like the tempest, downward and nearer. Louder and louder grew the tumult, rarer the mist, prouder and sterner the menace of their aspect. Sunlight gleamed upon the spear-head, the ax-head, upon the long flaming brightness of the brand. Downward and inward, sweeping and circling they whirled, impetuous as the conflagration among the pine-trees of the valley, louder than the proud storm of the north. Streaming were their silken banners, with due adornment of lurid dragons. They were upon him; the immense chariots imminent, the menacing, flaming spears at point. There rose a shout, a crashing, a thunder, like the ninth tempest-driven billow upon the craggy headlands of the north. The sun shone out over a broad plain, and beyond it, over a lake of the width of the world. The feather

of Aden Fwynach hung in the air above the shore; there
was no sign nor rumor of an army anywhere. Gwri went
forward.

As he was nearing the shore he heard a sudden shout, and
beheld a chariot with its huge horses, motionless between him
and the shore; and in it behind the kneeling charioteer, a
warrior, dark, stern-visaged, handsome, and vaster in stature
than any in the world since the days of the Emperor Arthur.
Gwri knew him for one of the host that he had seen driving
down out of the air. The wings upon his helmet were of
lurid flame. His long, wind-blown mantle was dark crimson,
and fastened with a brooch of rubies; his coat was of dark
blue linen, adorned with silver ornaments of the value of
fifty kine.

" The greeting of the god and the man to you," said Gwri
Gwallt Euryn.

" The greeting of the god and the man to you also," said
the warrior. " Go back, if it please you, to the Island of the
Mighty, while life remains in your body."

" Courteously I refuse this request," said Gwri. " I came
here following yonder feather, and following it I will go forward beyond the border of the world."

" There will be no going forward without encountering
the opposition of hosts."

" Make known to me what hosts they will be, if it please
you."

" Mighty and invincible hosts they will be; the men of
the King of Bargod y Byd," said the warrior. " Yonder is
the Lake of the Bargod, and beyond it is Caer Hedd; therein
dwells a company of the Immortals that have known no strife
since the Crying of the Name. It would be unfitting that
their delight should be broken by men from the Island of
the Mighty, and therefore no one may pass the lake without

overcoming the whole host of the Bargod; and it would not be possible for any man to overcome them."

"Opposition I desire, and extreme fighting, and not to go forward until usage shall have been complied with."

With that the warrior came down out of his chariot. "I am the King's Distain of Bargod y Byd," said he. "It is my right to be the first upon the field of conflict, and to encounter the stranger, body against body, before any other man of the host shall encounter him."

"It will be an honor to me to make combat with you," said Gwri. Thereupon he made bare his breast for the battle, according to the custom of the Gods and men of the Island of the Mighty. He raised the Dragon Shout, and went forward against the distain, and the distain against him. Body against body, they fought upon the shore until nightfall; it seemed to Gwri that he had dwelt in profound peace from the moment of his birth until then. At nightfall he slew the distain, and made a pile of his armor on the shore.

Then he turned to the charioteer. "Take you the armor," said he, "and bear it for a gift to the King of the Bargod."

He did so; and as soon as the armor was loaded upon the chariot, man and car and horses vanished. Then there came up out of the water another chariot, drawn by two immense, pearl-white, dimly luminous steeds. It was three times larger than the chariot of the distain, and formed of dark bronze adorned with shining sapphires. The warrior that stood in it was vaster of stature than the other, more handsome, prouder and darker of mien. His long mantle blew out from his shoulders towards the lake; it was of the color of pearl and mother-o'-pearl, and shone wanly in the dusk of the evening; on it was embroidered a carmine, ramping, fierce-eyed dragon, brighter and redder than the sunset cloud. His brooch was of the size of a king's breastplate, a vast, light-giving carnelian set with opals. His helmet glowed and burned against the night-sky, redder than the rising harvest moon. As for the spear whereon he leaned, it was a long, lithe, keen, impatient gainer of victories.

"The greeting of the god and the man to you," said Gwri Gwallt Euryn.

"Good greeting to you also," said the other. "Yonder upon the hill is the guest-house," said he; "and therein there is feasting prepared for you tonight, and the songs of seven skilful institutional bards, and a bed of skins and silk upon the sleeping-bench. With the dawn of the morning you shall be free to go back into the Island of the Mighty if it please you; or if it please you, you shall experience fighting here."

"May it be requited to you for this excellent courtesy," said Gwri; "I will experience the fighting. And may it be requited better, if the courtesy is extended."

"In what way might it be extended?"

"Rest is better after labor than before it," said Gwri. "Were I given my free choice, I would have the fighting first."

"You shall have it," said the other, "and no cause for complaint of stint; ample fighting shall you have. Where one opposed you in the daytime, ten shall make war upon you during the night, and the least of them stronger, and more valiant, and better at strategy than the man you have slain. I am the Penteulu of the War-host of the King of Bargod y Byd," said he; "it will be my right and privilege to be the tenth man at the head of them."

Thereupon he turned towards the lake, and sounded the hai atton of the men of the Bargod upon his horn; and having sounded it, came down out of his chariot. Nine

stern, tall, princely warriors rose up out of the lake, and came
forward. They were equal in strength and beauty, and in
richness of dress and armor, to their lord the penteulu. The
dullest of their ten horned helmets glowed like the crimson
setting sun. The poorest of their glimmering, pearl-pale
mantles was embroidered with a ruby-colored, rose-rich
dragon. The least of their keen, silver-headed spears would
have been capable of victories on the confines of hell. Courteously they greeted Gwri; courteously in return he greeted
them.

"It is a delight to us," they said, "to afford you this
warfare; we take pleasure in your pleasure of being one man
against ten."

"Greater will be the honor of opposing you," said he,
"than would be the honor of opposing a hundred mortals."

Then he raised up the Dragon Shout, and went forward
against them; and the ten of them went forward against
him, and the penteulu the tenth at the head of them. He
remembered the warfare he had waged against the distain;
it seemed to him to have been a peaceful and soothing dream.
He slew three of them before the rising of the moon. He
slew three of them between her rising and her setting. He
slew three in the darkness before the dawn. At dawn he
slew the penteulu also and made ten piles of their armor
beside the shore.

Then he turned to the charioteer of the penteulu, that
waited in the chariot. "Take you the armor for a gift to
the King of the Bargod," said he. The charioteer came down
and gathered up the armor; as soon as it was loaded in the
chariot, man and car and horses vanished.

"Will there be going forward now?" thought Gwri;
and turned towards the dawn-white water. As he turned,
a vast chariot rose up out of the lake, drawn by two beauti-

ful, mist-gray steeds, compared with which the horses of the penteulu were no better than ill-kept yearling foals. The chariot was three times greater than the chariot of the penteulu had been; it was formed of unpolished silver inlaid with turquoise stones for the sake of adornment and magical virtue. The warrior that stood in it was three times more handsome and better equipped than the penteulu; and he was greater in stature. His long, wind-blown, silken mantle was of the color of the sky, with whiteness of clouds drifting and wandering over it. His swan-winged, beautiful, regal helmet was of silver, whiter than the Wyddfa when the sunlight glitters on the snows of January on it. His brooch was of peerless pearl, and it was larger than a warrior's shield. The well-combed hair hung down over his shoulders, darker and more lustrous than the starling's wing. His shield was one great gleaming moon of silver; the sight of his spear alone would have put the leagued and hosted demons of Abred to flight.

"The greeting of heaven and man to you, in princely courtesy and warlike kindliness," said Gwri Gwallt Euryn.

"Even better be it to you than to me," said the other. "I am the King's Heir of Bargod y Byd, and I come to counsel you to return to the Island of the Mighty before harm befall you."

"Courteous is the counsel," said Gwri; "and courteously it will be refused."

"Even if it be refused," said the king's heir, "there is further courtesy to follow it. The King of the Bargod has received the gifts of armor that you have sent him, and he desires to requite you for them regally. For that reason the need of fighting will not be imposed upon you today, nor tomorrow, nor until such time as you may desire it. Yonder on the hill is the guest-house; therein you shall feast until noon and drink until night, when food for a hundred men shall be set before you. There shall be ten skilful institutional bards to sing verses to you, and ten more to relate stories; and whensoever you may desire rest, there shall be silk and furs laid upon an ivory sleeping-bench for you, and the ivory inlaid with bronze and opals."

"Rarely have I been offered the like of this regal courtesy," said Gwri. "May it be requited to you profusely; and may it be requited to you even better, if the courtesy is extended."

"What extension might there be, in the name of heaven?"

"Rest after labor is better than rest before it," said Gwri. "I shall have little appetite for feasting, until I have crossed and re-crossed yonder lake."

"There will be no crossing of it, without encountering opposition first," said the king's heir.

"I should enjoy the feasting better, if I came to it after encountering the opposition," said Gwri.

"It shall be according to your desire," said the king's heir. "Where you opposed ten in the night, you will encounter a hundred during the day, and the worst of them stronger and fiercer and more skilful than the best of the ten, and I myself will be the hundredth at the head of them."

"This will be a main privilege for me," said Gwri. "An unwonted delight will it be, indeed."

Thereupon the king's heir of the Bargod came down out of his chariot and blew the hai atton on his horn. For answer there came a mighty warshout, and a company of nineteen and fourscore men came running up out of the lake. In strength and beauty of aspect, in dignity of mien and splendor of accoutrements, they were none of them less than their lord the king's heir. With extreme courtesy they greeted Gwri, and not less courteously he greeted them. Any one would have known that they were all the sons of sovereign rulers, accustomed to wars upon the borders of the world. As soon as the greetings were finished, they formed in battle-array on the shore. Gwri raised the Dragon Shout, and went forward blithely against them, and they went forward against him. The least of them were much better men than the best of the men of the penteulu. Exceedingly vehement was their onslaught; with exceeding vehemence Gwri opposed them. He slew twenty of them before noon, and twenty more between noon and dusk. Between dusk and moonrise he slew twenty, and twenty before the moon set. Between that and dawn the twenty that were left gathered together their strength, and remembered their prowess, and thundered upon him a rage to shake the mountains. Man by man he put quietude upon them, and released them from their bodies, and at dawn he slew the king's heir also. Then he made ten huge, glittering piles of their armor upon the beach, and gave them to the charioteer to take to the king.

"There will be no need for him to take them," said a voice from the lake. "I myself am here to receive them, and to give thee counsel also."

Gwri turned, and beheld a chariot drawn up out of the lake by three immense, chestnut-colored stallions of supreme strength and beauty. With every motion of their shell-formed hoofs, they raised up waves of spray and foam as high as the shaft of the chariot. The dawn sun burned upon their burning, tossing manes. The chariot was of gold, richly adorned with precious rubies. He that stood in it, leaning on his golden, flame-bright, terrible spear, was huger of form and limb, sterner and nobler of bearing, loftier of beauty, and more magnanimous of soul than any of the

others had been. His winged helmet was brighter than the
noon sun. His hair and his long beard were of the color of
the wheat-field at bright noonday, three days before the harvest. His long mantle was more purple than the purple-
flowing wave; on it was embroidered a regal dragon in the
purest gold. His brooch was of diamonds, topazes and rubies. His coat was of woven gold, ruddier than the gold of
the dragon. His breastplate was like the sun; the sheath of
his sword brighter than the lightning.

"The greeting of the god and the man to the King of
the Bargod," said Gwri. "Courteously and with respect is
it given. Make known to me the counsel, if it please you."

"Courteous and honorable be the greeting to you also,"
said the King of the Bargod. "The counsel will be, that you
return to the Island of the Mighty, after receiving courtesy
and entertainment here, and before the nature of war and
strife and fighting is made known to you."

"Courteous and kindly is the counsel," said Gwri.
"Courteously and in a kindly manner will it be refused. I
came here for the sake of going forward, after encountering
what opposition might be prepared."

"Opposition you shall have, at the hands of a thousand
men," said the king; "and I myself will be the thousandth
at the head of them. The puniest of them all will be ten
times better and stronger than any of the men you have
slain."

"An exceptional delight and honor will this be to me,
truly," said Gwri.

"Without stint or reservation it shall be accorded to
you; all the battles you have fought hitherto shall seem like
peace and quietude in comparison with this. But first courtesy shall be extended to you, in accordance with custom,
and in consideration of your valor and generosity and mighty

deeds. I myself will accompany you to the guest-house, and therein you shall abide for seven days and seven nights. Each day I shall see that collops cooked and peppered are set before you, and an abundance of luscious wine and mead; food for fifty men in the morning, and food for a hundred at night. Each day there shall be seven-score skilful, wise institutional bards, the best in the world, to sing songs to you, and seven-score more to relate stories; and at dawn and at sunset you shall bathe in a cauldron of cure to strengthen you; and there shall be a sleeping-bench of gold for you at night, inlaid with the turquoise and encrusted with the diamond; greater will its value be than the value of ten thousand kine, and on it shall be spread coverings of embroidered silk, and pictures of the Gods and of dragons worked upon them; and beneath the coverings, the down of sea-birds deeper than the height of a man."

" Excellent is this courtesy indeed," said Gwri; " may it be requited to you in ample measure; may you lack hereafter nothing that you desire. Hardly might such hospitality be surpassed even in the Island of the Mighty; even in the house of the King of London; yet it might be surpassed."

" Make known to me how it might be surpassed," said the king, " and out of gratitude, nothing shall be refused to you."

" It might be surpassed in this way," said Gwri. " Rest after exertion is pleasant and honorable; but rest before it is a sorrow to the brave. Disgrace would fall upon the whole kindred of the Cymry, were I to accept feasting before experiencing warfare. I came not here for the sake of consuming food, truly. If the fighting might continue without intermission, the courteous hospitality you have offered me would be surpassed."

" Be it requited to you for making this known to me,"

said the king. " The courtesy shall be extended in accordance with your desires." Thereupon he lifted a dazzling horn
of diamond to his lips, and sounded the hai atton of the
Bargod; and having sounded it, came down out of his chariot.
The lake side lighted with the glory of a thousand dawns;
nine hundred and nineteen and four score were the men that
came up out of the water. The smallest of them was huger
of stature than the king's heir had been; the poorest in
adornment shone more resplendently. Courteously they
greeted Gwri; courteously in return he greeted them. Noble
were the words they spoke concerning the men of the Island
of the Mighty; noble words he spoke again concerning the
magnanimity and lofty lineage of the men of Bargod y Byd.
It seemed to them all that his friendship or his enmity would
be equally delightful to them; it seemed to him that it would
be equally pleasant to him to oppose them in conflict or to
feast with them in the hall.

" Will it please you that the strife should have its opening?" said they.

" It will," said he.

With that they drew up in battle array on the shore, and
sounded the warshout of the Bargod; and Gwri raised up
the Shout of the Dragon, and mutually they went forward
against each other. Proud and vehement was the flight of
spears; hosted Abred would have been frightened at the
sight of it. But he made circles about him with his sword,
and reaped the heads from the spears as they flew. Such
were his skill and strength and courage, and his complete
valor, and the learning he had obtained from Twrf Fliant his
foster-father, and the lofty, indomitable nature of his soul,
that they obtained no success or advantage against him. He
fought until noon and slew two hundred; he fought until
dusk and slew three hundred more. Between dusk and mid-

night he put quietude upon two hundred and fifty of them. Between that and dawn, the two hundred and fifty that were remaining gathered their strength, and remembered their old-time exploits and renown, and came against him in such a manner that it seemed to him that they had been at playful sport until then. Man by man he prevailed against them, and reaped them, and caused them to quit their bodies in delight at the nature of the fighting they had experienced. By dawn he had slain two hundred and two score and nine.

"Are you content with the fighting?" said he.

"I am not content," said the King of the Bargod; "even though it has been such fighting as I have not remembered. There will be no going forward for you until I am slain also."

They went forward with their fighting until the sun had shaken himself free from the edge of the world, and shone wanly over the mist-hidden waters. "Are you content now?" said Gwri Gwallt Euryn.

"Indeed, I am content, being slain," said the King of the Bargod. Then he said, "Pleasant is death to me truly, having become at last acquainted with the nature of fighting and war. Delightful it is to me to have received this satisfaction."

With that he rose up unwearied from his slain body; and he and the whole of his host were taken into the viewlessness. As for Gwri, he went up to the guest-house, and bathed in the cauldron of cure, and ate what food he needed, and slept for three days and three nights without waking. Here is what was made known to him in his sleep and dreams: he saw the King of the Bargod, and the king's heir, and the penteulu, and the lordly distain, and the whole of their proud, magnanimous host; they circled about him in the air, driving their flame-rich chariots; unwounded they had arisen; in great splendor they went forth, circling, wheeling,

flaming, raising song. Here is the song they raised, so far
as he was able to remember it afterwards:

Though we were slain full many a time,
  Full many a time have we risen again;
He that would harken the ages' rhyme
  Must meet us here by the border main,
Must bare his breast to the spears sublime
  Till the mortal life in his life be slain.

And some shall fail for a thousand years,
  And some shall win in a night and day;
And the eyes of some shall be blind with tears,
  And the hearts of some shall be always gay;
But come they singing, or dumbed with fears,
  They shall win, ere they wend their onward way.

And he that comes and is slain on the shore,
  Shall he meet no more with the Guardian Clan?
Hath he come to the peace at the end of war,
  The peace that was ere the worlds began?
Nay, — age on age shall the combat roar,
  Till that which was man is more than man.

For we that bide by the brink of time,
  That have fallen so oft, and arisen again,
Should we leave unhedged with our spears sublime
  The world's far edge — should we rest, being slain,
The ages were reft of their rhythm and rhyme,
  And the star in the heart of the world would wane.

IV. THE THREE KINSMEN OF THE FERRYMAN OF THE LAKE OF THE BARGOD, AND THE SPELL OF THE THREE PLACES IN WALES

AT the dawn of the fourth morning he awoke, and rose up stronger than ever he had been in his life, and went down to the shore. The waters of the lake were hued like the turquoise and the beryl, clearer and sweeter than any waters in mortal lands. Neither to the right nor to the left was there any sign of boundary or limit to them; nor was there any farther shore visible between the lake and the sky before him. The feather of Aden Fwynach, that had floated in the air without falling since he came to the Bargod, now drifted out from land, blown by the gentlest wind in the world. " There must be crossing this sea," he said; " and a marvel if there is no ferry."

Then he shouted: " Is there a ferryman? " " There is," came the cry. It seemed as if a pink rose dropped from heaven on to the far water, and began to glow and grow there. Out of the heart and middle glory of it, a boat drew towards the shore; it was shaped like the petal of a wild rose from the hedgerows of Cemais, and fashioned of one great, luminous rose-pearl, of beautiful curves and lines. In the boat stood the ferryman, dark, quiet-eyed, of subtle grace and dignity; he was one of the Beautiful Family of Gwyn the son of Nudd, and for hair on his head he had plumes of azure flame.

"The greeting of heaven and of man to you," said Gwri Gwallt Euryn. "Will there be any crossing the lake?"

"There will," said the ferryman; "and you shall not be chargeable for it." With that he drew in to the shore, and Gwri went into the boat with him.

"If it please you," said Gwri; "I desire to follow yonder feather."

"We will follow it," said the ferryman. He sat down in the front of the boat, and began his rowing. They went forward until noon in silence; then the ferryman said:

"Have you come here from the Island of the Mighty?"

"I have," said Gwri.

"There was a kinsman of mine dwelling there in the days of the Emperor Arthur," said the ferryman. "He was a man of whom no one ever spoke less than good. I desire to hear tidings of him."

"What name was with your kinsman?" said Gwri.

"Ol the son of Olwydd, according to his nature," said the ferryman. "Seven years before he was born, his father's swine were stolen; and when he grew up to be a man, he tracked the swine through the three worlds, and brought them back in seven herds without losing one of them. He had a keen sense of smell. He could track the bee from the blossom to the hive three days after her gathering the honey; and he could tell whether she had taken it from the rose or from the

meadowsweet, from the hawthorn or from the heather. The
path of last year's salmon through the sea, Ol could easily
follow it swimming blindfold. Indeed now," said he, " I
should be discourteous beyond bounds if I permitted you to
remain longer without hearing the story of Ol."

Thereupon he began narrating it with marvelous bardic
skill, chanting it, and weaving it together with pleasant consonances and assonances, delightful to the hearing. As he
went forward with it, the air darkened with pansies blooming out of invisibility, reddened with crimson roses that had
no stem nor root. The scent of them spread out over the
lake; it filled the whole region between the water and the
sky; it was sweeter than honey; it was far sweeter than
honey. Sweet and heavy, laden with soft heaviness, it
breathed out from the purple of the pansies, from the rich
imperial crimson of the roses. The ferryman stopped his
rowing, that he might have his two hands free for narrating
the story. With pleasant consonance and assonance, with
delightful rhythm, he unfolded the achievements of the son
of Olwydd, and multiplied the slumber-laden breathing of
the flowers. Sleep came drifting down about the boat. The
scent of roses and pansies rose up like mists along the edge
of the world in the evening; there was no seeing the feather
where it floated in the air; the boat followed it no longer,
but wandered northward with the current. " There must
be an end of this narrating the story of Ol," thought Gwri.

" The third day," said the ferryman, " he came into the
Cantref of Mabwnion, and there was a caer there — "

" Not so," said Gwri; " it was not to the Cantref of Mabwnion that he came."

" Wherefore sayest thou this? " said the ferryman, and
sighed.

" Out of regard for accuracy, and the art of story-tell-

ing," said Gwri. (And true it was, that Ol was never in the
Cantref of Mabwnion during his life, so far as there is knowing). "Although he came not to Mabwnion, either on the
third day or on the fourth, yet it was to a place in Wales
that he came; and indeed, to three places. Unless the nature
of them were known, no one could tell the story."

"What was the nature of them?" said the ferryman.
"What places were they, in the name of heaven?"

"I will make the first of them known to you," said Gwri,
"that you may relate this story accurately from this out."
Then he brought into his mind the power of the Spell of the
Three Places, and whispered it on the wind; and as he did
so, dipped his right forefinger into the horn. "Look you
now," said he; "and further, give you heed!" Therewith
he shook out his forefinger at the ferryman, to cause heeding and remembrance in him; and it happened that, with
the shaking, a drop of the water fell on the ferryman's forehead. "The place that he came to on the third day was the
Wood of Mon," said he; "it was the Wood of Mon, by the
power of the Gods that dwell there."

Sleep and all sweet scent and dimness were blown away
in an instant from the face of the lake; the feather shone
again in the air to the south and east of them, and the boat
turned of its own will to follow it. "Ah!" said the ferryman, sighing; "the story is known to thee. We will go
forward."

"And well it was that the story was known to me,"
thought Gwri; "and well that it was to the Wood of Mon
that he came."

They went forward in silence until the sky was aflame
with the sunset behind them, and the feather gleamed pale
like a rising star in the opal dimness of the east. The ferry-

man stopped his rowing, and fell to musing and cogitation.
" Wherefore stay you your rowing? " said Gwri.

" Considering I was," said the ferryman. " Seeking remembrance what island it was you left, before you came to
the Lake of the Bargod."

" It was the Island of the Mighty," said Gwri.

" If you come from that island," said the ferryman; " I
should desire to learn from you tidings concerning a kinsman
of mine that dwelt there in the days of the Emperor Arthur,
if you know any."

" What name was with your kinsman? "

" Clust," said the ferryman; " Clust fab Clustfeinydd,
truly. He was a musician. If he were buried fifty cubits
beneath the earth, he could hear the ant when she rose from
her nest in the morning, as far as from Gelliwic in Cornwall
to Pen Blathaon in North Britain. He could hear the dew
falling, and the wheat ripening, and the star shining, and the
rose breaking into bloom. He could hear the language of the
pilchard and the salmon. He could hear the hammer and
chisel of the bee, when she builds a storeroom for her plunder
from the flowers. Also he could hear the imagination of the
oak-tree. Evil be upon me, if I refuse to relate to you this
story."

Thereupon he began it. Music rose up in the east and in
the west, and floated and drifted towards them over the pearl-
pale water. It came from the roses and gold of the west, as
if the sun were harping beyond the brim of the world; marvelous spells, secret, druidic, mystery-laden music, drifted in
towards them over the rosy-rippling water. It came from
the blue dimness of the east, as if night were harping beyond
the brim of the world; as if seven secret enchanters were
whispering spells there; cold, lone whisperings of music,
more melodious than dream, drifted in towards them over

the wavering turquoise of the water. The ferryman forgot his oar, that he might have his two hands free for narrating the story. The boat forgot her following the feather, and wandered southward with the current. The feather herself forgot her glimmering in the east. The story of Clust was seventeen times better than the story of Ol; and the art and skill of the ferryman were seventeen times greater in relating it. No words but were linked together with subtle consonance and assonance and rhyme. With the music of his voice, his chanting, the whole lake became slumberous and a mystery. The power in the music for raising slumber was seventeen times greater than the power in the scent of the flowers had been. Drowsiness overtook the pallid stars, and the wan sickle of the moon at her rising. "There must be an end of this narrating the story of Clust," thought Gwri Gwallt Euryn.

"He came to Caer Deirtu in the Cantref of Gwinionydd, on the thirteenth day," said the ferryman, "and as soon as he came into the valley of the caer, he heard music from the Harp of Teirtu —"

"Woe is me for my birth and pre-existences," said Gwri. "There is no sorrow in the world so keen and bitter to me, as the hearing of lies and inaccuracy."

The ferryman sighed deeply. "What lies or inaccuracy were you hearing?" said he.

"Inaccuracy in the relating of this story," said Gwri. "Heaven knows it was not in Caer Deirtu, nor in the Cantref of Gwinionydd that he heard that harp; and he did not come there during his whole life, so far as is known, much less did he come there on the thirteenth day. Yet it was to a place in Wales that he came; and indeed, to three places."

"I marvel that you should say this," said the ferryman. "What places were they, since it is known to you?"

Without concealment or inexactitude Gwri answered him; it was unlikely that a foster-son of Twrf Fliant should have been without knowledge. " The first was the Wood of Mon," said he; " I made known that to you before. Now heed you what the second of them was." He whispered the Spell on the wind, and caused the power of it to be like an unseen mist in the air about them. Then he shook out his finger at the ferryman again, to enforce heeding and remembrance of what should be revealed; and with that, shook out water from the horn on to his breast. " The second place was a Field," said he. " The Field of the Fountain of Tybie at Llandybie it was, by the power of the Gods that dwell there."

In a moment the whole marvel of music went shuddering down and away into silence. The boat turned of its own will to follow the feather, that shone now like a little moon low in the heavens eastward. The ferryman picked up his oar from the bottom of the boat, and went forward with his rowing. " The story is known to you already," he said, and sighed even more sorrowfully than before.

During that night they traversed the water in silence, and at dawn there was no land to be seen anywhere, either in front or behind them. At an hour after dawn the ferryman was taken with musing and meditation again, so that he paused in his rowing.

" Wherefore is there pausing? " said Gwri Gwallt Euryn.

" Considering and cogitating I was," said the ferryman. " Is it from the Island of the Mighty that you come? "

" Indeed, it is from the Island of the Mighty," said Gwri.

" It would be better to me than receiving gifts," said the ferryman; " and that though they were generously given, by one accustomed to ample bounteousness, and neither stint nor afterthought in the giving, nor expectation of return — if I might obtain news of a kinsman of mine that dwelt in that island in the days of the Emperor Arthur. From that time until now I have heard no tidings of him, and it is unknown to me whether he is alive or dead."

"What?" said Gwri, "have you three kinsmen?"

"I have," said the ferryman; "and the third was dearer to me, and more gifted than either of the others; and his mind was of a more penetrating quality. Drem the son of Dremidyd was the name with him," said he; "he was an astronomer. When the gnat arose in the morning with the sun, Drem could see her from the top of Pengwaed in Cornwall to the bottom of Dinsol in the North; and furthermore, he could easily count the hairs of her beard. Of a winter's night, when the sky was cloudiest, it would be easy to him to count the stars of heaven, both the brighter and the dimmer ones."

While he was talking, the air above the lake bloomed out into flowers lovelier of aspect than the wild March daffodil, than the foxglove of Garth Maelor, than the blossom of the meadowsweet beside the river, than the frail, white woodanemone beside the meadow fountain. The waters about them glowed and burned with the hues of the opal, the ruby and the amethyst. Faces looked up out of the waves, of such beauty as might blind the eye that beheld them; faces looked down out of the unclouded sky, whose beauty might have caused strife among the holy Druids of the Gorsedd. The ferryman laid down his oar that he might free his two hands for the story; the boat began drifting backwards with the current to the west. Seven times greater was the peril of dreams and forgetfulness then, even than it had been before; on account of the potency of the faces in the waves and in the sky, and of the slumber-laden spell in the blossoms. "Indeed, indeed," thought Gwri; "there must be preventing this relating the story of Drem fab Dremidyd."

"Listen you now while I make this known to you," said the ferryman; "accurately and with extreme veracity shall it be told." He chanted it with such bardic skill, as made the skill he had used before seem mere ignorance and uncouth narration. "From Gelliwic," said he, "Drem could, in a twinkling, shoot the wren between the two legs upon Esgair Oerfel in Ireland, and that either by day or by night, either with eyes open or with eyes closed."

"Woe is me!" said Gwri; "what sorrow is this wherewith I am afflicted."

"What sorrow is it?" asked the ferryman.

"Accurate veracity you promised me, in the narration of this story; and what you are saying is but half true and half untrue."

"It seemed to me that it was true," said the ferryman, mournfully.

"It is not true," said Gwri. "Not from Gelliwic could he shoot the wren; his eyesight was not equal to that."

"From whence was it that he could shoot her, in heaven's name?" said the ferryman.

"From a place in Wales it was; indeed, from three places. He was such a one, that it would have been beneath his dignity to have traveled in other lands. It is a marvel to me that you should not have known this."

"I knew it not," said the ferryman. "What places were they?"

"The first and the second I made known to you before; they were the Wood of Mon, and the Field of Tybie, at Llandybie in Iscennen; marvelous is your power at forgetting." Then he dipped his finger again, making the power of the Spell. "Heed now what the third place was," said he; and shook out his finger to enforce it, causing water from the fountain to fall upon the crown of the ferryman's head. "It was the Wyddfa Mountain in Gwynedd, and in Arfon, that it was," said he; " and in the four quarters of the world there is not the equal of it, and hath not been, and will not be throughout the age of ages. The Wyddfa Mountain it was, by the power of our Father Hu Gadarn that dwells there. Those were the Three Places," said he; " heed you them, and remember, and it shall be the better for you while you remain alive: the Wood, the Field, and the Mountain."

"Alas!" sighed the ferryman; "this also is known to you. We will come to land."

V. THE SPELL OF THE WOOD, THE FIELD, AND
THE MOUNTAIN, AND THE FREEING OF ADEN
FWYNACH AT LAST

T was midway between dawn and noon when
Gwri landed and set forth to journey over
sunlit hills and valleys of apple-trees; an
orchard vaster than any in the world at that
time; and if vaster, more beautiful. It was
the peculiarity of the trees that they
were adorned with clouds of bloom, the
white bloom and the pink; and not only
bloom, but green young apples; and
furthermore, ruddy golden fruit such as
even the unhungry and ungluttonous
would desire. Amidst them the linnet
flitted perpetually, and ousels gifted
with supernatural song; and the missel-
thrush perched on the branches, strew-
ing penillion. There would be lawns and valley-bottoms,
beauteous with a million daffodils; and beneath the trees,
flaming hosts of the crocus, purple and white and saffron;
such beauty and delight have hardly been made known to
the eye of man at any time. On among the apple-bloom,
through the bird-music, the feather drifted shining; and
beauty and music increasing, increasing, with every step that
he took following it. When the sun was nearing the west of
heaven, he came to the edge of the orchard and looked down
over a soft, lawny valley, not deep; beyond it rose a palace
glowing against the sunset, that had the appearance of being
built of the rose-pearl and the mellow topaz. On the lawn
before the palace were a hundred youths and a hundred
maidens; their laughter was without loudness or harshness,

their motions fairer than the motions of the swan upon the lake, statelier than the motions of the crane in the marshland. The least and worst of them was equal in grace and beauty to the best of the Family of Gwyn ab Nudd who ride the night winds and the water foam among the mountains, and enjoy unbroken beauty and merriment until the Day of Doom. With dignified courtesy they met him, and greeted and praised him; commenting upon the fame and noble lineage of the men of the Island of the Mighty, and desiring that it would please him to quit wandering, and abide there with them in delight from that out.

They led him towards the door of the palace; " for the feast will be prepared," said they. At the door as he was going in with them, the feather of Aden Fwynach lighted down in his breast, and he knew that the bird herself would be within. Richer and more beautiful was everything that he saw there than anything he had attained seeing until then. Never should the footsole fall upon the flagstone, by reason, not of strewn rushes, but of rich skins of the bear and the beaver, of beautiful skins from the east and west of the world. Never should the eye behold the wall, by reason of armor carven of the amethyst and the diamond, and of priceless hangings of silk and taffeta adorned with stories of Ceugant, Gwynfyd, and Abred, the Three Circles of the World.

On the dais at the head of the hall the King of Caer Hedd was enthroned. His throne was of sun-kindled amethyst, and the mere setting eyes on it was equal in satisfaction to having seven ships of wealth and merchandise in the harbor, after their wandering the wide waters, and meeting with neither harm nor loss. On his head was a crown with nine proud acorns of polished diamond in it, the least of which, for pure beauty, was beyond the evening or the morning star; there was more satisfaction in looking at the crown, than in winning seven victories over war-wise sovereigns. As for the king himself, there was no one in the hall that was the equal of him, or nearly the equal of him, either for an aspect of serene dignity, or for handsomeness of visage, or for the knowledge of weaving spells, or for the power and peril of them when they were woven. Here is the likeness of him, so far as it may be given: his hair and beard were long and curling, and yellower than the outer petals on the bloom of the daffodil; his voice was more harmonious, and of sweeter modulation, than the coo and croon and rippling murmur of a runlet amid the rushes, in a peaty field on the mountain. His dark and starry eyes were now bright with a laughter beyond sound, now far and dimly glimmering with quietude and dreams of arcane magical beauty.

But if it should be thought that there was a cage above his throne, and Aden Fwynach imprisoned in it, false that thought would be, for there was no cage there. The whole hall was melodious with bird-music, as if there were a thousand such as she there; and indeed, unnumbered twinkling, jewel-luminous birds were flitting and sweeping and gleaming among the rafters, keeping alive their rich, harmonious, dream-wild confluence of sounds continually. They were all of them equal in beauty to the Birds of Rhianon; no one would have known if Mwynach were among them or not.

" The greeting of the god and the man to the King of Caer Hedd," said Gwri Gwallt Euryn.

" The best of greetings, and the kindliest of welcomes to you also," said the king. "As long as you remain in the caer, there shall be courtesy and entertainment, feasting and music for you; and when the gifts are given to the guests in the morning, they shall be in your hands at the beginning; and neither on the third day nor in the third year will it be asked of you to make known the nature of your quest."

" May it be requited to you for this courtesy," said Gwri.
" Less than fitting would it be, were I not to make it known
to you now. I come here as an ambassador from Tybie the
daughter of Hu, from the Well at Llandybie, in quest of
Aden Fwynach the Bird of Rhianon. Her music is the passing of the heart from its bondage, the fulfilment of the ultimate concerns of the soul; and therefore it is an ill thing for
the Island of the Mighty to be without her."

" There are a thousand birds here whose music is that,
and more than that," said the king. " We have never heard
even a rumor of Aden Fwynach."

" It is the place where falsehood is spoken," thought Gwri.
Thereupon they sat down to meat.

" Let the place of the king's heir of Caer Hedd be given
to this chieftain of the Cymry," said the king. " Let every
one that opens and shuts the eye, and every one that beholds
the light, show him respect, and serve him. Let not collops
cooked and peppered be lacking to him."

The feasting went forward, and Gwri in the place of the
king' heir opposite to the king. Neither among the foster-
sons of Teyrnion Twrf Fliant, nor in the court of the
Crowned King in London, when the chief bards and princes
of the Island of the Mighty were gathered there; neither in
Europe nor in Africa nor in the Islands of Corsica, had he
seen food of such delicate aspect so well served in such beautiful food-vessels. Always during the feasting and conversation, the birds amidst the rafters strewed forth their low,
sweet, harmonious utterance; neither so loud as to break
across the spoken word or the laughter, nor so quiet as not
to come between those and silence, and adorn every one of
them with such adornment as the foxglove has from the
mountain hedgerow; or the green shore-wave from the gleaming sand before, and the glittering, unstable, purple-running

blueness behind it; or the turquoise stones of Asia from their
place in the bronze brooch of a war-loving king; or the song
of the blackbird at dawntime, from the motions of the breeze
amid the sun-dappled leafage, in the green and wildwood
palaces of May.

The King of Caer Hedd looked at Gwri, and saw that
he left the best of the food untouched; that was vexation to
the king, by reason of the magical subtleties in the food; whoever might eat it, it would cause forgetfulness in him of the
places where he had played in his boyhood, and of the faces
that had been about him in the world.

"What troubles the mind of the foster-son of Teyrnion?" said he. "What troubles the mind of the prince
from Ynys Wen? The most delicate food is as little desirable to you, as chaff and stubble from the fields of September
after the harvest."

"Excellent it is truly," said Gwri Gwallt Euryn. "There
will hardly be the equal of it in the Island of the Mighty,
much less in the rest of the world. Even the scent of it
would be contentment for the hungry. Thinking and considering I was; not accusing the food."

"Unless the thought were made known to us, we should
deem that the food was unpleasing to you."

Then Gwri began to prepare in his mind the Spell of the
Three Places. First he mused upon the secrecies of the
Wood of Mon, where Math fab Mathonwy engages in enchantment for the purification of the world. He thought of
the bluebells there, that are endowed with supernal deep
thought by the Immortals; and their ponderings maintain
the science of the holy ovates of the Gorsedd; by reason of
his possessing the Spell of the Wood, the Field, and the
Mountain, he was able to let loose about him with a word
the whole power of their meditations, and to put compulsion

with it upon things animate and inanimate, and to ward off spells and harm.

"Last October I traveled in the north," said he. "The leaves of the oaks were falling, and blown hither and yonder along the floor of the forest, drifting and whispering on the wind. It was in my mind to cogitate and muse upon the learning I heard from them. Until I obtain knowledge of the meaning of it, I shall take little pleasure in food."

"It might well be that we could give you the knowledge," said the king. "Make known to us where you were traveling when you heard them."

"By the Wood of Mon," said Gwri; "by the Wood of Mon."

With that word a sigh passed through the hall, softer and sadder than the whispering of the west wind through the dry reeds and the sand hills of Teifi, on the first evening of autumn, when the sun is going down behind rain-gray clouds over Ireland. "Let the food be taken away," said the king. "Let drinking-horns be brought, adorned with silver and opals, and mead in goblets of crystal and pearl."

They brought them. The foam on the mead in the hirlas and the goblet was whiter and brighter than the foam on the ninth wave, when it rises against the black rocks of Gwbert, and breaks against them, and shakes out its long, white, glimmering mane against the blackness. The mead was of the color of the sunlight through topaz and amber; there was a sound in it like the murmur of bees through the lime groves and orchards; and a scent of all the flowers in the world, of heather and roses, of apple-bloom and daffodils and pansies. If there were potent spells in the food, ten times more potent and subtle were the enchantments in the drink; there was peril for the mighty, the careful, the well-governed in every drop that shone in the wonderfully-carven, jewel-adorned goblets and hirlas horns.

"For what reason is this abstinence on the lord of the Brython?" said the King of Caer Hedd. "The mead in the hirlas was brewed from honey nine times sweeter than the honey of the virgin swarm in the heatherlands of the Island of the Mighty, and there was neither scum nor bees in it. The mead has this peculiarity: that whoever drinks even a little of it, dreams what he desires to dream, and remembers what he desires to remember, and is made certain of the attainment of whatever he may seek."

"Excellent is the mead truly," said Gwri Gwallt Euryn. "Only fools would accuse it. The sight and the scent of it alone would be the multiplying of thirst, and the quenching of the thirst they multiplied. It was thought that had over-taken me; thought and cogitation."

Then he prepared the second power of the Spell, musing upon the secrecies of the Field at Llandybie, and the golden kingcups that grow there, endowed by a company of Immortals with a spirit of swift, shining and certain wisdom, so that by their mere blossoming they breathe out spiritual delight upon the air, and maintain the inspiration of the Bards of the Holy Gorsedd. "Yes indeed; I was troubled by cogitation, and inquiry into secret things," said he.

"Alas!" said the King of Caer Hedd, "unless we know the matter of the cogitations, we shall deem that it is an accusation against the mead."

"I will make it known, for your satisfaction," said Gwri. "A week ago I was traveling in the south, and I came by a place where the bees were raising song and monody among the marsh-marigolds. The weight of the news I heard from them was brought to my mind by the scent of mead. Until

I obtain knowledge of the meaning of it, I shall get no delight
out of drinking."

"It might well be that we could give you the knowledge,"
said the king. "By what place were you traveling in the
south?"

"By the Field of Llandybie," said he. "By the Wood
and the Field."

Hardly were the words out of his mouth, when a sigh
passed through the hall, softer and sadder than the rustling
of yellow leaves, and the dropping of mist-drops from them,
in the evening, when the wildwood is all a pale and ghostly
flame in October, and the mists over the mountains and valleys of the world. "Let the mead be taken away," said the
King of Caer Hedd sorrowfully.

Then the chief bard of the caer stood forth and began
to relate a story. Such was the nature of its assonance and
consonance, and its perfection of melodious sound, and its
clarity in the depiction of heroic men and actions, and marvelous places, that even the stories of Ol the son of Olwydd,
and Clust fab Clustfeinydd, and Drem the son of Dremidyd,
seemed dull and worthless in its comparison. When he had
made an end of it, the King of Caer Hedd said:

"For what reason is this abstraction, and lack of delight
in hearing stories, on the king's son from the Island of
Mighty? By relating tales such as this, the bards maintain
bloom and fruitage on a million trees, and spread unfading
beauty over the seven cantrefs of Caer Hedd. Yet it was
no better with you, hearing it, than would be hearing a crow
calling among the yellow elms on an autumn morning, or the
voice of the corncrake in the valley, on the night of the full
moon of the hay harvest."

"Wonderful was the story, truly," said Gwri Gwallt
Euryn. "Better would not be told in the Island of the

Mighty, or in Ireland; much less in the rest of the world. Considering and meditating I was; not accusing the story. The cogitations of my own mind had overtaken me."

Then he began preparing the last power of the Spell. He remembered the Wyddfa Mountain, the summit of the world, the House of Hu Gadarn; he bethought himself of the snow on the peak of the Wyddfa, and the pure nature of it, and the endowment it had of spiritual might from the Immortals, whereby is enhanced the spirituality in the hearts of the Holy Druids of the Sacred Circle. Owing to his possession of the Spell of the Three Places, he was enabled to speak as if it were from the Wyddfa, and to wield the lonely and lofty power.

"Alas that we know not the matter of the cogitations," said the king.

" I will tell you," said Gwri. " Last year when I traveled in Arfon, although there was snow, I heard an ousel singing. What with the blackness of his wing, and the whiteness of the snow, and the mysterious nature of the learning in the verses of the song, I have had little freedom from cogitation from that time until now; and until I learn the meaning of them, I shall get no satisfaction either out of song or story."

" Unless we knew the place where you heard the ousel, we could not interpret it for you," said the king. " By what place were you riding? "

" By the Wyddfa Mountain," said Gwri. " By the Wood, the Field and the Mountain."

With the utterance of the words of the Spell, and their regally leaping from between his teeth, and driving their glory and stern resonance through the hall, the magic of the king withered, and the music of the birds amid the rafters was hushed, and a sigh went through Caer Hedd, sadder than the cheeping of the robin in December when there is no gleam in the grayness of heaven, and no dry place on earth for the footsole of man. Care and lack of ease took the mind of the king; unknown to him until then was the failure of his spells. "Wonderful is the might of this druid-taught youth from the Island of Hu Gadarn!" thought he. Then he betook himself to considering whether there would be any means of overcoming and putting spells on him. "Unless it would be through delight and forgetfulness coming upon him with the hwyl of his own speech and song, there will be no means," thought he.

"Will it please you to give us full news of what you heard from the leaves, and from the bees, and from the ousel?" said the king. "It is well known to us that there are no songs in the world to equal the songs of the Cymry, and no stories comparable to the stories of the Island of Britain."

"If I had a harp, I would sing them," said Gwri Gwallt Euryn. "They are not of a nature to be related, except in song."

Thereupon they brought a harp, and set it before him; and he began to get music out of it; and made these verses, and sang them to the music:

> *The fall of the leaves*
> *In the woods of the world;*
> *And the heart in me grieves*
> *Where they drift and are whirled,*
> *For the silence of her, in the springtime,*
> *Whose wings are enrainbowed, empearled.*
>
> *And where is the might*
> *In the limbs of the tree?*
> *And his dreams of delight,*
> *And imaginings free?*

It's he longs for thy songs, Aden Fwynach,
Shaken out o'er the hills and the sea!

For the Three Pearls of Singing
Were lost from the land.
They were fairies far-winging;
The winds that were fanned
By the fall of their wings, were enroyaled.
By what craft were ye stolen, by what hand?

Shall I multiply words
Without ending the wrong?
From the midst of the birds
That have held thee so long,
By the Wood that thou knowest, O Mwynach,
Come, Princess of beauty and song!

When he had sung as much as that, he looked up, and
saw that the birds had lighted down where they might among
the rafters, and covered their heads with their wings; all
but one of them, and she the most beautiful of all, and her
plumage like the rainbow, like the clouds of sunset and dawn.
She had been songless and hidden during the whole time of
the feast; but now she was circling through the air uneasily,
and fluttering to and fro there.

" Now I will sing to you the news I had from the bees at
Llandybie," said he.   Then he made these verses and sang
them:

There's a Field mid the mountains,
And streams have their rise there
In the diamond of fountains,
Spell-hidden from men's eyes there;
And the bees in the cuckoo-flowers heed it,
And ponder and dream and grow wise there.

And I heeded, much yearning,
Their murmur and croon,
And the drift of their learning,
A wandering tune;
And here's what I heard, Aden Fwynach,
By the Fountain of Tybie in June:

There was one without rest
From her beating of wings,
In a silence unblest
In a palace of kings
That had stirred not from sloth since the Three Shouts
Woke life in the voidness of things.

But westward and westward
Ere this, she is winging;
And a Queen turneth restward,
Heart-healed by her singing;
For War amidst Peace unenspelled her.
Heed thou, too, this gift of my bringing!

This gift of small words
Wherein all powers abound,
So that stars, seas and birds
Must submit to their sound,
And rivers, and islands, and forests,
Yea, and man, and his steed and his hound.

And is there no lurement
In this, then, for thee?
Was the White-winged, the pure, meant
In loneness to be?
By the Wood, and the Field of the Fountain,
O Mwynach, thou too shalt be free!

When he had sung as much as that, the bird that had been silent slanted down suddenly through the air, and lighted on the helmet of a group of armor that hung high on the wall above the king's throne.   No one heeded her, except Gwri; and that by reason of the magic he had been slowly weaving about them with his song, and with the first two words of the spell, and with the rich, heroic glory of his voice in the singing, and with his unequalled bardic skill with the harp.

"Now I will sing you what I heard from the Blackbird of the Wyddfa Mountain," said he; and with that, went to the harping again, and made these verses, and sang them:

> There's a mountain in Wales
> Where an Ousel is biding,
> And I heeded the tales
> From his bill that came gliding,
> That so I might pierce the enchantment,
> And find thee in thy fairyland hiding.

> 'Twas of one that was cumbered
> By dreams without light,
> In oblivion she slumbered
> The long, barren night,
> Till with Peace amidst War for a weapon
> I gave back the sun to her sight.

> Yea, their bonds are outworn,
> Thy bright sisters are free;
> They may wing through the morn,
> They may sing o'er the sea —
> Wilt thou leave them to droop in the sunlight
> With sadness of mourning for thee?

> For the sake of the Queen
> In whose service of old

Ye went dazzling in sheen
Of dawn-glory and gold,
By the Wood and the Field and the Mountain,
Ah, come forth, Glamor-ensouled!

With that, remembrance burst upon Aden Fwynach. The beauty of the hall and the lawn-lands seemed to her to be nothing; the birds that had been her companions since she was stolen were no better to her than a flock of starlings on a morning in April; their music that had enchanted and put shame and silence and dreams of pleasure on her during all those years, seemed only the loud converse of starlings, when they may be chattering and quarreling over the things that concern them. She bowed her beautiful crowned head beneath her wing; sorrow and remorse were upon her; she had had much delight, she remembered, in the place of her enchantment, and no memories of Rhianon her Lady: that was by reason of the spells that had been put upon her, and their being ten times stronger than the enchantments of Aden Lanach and Aden Lonach. As for the men of Caer Hedd, they were beyond heeding her; power and magic had faded from them; they only remembered the ages of the world, and the toil of the Gods, and their own life without warfare or labor. Glory they had never earned; time was taking from them the semblance of it that they had cherished.

But as for Gwri himself, he did not stay in his singing. The great power of song had come on him; the hwyl of the bards was filling his soul, as the wind fills and drives the sails of a ship. He saw that Aden Fwynach had awakened from her dreams; he saw her bow her crowned head; he knew that in a little while song would come to her, and she would go forth singing before him. He sang these verses to restore her:

For I saw in my dreams
In the halls of her sire,
One crowned with sunbeams
And engirdled with fire;
She was brighter than dawn is in summer;
More lovely than dawn her attire.

And I saw her again
Where high pity had brought her;
She was compassed with pain,
She, a Goddess's daughter.
And wilt thou not come, Aden Fwynach,
To make end of the wrong that was wrought her?

Was she Queen of the World,
Or the realms of the Air?
Where the sea-foam is whirled,
Was her sovereignty there?
And what might was enkindled against her,
That her world was made barren and bare?

Speak thou! hast thou known?
Is it given thee to know
What so dimly was shown
When my dreams were aglow?
By the Wood and the Field and the Mountain,
Oh sing thou the end of her woe!

Thereupon the beautiful wings of Aden Fwynach were
spread, and beat down the air beneath her, and she rose in
her glory singing. Her song was incomparable; true was
that saying, that it would be the passing of the heart from
its bondage, the fulfilment of the ultimate concerns of the
soul. It was seven times more melodious than the singing
either of Glanach or Llonach. As she sang, here is what

happened: the men of Caer Hedd rose up, and their king
with them; they remembered the dawn of the world, when
the Blessed Ones went forth from Gwynfyd, and *they* went
not forth with them; they remembered that they had chosen
delight then, and now their delight was withered. But Aden
Fwynach sang and sang.

Then there rose up a star and purple brilliance in the far
part of the hall; it was a God; the harp in his hands was
brighter than the sun. Gwri heard him sing this verse to
the men of Caer Hedd:

> *Oh ye that not stirred*
> > *when ye heard our Hai Atton,*
> *When first the dark world*
> > *of Abred we trod;*
> *When for warward attire*
> > *the flame-plumes we wrapt on,*
> *And Chaos caught fire*
> > *with the radiance of God;*
> *Will ye dream here in peace*
> > *while the death-fumes encumber*
> *Your brethren that went forth*
> > *of old time, and fell?*
> *Shall ye sweep not in aid*
> > *to those Stars dimmed in slumber,*
> *Those heroes enchained*
> > *in oblivion and hell?*

And he heard the men of Caer Hedd answer him with
this one:

> *O Bright One flame-plumed,*
> > *what fate hath o'erborne them?*
> *What dark power hath doomed*
> > *them these slumber-wrought chains?*

They were brave, though they heard
  not our wise words who warned them —
Ah, say not the glow
  of their sun-brightness wanes!
Ah, we too, that sought not
  High Ceugant's surrender,
That quested no perilous
  heaven for our hold,
We too have seen wane
  our old cherished splendor,
And delight hath turned pain,
  and the whole world grown cold.

And he heard these verses again from the beautiful Immortal:

They rode forth from Bliss
  in the world's golden morning,
When the lone, bardic stars
  sang hymns in their praise;
The insignia of Gods
  were their proud brows adorning,
The waste of night glowed
  as they passed on their ways.
What though, while through hell's self
  their war-way they winged on,
In ages oblivion-
  o'erladen, they fell?
It was Gwynfyd they deemed
  too inglorious a kingdom,
It was they that made choice
  to build new heavens in hell.

There be some that o'ercame
  when the deep rose to slay them,

And flame against flame,
     waged high war with Night;
Leagued chaos and hell
     without might to dismay them,
  Nor subtly wrought spell
     that might dim their proud sight;
The ranks of the Warrior Gods
     shine with their glory,
  They turn from delight
     to their stern, agelong war,
Lest the brightness at heart
     of the ages grow hoary,
  And the Spirit Sun rise
     o'er the world's brink no more.

And again the men of Caer Hedd, the Gods without toil,
answered him:

Our peace hath grown old,
     like a flower past its bloom-time,
  And wan-rimmed and cold
     hath fallen low on the ground.
And we gird us with swords
     and go forth to our doom-time,
  To free them that fell,
     or ourselves to lie bound.
Ah ye, on whose dark brows
     long pain and compassion
  Have kindled sad splendors
     of star-flame to crown;
We, the pure ones unstained
     with the long moil of passion,
  To your godhood war-worn
     and war-glorious, bow down.

Here is the Third Branch of
The Story of Rhianon and Pryderi, called

The Return of Pryderi

1. THE PECULIARITIES OF THE RING AND THE FILLET OF THE FAMILY OF HEFEYDD, AND THE THREE PRIMITIVE BARDS OF THE ISLAND OF THE MIGHTY.

YBIE rose up, glimmering darkly, out of her fountain, when he came to the Field of Llandybie on the evening of the third day. Her aspect was even sterner than it had been before. "Wherefore come you?" said she.

"Aden Fwynach is made free from the sorceries," he answered.

"Yes is she made free," said Tybie; "Pryderi fab Pwyll freed her. Unless I obtain service from you, I shall never be requited for the loss of the water."

Gwri marveled in his mind; it seemed to him that it would have been he himself that freed Aden Fwynach; but it would have been unfitting for him to have spoken of it. "Whatever service you may require of me," he said, "it will be an honor to me to perform it."

"It will be the succoring of my kinswoman, Rhianon ferch Hefeydd," she said. "From dawn to dusk her place is at the palace gate in Arberth, doing the least just penance in the world; and her enemies plotting against her continually. Pryderi her son will be going forward to save her; but so many will be against him, that it is not known whether he would obtain success without aid."

"I never had any desire in my life, equal to my desire to do this," said he. "I will ride forward now, and storm the palace in the morning."

"Misfortune often overtakes the rash," said she. "It will be better to remain here until dawn. There would be no seeing, by night, the feathers that are to guide you."

Thereupon she gave him the feathers, one from each of the birds. "Follow the white one when the blue is lost," she said; "and the rainbow-colored when there may be no recovering the white. By the time that you have parted with the rainbow-colored, it will be a marvel if you are not within sight of Arberth." With that she melted into the glow and gloom of the dusk.

He lay down by the well, the beauty of the stars a tent for him. Scarcely had his eyelids fallen over his eyes, when he heard voices and conversation from the road. The voices were so melodious, that no music in the world would be equal to them.

"Is there any cure for old age?" said the first of them. "Is there any making the weak limbs strong, and taking whiteness from the hair, and the deep furrows from about the eyes and the mouth?"

"There is," said the second; "if one could find Pryderi fab Pwyll."

Then the third of them said: "How would he accomplish it?"

"With the peculiarities of the Fillet of the Family of Hefeydd Hen, from the Country of the Immortals," said the second.

"Put news of them on the wind, Lord Brother," said the first.

"Rhianon his mother brought it with her from the palace of Hefeydd, at the time she came into the Island of the Mighty. She bound it about the swaddling clothes of Pryderi on the day that he was born."

"Would there be using the fillet, without knowledge of spells?"

"There would not; and even with the Spell of the Three Places there would be no using it, unless the secret of it were made known to him." It was the third of the voices that said that.

"I will tell you," said the second voice. "There was a family that loved delight and beauty, and had not bestirred themselves, nor won any victories since the Morning of the Three Shouts. He came to them, and caused them to become eager for the battle of the world; and to reward him for this I shall make it known to him in the morning."

Gwri considered within himself; it was not in his power to rise up or question the voices. "The fillet was about my swaddling-clothes when I was found," thought he. "Beyond that, there is knowledge of the Spell of the Three Places. The men of Caer Hedd were such a family as was spoken of." He took the fillet from his breast where he wore it; never had he been without it during his life. "It might well have peculiarities with it," he thought. He fell to musing upon the fillet, and from musing, to sleep.

How long he might have been sleeping is not known, when he heard the voice again, and listened; it was still beyond his power either to rise, or to turn his head, or to question them.

"Lord Brother," said the third voice; "if there were, in the Island of the Mighty, any giving sight to the blind, it would be one of the priceless wonderful gifts of the island."

" There is such a gift," said the first.   " It is with Pryderi fab Pwyll."

" Put news of it on the wind, Lord Brother," said the second.

" He would do it with the Spell of the Wood, the Field and the Mountain," said the first; " and by means of the peculiarities of the Ring of the Family of Hefeydd Hen."

" Is that ring with him also? " said the Second.

" Rhianon his mother threaded it on a golden thread, and tied it about his neck on the morning when he was born. The ring was inscribed in the coelbren letters of the bards: *Bydd i ti ddychwelyd.*"

"And a return there shall be for him," said the third voice. " There was a family that dwelt in confusion, and turmoil, and hideous sound; they had been at senseless warfare since the Crying of the Name.   He came to them, and caused music to be heard in their caer, and brought harmony there, so that now they are doing service for the Immortals on the borders of space.   To requite him for this I shall appear to him in the evening, and cause the path of his returning to be clear before him."

" I will tell you," said the first voice.   " I shall cause the secret of curing blindness to be known to him; I shall appear to him at noonday and make it clear.   There was a caer wherein there was heavy sloth and unbreakable slumber, and he brought the brightness of day, and clear vision there; it is to requite him for this that I shall appear to him and make known the secret of the ring."

" He is the song-bringer," said the second voice; " and therefore I shall aid him."

" He is the light-giver," said the first; " and therefore I shall reward him."

"He is the hero," said the third; "and therefore I also shall be with him."

Gwri put his hand in his breast, and touched the ring that he still wore there, on the golden thread on which it was threaded when he was found in the stall of Fflamwen the mare of Teyrnion. "All this is a marvel to me," thought he; and desired the more that Pryderi might become known to him. "There might be peculiarities with this ring also," he mused; "and the one inscription in the coelbren inscribed on it, and on the ring of the Family of Hefeydd that is with the son of Pwyll." From musing upon the ring, he fell asleep.

The sky was abloom with dawn tulips when he awoke; no memory of the voices remained with him, at that time. But it chanced that he had the fillet in his right hand, and his forefinger thrust through the ring; and when his eyes fell on those two adornments, it seemed to him that there was magic quickening in them, and elemental being; they flashed suddenly in the sunlight as far as from Bettws Mountain to Dinefawr.

He threw the feather of Aden Lonach into the air, according to the counsel Tybie had given him; a wind from the east took it and bore it on, and he rode forward following it through the valleys and over the hills of the Great Cantref till mid-morning. Then he saw it drop by the road-side; and at a word from him, away with the Wind-driver at his swiftest to the place where it fell. Here is who Gwri saw there: an old, infirm man sitting by the hedge. The flesh of his face and hands was withered, yellow, and with a thousand wrinkles; his back was bent double with age; he was grievously afflicted with coughing; his hair was as white as the wind-driven foam.

"The greeting of heaven and of man to you, Pryderi fab

Pwyll," said the old man. " Sorrow upon me," thought Gwri Gwallt Euryn, a moon of memory suddenly shining forth in his mind, " if I heard not such a voice as that in my dreams in the night."

" The greeting of heaven and of man to you also, and better to you than to me," said Gwri. "And no worse with you because Gwri Gwallt Euryn is the name to name me with, and not Pryderi fab Pwyll."

" Many times would it be worse," said the old man. " It would be the continuance of the burden of old age, when youth might be had for the asking from Pryderi."

" Could he accomplish that, indeed? " said Gwri. " Could he restore youth to the ancient? "

" Yes could he restore it," said the old man. " He has the golden fillet of the Family of Hefeydd Hen in the Country of the Immortals; and therein there is restoring youth to the ancient, and strength to the worn out limbs, and furthermore, blackness to the hair that has grown white these years."

" I marvel at this," said Gwri. " Make known to me, in heaven's name, if it please you, the manner of restoring youth with the fillet."

" Yes, yes will I make it known," said the old man. " Pryderi would set the fillet on my head, and he would repeat spells, and he would order the hair to assume its natural color, the black to be black, the brown brown, and the golden golden; and he would command the limbs to regain their former youth and vigor, as if the years had never passed over them; and in my deed he would put compulsion upon them all, and they would obey him."

" Well, well, in my deed, a marvel is this truly," said Gwri. " Would he put compulsion upon them in this way? " said he. He took his own fillet from his breast, and set it on the white hair of the old man, and as he did so, said: "*By the Wood, the Field and the Mountain, forsake whiteness, every hair of you, and assume your natural color; let the black be black, and the brown brown, and the golden golden; and let the limbs regain their former vigor and youth, as if the years had never passed over them.* Would he command them, and put compulsion upon them, in that way?" said Gwri.

But before the other could answer him, it was as if a wind arose and blew the old age from him; he stood forth there by the roadside, young and strong and handsome; one to be feared by the hostile, one to be loved by many. "By heaven, he would put the compulsion on them in that way," said he. His laughter rang out through the valley; except the sun in heaven, nothing was so bright and golden as the hair upon his head.

"It is a good fillet enough, and excellent peculiarities in it," he said, giving it back to Gwri. "It is a marvel if it be any other than the fillet of the Family of Hefeydd Hen." With that he raised his two hands towards the sky, and golden and roseate flames leaped up from the earth, and played and circled about him. Gwri watched him in delight and wonder. As the flame rose, so he increased in stature, till he had the height of pines and poplars with him. They leaped and played about the glory of his head, and took the form of soaring eagles of golden fire. Innumerable harps sounded out of the invisible air; their music was such as the Gods desire to hear, when They move combatward in their burning cars. On his two hands were two marvelous gloves; it seemed as if even the puny, wearing them, might easily pluck up Pumlumon. A blue cloak of immortal bardhood was on his shoulders; it was as if woven of the fire of the sapphire, the turquoise and the amethyst. Higher and higher the flame circled and blossomed, and he rose with it into the air. As soon as he overtopped the mountains, the form and beauty of him changed; wings of excessive glory branched out on this side and on that, and he became a Dragon of flame against the blue brightness of the firmament. Soaring and flaming and circling, his eagles like stars scintillant around him, his music waning from the world, he ascended resplendently into the empyrean. Then the two glories of the sky were made one; the Dragon was lost in the brilliance of the morning sun.

"It was Gwron Brif-fardd," said Gwri. "In my deed, it was the Heartener of Heroes. Marvelous is my good fortune this day, to have held converse with such a one." Since the blue feather was lost, he put the white one on the wind, and mounted Gyrru'r Gwyntoedd slowly, and rode forward after the feather, deep in his meditations. "As for old age, and the restoration of his youth to him, never would he have needed the services of any one for that. The Immortals grow not old; they assume what guise will please them at any time." So he rode on, musing. "For what reason will the Prif-fardd have appeared to me?" he wondered.

At noonday, a mile from him along the road, he saw a blind man coming towards him slowly, tapping the ground with his stick. Immediately a gust took the feather, and whirled it away till it fell like a star into the breast of the blind man's coat. Away with the Wind-driver with that, leaving the wind behind him; the blind man had not taken the ten steps after receiving the feather, before Gwri and the Wind-driver had come up to him.

"The greeting of heaven and of man to you, Pryderi fab Pwyll Pen Annwn," said the blind man.

"May it be better to you than to me," said Gwri; "and none the worse if the name with me is Gwri Gwallt Euryn."

" If this be true, it is the sorrow of my life. More than anything I desire to meet with Pryderi fab Pwyll, and that on account of the service he would do for me."

" I would do you service, if it were in my power to," said Gwri. " What service would Pryderi do for you? "

" Sight he would give to my eyes," said the blind man. " He would do it by means of the peculiarities of the ring of the Family of Hefeydd Hen in the Kingdom of the Immortals, that has the gift of restoring the blind to their eyesight, and even to seeing better than they saw before they became blind."

Gwri dismounted, and took the ring that had been found with him out of his breast. " Marvelous is this, indeed," said he. " Make known to me, if it please you, how he would restore eyesight with the ring."

" He would touch the eyelids over the eyes that might be afflicted," said the blind man. " It is a marvel to me that any one should be ignorant of this. He would put the ring on the forefinger of his right hand, and touch the eyelids."

" Which eyelid would he touch first? " said Gwri.

" The right eyelid, as would be natural and fitting," said the other; ." few would dream that it would be the left. And he would put the Spell of the Three Places upon the one and the other of them, and command them; and a marvel if they were not obedient."

" Would he do it in this way? " he said, and touched the right eyelid of the blind man with the ring. " *By the Wood, the Field and the Mountain, quit you your blindness,*" he said; and then to the left eye: " *By the Wood, the Field and the Mountain, quit you your blindness also; and neither stubbornness nor cheating with you, either of you; and the sight of the eagle, the God and the Dragon to the two of you from this out.*"

" By heaven, he would do it in that way," said the other. A wind rose up out of the Isle of Apples, and blew the blindness from him; whatever lack of beauty there had been upon him, vanished with it. His two eyes became brighter than the eyes of man; they became like two gleaming dragons afar, like two diamonds kindling in the sun, like the brightness of two sea-waves when the noonday sunlight is reflected from them. He laughed and looked sunward, and lifted his two arms towards the sky; he seemed to draw blueness out of the sky, and a flame out of the ground beneath his feet. His beggar's rags became a blue cloak of bardhood, woven of the fire of jewels, bluer than the bloom of the noonday in June; his body itself wavered and glimmered into intense, gleaming, excellent fire. He lifted his head; it rose to the level of the mountain-tops, so great was his stature. Because of his eyes, no one would have known that there were not three suns in heaven. Beautiful he appeared, and Oh, beautiful and worthy of praise; kindling the silvering gold of the noon light, kindling the mountains and the valley; the Glory of Wales, a meteor out of the firmament of Godhood. In the white, extreme blazonment of glory about his bardic, sunbright head, birds brighter than the lightnings flashed and sang. He had a golden breastplate upon his breast, adorned with the opal, the sapphire and the diamond; its peculiarity was the gift of insight, and that no magic should ever prevail against the one wearing it. It was unknown to Gwri whether ever so much beauty had been revealed before, unless it was when Gwron appeared to him in the morning.

"A good ring it is with you," laughed the God; " and a marvel if it be not the ring of the Family of Hefeydd. Useful are its peculiarities." Laughing, he rose up into the air, and assumed the form and glory of the Dragon. From the north to the south above the mountains, burned his bright

blue, bounteous, vision-giving wings. Beautifully he was
poised there for a moment; the proud and arching neck,
the quivering, flaming, sapphire scales, the head with the
aspect of complete vision, wisdom, empire and command.
Away with him then into the ether, into the empyrean, to play
and kindle and leap forth among the constellations as it might
please him.

" Indeed, indeed, and in my deed," thought Gwri, watching him, " fortunate is this beyond any falling of good fortune. To meet Gwron in the morning, and Plenydd before
the passing of noon. Plenydd it was,"said he; " the blind
and foolish would have known him; undoubtedly it was Plenydd the Sight-giver, Plenydd Brif-fardd Prydain. Indeed,
indeed, fortunate is this."

Deep in his musings he rode forward again, setting first
the feather of Aden Fwynach on the wind to guide him.
" Indeed," thought he, " marvelous revelations are made
known to me this day. As for healing blindness, it would
not be that Prif-fardd that would have suffered the loss of
vision. Dear and blessed are these Immortals, and the hidden reasons they will have for their appearings and vanish-
ings, and for this guise and that that they will wear as it
pleases them." Then he sang the song that Taliesin Benbardd made at one night old, when Elphin the son of Gwydd-
no found him in the weir:

" O foroedd ac o fynydd,
Ac o eigion afonydd
Daw Duw a da i ddedwydd " —

— " and fortunate am I, truly," thought he; " to whom two
Gods have appeared in the one day." So musing, he rode
forward in a deep and golden content.

At sunset he was riding beside the river, and passed the

hill of Gorsedd Arberth on his right. He saw that there was
a company of men watching on the hilltop, but paid little heed
to them. When the darkness came down over the mountains,
the feather of Aden Fwynach became beautifully luminous
before him, and failed not in its guiding him. He rode forward until he came within sight of a city, dim-walled in the
light of stars. He saw a man come out of the city, and make
his way towards him along the road. He had a little harp
at his breast, that shone strangely; the feather blew towards
him, and was caught in the harpstrings. Gwri rode up to
him.

"The greeting of heaven and of man to you, Pryderi fab
Pwyll," said the Harper.

"The greeting of heaven and of man to you also," said
Gwri. "And much better to you than to me, Lord Alawn
Brif-fardd," said he.

"What names are these you are putting on me?" said
the Harper. "I marvel at this."

"What names are these you are putting on me?" said
Gwri. "Gwri Gwallt Euryn my foster-parents called me."

" — And the aspect on you of the one that should be
riding to the court of Arberth this night and all," said the
Harper.

"Lord Prif-fardd," said Gwri; "Lord god," he said;
"I am riding thither."

"Careless are you in the matter of speech and name-
giving," said the Harper. "This is a cause for marveling."

"As to name-giving, and as to carelessness therein, the
feather will know the one to whom it flies. I met Gwron in
the morning, in the guise of an old man afflicted with coughing, and did not know him till he was taking dragon aspect.
I met Plenydd at noonday, in the guise of a blind man. To
both of them the feather flew, and rested with them. For

that reason, when I meet a harper in the evening, and the feather flies to him, it will please me to call him *Alawn* and *God,* without consultation, or waiting for the dragon-change to come on him. Therefore, the greeting of the god and the man to you, Lord Alawn Brif-fardd," said Gwri.

Alawn laughed.

" Well, well," said he; " would you take advice and counsel from the harper that the feather flew to, whether he had the dragon-guise or not? "

" Evil upon me if I would not," said Gwri, laughing.

" Here is what the counsel will be, then," said Alawn. " Go forward into Arberth, to the palace; and obtain entry in the name of a craftsman bearing his craft. And when it may be desired of you to make known the nature of the craft, name you the three Unusual Arts."

" Gladly will I do so," said Gwri.

" Is it known to you what those three arts will be? " said Alawn.

" It is not known," said Gwri.

" Here is what they will be then; give you heed to them. The first will be restoring youth to the aged; it is known to you how it may be accomplished. The second will be restoring sight to the sightless; Plenydd my brother made the secret of it known to you. See that you exercise those two arts between the outer portals and the door of the hall."

" What will the third art be? " said Gwri. " Make the third known to me also, if it please you."

" When they ask you for the third, say you that it will be restoring thrones to their rightful owners."

" I will say that," said Gwri. "And I will say, when the queen asks me, that I saw Alawn Alawon at the gates of her town in the starlight, and that I had counsels from the Priffardd of the Harmonies."

"Say it you," said the Other, laughing, and stroked his
harpstrings with his fingers. As he touched them, they gave
forth light and immortal melody; pale green and purple
flames rose out of the earth and encompassed him; and it
was to be seen that he was indeed the brother of Plenydd
and of Gwron, not less marvelous than they. He stood there
in his body of purple fire, darkly glowing, paling, gleaming,
kindling and brightening; his two eyes complete in glory and
beauty, in the most ancient wisdom, the deepest compassion
in the world.

"Say it you," he said laughing. "And let it be known to
our sister, Rhianon, that we the Prif-feirdd Prydain have
served her, and will serve her until the ending of her sorrows. And now go forward," said he; "and success and
advantage be with you according to your desert."

Then he, too, took the guise of the Dragon, his body of
the fire of the amethyst glowing through the darkness, and
his wide, beautiful flame wings kindling and flashing, hued
like the beryl and the emerald, through the gloom. In a moment he too was lost, encompassed in the night amidst the
stars.

Then Gwri rode forward, and through the gates of Arberth, and by the silent streets, until he came to the portals
of the palace of Pwyll Pen Annwn.

II. THE PETULANT IMPATIENCE OF PENDARAN DYFED, AND THE MAINTAINING OF THE SOVEREIGNTY OF RHIANON

HIANON sat at the palace gate in Arberth; day after day she had had her place there between dawn and dusk during twenty years. There was no queen's robe on her, no adornment in the world. When she chose the fate of waiting and penance, she acquired the nature of mortality, and knew there would be no escaping it unless she should go to the Gods, or until Pryderi should return. By reason of that, her hair was gray, and the lines of sorrow were on her forehead; and before the ten years were over, she was blind. Yet there was no concealing her majesty; nothing in fair Dyfed was fairer than she. Her calm, deep, beautiful eyes were bereft of their outward vision, but not of their lone, untroubled glory; not of their color like the sunlight through the oak-leaves on the waters of a deep pool in the forest. Whoever beheld her, knew that she was a queen.

No one had remained faithful to her, when she chose the penance, except Gwawl ab Clud and the hundred men of the teulu of Pwyll Pen Annwn, with Pendaran Dyfed for penteulu at the head of them. They had been men in the prime of their worth at that time; not too young to be the best in council; not too old to be the best in war. But the loss of his lord was equal to the taking of twenty years from the life of each one of them, and the penance of their queen had whitened their hair.

When she was accused, they were eager to do battle for her; but she forbade them. She would have no warfare until Pryderi or Pwyll Pen Annwn should return. She made a treaty with her enemies on behalf of Pwyll; she would claim no right for herself; she would remain in penance at the palace gate daily; but the throne on the dais should be kept for the king or for his son. As for the governing of Dyfed, it should be in the hands of Pendaran and the Crintach between them, and each with three men to uphold him in the council.

When Einion Arth Cennen heard of this, he rose up in furious impatience. "Are the men of the king's teulu dead?" said he. "While I live, this wrong shall not be done to the sovereign lady of the Dimetians. If she elects to do penance where no penance should be done, let her have praise and honor for it. But in my deed she shall have the name of queen, and she shall have the king's place at the feasts. I will not let sleep come to the eyes of any man, until this is granted."

"We will humor you," said the Crintach, remembering the furious nature of Einion's onslaught in the conflict, and how he was accustomed to go one against many, and drive his foemen into the wave. "The daughter of Hefeydd shall have the name of queen between dusk and dawn, and she shall hold the throne on the dais at feast time."

Madog and his men were proud enough of that treaty when they made it, on account of the rising of the teulu in the hall at Einion's words, and the fierce light in their eyes, and the difficulty that Rhianon had had in restraining them.

But with every year they grew less proud and more impatient
over it; with so little between their lord and the kingship:
no more than word given to this woman at the palace gate;
and she blind and gray after ten years of it, although she had
seemed no older than the king, at the time she took on grief
and mortality. No more than word given to her, and the will
of those few fierce warriors that were growing older year
by year; and if older, fewer also. For by the time that the
twenty years were over, there were not more than nine and
twenty of them left alive, and Gwawl ab Clud for the thirti-
eth. Here is relating, now, how it came to be that there were
so few:

During the first seven years, not one day had passed but
that the queen had had plots and designs to combat in it: the
whole power of Llwyd ab Cilcoed set against her. It was
marvelous how she might meet and undo all without open
warfare, and giving no one reason to accuse her. At times,
indeed, her enemies obtained success against her; it was
when any of the men of the teulu had forsaken following
her counsel.

Every Eve of May she would send ten men to watch on
Gorsedd Arberth, and until the seventh year, none of those
she sent had ever failed in the watching. But it happened
then to Einion Arth Cennen, that two days before May Eve
he received tidings of the greatest wild boar in the world,
that had its haunts on Mynydd Amanw, opposite Carreg
Cennen, and was laying waste the whole of the cantref. The
desire of his life came upon him to hunt it; and for that
reason he rode away from Arberth without the queen's having knowledge of his going.

"Where is the lord of Iscennen?" said she, on the morning of May Eve. "It would be well for him to lead the
watchers on Gorsedd Arberth this day."

" Hunting the wild boar on Mynydd Amanw he is," said Pendaran Dyfed.

" Indeed, alas for that hunting," she answered; " it is the pity of my life that he should have gone to it." The day after, news came that Einion had been found slain at the head of the mountain. The boar had slain him when he was parted from his huntsmen; Catwg Gwaeth had come upon him lifeless.

Pendaran Dyfed considered within himself. The loss of his lord had been a more grievous burden to Pendaran than to any of the men of the teulu; his hair was white and his brow furrowed, and he was never heard to laugh. "As for wild boars," said he, " many will be of the nature of swine, that have but two legs to go upon. It will be well to consult the queen."

He came to the gate and stood before her. " Lord Pendaran," said she, " the greeting of heaven and of man to you."

" And to you also," said he; " and better to you than to me or to any of us. I come for counsel."

" Concerning what? " said she.

" Concerning the slaying of wild boars," he said. " There was not the better of Einion Arth Cennen in Dyfed, except Gwawl ab Clud. Proud and fierce and kindly he was; there was no withstanding him in battle, there was no resisting him at the hearth in the hall."

" It is true," said Rhianon. " Unfitting it would be to say less concerning him."

" It appears to me that it would be better for Catwg Gythraul to be slain," said he. " He has the nature of a wild boar on him, and I can not abide these killings by swine."

" He shall not die," said she. "Albeit it is known to me that it was he who slew the chieftain of Iscennen."

" Even if you were other than the sovereign lady, I should

follow your counsels," said he. " Yet there may be a way of
appeasing Einion."

"What way will it be?" said Rhianon.

" I will not disobey you," said he. " Let it be permitted
to me to maintain silence concerning this."

"Maintain it you," she said. "Well known to you are
the fruits of rashness."

" Yes," said he, and the shadow, of laughter on his face.
" I was two days in the Basket of Gwaeddfyd Newynog, and
it is not unremembered with me."

The next day the chieftains held council. Madog and
Deiniol, Catwg and Gwylltyn were there; and against them,
Pendaran Dyfed and Gwawl ab Clud, and Ceredig Cwmteifi,
and Meurig Mwyn of Bronwydd in the place of Einion.

Madog Crintach rose up. " It was for the sake of pacify-
ing the lord of Iscennen," said he, " that the throne at the
feast times was given to the daughter of Hefeydd. For no
reason was this, but for quieting his turbulent nature. Now
that he is slain, let the treaty be kept. There is no sovereign
in Dyfed, and no one shall be seated on the throne."

" Evil was the day on which Arth Cennen was slain," said
Pendaran, not heeding him. " Were it not for the queen, I
would hunt the boar that slew him as far as from here to the
Sea of Mists, and from the top of Pengwaed in Cornwall to
the bottom of Dinsol in the North. Though the boar were
greater than Twrch Trwyth himself, it should come by ill-
health and extreme weariness, if not by death, because of me.
In my deed to God," said he, " were it not for the commands
of Rhianon Ren, the sovereign lady of the Dimetians, to
whom obedience is due, I would be the cause of endless sorrow to that boar."

Said Catwg Gwaeth: " Heedless are you of the council,

truly. There is no queen in Dyfed. It is unfitting to put the title of queen on the daughter of Hefeydd Hen."

"There was the treaty," said Pendaran, turning upon him.

"She has borne the name on account of the turbulence of Einion. It was not in the treaty."

"Well, well, and in my deed now," said Pendaran; "my mind is lightened of its burden by this." He had his bow strung beside his chair; he took it in his hands now, and drew an arrow from his quiver, as if for diversion merely, and without anger or vehemence. "She has no right of queenhood," said he, "and did ill to command me. Evil fall upon me unless I hunt that boar."

"For what reason is this fitting an arrow to the string?" said Madog, and anxiety enough in his voice as he said it. "There is no boar here."

"In my deed there is a boar here," said Pendaran. He was on his feet in a moment, towering over them and dominating them, his aspect regally warlike, menacing; the drawn bowstring at his right shoulder, the shaft aimed between the eyes of Catwg. "When the arrow hath pierced him, the enchantment will fall from him, and you shall see the swinish nature of yonder man."

"The queen ordered you not to shoot," said Catwg. Though he had opposed ten good shields to the arrow of Pendaran, it was well known that the shields would have been pierced, and he himself likewise, without hindering the arrow in its course. "For the sake of the queen, shoot not," said he.

"Not so," said Pendaran; "thou art a wild boar, and it was no more than the daughter of Hefeydd that ordered me."

"She is the queen," said Catwg.

"Say you so, indeed?" said Pendaran, not lowering the shaft.

"We say it," said the four of them. "She shall have the throne at the feasts."

"Einion would be appeased now," said Pendaran, when he was making it known to Rhianon. "If he should have to hear what has been gained by it, he would have no sorrow because of being slain."

"Were it in my power, I would relate it to him in the Gwerddonau Llion," said she. "A magnanimous hero he was; sorrow upon me that he should have been slain."

(The story relates that that evening a Dragon lighted down on the shores of the Gwerddonau Llion in the magical west of the world. "Where is the one that was Einion Arth Cennen?" said the Dragon. "I am here," said Einion; "sorrow upon me that I am not in Dyfed for the defense of my queen." "Sorrow not for it," said the Dragon, and related to him what had befallen. Einion was a stern, silent man at all times; nobly courteous in his demeanor, but few would jest with him, and he with few; seldom was he heard to laugh. But when he heard the news of that council, there was no restraining his laughter until the rising of the sun.)

Three years passed after that; at the end of them the men of the teulu were older and fewer than at the beginning, and it troubled the Crintach more and more daily to see any one on the throne at feast times, and he going throneless himself. It happened on the day before May Eve that news came to Ceredig Call at Boncath, that his lordship was being harried by sea-demons. "I must keep watch upon Pen Cemais tomorrow night," thought he; but if he should ride back to Arberth to give the news to Rhianon, there would be no keeping watch there. "This is a difficult matter," he said; "sorrow upon me if I know which course to take." But in the end he determined to ride forward into Cemais; he knew well that it was on May Eve that the demons would be at their worst.

"Where is Ceredig Cwmteifi?" said Rhianon in the morning. "It will be well for him to lead the watchers on Gorsedd Arberth."

"News has come from him that he has ridden to Aberteifi," said Gwawl. "The sea-demons are troubling his lordship."

"Woe is me on account of this," said she.

Two days after, Deiniol the Wicked came into the court. "Pendaran Dyfed," said he, "Ceredig is dead. He was found at the foot of Pen Cemais at low tide, on the morning of the first day of May."

"Who was it that found his body?" said Pendaran.

"It was I," said Deiniol. "It was a night of sea-mists, and he would have fallen from the headland."

"Evil upon the sea-mists," thought Pendaran; "it shall be the worse for them." He went out to the palace gate.

"It would be well to loose an arrow at Deiniol Drwg," said he. "He was ever an enemy of Ceredig; and there is much that is mistlike and treacherous, both in his mind and in his passions. Were an arrow to be loosed, and to chance to harm him, there might well be clearer nights upon the coast."

"Loose it not," said Rhianon, "or there will be no hindering warfare."

Pendaran went into the council; Gwawl and Meurig went with him, and the Lord of Aberdaugleddau in the place of Ceredig Call Cwmteifi. Now that another of the men of the teulu was slain, and he Ceredig Cwmteifi, the best of the Dimetians after Pendaran himself; a man beloved by Pwyll Pen Annwn, and holding high honor with him in the old days, and renowned even as far as the court of the King of

London — it was intolerable to the Crintach that he should hold back any longer. " The Dimetians grow impatient of the breaking of laws and precedents," said he. " Let the treaty be kept from this time forward. It is unfitting that a woman should be throned at the feast times."

" Let it be kept, and evil fall upon it," said Pendaran. " If Ceredig Call Cwmteifi were here, ye should be hindered; as for me, I have no fortitude left wherewith to oppose ye, on account of being plagued by sea-mists."

Meurig Mwyn and the Lord of Aberdaugleddau marveled at the compliance of Pendaran. " Lord Pendaran," said Meurig, " old age is oppressing you."

" Truly is it oppressing me," said Pendaran. " On account of it, I can not hear of fallings into the sea without petulant impatience, and a desire for revenge upon the sea-mists. By the war-shout and Hai Atton of the Gods, I would shoot until there were no mists left along the sea-border, were it not that the queen forbade me."

While he was speaking, Deiniol Drwg came into the council hall. " What talk is this of queenhood? " said he. "According to the treaty, there is neither king nor queen in Dyfed."

" That is true," said the Crintach. " The treaty shall be kept from this out. Let no man speak of the queen in this council."

Pendaran took his bow lightly, and fitted an arrow to it without pomp or ostentation. " I am growing old," said he; " miserably fitful is my memory. It was but the daughter of Hefeydd forbade me; I had forgotten that she forfeited her sovereignty." No sooner was *sovereignty* out from between his teeth, than he was on his feet, dominant, a warlike hero intensely to be feared. His right hand with the bow-string was at his shoulder; the point of the shaft would take

Deiniol between the eyes, were the string loosed, and thereafter would pass through his head and through the wall of
the council chamber. " By heaven, I never will refrain from
shooting except upon command of a lawful sovereign! The
fickle rashness of my old age is too much for me."

Confusion took the four of them in a moment, and Deiniol more than any of them. " The queen ordered thee not
to shoot," said he; and trembling with the fear of death as
he said it.

" The queen?" said Pendaran. " What talk is this of
queenhood, in the name of heaven? Was there no treaty?
Was there no forfeiting queenhood? There is no sovereign
in Arberth, and no one with a right to command me; and
there are three arrows in the quiver, and one upon the string,
that I shall shoot, to prove that ye are but sea-mists enchanted in the guise of men. It is evil to take advantage of
my old age and infirmities, and to seek to deceive me because
my wits are failing."

" Shoot not, on account of the queen's forbidding thee,"
said Madog. " Rhianon ferch Hefeydd is the queen."

In that way the sovereignty of Rhianon was maintained
that year also. Gwydion ab Don, in the form of a dragon,
took the news to Ceredig Call in the Gwerddonau Llion;
and he, and Arth Cennen, and as many of the teulu of Pwyll
Pen Annwn as were there, made merry over it, and over
Pendaran's infirmities, between dawn and sunset during three
days.

" Less well should I have served her, had I remained
alive," said Ceredig.

In the fifteenth year, it happened that Meurig Mwyn was
in his house at Bronwydd, and as they were sitting down to
the feast, a messenger came into the hall from Rhianon, with
news that there was need of the chieftain at Arberth. " Yes,"

said Meurig; "I will ride forth tomorrow when it dawns."

"It would be better to ride now," said the messenger. "Often the unprompt will be overtaken by misfortune."

Said Meurig: "For what labor will the need of me be?"

"For the watching on Gorsedd Arberth," said the messenger.

"We will set forth at dawn," said Meurig, "and be at Arberth by mid-morning. Inhospitable it were, truly, that a prince should come to the hall, and meet with no entertainment."

"You are to choose," said Gwawl ab Clud; "but it would be better to set forth now."

"Not so," said Meurig; "we will ride at dawn."

That night the house of Meurig was burnt over his head, and he himself perished in the smoke, and Gwawl ab Clud powerless to save him.

Gwawl gave the news to Rhianon and the penteulu. "There was a man lurking beyond the gate," said he, "that had the aspect of Gwylltyn Gwaethaf."

Pendaran Dyfed mourned for the slaying of Meurig; except Gwawl ab Clud, there was no one in Dyfed that he loved more. "The hospitality of the Immortals was with him!" said he. "I delighted in his conversation at all times, and in his generosity, and in his magnanimous bearing in the onslaught, and in the gay nature of him, and the regal songs and the laughter. Hateful to me above all things are these deaths by flame and suffocation."

"Noble are the words spoken," said Rhianon. "It would be unfitting to say less of him."

Pendaran turned to her. "Sovereign princess," said he, "do not deny me this. Unbounded is my desire to loose an arrow this day in the council. The anger of that Gwylltyn is of the nature of flame, and his deceits are darker and more treacherous than the smoke and fumes that destroy the sleeping."

"If Gwylltyn were slain, there would be war," said she, "Unless Pwyll Pen Annwn were here, or Pryderi fab Pwyll to lead you, there would be no advantage even in victory. Those two are of the kingly race, descendants of the Gods and the Cymry; there are many that would support and follow them, that will take no side now; and the Dimetians will be weary of lacking their king by the time Pryderi returns. And return he will," said she, "and will have need of you. But now you would destroy these men, and lay the land in ruin, and neither Pwyll nor Pryderi would have advantage from it."

"We desire no advantage for any one but you," said he. "It is the sorrow of our lives that you should do the penance."

"I am content with waiting and patience," said she. "This fate I foresaw. I pray you to be content with waiting also."

"Old and fierce and hasty am I grown," said Pendaran. "Fiercely I desire to loose this arrow, and three more after it. But I am not without knowledge what is your due."

He went into the council, and as he went, fell to his considering and cogitations. "They shall acknowledge her queenhood this year also," thought he; "Meurig Mwyn would not grudge the price of it."

Pendaran rose up in the council hall. "But for the orders I have received from the queen, the Daughter of Hefeydd Hen in the Kingdom of the Immortals, the sovereign ruler of the Dimetians, your lady and mine, and the lineage of the Gods with her, and herself a Goddess — " (slowly, and haughtily, with defiant menace, the words rolled out from between his teeth and lips) —

" You shall not speak of her thus," cried Gwylltyn Gwaethaf Oll; " unbearable is this."

" By the Son of the Three Shouts, were it not for the
orders I had from her, I would quench certain fires with this
arrow."

The point of it was aimed between the eyes of Gwylltyn;
there was no one worse than he between the sea and the Tywi
and the Teifi, and therefore was he called Gwaethaf Oll.

" Shoot not; the queen ordered thee," said Gwylltyn,
trembling.

" Not so; it was Rhianon ordered me."

" She is the queen."

" I will show thee," said Pendaran, and lowered his aim.
He loosed the arrow, and it took the two folds of the mantle
of Gwylltyn between his right arm and his ribs, and pinned
him by the mantle to the wall. Before the arrow struck,
another was fitted to the bow. " I will show thee again,"
said Pendaran, and loosed it. It took the folds of his mantle
between the left arm and the heart, and pinned him to the
wall on that side also. The third arrow was aimed before
the second struck. " Who is the queen? " said Pendaran
Dyfed.

" Rhianon is the queen," said Gwylltyn.

" Ever I loved formalities," said Pendaran. "Appease
you my irritable nature now, out of courtesy, by speaking
according to her dignity and your own unworthiness. Let
your words be: *The queen, Rhianon Ren the daughter of
Hefeydd, from the Land of the Immortals.*"

" The queen, Rhianon Ren the daughter of Hefeydd in
the Land of the Immortals," said Gwylltyn.

" *The sovereign ruler of the Dimetians, your lady and
mine, and the lineage of the Gods with her, and herself clearly*

a Goddess — speak you the words as they are given you,"
said Pendaran.

Gwylltyn repeated the words.

"Madog and Catwg and Deiniol, to your feet with you,
and repeat the titles of your lady and mine," said Pendaran.
The fear of his swift bow was upon them, with his not ceasing to menace them with it, and they rose up and repeated the
titles.

"That is well," said Pendaran.   "It is delightful to me
that the rash impetuosity of my nature should have been
appeased, without committing violence and ill-considered action.   You see how it is with me," he said.   "I am grown
old and hasty, and am troubled with forgetfulness and am
fickly rash.   When any of the servants of the queen meet
their death by treachery, I am filled with the burning desire
to shoot; and this desire takes me whenever I come into the
council, and it is needful that you should constantly remind
me who it is that has ordered me to restrain the arrows.
And beyond that," said he, " it has been revealed to me that,
should another of us be slain, I shall fall short of restraining
them, and forget the orders of the queen, and shoot in this
council, and that vehemently and without warning; and that
the one I shall shoot at will be the Crintach himself; and
heaven knows, if I did that, it might well be the cause of pining away and distaste of food with me."

So Rhianon had her queenhood acknowledged, what there
was of it after doing penance from dawn to dusk, for that
year also.   As for Meurig Mwyn of Bronwydd, when the
news was given him in the Gwerddonau Llion, there was no
controlling his delight and laughter on account of the arrows
and impatience of Pendaran, and of the infirmities of his old
age.

It happened in the eighteenth year that there was a raid

of giants at Aberdaugleddau, from beyond the raging sea.
Few would go against them, except the men of the teulu of
Pwyll Pen Annwn. Thirty remained to guard the queen at
Arberth, and thirty went against the giants. They obtained
the victory, such as it was, and destroyed the host that opposed them; but twenty of them were slain, and five so deeply wounded that neither physician nor cauldron of cure could
heal them. On the Eve of May Rhianon sent ten men to
guard the Gorsedd, so that there were no more than five and
twenty left at Arberth that night.

The men of the Crintach had become more impatient
than ever by that time; they had determined that on the Eve
of May, when the teulu was at its fewest, their lord should
take the throne at the feast. Pendaran Dyfed came into the
hall early; he took the place of the king's heir opposite to the
dais. Fourteen of his companions were with him; the rest
would lead the queen from the gate, when she might leave
it at sunset.

Madog came in at the head of his men; they did not take
their places about the table, as would have befitted them,
but went forward towards the throne. Pendaran waited until
they were on the dais; then he was on his feet, and his bow
drawn and aimed (it had not its equal in Dyfed either for
swift suddenness, or for driving power, or for sureness of
aim; nor in the whole of the Island of the Mighty, as was
well known, nor in the rest of the world).

" Woe is me! " cried Pendaran; " old and rash and full
of whims have I grown. I am seized with an intolerable desire to drive shafts through the back of yonder chair."

Madog turned and saw him, and stepped aside quickly
from the throne.

" Fickly rash are the desires of old age," cried Pendaran
again. " Bear you with me in all courtesy and consideration,

and it shall be the better. It was revealed to me in dreams during the night that I should be speeding arrows senselessly at the dais throughout the feast time, unless there were one from the Kingdom of the Immortals upon the throne." His voice was like the roaring of the flood among the mountains; his aspect was that of a breaker of battles, a driver of thousands into the wave; there was no one in the hall that would have dared to oppose him.

In that way he preserved the queenhood of Rhianon during the twenty years. There were many that plotted to destroy him; but he was wise continually, and went nowhere but where Rhianon might have counseled him to go, and did nothing but what was service for her. With that, and with the ready, swift terror of his bow, it was as if there were unseen dragons of protection encircling him; there was no one that dared to come against him openly, and no one that could obtain success or advantage against him in secret.

III. THE COMING OF PRYDERI

HE twenty-one years of the penance of Rhianon were at their end, and two months after it. By that time there were no more than thirty left to maintain the sovereignty of their queen: Pendaran Dyfed, and Gwawl ab Clud, and eight and twenty of the teulu of Pwyll Pen Annwn with them. From the Eve of May onward, she had let no day pass without ten of them guarding the Gorsedd from noon until sunset. Glanach and Llonach and Mwynach, her three birds, had returned to her; she had not kept them, to take delight in their singing, but had sent them questing over the world after her lord, the Son of the Boundless, that had been Pwyll Pen Annwn before the falling of the sorrow of the Dimetians. She had made known to the men of the teulu that the birds had returned, and that it would mean the coming of Pwyll or of Pryderi; and indeed, great was the need on them for good tidings; with their having grown so few and old, and their enemies waxing stronger and more insolent around them always.

Here is what happened to them at last: they were leading her into the hall for the feast, Pendaran on her right and Gwawl ab Clud on her left, and she leaning on their arms dependent on them; eighteen men followed those three. As they came in, they saw what had befallen. The place was filled with five hundred of the men of Madog, and the Crintach himself was on the throne. Five hundred bows were strung, and five hundred arrows aimed at Rhianon. Even if Pendaran had had his arms free for shooting, the queen would have been slain before his bow-string could have obtained its stretching.

Madog Crintach laughed. "Pendaran Dyfed," said he, "five hundred are the shafts that are aimed. Is there curbing your petulance in it? Is your rash impatience quenched?"

Pendaran moved forward between the arrows and Rhianon. "Their bows are aimed," he whispered to her; "there is no resisting them now. What answer will I give him?"

She laughed quietly. "A peaceful answer," said she; "give him a peaceful answer. Say that he has won, and may get to his feasting. Say that we will go into exile in Ireland, if it please him. He will not slay us here, but will make pursuit of us secretly."

"Indeed, my impatience is quenched, good soul," said Pendaran. "Never had I a greater desire for peace than now. The aged long for quietness. Take you the throne of the Dimetians. As for us, if it please you, we will go into exile in Ireland."

Then said Rhianon: "Lord Madog, I shall come again to oppose you; and it will be with Pwyll Pen Annwn or with Pryderi fab Pwyll."

Uproariously they laughed in mockery at that, the whole five hundred of them and Madog their lord. "Were it not for pity, ye should be slain," said he. "Ye are given until the morning to leave Dyfed."

"Lord Madog," whispered Gwylltyn to him; "it would be better to slay them before they can take ship at Aberdaugleddau."

"That is true," said Madog, whispering again. "Men shall go in pursuit of them, and slay them secretly."

The twenty turned sadly, and led their queen out from the hall. They came into the courtyard without speaking.

"The ruin of Dyfed is this," said Pendaran. "There is no more hope for it henceforward. Without fighting, it would have been hard for the thirty of us to have resisted them further. An evil fate is this."

"Not so," said Rhianon. "Fortunate are you, truly. The Immortals will have heard of your service; not one of you will be without his reward."

"By the Shield of Hu Gadarn, let there be no talk of reward," said Pendaran. "To have served you has been a better reward than was given to any one before. Less than human should we be, if we desired rewards beyond this."

The eighteen old men sighed; none of their keen, fierce, aged eyes but had the tears in them. "That is true," said they. "We will have no rewards. Alas that we are alive, to behold you bereft of sovereignty."

"Go you back to your immortality; this world is too evil for you," said Pendaran. "Be it granted to us to know that you are among your own Dragon Kin, and we will take what reward we desire. We are old men that love you," said he; "grant us the sight of the wings that shall carry you to the House of Hu Gadarn. After that, our own hands will take what our hearts desire."

The eighteen nodded; their old eyes fell, or were set, shining, for far vision. "Indeed, we could take it then," said they.

"It is known to me what ye would take." With that she turned to Gwawl ab Clud. "Lord Gwawl," she said; "is it your will to return to your own land?"

"It is not," said he. "I desire new lives in the Island of

the Mighty. My fate will be one with theirs. Call you upon the dragon chariots; we are not able to serve you further."

They were standing beneath the apple-tree in the court-yard, under the moon. She lifted her face; although sight-less, she saw what was not made known to any of them. She was aware of flaming mists, green and golden, that leaped and streamed over the firmament. They drew nearer and took the form of a dragon, that circled in the air above the Dimetians, and lighted down at last in the limbs of the tree.

"It is given you now to behold an Immortal," said Rhia-non. "It is given you to hear the conversation of Gwydion the son of Don."

They looked up, and the tree was one white flame and intense glory above them; and there in the midst of it was Gwydion ab Don in his bardic guise, the most beautiful youth in the world.

"It is now that you will come to the Wyddfa, Daughter of Hefeydd," said he. "Hu the Mighty is enthroned there awaiting you. The knife is in the meat and the mead is in the horn, and there will be revelry in the Hall of the Gods, when the best of their race is made one with them. Every night during these one and twenty years it has been offered to you; you will not refuse it now. The dragon wings are made ready; come you with me now to the Ones that await you."

Proud and gentle was the laughter of Rhianon Ren. "Ah dear!" she said; "Gods and men, you are without under-standing of this. Did you think that I had suffered defeat?"

The light waned from the tree, and Gwydion was gone. They went on towards the outer gate. Before they came to it, a sound of knocking arose from without.

"Is there a porter?" cried the one that knocked.

"There is not," said Pendaran Dyfed. "There is revel-

ry in the court of Madog Crintach; the porters will be feasting with their lord."

"The greeting of heaven and of man to the one that made
answer. Open the portal, if it please you."

"It is better for a good man not to enter the house of
the wicked," said Pendaran. "Who is it that desires to come
in?"

"A craftsman bearing his craft."

"What craft?"

"Three Unusual Crafts, and the first of them, restoring
youth to the aged."

"Madog the Crintach would be better without it. Not
well would it be for you to come in here."

"The second is restoring sight to the sightless."

"Shall I open it?" he asked Rhianon.

"Let him make known the third craft first," said she.

"The Crintach would be better with less sight than he
has," said Pendaran. "What will the third craft be?"

"O chieftain, it is not on the Crintach that I shall exercise my crafts. As for the third, it will be restoring thrones
to their rightful owners," said Gwri Gwallt Euryn.

"Open thou the portal, dear soul," said Rhianon.

He opened it, and Gwri dismounted at the horse-block, and
came in. As soon as he saw Rhianon, he kneeled down at
her feet. "Lady," said he, "is it your will that I make
known to you the manner of exercising the first of the arts?"

"It is my will," she said.

He rose up, and took the fillet, and fastened it about her
white hair as Gwron Brif-fardd had directed him. "By the
Wood, the Field and the Mountain," he said, "quit whiteness, every hair of you, and assume your natural color; let
the black be black, and the brown brown, and the golden

golden; and let the limbs regain their youth, as if years had never passed over them."

She stood there, as young and glorious of aspect as she had been when Pwyll first saw her riding through the valley of the Gorsedd; her rightful immortality kindled in all her limbs.

" The years are undone, and the sorrow with them," said Rhianon. " This also was foreknown. Do you deem now that I have suffered defeat? "

" This is a marvel," said the twenty of them. " Praised and honored be this young man, beyond all the youths of the world."

" Lady," said Gwri Gwallt Euryn, " is it your will that I make the second art known? "

" It is my will, dear," said she.

He put the ring on the forefinger of his right hand, and lifted it to her right eyelid, as Plenydd the Sight-giver had directed him. " By the Wood, the Field and the Mountain, quit you your blindness," said he. Then he touched the left eyelid, and said to it: " By the Wood, the Field and the Mountain, quit you your blindness also "; and then: " The vision of the God, the dragon and the eagle to the two of you from this out."

Rhianon turned to the twenty. " Souls, souls," said she; " excellent and delightful to me it is to behold you." There were two score eyes with them, that were shedding the tears of joy and delight. " Do you deem now that I have suffered defeat? " said she.

"As for you, dear," she said, turning to Gwri again; " am I made known to you now, as clearly as you were made known to me from the moment I heard you knocking on the portal? "

He was at her feet again, his arms compassing her knees.

"Indeed, yes, dear," she said, raising him. "You are my own son Pryderi."

. . . . . .

"By heaven," said Pendaran Dyfed; "it is Pwyll Pen Annwn's son."

. . . . . .

They heard hoof-beats on the road near by, and the voice of the Lord of Aberdaugleddau. "Come," said Pendaran, quietly; "we will meet them on the road with the tidings." They stole forth through the gate, and met the ten from Gorsedd Arberth.

Said Pendaran Dyfed: "Is there any news with you from Gorsedd Arberth?"

"We saw a youth riding by through the twilight, and half of us said that he would be Pwyll Pen Annwn; and half of us held that he would be one of the Immortals," said the Lord of Aberdaugleddau. "Is there any news from the hall?"

"There is," said Pendaran. "Madog Crintach is enthroned there."

"The sorrow has fallen at last," said the ten. "Never was there misery to equal this."

"There never was joy to equal it," said Pendaran Dyfed. "Come you into the courtyard."

They went in, and beheld Pryderi and Rhianon. "By heaven," said the Lord of Aberdaugleddau, "it is Pwyll Pen Annwn's son."

. . . . . .

The nine and twenty old men, the last of the best of the Dimetians, and Gwawl ab Clud that had not grown old, and never would, came about Pryderi, eager to delight their eyes with his strength and his beauty, with the mien and regal bearing of Pwyll Pen Annwn that they beheld with him;

eager for the touch of his hands. They remembered all the
delights they had ever known during their lives; the best
that they remembered seemed to them akin to sorrow, compared with the delight of beholding Pryderi fab Pwyll Pen
Annwn.

"Lord," said Pendaran Dyfed; "here is your teulu.
There will be barely five hundred within the hall to give you
the welcome of opposition. Is it permitted to us to storm the
hall?"

"Souls, souls," said Rhianon, "I will have you restored
to the best of your manhood first." She turned to Pryderi.
"Dear," she said; "there never were the equals of these
Dimetians. Set you the fillet about their foreheads, one
after another of them; it was for this that I bound it about
your swaddling-clothes, the morning you were born. Souls,
souls," she said; "did you deem that I would desert you?
Did you deem that the companionship of the Immortals
would be better to me than the companionship of such Cymry
as you are?"

One by one, beginning with Pendaran Benteulu, Pryderi put youth on them; until there were thirty warriors with
him in the courtyard, and they all in the prime of their
strength and youthful manhood, of their warlike beauty and
glory and vigor.

Pendaran Dyfed sighed. "Dear soul," said Rhianon,
"what will be troubling you?"

"Inordinate desires," said Pendaran.

"What desires are they?" said she.

"I lament that I rejected that which was offered me.
In spite of this young manhood, it is the fickle nature of the
over-old that remains with me."

"Speak you without concealment," said Pryderi.

Then Pendaran said: "Heretofore I was penteulu for

Pwyll Pen Annwn thy father. During one and twenty years have I been penteulu for the queen. For her sake I have desired often to shoot; for her sake I have refrained from shooting. Sorrow upon me, I desire a reward for this."

"Lord," said the nine and twenty; "the best of us will not compare with Pendaran."

"What reward do you desire, dear soul?"

Pendaran answered hesitatingly, and with the bashfulness of a young boy. "This," said he; "that I may make the way for my lord into the hall of his fathers. Delightful to my soul beyond all things would be this pleasant diversion. It is so long since I have made the bowstring sing."

All this while they had heard the shouting and revelry from within the hall. Suddenly the door was flung open, and a flare of light came out to them. "Stand in the shadow of the tree," said Rhianon, and they did so. "Forgo you the reward for a little while, Pendaran dear," said she. "My son has three Unusual Arts with him; and if the truth were told, he has barely made one of them known to us yet. Go you forward into the hall, Pryderi," said she. "There are your three arts that must be exercised."

"Who is it that makes disturbance in the courtyard?" shouted the porter. "Let him begone, whosoever he is. The knife is in the meat and the mead is in the horn, and no one may enter."

Pryderi fab Pwyll went forward towards the door. "Say you so, indeed?" said he. "A craftsman bearing his craft may enter at any time."

"Neither craftsman nor bard, neither king's son nor chieftain," said the porter.

"It is a marvel to me that this should be spoken," said Pryderi. "Come you into the hall with me, that you may make it clearer by the light of the torches."

He took the porter by the arm, and led him into the hall; it was more dragging than leading, and neither good will nor silence with the one dragged. "Lord Madog," cried he; "here is one that hath entered by violence when the door was opened."

"If he had no regard for usage, he ought to be slain," said Deiniol Drwg.

"Make an end of him quickly," said the Crintach; "we will have respect paid to the precedents of the court." A hundred men rose up, eager for the diversion; when they saw Pryderi, they paused, although their swords were drawn and his sheathed.

Pryderi laughed merrily. "As for usage and precedent," said he, "there will be regard paid to them everywhere except here. It is as if some upstart alien held court here, and no rightful king of the race of the Cymry."

"What disregard of them is found here?" said Madog. He knew that he had never learned kinghood.

"Disregard enough, and the greatest in the world," said Pryderi. "Two men may enter a court at any time: an institutional bard and the son of a king. Two men may enter if there is need of them; a warrior bearing his arms and a craftsman bearing his craft. I am a bard and a king's son, yet entrance was refused me. I am a warrior of whom there is need, yet I was not made welcome. I am also a craftsman bearing his crafts, yet I was not asked concerning the nature of them. Unkinglike and uncourtly is this."

"Let a place be made for him next to the penteulu," said Madog. It was his nature to be without hospitality, and therefore was he called the Crintach. No one had ever had generous kindliness from him; what he had, he kept, and desired more. Now that kinghood had come to him, nothing would please him but to seem kingly; he desired to put on the bearing of the kings of the Cymry, lest it should be remembered that he was the son of a merchant from beyond the sea. He would accord honor to this guest; but it was fear and meanness that drove him to it. He would have the most splendid feast that had been given in Dyfed since the reign of Hu Gadarn; but what seemed to him regal generosity was no better that gluttonous waste. There was triumph and delight in the hall that night, and consuming meat and mead without measure; but it was such feasting as would be hateful to heroes, and the songs sung would be the sorrow of bards.

Pryderi took his place; Gwylltyn Gwaethaf was in the seat of the Penteulu next to him. "The greeting of heaven and of man to you, Pendaran Dyfed," said Pryderi, and obtained no answer from him. The feasting went forward.

" Throughout these islands I have heard the renown of Pendaran Dyfed," said Pryderi. "This is a marvel to me."

" What is a marvel to thee?" said Gwylltyn.

" That a man with such fame for valor and courtesy should practise ill manners towards a guest," said Pryderi.

" Who practises ill manners?" said Gwylltyn.

" It is you that practise them, Pendaran," said Pryderi. "Ungreeted have I taken my place at your side. A cause of grief with me is this."

" Insolent thou art," said Gwylltyn. He rose to his feet, and struck at Pryderi with his hand. "Insolent thou art, truly," said he.

Pryderi rose up. "The penteulu of the court has given me blows and violence," said he. "According to precedent, it is a cause of fighting between him and me, and if I overcome him, I shall be the penteulu. It is the courtesy of king's houses," said he.

Gwylltyn waited for nothing, but drew his sword, and

smote at Pryderi. Pryderi struck it out of his hand lightly, and it fell broken afar in the hall. " Forgo you the office of penteulu," said he; " it will be the better for you."

Gwylltyn slunk away ashamed; he would have fought well enough, but for overmuch meat and mead. Pryderi took the place of the penteulu; and Madog called Gwylltyn to him.

" This can be righted in the morning," said Madog. "At the first feast, there are the usages that must be considered."

Then he said: " The victorious shall be penteulu. Keep you this office, whosoever you are. Let the feasting go forward. Let the household bard sing, that we may have peace here."

As for who the household bard was: he was Deiniol the Wicked; there was no one better among them at bardism than he. Institutional bards of the holy Gorsedd of Ynys Prydain were not to be found in Dyfed at that time.

This much may be said of Deiniol's singing: it was without the three necessities of bardic song. The best truth in it was a lie; and truth is well known to be the first necessity. It was framed more in rancor against the queen, and Pwyll Pen Annwn, and Pendaran Dyfed, than in praise even of the Crintach; of whom, heaven knows, there was little praise either to be spoken or sung; the second necessity is, that the noble shall be extolled, and the small-souled and meagre left without mention. There was no sweet sound nor beauty with it; and the third necessity is, that a bardic song shall be well-framed and melodious, closely knit with sweet consonances and assonances, and no less agreeable to the ear than the music of the blackbird at dawn, or the whisper of the west wind among the reeds on the fairest evening in August, or the carolling of the mavis in the woods in May. Unless those necessities are observed the Immortal Kindred cannot maintain their friendship with the bards; neglect of them would have been the corruption of the whole virtue of the Island of the Mighty, in those days.

Pryderi rose to his feet. " Vile singing is this," he said, pleasantly. He made his way to the dais, where Deiniol stood. " Peace be with you all," said he; " I myself will show you singing. It is unfitting that the king's feast should be defiled by songs without truth, extolment or assonance. Give me the harp, good soul, and I will make known to you the true method of bardic singing."

Deiniol stopped and stared at him. " By heaven," said he, " is this to be permitted? What insolent youth is here? "

Pryderi laughed lightly and pleasantly. "A bard, such as it is," said he. " Go you down there, good soul, and I will show you singing."

No one had the desire to hinder him, so regal was his mien, and so careless his laughter and cheerful audacity. He took the harp from Deiniol; who went down slowly from the dais. With the first note that he struck, he put wonder and silence on every one. Then he made these verses and sang them:

> *When darkness came down*
> *On the lord of the west,*
> *And, bereft of renown,*
> *He went forth on his quest,*
> *When he wandered the world, and was nameless,*
> *Long years without joy, without rest;*

> *Did ye deem that he went,*
> *And left after him none?*
> *That his life was all spent,*
> *And your warfare all won?*

When ye dreamed of the passing of Pwyll,
  Took ye thought for Pryderi his son?

Madog started forward. " Pryderi!" he cried," where hast thou heard news of Pryderi fab Pwyll?"

"Peace!" said Pryderi. " Kings are silent, when bards may be singing." Then he made these verses and sang them:

When the queen of the land
  Was driven forth from her own,
That the puny might stand
  On the steps of the throne,
Did ye deem there was none to redeem her?
Did ye search betwixt Mynwy and Mon?

A little gold band
  From the regions of light,
And a ring from her hand
  That had power over night,
And a babe that was stolen from the cradle —
Can ye fathom the riddle aright?

Thrice dark was the world
  When they stole him away,
To be hidden, to be hurled
  In the flame, in the spray;
Save for one that was watching to save him
He should not have looked on the day.

— He multiplied the glory of his hwyl upon them with the singing; they were enthralled, they were enspelled, they were enchanted; they did not move nor speak; many of them remembered with yearning the splendor of the days of Pwyll Pen Annwn. Little wonder in that; since unseen behind and over him on the dais stood One bodied in purple

flame, even Alawn Brif-fardd Prydain; even the Immortal
Ruler of Song.

> *By this ring that was found*
> *In the stall when they found me,*

— he held up the ring of the Family of Hefeydd; they knew
it for Rhianon's ring; it was as if carven out of sun-stuff;
it flashed lightnings of brilliance through the hall —

> *By this small fillet bound,*
> *Gold-buckled around me,*

— he held up the fillet; they trembled when they saw its
beauty and magical nature, and remembered how of old it
had shone about the hair of Rhianon —

> *Ye shall know me in anger and fear*
> *Ere the hands of my druids have crowned me.*

> *Hath the saying been heard?*
> *Hath the fate been made known?*
> *Must I speak the brute word*
> *Ere I come to mine own,*
> *That myself am Pryderi fab Pwyll*
> *That should come, that should reign on his throne?*

Madog started up from the king's place. "Catwg,
Gwylltyn, Deiniol," he cried, "without conflict there will
be no kinghood for us. It is the son of Pwyll."

"Be silent as to that," cried Catwg Gwaeth. "Cowards
obtain nothing. Every one to his arms!" he shouted; "the
man hath a host of Gwyddelians about the city." They
raised up their warshout, such as it was, and forced the Dimetians to their arming. But for the enchantments of Ab Cil-

coed, there were many who would not have armed against the son of Pwyll.

But Pryderi strode towards the middle of the dais and towards Madog. "Quit thou the throne," said he. The Crintach drew sword, and struck at him, and he lifted neither shield nor blade to meet the blow. But it seemed to Madog as if a great battle-brand of flaming sapphire-stuff flashed down from the rafters of the roof, swifter than the lightning and more beautiful, and met his own sword, and shivered it into fragments in the midst of its falling. He looked up, and there was One standing over Pryderi that had the poplar-stature with him, and the beauty of the dawn, and his body of golden flaming fire. He shrank back from the menace of Gwron Gawr the Heroic Prif-fardd.

"Quit thou the throne when the king's son orders thee," said Pryderi fab Pwyll; and Madog slunk back into the sha-dows behind the throne.

Then Pryderi took his place before the throne, and watched those who were arming against him in the hall. "There may be peace here yet," he said. "It is permitted to the Crintach and the three that are with him to leave Dyfed this night; the rest shall have peace and pardon, if they desire it."

"So shall it never be permitted to you; and you shall have neither pardon nor peace," cried Catwg. He and Gwyll-tyn and Deiniol were well armed by that time; they were going about among the Dimetians, ordering and inciting them. It was as if they prepared for battle with a host, not for the slaying of one man; they knew that that one was Pryderi fab Pwyll. The three of them were powerful men, accustomed to conflict; but they would have their whole host about them armed, before they would give battle to the son of Pwyll Pen Annwn. They overthrew the tables of the feasting, and dragged them to the walls for the sake of war-space. Pryderi stood, and watched them proudly.

Catwg raised his warshout; five hundred of them raised it after him; shouting they rushed forward. When their rush was at its beginning, an arrow sped out from the back of the hall behind them, and passed Pryderi between his right arm and his ribs. It appeared to them that it would have been one among themselves that had shot, and that their enemy would have been already wounded, if not slain. But it was not Pryderi that moved or trembled because of the arrow, nor that groaned when it struck; nor that ceased then from nefarious projects, and from stealing upon men from behind, and from plotting treacherous dagger-blows, repugnant to the warlike and the courteous; nor that fell where he was lurking and creeping behind the throne.

"Evil upon the arrow," groaned Madog Crintach; "a miserable death is this."

They heard him, and paused in the first of their rush, shaken by indecision. But Catwg and his companions leaped forward, shouting them on. Deiniol and he were at the foot of the dais; Pryderi stood before the throne, unshaken, his sword undrawn, his shield at his back; the points of their spears were a hand's length from his breast. Two arrows sped out of the far end of the hall; Catwg fell for the first, and Deiniol for the second, at the very feet of the son of Pwyll. The third arrow flew, and Gwylltyn Gwaethaf fell upon his brethren. There was no remaining in doubt as to who might be the speeder of those arrows.

The men in the hall hesitated; there rose up from behind them a regal, triumphant shouting of warshouts; a warshout that they remembered of old, and a warshout that was new to them: *For the sake of Pwyll Pen Annwn!* and *For the sake of Pryderi fab Pwyll!* They turned; they saw there thirty men under Pendaran Dyfed, who had been old men when the feast began, but were now in the glory of their vigor and manhood, terrible of mien and aspect. There was the bow of Pendaran to consider, and how the shafts would come from it, if he had a mind to send them, swifter than the driving of hail before the north wind in January, when the blasts of winter are at their fiercest.

Pendaran laughed. "I shall never restrain the rash passions of my age," he cried; "I have no more power over the arrows." It seemed to them all that shafts from him were raining about them continually; no man dared to move because of them. "Evil upon the bowstring that I can not keep it from speeding them! Evil upon my right hand, that will forever be drawing the string!" He shot, and laughed, and shot. "Old age is a curse," he cried; "let none of ye desire it! Full it is of whims irrestrainable." The arrows took the sword blades in their hands and split them lengthwise; they shaved off the hair from their lips without grazing the skin. "I have destroyed the Crintach; I have destroyed Deiniol Drwg, and Catwg Gwaeth, and Gwylltyn Gwaethaf Oll; yet still the bowstring twangs and sings. Woe is me, it may well be that I shall pine away on account of this!" So he put confusion and terror upon them all, without slaying, or so much as wounding one of them. His shooting was unlike the shooting of a mortal; not one of them, but it seemed to him that arrows were grazing him at every moment. The men of the teulu of Pwyll Pen Annwn put their mantles over their faces, and rocked with laughter, silently. Pryderi took his place on the throne, and watched them; it was marvelous that he could keep from laughter. To him, and to Rhianon, was revealed what it was given to no one else to see. They saw the flame form that leaned over Pendaran from behind, and rained the arrows upon the string of his bow more swiftly than the wave-foam is driven by the tempests of November. They saw the glory of Plenydd Brif-fardd Prydain.

"Let a passage be cleared through the midst of ye," roared Pendaran. "For the sake of my peace let it be cleared; I shall not be able to refrain from driving arrows along the middle of the hall, such a storm of them as will sweep it clean. Get to the walls, if ye love your peace and mine." They obeyed him hastily.

Then Rhianon Ren went forward, passing through the middle of the hall towards the dais. "Ah, peace now, Pendaran Benteulu," said she.

The bowstring ceased its twanging, the arrows their flight. The Dimetians marveled when they saw her without blemish of old age or blindness, more beautiful than ever she had been. Pryderi came down from the dais, and led her to the throne. She took her place on the throne of the Princes of Dyfed.

"Indeed, indeed," thought Pendaran; "it was a marvel even to me, was that shooting. Never have I had pleasure out of bowstrings until now."

Then Pryderi spoke to the Dimetians that had followed Madog. "It is permitted to you all to leave this land," said he. "You shall ride towards Morganwg this night, and Pendaran Dyfed behind you, with his bow strung, for protection."

One of them stood forth. "I will not leave Dyfed," said he. "I served my lord Pwyll Pen Annwn of old, and he never had cause to complain of me. I will not leave Dyfed now that Pryderi fab Pwyll is here. If you are unwilling that I should be your man, order Pendaran to shoot."

Five of them took their places beside him; then ten more, then a hundred. "We have been under evil," said they;

"an evil compulsion was put upon our minds. We will not leave Dyfed, and the true king on the throne."

"Evil upon me if there is any king here," said Pryderi. "Evil upon me if I will have one man to follow me. Rhianon Ren my mother is the queen; there is no sovereignty here except with her."

They bowed their heads; they covered their faces with their mantles. "It is made known to us now," said the first of them, "how she has been made to suffer because of us. It would be impossible for her to take service from such as we are."

In silence the tears fell from their eyes. They remembered the good they had had from Rhianon; they remembered her wisdom and kindness; the thought of her long sorrow was a greater sorrow to them than they had ever known.

"Lady," said they; "order Pendaran to shoot."

But Pendaran's bow was unstrung, and he was hanging it on the wall behind the chair of the penteulu, where it had not hung since Pwyll Pen Annwn's time.

"Not so," said Rhianon. "Pendaran Benteulu will shoot at my enemies, not at the men of my own teulu; not at the men who are my own well-loved friends."

.   .   .   .

With that the hall was suddenly filled with light and music; three bright jewels of song fluttered among the rafters, more light-giving than the moon of heaven. A murmur of delight went through the Dimetians.

"They are the Birds of Rhianon," said Pendaran Dyfed.

"They are Aden Lanach, Aden Lonach, and Aden Fwynach," said Pryderi; "they are the three beautiful Singers of Peace."

While they sang, all mournfulness departed from the Dimetians; it was to every one as if the whole evil of his life had gone from him. For an hour they flashed and sang there, then went forth again in quest of Pwyll Pen Annwn.

With their going forth from the hall, the Story of Rhianon and Pryderi ends. On account of its relating by what means Pryderi accomplished setting the birds free and overthrowing the men of Madog Crintach, it is often called *The Book of the Three Unusual Arts of Pryderi.*

Key to Pronunciation
and
Glossary

KEY TO PRONUNCIATION

The vowels in Welsh are a, e, i, o, u, w, y. In pronouncing these, none should ever be slurred or neutralized, as in English one neutralizes the final *e* in *little*, or the *a* and the *o* in *attention:* each must always have full value. *A*, when long, has the sound of *a* in *father;* when short, it has the sound of *a* in *fat.* So *e* varies between the sound of *ai* in *pain* and that of *e* in *pen; i*, between *ee* in *feel* and *i* in *fill; o*, short, is as *o* in *hot;* the long sound of it is between the *a* of *all* and the *ow* in *know. U* has the sound of the French *u* in *une* or the German *u* modified; those who know not this sound can pronounce it in the same way as the Welsh *i*, taking *feel* and *fill* as key words. *W* varies between the sounds of *oo* in *fool* and *u* in *full:* we should write either word *fwl. Y*, in final syllables or monosyllables is commonly the equivalent of the *u* (*feel, fill*); in other places it varies between the *u* in *burn* and the *u* in *bun;* as a word by itself, meaning *the*, it has the sound of *u* in *fur*.

It will be seen that the two sounds given for each vowel are in reality the same in kind; they differ only in quantity. Of course all rules given for the pronunciation of any language in terms of another language can only be approximate; so here one may say that in pronouncing any Welsh vowel the safest plan will be to steer a middle course between the long sounds and the short ones as given above; making your *a's* neither so broad as the broad English *a* in *father*, nor so short as the one in *fat*. Then one should remember that the accent falls always on the last syllable but one — except perhaps in such words as Penclawdd, Penbardd, Prif-fardd, in which two words are joined together, and the accent would tend to fall equally on either.

Of the consonants, b, d, l, m, n, p, t, are pronounced as in English. *C* is always equal to English *k; ch* is pronounced as in Scots *loch*, it is something like the German *ch*, or the Spanish *j. Dd* has the sound of *th* in *that, thy, this* or *breathe. F* is the English *v; ff* is the English *f;* the two words *of* and *off* are keywords for these two consonants; though English words they are written with Welsh letters. *G* is always like *g* in *gave, give*, or *get. Ng* is always like *ng* in *sing;* never as in *singe* or *finger. H* is always well aspirated. *Ll* is simply an aspirated *l;* there is no *th* in it, no *sh* in it, no sort of splurge or splutter in it; it presents no difficulty until one tries to pronounce it by twisted and sidelong motions of the tongue. So *mh* and *nh* are aspirated *m* and *n* respectively; *ph* is *f* (as in English); *rh* is an aspirated *r*, and *r* is well trilled on the end of the tongue as in Spanish or Italian; it is not a guttural *r*, as in the American pronunciation of English; nor a knock-kneed nonentity as in the English pronunciation of it. *S* has never the sound of *z*, always that of English *ss;* when followed by *i* and another vowel, however, the *si* becomes equal to English *sh;* thus *Moel Siabod* we pronounce (nearly) *Moyle Shab'-od. Th* is like the English *th* in *breath, thigh; breathe* we might write in Welsh letters *bridd;* but *breath* we should write *breth.*

Of the diphthongs: ai, ae, au, ei, eu, ey, may all be pronounced like the *i* in *fine, quite* or *pile;* there are of course differences between these diphthongs, but there is no English sound, except in dialects, that will express them. *Aw* is like *ow* in *cow; ew* is a combination or unification of the sound of *ay* as in *day* as the first part and the sound of *oo* as in *fool* as the second; make one sound, a true diphthong, of these two, and you have it. (This sound is common enough in the cockney dialect). *Iw is eeoo* — like the *ew* in *new. Wy* is *ooee* — but made one sound, not as in coo-ee. *Oe, oi, ou* may be pronounced as *oy* in *boy.* Lastly, *w* becomes a consonant generally when it follows *g; i,* when it precedes another vowel: thus *Gwyn = Gwin; Taliesin* is *Tal-yes'-in,* not *Tally-esin.*

Perhaps it will make this clearer if we give approximate pronunciations for the chief proper names in the book.

DYFED: the dyf is equivalent to the English *dove;* it rhymes with *love, above, shove,* and so on. Also the accent falls on it. The *ed* is equivalent to English *head,* when once the initial *h* of that word has been dropped.

PWYLL: Pooeelh; there is no better way of writing it in English characters.

RHIANON: Rhee-ann'-onn.

GWRI GWALLT EURYN: Goor'-ee Gwalht Eye'-reen.

DIENW 'R ANFFODION: D'-yenn'-oorr Anfod'-yon.

HU GADARN: Hü Gad'-arrn (or one may call it Hee, if necessary).

CERIDWEN: Kerr-id'-wen (Ceridwen Ren ferch Hu: Kerrid'-wen
Rain vair — rhymes with *fair* — kHee).

TEULU: tilee; it rhymes (more or less) with Smiley or highly.

MANAWYDDAN: Man-ah-wee'-than.

PRYDERI: Pree-dairy.

GWYDION: Gwid'-yon.

GLOSSARY

AB, FAB, MAB. Son, youth, the son of.

ABRED. The Cylch yr Abred or Circle of Inchoation was the lowest
of the three circles or planes of existence according to Druidic
philosophy. In it the host of souls go through the cycles of incarnation, passing from the mineral to the vegetable, thence to the
animal and finally to the human kingdom; in which last they have
the power of choosing good and warring against evil (cythraul),
and at last attaining godhood or immortality. The four stages of
Abred are: Annwn, Obryn, Cydfil, and Dyndeb.

AFANC. A monster that dwelt in the Lake of Floods (Bala Lake),
and caused the water to rise till the land was drowned. Hu
Gadarn, when he led the Cymry into the Island of the Mighty,
dragged the Afanc out of the lake with his two oxen, Nynnio and
Peibio; thus saving the land from the oppression of waters.

ANNWN. The Underworld, the lowest plane of Abred.

AWEN. The muse, the inspiration of the poets. Tydain Tad Awen,
Tydain father of the Muse, according to the Iolo MSS., the
founder of Druidism.

BACH. Little, used commonly as a term of endearment.

BENADUR (PENADUR). Chieftain.

BENBARDD (PENBARDD). Chief of Bards.

BRIF-FARDD (PRIF-FARDD). Primitive Bard, a term applied to Plenydd, Alawn, and Gwron, the three disciples of Tad Awen (see Iolo MSS.).

BYD. The world.

CAER. Castle, stronghold. Caer Hun, the Castle of Sleep; Caer Drais, the Castle of Violence; Caer Hedd, the Castle of Peace. Caer Sidi, Caer Ochren, Caer Fedifyd, have their mention in Taliesin's *Preiddieu Annwn* (The Spoils of the Deep).

CANTREF. A division of the land; there might be two or three to six or seven of them in a modern county. A commote is a smaller division than a cantref. See the *History of Wales* by Professor Lloyd of Bangor; also for the location of the various cantrefi mentioned; and for explanations of the duties, etc., of the various officials of the Welsh court, such as the Distain, Chief Judge, Penteulu.

CEUGANT. The highest of the three druidic circles of Existence: the World of the Absolute.

COELBREN. The ancient alphabet of the Druids, according to the Iolo MSS. It bears a close resemblance to the alphabet of the Celtiberian inscriptions found in Spain.

CRINTACH. Curmudgeon.

CYTHRAUL. The principle of evil; nowadays, the devil.

CYMRAEG. The Welsh language. Cymru, Wales. Cymry, the Welsh; traditionally, the first of the three races that occupied Britain by peaceful invasion and consent. The other two were the Brythons and the Lloegrwys. Science also speaks of the Ancient Britons as composite of three racial stocks, calling these Iberians, Gaels, and Brythons.

CYNGHANEDD. The system of consonance used in certain of the Welsh meters, e. g.:

> Yr alarch ar ei wiw lyn
> Abid galch fel abad gwyn.
>
> (*Dafydd ab Gwilym*)

DISTAIN. An official of the king's court, according to the Laws of Hywel Dda.

DRWG, GWAETH, GWAETHAF OLL. Bad, worse, worst of all.

FAB. See Ab.

FERCH (MERCH). The daughter of.

GADARN. Mighty.

GAWR (CAWR). Giant.

GOREU. The Best. Goreu fab Ser, the Best One, the son of the Stars. The Caer of Gwydion ab Don was the Milky Way.

GORSEDD. Primarily a throne, in which sense it is used in the term Gorsedd Arberth. Secondarily, the throne or Chair (somewhat in the sense of a chair at a University) of a bard; thence, a School of Bards, as the Gorsedd of Glamorgan; thence, an assembly of Druids and Bards for the carrying out of sacred rites.

GWENT ISCOED. A kingdom in the neighborhood of Monmouthshire.

GWERDDONAU LLION. The Green Places of the Floods, the Islands of the Blessed in the West of the World.

GWINIONYDD. A cantref on the north bank of the Teifi in Cardigan.

GWYDDEL. Goidhel, Gael or Irish.

GWYDDON. Scientist or philosopher. Here used as an adjective, with the meaning of pertaining to the Gwyddoniaid, according to the Iolo MSS., a school of predruidic sages and enchanters.

GWYNFYD. The second of the three circles of Existence, the Circle of Bliss. At the time when the Deity, waking in Ceugant from the Universal Night (which had been preceded by other universal days and nights) sounded His own Threefold Name — the *Tair Gwaedd* or Three Shouts of the story — in order to waken the Universe from latent into manifested being, so that the stars and suns and systems " flashed into manifestation more swiftly than the lightning reaches its home "; the Blessed Ones or Gwynfydolion, who are ourselves, awoke in Gwynfyd, and looked forth over the gulf of Abred, the Great Deep; and saw the heights of Ceugant unattained; and determined to ride forth through space and take Ceugant by storm. On that expedition we still are traveling; for passing through Abred we were unable to withstand its tempting hosts, and fell into matter and incarnation; and it is with the gathered spoils of the deep, the experience of ages upon ages, that we shall come at last to the peaks of Ceugant, victors. (See *Barddas*, Iolo MSS., and other writings of the Glamorgan School).

HAI ATTON. Literally, *Heigh to us!* The bugle call for gathering the hosts. (See Allen Raine's *Hearts of Wales,* our sole authority for the use of this term. We have much to be thankful to Allen Raine for; and still more if she invented this glorious phrase.) Hai is pronounced like English *high.*

HEN. Ancient.

HIRLAS. A drinking-horn; literally, " long blue."

HU GADARN. According to Richards' Dictionary, *hu* means " the all-pervading."

HWYL. The method of chanting used in Wales for poetry and rhetoric. The word means " sail "; the idea being that the inspiration drives and fills the spoken words with a certain vibrant, singing quality of sound, as the wind fills and drives and swells the sails of a ship.

LLOEGR. England.

MABWNION. A cantref in Cardigan.

MON. Anglesey.

MYNWY. Monmouthshire.

MYNYDD. Mountain. Mynydd Amanw, the Black Mountain in Carmarthenshire.

O FOROEDD AC O FYNYDD, etc.

> " Out of the seas and the mountain,
> And the waves of the rivers,
> Comes a God with gifts for the fortunate."
> (Taliesin, *Dyhuddiant Elphin*)

PAIR DADENI. The Cauldron of Reincarnation, the Cauldron of Ceridwen.

PEN. Head, Chieftain.

PENBARDD. See Benbardd.

PENDEFIG. Prince, Chieftain.

PENNILLION. Verses.

PENTEULU. The Chief of the Teulu.

PRIF-FARD. See Brif-fardd.

TEULU. In modern Welsh, Household; but here it has the old meaning of the standing army or bodyguard of the Welsh Princes. The teulu consisted generally of a hundred and twenty men of the noble class, whose duty it was to be exterminated in battle before the king should be slain. (See Professor Lloyd's *History*, to which we are indebted for this and much other information.)

YNYS. Island. Yyns Prydain, Ynys Wen, Ynys y Cedyrn: the Beautiful Isle (or Island of Prydain ab Aedd Mawr, an ancient king), the White or Sacred Isle, the Island of the Mighty: names of Ancient Britain. I suppose that the phrase " the three Islands of the Mighty," used in the Mabinogion, would be really the equivalent of " the threefold or three-divisioned Island of the Mighty, and would refer to the three divisions of that island, ancient as well as modern: Cymru, Lloegr, and Alban; Wales, England, and Scotland.

YSTRAD TYWI. Part of Carmarthenshire.

Lightning Source UK Ltd.
Milton Keynes UK
UKHW022341060223
416580UK00004B/192